Praise for

Death Masks

"Butcher maintains a breakneck pace in Harry's exciting fifth adventure. This imaginative series continues to surprise and delight with its inventiveness and sympathetic hero." —*Booklist*

"*Death Masks* is his most assured book yet, a smooth melding of inventive storylines, dark supernatural themes, edge-of-your-seat adventure, strong characterizations, and irreverent humor. . . . The balance is perfect. In between the kickass adventure and supernatual fireworks, there's some pretty serious stuff about loyalty, love, faith, and loss." —*SF Site*

"Intense and wild, *Death Masks* is another roller-coaster ride from Jim Butcher, a skillful blend of urban fantasy and noir, sure to satisfy any fan and leave them begging for more." —*Green Man Review*

Summer Knight

"As usual in Butcher's books, the action begins on page one and moves rapidly from there . . . an excellent, and in my opinion powerful, chapter in the Dresden case files." —*The Best Reviews*

continued . . .

"Butcher is definitely among the best. *Summer Knight* starts with a bang and doesn't let up. . . . A very good detective series . . . Fans of any kind of fiction can enjoy Butcher's fun and fast-paced style. . . . I can't wait until Harry Dresden is on the case again."
—*The News-Star* (Monroe , LA)

Grave Peril

"A haunting, fantastical novel that begins almost as innocently as those of another famous literary wizard named Harry." —*Publishers Weekly*

"Harry is a likable protagonist with more than his share of troubles, and *Grave Peril* will keep readers turning the pages to find out how he overcomes them."
—*Booklist*

"A great supernatural who-done-it . . . few horror, fantasy, or mystery tales get any better than this wonderful plot that smoothly combines all three genres into one novel." —BookBrowser

Fool Moon

"It's even more entertaining . . . than the first in the series, good fun for fans of dark fantasy mystery."
—*Locus*

"*Storm Front* was one of the most enjoyable books I read last year, and *Fool Moon* is even better. Butcher keeps the thrills coming, with plenty of mystery, suspense, and edge-of-your-seat action." —SF Site

"A fast-paced fascinating noir thriller." —BookBrowser

"A really enjoyable read . . . Jim Butcher strikes just the right narrative balance between wizard and wiseguy, mystic and mobster."
—Lynn Flewelling, author of *Traitor's Moon*

Storm Front

"A very promising start to a new series, not to mention an unusually well-crafted first novel." —*Locus*

"Interesting characters, tight plotting, and fresh, breezy writing . . . an auspicious start to an engaging new series." —SF Site

"Butcher deftly blends the fantasy and detective genres in this entertaining yarn."
—*Publishers Weekly* (review of the audio edition)

"A strong contender for Best Sorcery Suspense Supernatural Paperback of 2000 . . . required summer reading for anyone who likes a few laughs."
—*The Reporter* (Vacaville, CA)

"Wish I'd thought of this myself. Try it. You'll like it."
—Glen Cook, author of *Faded Steel Heat*

"Exciting, well-plotted, complex, an excellent read . . . amazingly good."
—Chris Bunch, author of *The Doublecross Program*

BLOOD RITES

BOOK SIX OF THE DRESDEN FILES

Jim Butcher

A ROC BOOK

ROC
Published by New American Library, a division of
Penguin Group (USA) Inc., 375 Hudson Street,
New York, New York 10014, USA
Penguin Group (Canada), 90 Eglinton Avenue East, Suite 700, Toronto,
Ontario M4P 2Y3, Canada (a division of Pearson Penguin Canada Inc.)
Penguin Books Ltd., 80 Strand, London WC2R 0RL, England
Penguin Ireland, 25 St. Stephen's Green, Dublin 2,
Ireland (a division of Penguin Books Ltd.)
Penguin Group (Australia), 250 Camberwell Road, Camberwell, Victoria 3124,
Australia (a division of Pearson Australia Group Pty. Ltd.)
Penguin Books India Pvt. Ltd., 11 Community Centre, Panchsheel Park,
New Delhi - 110 017, India
Penguin Group (NZ), cnr Airborne and Rosedale Roads, Albany,
Auckland 1310, New Zealand (a division of Pearson New Zealand Ltd.)
Penguin Books (South Africa) (Pty.) Ltd., 24 Sturdee Avenue,
Rosebank, Johannesburg 2196, South Africa

Penguin Books Ltd., Registered Offices:
80 Strand, London WC2R 0RL, England

First published by Roc, an imprint of New American Library,
a division of Penguin Group (USA) Inc.

First Printing, August 2004
10 9

ROC REGISTERED TRADEMARK—MARCA REGISTRADA

Printed in the United States of America

PUBLISHER'S NOTE
This is a work of fiction. Names, characters, places, and incidents either are the
product of the author's imagination or are used fictitiously, and any resemblance
to actual persons, living or dead, business establishments, events, or locales is
entirely coincidental.
    The publisher does not have any control over and does not assume any respon-
sibility for author or third-party Web sites or their content.

For my nieces and nephews: Craig, Emily, Danny, Ellie, Gabriel, Lori, Anna, Mikey, Kaitlyn, Greta, Foster, and Baby-to-Be-Named-Later. I hope you all grow up to find as much joy in reading as has your uncle.

ACKNOWLEDGMENTS

I would like to thank a whole bunch of people for their continuing support, encouragement, and tolerance of me personally: June and Joy Williams at Buzzy Multimedia, Editor Jen, Agent Jen, Contracts Jen, and any other Jens out there whom I have missed, the members of the McAnally's e-mail list, the residents of the Beta-Foo Asylum, the artists (of every stripe) who have shared their work and creative inspiration with me and lots of other folks, and finally all the critics who have reviewed my work—even the most hostile reviews have provided valuable PR, and I'm much obliged to y'all for taking the time to do it.

I need to mention my family and their continued support (or at least patience). Now that I'm settled back at Independence, I have a whole ton of family doing too many things to mention here—but I wanted to thank you all for your love and enthusiasm. I'm a lucky guy.

Shannon and JJ get special mention, as always. They live here. They deserve it. So does our bichon, Frost, who makes sure that my feet are never cold while I'm writing.

Chapter One

The building was on fire, and it wasn't my fault.

My boots slipped and slid on the tile floor as I sprinted around a corner and toward the exit doors to the abandoned school building on the southwest edge of Chicagoland. Distant streetlights provided the only light in the dusty hall, and left huge swaths of blackness crouching in the old classroom doors.

I carried an elaborately carved wooden box about the size of a laundry basket in my arms, and its weight made my shoulders burn with effort. I'd been shot in both of them at one time or another, and the muscle burn quickly started changing into deep, aching stabs. The damned box was heavy, not even considering its contents.

Inside the box, a bunch of flop-eared grey-and-black puppies whimpered and whined, jostled back and forth as I ran. One of the puppies, his ear already notched where some kind of doggie misadventure had marked him, was either braver or more stupid than his littermates. He scrambled around until he got his paws onto the lip of the box, and set up a painfully high-pitched barking full of squeaky snarls, big dark eyes focused behind me.

I ran faster, my knee-length black leather duster swishing against my legs. I heard a rustling, hissing sound and juked left as best I could. A ball of some kind of noxious-smelling substance that looked like tar went zipping past me, engulfed in yellow-white flame. It hit the floor several yards beyond me, and promptly exploded into a little puddle of hungry fire.

I tried to avoid it, but my boots had evidently been made for walking, not sprinting on dusty tile. They slid out from under me and I fell. I controlled it as much as

I could, and wound up sliding on my rear, my back to the fire. It got hot for a second, but the wards I'd woven over my duster kept it from burning me.

Another flaming glob crackled toward me, and I barely turned in time. The substance, whatever the hell it was, clung like napalm to what it hit and burned with a supernatural ferocity that had already burned a dozen metal lockers to slag in the dim halls behind me.

The goop hit my left shoulder blade and slid off the protective spells on my mantled coat, spattering the wall beside me. I flinched nonetheless, lost my balance, and fumbled the box. Fat little puppies tumbled onto the floor with a chorus of whimpers and cries for help.

I checked behind me.

The guardian demons looked like demented purple chimpanzees, except for the raven-black wings sprouting from their shoulders. There were three of them that had escaped my carefully crafted paralysis spell, and they were hot on my tail, bounding down the halls in long leaps assisted by their black feathered wings.

As I watched, one of them reached down between its crooked legs and . . . Well, not to put too fine a point on it, but it gathered up the kind of ammunition primates in zoos traditionally rely upon. The monkey-demon hurled it with a chittering scream, and it combusted in midair. I had to duck before the noxious ball of incendiary goop smacked into my nose.

I grabbed puppies and scooped them into the box, then started running. The demon-monkeys burst into fresh howls.

Squeaky barks behind me made me look back. The little notch-eared puppy had planted his clumsy paws solidly on the floor, and was barking defiantly at the oncoming demon-chimps.

"Dammit," I cursed, and reversed course. The lead monkey swooped down at the puppy. I made like a ball-player, slid in feetfirst, and planted the heel of my boot squarely on the end of the demon's nose. I'm not heavily built, but I'm most of a head taller than six feet, and no one ever thought I was a lightweight. I kicked the demon hard enough to make it screech and veer off. It slammed into a metal locker, and left an inches-deep dent.

"Stupid little fuzzbucket," I muttered, and recovered the puppy. "This is why I have a cat." The puppy kept up its tirade of ferocious, squeaking snarls. I pitched him into the box without ceremony, ducked two more flaming blobs, and started coughing on the smoke already filling the building as I resumed my retreat. Light was growing back where I'd come from, as the demons' flaming missiles chewed into the old walls and floor, spreading with a malicious glee.

I ran for the front doors of the old building, slamming the opening bar with my hip and barely slowing down.

A sudden weight hit my back and something pulled viciously at my hair. The chimp-demon started biting at my neck and ear. It hurt. I tried to spin and throw it off me, but it had a good hold. The effort, though, showed me a second demon heading for my face, and I had to duck to avoid a collision.

I let go of the box and reached for the demon on my back. It howled and bit my hand. Snarling and angry, I turned around and threw my back at the nearest wall. The monkey-demon evidently knew that tactic. It flipped off of my shoulders at the last second, and I slammed the base of my skull hard against a row of metal lockers.

A burst of stars blinded me for a second, and by the time my vision cleared, I saw two of the demons diving toward the box of puppies. They both hurled searing blobs at the wooden box, splattering it with flame.

There was an old fire extinguisher on the wall, and I grabbed it. My monkey attacker came swooping back at me. I rammed the end of the extinguisher into its nose, knocking it down, then reversed my grip on the extinguisher and sprayed a cloud of dusty white chemical at the carved box. I got the fire put out, but for good measure I unloaded the thing into the other two demons' faces, creating a thick cloud of dust.

I grabbed the box and hauled it out the door, and then slammed the school doors shut behind me.

There were a couple of thumps from the other side of the doors, and then silence.

Panting, I looked down at the box of whimpering puppies. A bunch of wet black noses and eyes looked back up at me from under a white dusting of extinguishing chemical.

"Hell's bells," I panted at them. "You guys are lucky Brother Wang wants you back so much. If he hadn't paid half up front, I'd be the one in the box and you'd be carrying me."

A bunch of little tails wagged hopefully.

"Stupid dogs," I growled. I hauled the box into my arms again and started schlepping it toward the old school's parking lot.

I was about halfway there when something ripped the steel doors of the school inward, against the swing of their hinges. A low, loud bellow erupted from inside the building, and then a Kong-size version of the chimp-demons came stomping out of the doorway.

It was purple. It had wings. And it looked really pissed off. At least eight feet tall, it had to weigh four or five times what I did. As I stared at it, two little monkey-demons flew directly at demon Kong—and were simply absorbed by the bigger demon's bulk upon impact. Kong gained another eighty pounds or so and got a bit bulkier. Not so much monkey Kong, then, as Monkey Voltron. The original crowd of guardian demons must have escaped my spell with that combining maneuver, pooling all of their energy into a single vessel and using the greater strength provided by density to power through my binding.

Kongtron spread wings as wide as a small airplane's and leapt at me with a completely unfair amount of grace. Being a professional investigator, as well as a professional wizard, I'd seen slobbering beasties before. Over the course of many encounters and many years, I have successfully developed a standard operating procedure for dealing with big, nasty monsters.

Run away. Me and Monty Python.

The parking lot and the Blue Beetle, my beat-up old

Volkswagen, were only thirty or forty yards off, and I can really move when I'm feeling motivated.

Kong bellowed. It motivated me.

There was the sound of a small explosion, then a blaze of red light brighter than the nearby street lamps. Another fireball hit the ground a few feet wide of me and detonated like a Civil War cannonball, gouging out a coffin-sized crater in the pavement. The enormous demon roared and shot past me on black vulture wings, banking to come around for another pass.

"Thomas!" I screamed. "Start the car!"

The passenger door opened, and an unwholesomely good-looking young man with dark hair, tight jeans, and a leather jacket worn over a bare chest poked his head out and peered at me over the rims of round green-glassed spectacles. Then he looked up and behind me. His jaw dropped open.

"Start the freaking car!" I screamed.

Thomas nodded and dove back into the Beetle. It coughed and wheezed and shuddered to life. The surviving headlight flicked on, and Thomas gunned the engine and headed for the street.

For a second I thought he was going to leave me, but he slowed down enough that I caught up with him. Thomas leaned across the car and pushed the passenger door open. I grunted with effort and threw myself into the car. I almost lost the box, but managed to get it just before the notch-eared puppy pulled himself up to the rim, evidently determined to go back and do battle.

"What the hell is that?" Thomas screamed. His black hair, shoulder length, curling and glossy, whipped around his face as the car gathered speed and drew the cool autumn wind through the open windows. His grey eyes were wide with apprehension. "What is that, Harry?"

"Just drive!" I shouted. I stuffed the box of whimpering puppies into the backseat, grabbed my blasting rod, and climbed out the open window so that I was sitting on the door, chest to the car's roof. I twisted to bring the blasting rod in my right hand to bear on the demon.

I drew in my will, my magic, and the end of the blasting rod began to glow with a cherry-red light.

I was about to loose a strike against the demon when it swooped down with another fireball in its hand and flung it at the car.

"Look out!" I screamed.

Thomas must have seen it coming in the mirror. The Beetle swerved wildly, and the fireball hit the asphalt, bursting into a roar of flame and concussion that broke windows on both sides of the street. Thomas dodged a car parked on the curb by roaring up onto the sidewalk, bounced gracelessly, and nearly went out of control. The bounce threw me from my perch on the closed door. I was wondering what the odds were against finding a soft place to land when I felt Thomas grab my ankle. He held on to me and drew me back into the car with a strength that would have been shocking to anyone who didn't know that he wasn't human.

He braced me with his hold on my leg, and as the huge demon dove down again, I pointed my blasting rod at it and snarled, *"Fuego!"*

A lance of white-hot fire streaked from the tip of my blasting rod into the late-night air, illuminating the street like a flash of lightning. Bouncing along on the car like that, I expected to miss. But I beat the odds and the burst of flame took Kongtron right in the belly. It screamed and faltered, plummeting to earth. Thomas swerved back out onto the street.

The demon started to get up. "Stop the car!" I screamed.

Thomas mashed down the brakes and I nearly got reduced to sidewalk pizza again. I hung on as hard as I could, but by the time I had my balance, the demon had hauled itself to its feet.

I growled in frustration, readied another blast, and aimed carefully.

"What are you doing?" Thomas shouted. "You lamed him; let's run!"

"No," I snapped back. "If we leave it here, it's going to take things out on whoever it can find."

"But it won't be *us!*"

I tuned Thomas out and readied another strike, pouring my will into the blasting rod until wisps of smoke began emerging from the length of its surface.

Then I let Kong have it right between its black beady eyes.

The fire hit it like a wrecking ball, right on the chin. The demon's head exploded into a cloud of luminous purple vapor and sparkles of scarlet light, which I have to admit looked really neat.

Demons who come into the mortal world don't have bodies as such. They create them, like a suit of clothes, and as long as the demon's awareness inhabits the construct-body, it's as good as real. Having its head blown up was too much damage for even the demon's life energy to support. The body flopped around on the ground for a few seconds, and then the Kong-demon's earthly form stopped moving and dissolved into a lumpy looking mass of translucent gelatin—ectoplasm, matter from the Nevernever.

A surge of relief made me feel a little dizzy, and I slid bonelessly back into the Beetle.

"Allow me to reiterate," Thomas panted a minute later. "What. The hell. Was *that*."

I settled down onto the seat, breathing hard. I buckled up, and checked that the puppies and their box were both intact. They were, and I closed my eyes with a sigh. "Shen," I said. "Chinese spirit creatures. Demons. Shapeshifters."

"Christ, Dresden! You almost got me killed!"

"Don't be a baby. You're fine."

Thomas frowned at me. "You at least could have told me!"

"I *did* tell you," I said. "I told you at Mac's that I'd give you a ride home, but that I had to run an errand first."

Thomas scowled. "An *errand* is getting a tank of gas or picking up a carton of milk or something. It is *not* getting chased by flying purple pyromaniac gorillas hurling incendiary poo."

"Next time take the El."

He glared at me. "Where are we going?"

"O'Hare."

"Why?"

I waved vaguely at the backseat. "Returning stolen property to my client. He wants to get it back to Tibet, pronto."

"Anything else you're neglecting to tell me? Ninja wombats or something?"

"I wanted you to see how it feels," I said.

"What's that supposed to mean?"

"Come on, Thomas. You never go to Mac's place to hang out and chum around. You're wealthy, you've got connections, and you're a freaking vampire. You didn't need me to give you a ride home. You could have taken a cab, called for a limo, or talked some woman into taking you."

Thomas's scowl faded away, replaced by a careful, expressionless mask. "Oh? Then why am I here?"

I shrugged. "Doesn't look like you showed up to bushwhack me. I guess you're here to talk."

"Razor intellect. You should be a private investigator or something."

"You going to sit there insulting me, or are you going to talk?"

"Yeah," Thomas said. "I need a favor."

I snorted. "What favor? You do remember that technically we're at war, right? Wizards versus vampires? Ring any bells?"

"If you like, you can pretend that I'm employing subversive tactics as part of a fiendishly elaborate ruse meant to manipulate you," Thomas said.

"Good," I said. " 'Cause if I went to all the trouble of starting a war and you didn't want to participate it would hurt my feelings."

He grinned. "I bet you're wondering whose side I'm on."

"No." I snorted. "You're on Thomas's side."

The grin widened. Thomas has the kind of whiter-than-white boyish grin that makes women's panties spontaneously evaporate. "Granted. But I've done you some favors over the past couple of years."

I frowned. He had, though I didn't know why. "Yeah. So?"

"So now it's my turn," he said. "I've helped you. Now I need payback."

"Ah. What do you want me to do?"

"I want you to take a case for an acquaintance of mine. He needs your help."

"I don't really have time," I said. "I have to make a living."

Thomas flicked a piece of monkey flambé off the back of his hand and out the window. "You call this living?"

"Jobs are a part of life. Maybe you've heard of the concept. It's called work? See, what happens is that you suffer through doing annoying and humiliating things until you get paid not enough money. Like those Japanese game shows, only without all the glory."

"Plebe. I'm not asking you to go pro bono. He'll pay your fee."

"Bah," I muttered. "What's he need help with?"

Thomas frowned. "He thinks someone is trying to kill him. I think he's right."

"Why?"

"There have been a couple of suspicious deaths around him."

"Like?"

"Two days ago he sent his driver, girl named Stacy Willis, out to the car with his golf clubs so he could get in a few holes before lunch. Willis opened the trunk and got stung to death by about twenty thousand bees who had somehow swarmed into the limo in the time it took her to walk up to the door and back."

I nodded. "Ugh. Can't argue there. Gruesomely suspicious."

"The next morning his personal assistant, a young woman named Sheila Barks, was hit by a runaway car. Killed instantly."

I pursed my lips. "That doesn't sound so odd."

"She was waterskiing at the time."

I blinked. "How the hell did *that* happen?"

"Bridge over the reservoir was the way I heard it. Car jumped the rail, landed right on her."

"Ugh," I said. "Any idea who is behind it?"

"None. Think it's an entropy curse?" Thomas asked.

"If so, it's a sloppy one. But strong as hell. Those are some pretty melodramatic deaths." I checked on the puppies. They had fallen together into one dusty lump and were sleeping. The notch-eared pup lay on top of the pile. He opened his eyes and gave me a sleepy little growl of warning. Then he went back to sleep.

Thomas glanced back at the box. "Cute little furballs. What's their story?"

"Guardian dogs for some monastery in the Himalayas. Someone snatched them and came here. A couple of monks hired me to get them back."

"What, they don't have dog pounds in Tibet?"

I shrugged. "They believe these dogs have a foo heritage."

"Is that like epilepsy or something?"

I snorted and put my hand palm-down out the window, waggling it back and forth to make an airfoil in the wind of the Beetle's passage. "The monks think their great-grandcestor was a divine spirit-animal. Celestial guardian spirit. Foo dog. They believe it makes the bloodline special."

"Is it?"

"How the hell should I know, man? I'm just the repo guy."

"Some wizard you are."

"It's a big universe," I said. "No one can know it all."

Thomas fell quiet for a while, and the road whispered by. "Uh, do you mind if I ask what happened to your car?"

I looked around at the Beetle's interior. It wasn't Volkswagen-standard anymore. The seat covers were gone. So was the padding underneath. So was the interior carpet, and big chunks of the dashboard that had been made out of wood. There was a little vinyl left, and some of the plastic, and anything made out of metal, but everything else had been stripped completely away.

I'd done some makeshift repairs with several one-by-sixes, some hanger wire, some cheap padding from the camping section at Wal-Mart, and a lot of duct tape. It gave the car a real postmodern look: By which I meant that it looked like something fashioned from the wreckage after a major nuclear exchange.

On the other hand, the Beetle's interior was very, very clean. My glasses are half-full, dammit.

"Mold demons," I said.

"Mold demons ate your car?"

"Sort of. They were called out of the decay in the car's interior, and used anything organic they could find to make bodies for themselves."

"You called them?"

"Oh, hell, no. They were a present from the guest villain a few months ago."

"I hadn't heard there was any action this summer."

"I have a life, man. And my life isn't all about feuding demigods and nations at war and solving a mystery before it kills me."

Thomas lifted an eyebrow. "It's also about mold demons and flaming monkey poo?"

"What can I say? I put the 'ick' in 'magic.' "

"I see. Hey, Harry, can I ask you something?"

"I guess."

"Did you really save the world? I mean, like the last two years in a row?"

I shrugged. "Sort of."

"Word is you capped a faerie princess and headed off a war between Winter and Summer," Thomas said.

"Mostly I was saving my own ass. Just happened that the world was in the same spot."

"There's an image that will give me nightmares," Thomas said. "What about those demon Hell guys last year?"

I shook my head. "They'd have let loose a nasty plague, but it wouldn't have lasted very long. They were hoping it would escalate into a nice apocalypse. They knew there wasn't much chance of it, but they were doing it anyway."

"Like the Lotto," Thomas said.

"Yeah, I guess. The genocide Lotto."

"And you stopped them."

"I helped do it and lived to walk away. But there was an unhappy ending."

"What?"

"I didn't get paid. For either case. I make more money from flaming demon monkey crap. That's just wrong."

Thomas laughed a little and shook his head. "I don't get it."

"Don't get what?"

"Why you do it."

"Do what?"

He slouched down in the driver's seat. "The Lone Ranger impersonation. You get pounded to scrap every time you turn around and you barely get by on the gumshoe work. You live in that dank little cave of an apartment. Alone. You've got no woman, no friends, and you drive this piece of crap. Your life is kind of pathetic."

"Is that what you think?" I asked.

"Call them like I see them."

I laughed. "Why do you think I do it?"

He shrugged. "All I can figure is that either you're nursing a deep and sadistic self-hatred or else you're insane. I gave you the benefit of the doubt and left monumental stupidity off the list."

I kept on smiling. "Thomas, you don't really know me. Not at all."

"I think I do. I've seen you under pressure."

I shrugged. "Yeah, but you see me, what? Maybe a day or two each year? Usually when something's been warming up to kill me by beating the tar out of me."

"So?"

"So that doesn't cover what my life is like the other three hundred and sixty-three days," I said. "You don't know everything about me. My life isn't completely about magical mayhem and creative pyromania in Chicago."

"Oh, that's right. I heard you went to exotic Oklahoma a few months back. Something about a tornado and the National Severe Storms Lab."

"I was doing the new Summer Lady a favor, running down a rogue storm sylph. Got to go all over the place in those tornado-chaser geekmobiles. You should have seen the look on the driver's face when he realized that the tornado was chasing *us*."

"It's a nice story, Harry, but what's the point?" Thomas asked.

"My point is that there's a lot of my life you haven't seen. I have friends."

"Monster hunters, werewolves, and a talking skull."

I shook my head. "More than that. I like my apartment. Hell, for that matter I like my car."

"You *like* this piece of . . . junk?"

"She may not look like much, but she's got it where it counts, kid."

Thomas slouched down in his seat, his expression skeptical. "Now you've forced me to reconsider the monumentally stupid explanation."

I shrugged. "Me and the Blue Beetle kick ass. In a four-cylinder kind of way, but it still gets kicked."

Thomas's face lost all expression. "What about Susan?"

When I get angry, I'd like to be able to pull off a great stone face like that, but I don't do it so well. "What about her?"

"You cared about her. You got her involved in your life. She got torn up because of you. She got attention from all kinds of nasties and she nearly died." He kept staring ahead. "How do you live with that?"

I started to get angry, but I had a rare flash of insight and my ire evaporated before it could fully condense. I studied Thomas's profile at a stoplight and saw him working hard to look distant, like nothing was touching him. Which would mean that something *was* touching him. He was thinking of someone important to him. I had a pretty good idea who it was.

"How's Justine?" I asked.

His features grew colder. "It isn't important."

"Okay. But how is Justine?"

"I'm a vampire, Harry." The words were cold and distant, but not steady. "She's my girlfri—" His voice stumbled on the word, and he tried to cover it with a low cough. "She's my lover. She's food. That's how she is."

"Ah," I said. "I like her, you know. Ever since she blackmailed me into helping you at Bianca's masquerade. That took guts."

"Yeah," he said. "She's got that."

"How long have you been seeing her now?"

"Four years," Thomas said. "Almost five."

"Anyone else?"

"No."

"Burger King," I said.

Thomas blinked at me. "What?"

"Burger King," I said. "I like to eat at Burger King. But even if I could afford to do it, I wouldn't eat my meals there every day for almost five years."

"What's your point?" Thomas asked.

"My point is that it's pretty clear that Justine isn't just food to you, Thomas."

He turned his head and stared at me for a moment, his expression empty and his eyes inhumanly blank. "She is. She has to be."

"Why don't I believe you?" I said.

Thomas stared at me, his eyes growing even colder. "Drop the subject. Right now."

I decided not to push. He was working hard not to give anything away, so I knew he was full of crap. But if he didn't want to discuss it, I couldn't force him.

Hell, for that matter, I didn't want to. Thomas was an annoying wiseass who tended to make everyone he met want to kill him, and when I have that much in common with someone, I can't help but like him a little. It wouldn't hurt to give him some space.

On the other hand, it was easy for me to forget what

he was, and I couldn't afford that. Thomas was a vampire of the White Court. They didn't drink blood. They fed on emotions, on feelings, drawing the life energy from their prey through them. The way I understood it, it was usually during sex, and rumor had it that their kind could seduce a saint. I'd seen Thomas start to feed once, and whatever it was that made him not quite human had completely taken control of him. It left him a cold, beautiful, marble-white being of naked hunger. It was an acutely uncomfortable memory.

The Whites weren't as physically formidable or aggressively organized as the Red Court, and they didn't have the raw, terrifying power of the Black Court, but they didn't have all the usual vampire weaknesses, either. Sunlight wasn't a problem for Thomas, and from what I'd seen, crosses and other holy articles didn't bother him either. But just because they weren't as inhuman as the other Courts didn't make the Whites less dangerous. In fact, the way I saw it, it made them more of a threat in some ways. I know how to handle it when some slime-covered horror from the pits of Hell jumps up in my face. But it would be easy to let down my guard for someone nearly human.

Speaking of which, I told myself, I was agreeing to help him and taking a job, just as though Thomas were any other client. It probably wasn't the smartest thing I'd ever done. It had the potential to lead to lethally unhealthy decisions.

He fell silent again. Now that I wasn't running and screaming and such, the car started to get uncomfortably cold. I rolled up the window, shutting out the early-autumn air.

"So," he said. "Will you help me out?"

I sighed. "I shouldn't even be in the same car with you. I've got enough problems with the White Council."

"Gee, your own people don't like you. Cry me a river."

"Bite me," I said. "What's his name?"

"Arturo Genosa. He's a motion-picture producer, starting up his own company."

"Is he at all clued in?"

"Sort of. He's a normal, but he's real superstitious."

"Why did you want him to come to me?"

"He needs your help, Harry. If he doesn't get it, I don't think he's going to live through the week."

I frowned at Thomas. "Entropy curses are a nasty business even when they're precise, much less when they're that sloppy. I'd be risking my ass trying to deflect them."

"I've done as much for you."

I thought about it for a moment. Then I said, "Yeah. You have."

"And I didn't ask for any money for it, either."

"All right," I said. "I'll talk to him. No guarantees. But if I do take the case, you're going to pay me to do it, on top of what this Arturo guy shells out."

"This is how you return favors, is it."

I shrugged. "So get out of the car."

He shook his head. "Fine. You'll get double."

"No," I said. "Not money."

He arched an eyebrow and glanced at me over the rims of his green fashion spectacles.

"I want to know why," I said. "I want to know why you've been helping me. If I take the case, you come clean with me."

"You wouldn't believe me if I did."

"That's the deal. Take it or leave it."

Thomas frowned, and we drove for several minutes in silence. "Okay," he said then. "Deal."

"Done," I responded. "Shake on it."

We did. His fingers felt very cold.

Chapter Two

We went to O'Hare. I met Brother Wang in the chapel at the international concourse. He was a short, wiry Asian man in sweeping robes the color of sunset. His bald head gleamed, making his age tough to guess, though his features were wrinkled with the marks of someone who smiles often.

"Miss sir Dresden," he said, breaking into a wide smile as I came in with the box of sleeping puppies. "Our little one dogs you have given to us!"

Brother Wang's English was worse than my Latin, and that's saying something, but his body language was unmistakable. I returned his smile, and offered him the box with a bow of my head. "It was my pleasure."

Wang took the box and set it down carefully, then started gently sorting through its contents. I waited, looking around the little chapel, a plain room built to be a quiet space for meditation, so that those who believed in something would have a place to pay honor to their faith. The airport had redecorated the room with a blue carpet instead of a beige one. They'd repainted the walls. There was a new podium at the front of the room, and half a dozen replacement padded pews.

I guess that much blood leaves a permanent stain, no matter how much cleaner you dump on it.

I put my foot on the spot where a gentle old man had given up his life to save mine. It made me feel sad, but not bitter. If we had it to do again, he and I would make the same choices. I just wished I'd been able to know him longer than I had. It's not everyone who can teach you something about faith without saying a word to do it.

Brother Wang frowned at the white powder all over

the puppies, and held up one dust-coated hand with an inquisitive expression.

"Oops," I said.

"Ah," Wang said, nodding. "Oops. Okay, oops." He frowned at the box.

"Something wrong?"

"Is it that all the little one dogs are boxed in?"

I shrugged. "I got all of them that were in the building. I don't know if anyone moved some of them before I did."

"Okay," Brother Wang said. "Less is more better than nothing." He straightened and offered me his hand. "Much thanks from my brothers."

I shook it. "Welcome."

"Plane leaving now for home." Wang reached into his robe and pulled out an envelope. He passed it to me, bowed once more, then took the box of puppies and swept out of the room.

I counted the priest's money, which probably says something about my level of cynicism. I'd racked up a fairly hefty fee on this one, first picking up the trail of the sorcerer who had stolen the pups, then tracking him down and snooping around long enough to know when he went out to get some dinner. It had taken me nearly a week of sixteen-hour days to find the concealed location of the room where the pups were held. They asked me to go get them, too, so I had to identify the demons guarding them, and work out a spell that would neutralize them without, for example, burning down the building. Oops.

All in all, my pay amounted to a couple of nice, solid stacks of Ben Franklins. I'd logged a ton of hours in tracking them down, and then added on a surcharge for playing repo. Of course, if I'd known about the flaming poo, I'd have added more. Some things demand overtime.

I went back to the car. Thomas was sitting on the hood of the Beetle. He hadn't bothered moving it to the actual parking lot, instead taking up a section of curb at the loading zone outside the concourse. A patrol cop had evidently come over to tell him to move it, but she was a fairly attractive woman, and Thomas was Thomas. He had taken off her hat and had it perched on his head at a rakish angle, and the cop looked relaxed and was laughing as I came walking up.

"Hey," I said. "Let's get moving. Things to do."

"Alas," he said, taking off the hat and offering it back to the officer with a little bow. "Unless you're about to arrest me, Elizabeth?"

"Not this time, I suppose," the cop said.

"Damn the luck," Thomas said.

She smiled at him, then frowned at me. "Aren't you Harry Dresden?"

"Yeah."

The cop nodded, putting on her hat. "Thought I recognized you. Lieutenant Murphy says you're good people."

"Thanks."

"It wasn't a compliment. A lot of people don't like Murphy."

"Aw, shucks," I said. "I blush when I feel all flattered like that."

The cop wrinkled her nose. "What's that smell?"

I kept a straight face. "Burned monkey poo."

She eyed me warily for a second to see if I was teasing her, then rolled her eyes. The cop stepped up onto the sidewalk and began moving on down it. Thomas swung his legs off the car and pitched my keys at me. I caught them and got in on the driver's side.

"Okay," I said when Thomas got in. "Where do I meet this guy?"

"He's holding a little soiree for his filming crew tonight in a condo on the Gold Coast. Drinks, deejay, snacks, that kind of thing."

"Snacks," I said. "I'm in."

"Just promise me you won't fill up your pockets with peanuts and cookies." Thomas gave me directions to a posh apartment building a few miles north of the Loop, and I got moving. Thomas was silent during the drive.

"Up here on the right," he said finally, then handed me a white envelope. "Give this to the security guys."

I pulled in where Thomas told me to and leaned out

of my car to offer the envelope to the guard in the little kiosk at the entrance of the parking lot.

A squeaky, bubbling growl erupted from directly below my seat. I flinched.

"What the hell is that?" Thomas said.

I pulled up to the guard kiosk and stopped. I reached for my magical senses and extended them toward the source of the continuing growl. "Crap. I think it's one of the—"

A sort of greasy, nauseating cold flooded over my perceptions, stealing my breath. A ghostly charnel-house scent came with it, the smell of old blood and rotting meat. I froze, looking up at the source of the sensation.

The person I'd taken to be a security guard was a vampire of the Black Court.

It had been a young man. Its features looked familiar, but dessication had left its face too gaunt for me to be sure. The vampire wasn't tall. Death had withered it into an emaciated caricature of a human being. Its eyes were covered with a white, rheumy film, and flakes of dead flesh fell from its decay-drawn lips and clung to its yellowed teeth. Hair like brittle, dead grass stood out from its head, and there was some kind of moss or mold growing in it.

It snatched at me with inhuman speed, but my wizard's senses had given me enough warning to keep its skeletal fingers from closing on my wrist—just barely. The vampire caught a bit of my duster's leather sleeve with the tips of its fingers. I jerked my arm back, but the vampire had as much strength in its fingertips as I did in my whole upper body. I had to pull hard, twisting with my shoulders to break free. I choked out a shout, and the sudden rush of fear made it high and thready.

The vampire rushed me, slithering out through the guardhouse window like a freeze-dried snake. I had a panicked instant to realize that if the vampire closed to wrestling range with me inside the car, they'd be harvesting my organs out of a mound of scrap metal and spare parts.

And I wasn't strong enough to stop it from happening.

Chapter Three

Thomas's senses evidently didn't compete with mine, because the Black Court vampire was up to its shoulders in the Beetle before he choked out a startled, "Holy crap!"

I threw my left elbow at the vampire's face. I couldn't hurt the creature, but it might buy me a second to act. I connected, snapping its head to one side, and with my other hand I reached into a box on the floor between the seats, right by the stick, and withdrew the weapon that might keep me from getting torn to shreds. The vampire tore at me with its near-skeletal hands, its nails digging like claws. If I hadn't laid those spells on my duster, it would have shoved its hand into my chest and torn out my heart, but the heavy, spell-reinforced leather held out for a second or two, buying me enough time to counterattack.

The vampires of the Black Court had been around since the dawn of human memory. They had acres of funky vampire powers, right out of Stoker's book. They had the weaknesses too—garlic, tokens of faith, sunlight, running water, fire, decapitation. Bram Stoker's book told everyone how to kill them, and the Blacks had been all but exterminated in the early twentieth century. The vampires who survived were the most intelligent, the swiftest, the most ruthless of their kind, with centuries of experience in matters of life and death. Mostly death.

But even with centuries of experience, I doubted any of them had ever been hit with a water balloon.

Or with a holy-water balloon, either.

I kept three of them in the box in my car, in easy reach. I snatched one up, palmed it, and slammed it hard against the vampire's face. The balloon broke, and the blessed water splattered over its head. Wherever it struck the vampire, there was a flash of silver light and the dead flesh burst into white, heatless flame as bright as a magnesium flare.

The vampire let out a dusty, rasping scream and convulsed in instant agony. It began thrashing around like a half-squashed bug. It slammed a flailing arm into my steering wheel and the metal bent with a groan.

"Thomas!" I snarled. "Help me!"

He was already moving. He tore his seat belt off, drew up his knees, and spun to his left. Thomas let out a shout and drove both feet hard into the vampire's face. Thomas couldn't have matched the Black Court vampire's physical power, but he was still damned strong. The double kick threw the vampire out of the car and through the flimsy wooden wall of the guard kiosk outside.

The squeaky growling turned into ferocious little barks while the vampire struggled weakly. It tried to rise, its white-filmed eyes wide. I could see the damage the holy water had inflicted. Maybe a quarter of its head was simply gone, starting above its left ear and running down to the corner of its mouth. The edges of the holy-water burns glowed with faint golden fire. Viscous globs of gelatinous black fluid oozed forth from the wounds.

I picked up another water balloon and lifted my arm to throw it.

The vampire let out a hissing shriek of rage and terror. Then it turned and darted away, smashing through the back wall of the kiosk without slowing down. It fled down the street.

"He's getting away," Thomas said, and started getting out of the car.

"Don't," I snapped over all the barking. "It's a setup."

Thomas hesitated. "How do you know?"

"I recognize that guy," I said. "He was at Bianca's masquerade. Only he was alive back then."

Thomas somehow grew even paler. "One of the people that creepy Black Court bitch turned? The one dressed like Hamlet's shrink?"

"Her name is Mavra. And yeah."

"Crap," he muttered. "You're right. It's a lure. She's probably hiding out there watching us right now, waiting for us to go running down a dark alley."

I tried the steering wheel. It felt a little stiff, but it still functioned. Hail the mighty Blue Beetle. I found a parking space and pulled into it. The puppy's barks became ferocious growls again. "Mavra wouldn't need a dark alley. She's got some serious talent for veils. She could be sitting on the hood and we might not see her."

Thomas licked his lips, keeping his eyes on the parking lot. "You think she's come to town for you?"

"Sure, why not. I cheated her out of destroying the sword *Amoracchius*, and she was an ally of Bianca's up until I killed her. Plus we're at war. I'm surprised she hasn't shown up before now."

"Christ on a crutch. She spooks the hell out of me."

"Me too." I bent over and reached beneath the driver's seat. I felt a fuzzy tail, grabbed it, and drew the puppy out as gently as I could. It was the insane little notched-eared pup. He ignored me, still growling, and started shaking his head back and forth violently. "Good thing we had a stowaway. Vamp might have gotten us both."

"What's that he's got in his mouth?" Thomas asked.

The puppy lost hold of whatever he was savaging, and it landed on the floor of the Beetle.

"Ugh," I said. "It's that vamp's ear. Holy water must have burned it right off."

Thomas glanced down at the ear and turned a bit green. "It's moving."

The puppy snarled and batted at the wriggling bit of rotted ear. I picked it up as lightly as I could and tossed it out. The grey-and-black puppy was evidently satisfied with that course of action. He sat down and opened his mouth in a doggie grin.

"Nice reflexes, Harry," Thomas said. "When that vamp came at you. Real nice. Faster than mine. How the hell did you manage that?"

"I didn't. I was trying to feel out this little nuisance after he started growling. I felt the vamp coming a couple seconds before it jumped me."

"Wow," Thomas said. "Talk about strokes of luck."

"Yeah. It's sort of a first for me."

The pup abruptly spun, facing the direction the vampire had fled. He growled again.

Thomas went rigid. "Hey, Harry, you know what?"

"No, what?"

"I'm thinking we should get indoors."

I picked up the puppy and scanned the darkness, but saw nothing. "Discretion is the better part of not getting exsanguinated," I said. "Let's go."

Chapter Four

Thomas and I went into the apartment building, and found the guard who should have been in the booth outside drinking a cup of coffee with a second man behind a desk. We took the elevator to the top floor. There were only two doors in the hall, and Thomas knocked on the nearest. Music rolled and thumped inside while we waited, and the spotless carpet had been cleaned with something that smelled like snapdragons. Thomas had to knock twice more before the door finally opened.

A pretty woman somewhere around her mid-forties answered Thomas's knock, and a tide of loud music came with her. She was maybe five-foot-six and had her dark brown hair held up with a couple of chopsticks. She held a pile of discarded paper plates in one hand and a couple of empty plastic cups in the other and wore an emerald knee-length knit dress that showed off the curves of a WWII pinup girl.

Her face lit with an immediate smile. "Thomas, how wonderful to see you. Justine said you'd be coming by."

Thomas stepped forward with his own brilliant smile and kissed the woman on either cheek. "Madge," he said. "You look great. What are you doing here?"

"It's my apartment," Madge replied, her tone dry.

Thomas laughed. "You're kidding me. Why?"

"The old fool talked me into investing in his company. I need to make sure he doesn't throw the money away. I'm keeping an eye on him."

"I see," Thomas said.

"Did he finally talk you into acting?"

Thomas put a hand on his chest. "A modest schoolboy like me? I blush to think."

Madge laughed, a touch of wickedness to it, resting her hand lightly on Thomas's biceps as she did. Either she liked speaking with Thomas or the hallway was colder than I thought. "Who is your friend?"

"Madge Shelly, this is Harry Dresden. I brought him by to talk business with Arturo. Harry's a friend of mine."

"I wouldn't go that far." I smiled a bit and offered my hand.

She fumbled with plates and cups for a moment, and then laughed. "I'll have to give you a rain check. Are you an actor?" Madge asked, her expression speculative.

"To be or not to be," I said. "How now brown cow."

She smiled and nodded at the puppy, who was riding in the curl of my left arm. "And who is your friend?"

"He's the dog with no name. Like Clint Eastwood, but fuzzier."

She laughed again, and said to Thomas, "I see why you like him."

"He's mildly amusing," Thomas agreed.

"He's up past his bedtime," I said. "Don't mean to be rude, but I need to talk to Arturo before I fall asleep on my feet."

"I understand," Madge said. "The music's a little loud in the living room. Thomas, why don't I show you both to the study, and I'll bring Arturo to you."

"Is Justine here?" Thomas asked. His voice held a note of quiet tension to it that I doubted Madge noticed.

"Somewhere," she said vaguely. "I'll tell her you've arrived."

"Thank you."

We followed Madge inside the apartment suite. The living room was fairly dim, but I saw maybe twenty people there, men and women, some of them dancing, others standing and drinking or laughing or talking, like most parties. There was a haze of smoke, and only some of it was from cigarettes. Colored lights shifted and changed in time with the music.

I watched Thomas as we walked through the room. His manner changed subtly, something I could sense without being able to define. He didn't move any more quickly, but his steps became more fluid somehow. He looked around the room as we went through, his eyelids a little heavy, and he started drawing the eyes of every woman we walked past.

I drew no such looks, even with the grey puppy sleeping in the crook of my arm. It's not like I'm Quasimodo or anything, but with Thomas walking through the room like a predator angel, it was tough to compete.

Madge led us past the party room and into a small room with bookshelves and a desk with a computer. "Have a seat and I'll go find him," she said.

"Thank you," I said, and settled down onto the chair at the desk. She left, her eyes lingering on Thomas for a moment before she did. He perched on a corner of the desk, his expression pensive. "You look thoughtful," I said, "which seems wrong somehow. What is it?"

"I'm hungry," Thomas said. "And thinking. Madge is Arturo's first ex-wife."

"And she's hosting a party for him?" I asked.

"Yeah. I never thought she liked the guy much."

"What did she mean about investing?"

Thomas shrugged. "Arturo broke off from a larger studio on the West Coast to found his own. Madge is real practical. She's the kind of person who could despise someone while still being professional and working with him. Acknowledging his talents. If she thought it was a winning bet, she wouldn't be worried that she didn't like the person in charge. It wouldn't be out of character for her to have invested money in Arturo's new company."

"What kind of money are we talking about?"

"Not sure," Thomas said. "Seven figures, maybe more. I'd have to get someone to look."

I whistled. "Lot of money."

"I guess," Thomas said. Thomas was rich enough that he probably didn't have much perspective on the value of a buck.

I started to ask him more questions, but the door opened, and a tall and vigorous man in his fifties entered, wearing dark slacks and a grey silk shirt rolled up over his forearms. He had a head of magnificent silver locks framing a strong face with a dark, short beard. He had a boater's tan, pale smile lines at the corners of his eyes and mouth, and large, intelligent dark eyes.

"Tommy!" the man boomed, and strode to Thomas. "Hey, I was hoping I would see you tonight." His voice had a thick accent, definitely Greek. He clapped both hands on Thomas's shoulders and kissed him on either cheek. "You're looking good, Tommy boy, real good. You should come work with me, huh?"

"I don't look good on camera," Thomas said. "But it's good to see you, too. Arturo Genosa, this is Harry Dresden, the man I told you about."

Arturo looked me up and down. "Tall son of a bitch, huh?"

"I ate my Wheaties," I said.

"Hey, pooch," Arturo said. He scratched the grey puppy behind the ear. The little dog yawned, licked Arturo's hand once, and promptly went back to sleep. "Your dog?"

"Temporarily," I said. "Recovered him for a client."

Arturo nodded, his expression calculating. "You know what a *strega* is, Mr. Dresden?"

"Practitioner of Italian folk magic," I responded. "Divinations, love potions, fertility blessings, and protections. They also can manage a pretty vicious set of curses with a technique they call the *malocchio*. The Evil Eye."

His eyebrows lifted in surprise. "Guess you know a thing or two, huh."

"Just enough to get me into trouble," I said.

"But do you believe in it?"

"In the Evil Eye?"

"Yes."

"I've seen stranger things."

Arturo nodded. "Tommy boy tell you what I need?"

"He said you were worried about a curse. Said some people close to you died."

Arturo's expression flickered for a second, and I saw grief undermine his confidence. "Yes. Two women. Good souls, both."

"Uh-huh," I said. "Assuming there is a curse involved, what makes you think it was meant for you?"

"They had no other contact with each other," Arturo said. "Far as I know, I was the only thing they had in common." He opened a drawer in his desk and drew out a couple of manila file folders. "Reports," he said. "Information about their deaths. Tommy says maybe you can help."

"Maybe," I agreed. "Why would someone curse you?"

"The studio," Arturo said. "Someone wants to stop the company from getting off the ground. Kill it before the first picture gets made."

"What do you want me to do?"

"Protection," Arturo said. "I want you to protect the people on my crew during the shoot. Don't want anything else to happen to anyone."

I frowned. "Can be a tough job. Do you know who would want to stop production?"

Arturo scowled at me and stalked across the room to a cabinet. He opened it and withdrew an already opened bottle of wine. He pulled out the cork with his teeth and took a swig. "If I knew that, I wouldn't need to hire an investigator."

I shrugged. "I'm a wizard, not a fortune-teller. Got any guesses? Anyone who might want to see you fail?"

"Lucille," Thomas said.

Arturo glanced at Thomas, scowling.

"Who is Lucille?" I asked.

"My second ex-wife," Arturo answered. "Lucille Delarossa. But she is not involved."

"How do you know?" I asked.

"She would not," he said. "I am certain."

"Why?"

He shook his head and stared down at his wine bottle. "Lucille . . . well. Let us say that I did not marry her for her mind."

"You don't have to be smart to be hostile," I said, though I couldn't really think of the last time someone stupid had pulled off powerful magic. "Anyone else? Is there another ex-wife around?"

Arturo waved a hand. "Tricia would not try to stop the picture."

"Why not?" I asked.

"She is the star."

Thomas made a choking sound. "Christ, Arturo."

The silver-maned man grimaced. "No choice. She had a standing contract. Could have killed me in court if I did not cast her."

"Is there an ex-wife number four?" I asked. "I can keep track of three. If there's four, I have to start writing things down."

"Not yet," Arturo muttered. "I am single. So far just the three."

"Well, that's something," I said. "Look, unless whoever is bringing this curse onto you does something right in front of me, there's not a lot I can do. We call a spell like the Evil Eye an entropy curse, and it's damned near impossible to trace any other way."

"My people must be protected from the *malocchio*," Arturo said. "Can you do that?"

"If I'm there when it goes down, yes."

"How much does that cost?" he asked.

"Seventy-five an hour, plus expenses. A thousand up-front."

Arturo didn't hesitate. "Done. We start shooting in the morning, nine o'clock."

"I'll have to be close. Within sight, if possible," I said. "And the less anyone knows about it, the better."

"Yeah," Thomas agreed. "He'll need a cover story. If he stands around in the open, the bad guy will just wait until he leaves or goes to the bathroom or something."

Arturo nodded. "He can boom for me."

"Boom?" I asked.

"Boom microphone," Thomas supplied.

"Oh. That isn't such a hot idea," I said. "My magic doesn't get on so well with machines and such."

Arturo's face clouded with annoyance. "Fine. Production assistant." Something in his pants made a chirping sound, and he drew a cell phone from his pocket. He held up a hand to me and stepped over to the other side of the room, speaking in low tones.

"Production assistant. What's that?" I asked.

"Gofer," Thomas said, "Errand boy." He stood up, his movements restless.

There was a knock at the door, and it opened to admit a girl who may not have reached drinking age. She had dark hair, dark eyes, and was a little taller than average. She wore a white sweater with a short black skirt that showed off a lot of leg, and even compared to the pretty people outside, she was a knockout. Of course, the last time I'd seen her she'd been naked except for a red, Christmas-present-type bow, so it was possible that I was biased.

"Justine," Thomas said, and there was the kind of relief in his voice that I would usually have associated with historical sailors shouting, "Land ho." He took a step over to the girl and pulled her to him in a kiss.

Justine's cheeks colored and she let out a breathless little laugh before her lips touched his, and then melted into the kiss like there wasn't anything else in the whole world.

The puppy in the curl of my arm vibrated, and I

glanced down to see him staring at Thomas, an inaudible, disapproving growl shaking his fuzzy chest.

They didn't kiss for a long time, really, but when Thomas finally lifted his mouth from hers, she was flushed and I could see the pulse beating in her throat. Nothing remotely like thought or restraint touched her face. The heat in her eyes could have scorched me if I'd been a little closer, and for a second I thought she was about to drag Thomas to the carpet right there in front of me.

Instead Thomas turned her so that she stood with her back to his chest, and drew her against him, pinning her there with his arms. He looked paler, and his eyes had become an even fainter shade of grey. He rested his cheek on her hair for a moment, and then said, "You've met Harry."

Justine regarded me with heavy, sultry eyes and nodded. "Hello, Mister Dresden." She inhaled through her nose, and made a visible effort to draw her thoughts together. "You're cold," she said to Thomas. "What happened?"

"Nothing," Thomas said, his tone light.

Justine tilted her head and then took a tiny step away from him. Thomas blinked at her, but didn't try to keep her there. "Not nothing," she said. She touched his cheek with her fingers. "You're freezing."

"I don't want you to worry about it," Thomas told her.

Justine looked over her shoulder at me.

I checked on Arturo, who was still in his conversation on the phone, then said in a low voice, "Black Court. I think it was one of Mavra's goons."

Justine's eyes widened. "Oh, God. Was anyone hurt?"

"Only the vampire," I said. I gave the puppy, now silent, a vague wave. "The pup saw him coming."

"Thomas," Justine said, looking back at him. "You told me you didn't have to worry about Mavra."

"In the first place, we don't know it's Mavra," Thomas said. He gave me a look over Justine's head that warned me to shut the hell up. "And in the second place, they were after Dresden. He's here under my invitation, so I helped him out a little."

"Boot to the head," I agreed. "Ran him off."

"My God. I'm glad you are all right, Mister Dresden, but this shouldn't have happened. Thomas, we shouldn't even be in town. If you don't—"

Thomas put a finger under Justine's chin and drew her eyes up to his.

Justine shuddered, her lips faltering to a halt, her mouth partly open. Her pupils dilated until there was practically no color showing around them. She swayed a little on her feet.

"Relax," Thomas said. "I'll take care of things."

Her brow furrowed with a tiny line, and she stammered, "But . . . I don't want you to . . . get hurt."

Thomas's eyes glittered. Deliberately he raised one pale hand and touched a fingertip to the pulse in Justine's throat. Then he drew it down in a slow, lazy spiral that stopped half an inch under her collarbone. She shuddered again, and her eyes slipped entirely out of focus. Whatever thought had been in her head, it died a silent little death, and left her swaying on her feet making soft, mindless sounds between quick breaths.

And she loved it. From the looks of things she didn't have a choice.

The puppy's silent growl buzzed against the skin of my arm. Anger flashed through me in a wave of silent outrage.

"Stop it," I said in a quiet voice. "Get out of her head."

"This doesn't concern you," Thomas replied.

"Like hell it doesn't. Back off on the mind-mojo. Right now. Or you and I are going to have words."

Thomas's gaze moved to me. Something vicious in his eyes flashed with a cold fury and one of his hands closed into a fist. Then he shook his head and closed his eyes for a moment. He spoke before they opened.

"The less she knows about the details," he said in a rough, strained voice, "the safer she's going to be."

"From who?" I demanded.

"From anyone who might not like me or my House," Thomas said. The words were laced with a hint of a feral snarl. "If she doesn't know any more than any other doe, there's no reason to target her. It's one of the only things I can do to protect her. Back off, wizard, or I'll be happy to start the conversation myself."

Just then Arturo finished his call and turned back to us. He blinked and stopped short of conversation distance. "I'm sorry. Did I miss something?"

Thomas arched an eyebrow at me.

I took a deep breath and said, "No. We just stumbled onto an uncomfortable topic. But we can put a lid on it until later."

"Good," Arturo said. "Now where were we?"

"I need to take Justine home," Thomas said. "She's had a little too much tonight. Best of luck, Arturo."

Arturo nodded to him and managed to smile. "Thank you, Tommy boy, for your help."

"It's nothing." He slipped an arm around Justine, drawing her with him, and nodded to me as he left the room. "Later, Harry."

I rose too, and asked Arturo, "Where do you want me tomorrow?"

He sat down his bottle of wine, grabbed a memo pad off the desk, and scribbled down an address. Then he withdrew a roll of money, peeled off ten bills and slapped a thousand dollars cash down on top of the address. I collected all of it.

"I do not know if I believe in your sincerity, Mr. Dresden," Arturo said.

I waved the bills. "As long as you're paying, I don't really need you to believe in me. See you in the morning, Mr. Genosa."

Chapter Five

I shambled back to my place around late o'clock. Mister, the bobtailed grey tomcat who shares my apartment, hurled himself at my legs in a shoulder-block of greeting. Mister weighs twenty-five or thirty pounds, and I had to brace myself against his ritual affection.

Mister tilted his head at me and sniffed at the air. Then he made a low, warning sound of his imperial displeasure. As I came in, he bounded up onto the nearest bit of furniture and peered at the puppy still sleeping in my arm.

"Temporary," I assured him. I sat down on the couch. "He isn't staying."

Mister narrowed his eyes, prowled over to me, and swatted at the puppy with an indignant paw.

"Take it easy. This little lunatic is a featherweight." I murmured a minor spell and lit a few candles around my apartment with my will. I dialed the number where I had been contacting Brother Wang while he was in town, but got only a recording telling me the number had been disconnected. The phones are occasionally wacky when it's me using them, so I tried again. No success. Bah. My bones ached and I wanted to rest, safe and cozy in my lair.

Said lair was in the basement of a creaky old boardinghouse built better than a hundred years ago. It had sunken windows high up on its walls, and largely consisted of a single living area around a fireplace. I had old, comfortable furniture—a sofa, a love seat, a couple of big recliner-type chairs. They didn't match, but they looked soft and inviting. The stone floor was covered with a variety of area rugs, and I'd softened the look of the concrete walls with a number of tapestries and framed pictures.

The whole place was sparkling clean, and the air smelled of pine boughs. Even the fireplace was scoured down to a clean stone surface. You can't beat the Fair Folk as housekeepers. You also can't tell people about them, because they'll pack up and clear out. Why? I have no idea. They're faeries, and that's just how it works.

On one side of the living room there was a shallow alcove with a wood-burning stove, an old-fashioned icebox, and some cabinets that held my cooking ware and groceries. On the other, a narrow doorway led to my bedroom and bath. There was barely enough room for my twin bed and a secondhand dresser.

I pulled up the rug that covered the entrance to the subbasement, a trapdoor set into the floor. It was deep enough underground to keep a subterranean chill the year-round, so I juggled the puppy while putting on a heavy flannel robe. Then I got a candle, opened the trapdoor, and descended the folding stepladder into my laboratory.

I had forbidden the cleaning service to move around my lab, and as a result it had been slowly losing the war against entropy for a couple of years. The walls were lined with wire racks, and I'd filled them with Tupperware, boxes, bags, tubs, bottles, cups, bowls, and urns. Most of the containers had a label listing their contents, ingredients for any number of potions, spells, summonings, and magical devices I had occasion to make from time to time. A worktable ran down the middle of the room, and at its far end was a comparatively recent concrete patch that did not match the rest of the floor. The patch was surrounded by the summoning circle set into the stone. I'd splurged on replacing the old ring with a new one made of silver and I'd moved everything in the room as far from it as I could.

The thing I'd locked up under the circle had been quiet since the night I had sealed it into a spirit-prison, but when it came to entombing a fallen angel, I was pretty sure that there was no such thing as too much caution.

"Bob," I said as I lit some more candles. "Get up."

One shelf didn't match the rest of the room. Two simple metal struts held up a plain wooden plank. Mounds of old candle wax spread in multicolored lumps at either end of the board, and in the middle rested a human skull.

The skull shivered a little, teeth rattling, and then a dim glow of orange light appeared in its empty eye sockets. Bob the Skull wasn't really a skull. He was an air spirit, a being with a great deal of knowledge and centuries of magical experience. Since I'd stolen him from Justin DuMorne, my own personal childhood Darth Vader, Bob's knowledge and skills had let me save lives. Mostly my own, maybe, but a lot of other lives, too.

"How did it go?" Bob asked.

I started rummaging through the various and sundry. "Three of the little bastards slipped through that paralysis charm you were so sure of," I said. "I barely got out in one piece."

"You're so cute when you whine," Bob said. "I'd almost think that— Holy cats, Harry!"

"Eh?"

"You *stole* one of the temple dogs?"

I petted the puppy's fur and felt a little offended. "It wasn't anything I meant to happen. He was a stowaway."

"Wow," Bob said. "What are you going to do with him?"

"Not sure yet," I said. "Brother Wang's already gone. I tried to call his contact number just now, but it was out of service. I can't call up a messenger and send it back to the temple, because that entire area of mountains is warded, and a letter might take months to get through. If it gets through at all." I finally found a big enough box, scrounged around a bit more, and dropped a couple of old flannel bathrobes into it, followed by the exhausted puppy. "Besides, I've got better things to worry about."

"Like what?"

"Like the Black Court. Mavra and her . . . her . . .

Hey, what's the term for a group of Black Court vampires? A gaggle? A passel?"

"A scourge," Bob said.

"Right. Looks like Mavra and her scourge are in town. One of them came pretty close to punching my ticket tonight."

Bob's eyelights flickered with interest. "Neat. So the usual drill? Wait for them to try again so you can backtrack the attackers to Mavra?"

"Not this time. I'm going to find them first, kick down their door, and kill them all in their sleep."

"Wow. That's an atypically vicious plan, Harry."

"Yeah. I liked it too."

I put the puppy's box on the table. "I want you to take Mister out on the town in the morning. Find wherever it is Mavra is holing up during the day, and for the love of Pete, don't step on any more warding spells."

Bob somehow gave the impression that he shivered. "Yeah. I've been a lot more careful. But the vampires aren't stupid, Harry. They know they're helpless during daylight. They'll have taken some measures to protect their refuge. They always do."

"I'll take care of it," I said.

"It might be more than you can handle alone."

"That's why I'm going Justice League on them," I said, fighting a yawn. I put the cardboard box with the puppy on the worktable, picked up my candle, and went to the stepladder.

"Hey, where do you think you're going?" Bob asked.

"Bed. Early day tomorrow. New case."

"And the temple dog is staying here why?"

"Because I don't want to leave him all by his lonesome," I said. "If I take him with me I think Mister would eat him after I went to sleep."

"Dammit, Harry, I'm a voyeur, not a veterinarian."

I scowled. "I need shut-eye."

"And I get to babysit the dog?"

"Yeah."

"My job sucks."

"Form a union," I said heartlessly.

"What's the new case?" Bob asked.

I told him.

"Arturo Genosa?" Bob asked. "*The* Arturo Genosa? The movie producer?"

I lifted my eyebrows. "Yeah, I guess. You've heard of him?"

"Heard of him? Heck, yeah! He's the best there is!"

My intuition piped up again, and I felt something in my insides drop. "Uh. What kind of movies?"

"Critically acclaimed erotic features!" Bob said, fairly bubbling with enthusiasm.

I blinked. "There are erotic film critics?"

"Sure!" Bob bubbled. "All kinds of periodicals."

"Like what?"

"Juggs, Hooters, Funkybuns, Busting Out—"

I rubbed at my eyes. "Bob, those are porno magazines, not trade journals."

"Four stars, four boners, what's the difference?" Bob asked.

I wasn't going to touch that one.

The skull sighed. "Harry, I'm not trying to call you stupid or belabor the obvious, but you *did* get hired by a vampire of the White Court. An incubus. What kind of job did you *think* this was going to be?"

I glowered at Bob. He was right. I should have known it wasn't going to be simple.

"Speaking of," I said, "how much do you know about the White Court?"

"Oh, the usual," Bob said, which meant he knew plenty.

"I saw Thomas get real weird tonight," I said. "I don't know how to describe it, exactly. But Justine was there, and she said that he was freezing and that it worried her. Then he hit her with some kind of mind-magic hypnosis whammy, and zoned her out entirely."

"He was Hungry," Bob said. "I mean, capital H kind of Hungry. The Hunger is a kind of . . . I don't know. Symbiotic spirit, inside a White Court vamp. They're born with it."

"Ah," I said. "That's where they get the strength and powers and stuff."

"Among them nigh-immortality," Bob said. "But it don't happen for free. That's why they do the whole feeding thing. The Hunger needs it to survive."

"I got it, I got it," I said, through a yawn. "They use their powers and it makes the spirit hungry so they have to feed." I frowned. "What happens if they don't feed?"

"Short-term? Moodiness, anger, violent behavior, paranoia. In the long term, they'll use up whatever reservoir of life energy they have. Once that happens, the Hunger pretty much takes over and makes them hunt."

"If they can't hunt?"

"They go insane."

"What about the people they feed on?" I asked.

"What about them?" Bob said. "They get little pieces of their life nibbled away. It does a form of spiritual damage, like when the Nightmare mauled Mickey Malone. It leaves them vulnerable to the Whites' mental allure and control, so it's easy for the Whites to come by for another bite."

"What happens if they keep getting fed on?"

"It's fed *upon,* o Bard, and if it keeps up the mortal burns out early. Sort of fades away into a kind of mindless daze. Heart attack during an intense feeding usually kills them."

"Killer sex," I said. "Literally."

"To die for," Bob confirmed.

An eerie thought, and one that disturbed me a lot more than I thought it should. "What if the vamp doesn't want to feed on someone?"

"Want doesn't matter," Bob said. "They feed on pure reflex. It's what they are."

"So if they stay with someone," I said, "eventually they kill them."

"Sooner or later," Bob said. "Always."

I shook my head. "I'll remember that," I said. "Tough to keep up the paranoia around Thomas. He's . . . well, hell, if he was human I might not mind buying him a beer once in a while."

Bob's tone turned serious. "He might be a great guy, Harry, but it doesn't change the fact that he isn't always in control of his power, or his Hunger. I doubt he can stop himself from entrancing that pretty girl of his. Or from feeding upon her." Bob paused. "Not that he'd really want to. I mean, she's hot. Who *wouldn't* want a little nibble of Justine now and then? Am I right?"

"Focus," I growled. "Just find Mavra's hiding place. I'll be back from the job before sundown if I can."

Bob sighed dreamily. "Some guys get all the luck. Genosa always casts the prettiest girls. Lots and lots of pretty girls. I'm going to be prowling the mean streets, looking for hideous creatures of the night. And you're going to be standing right there next to the most beautiful women in erotica, getting to watch everything going on. Big as life."

I felt my face flood into a feverish blush. "Keep an eye on the dog. You have my permission to take Mister on the town after the sun rises. Be back by sundown."

"Will do," Bob said. "Harry, Harry, Harry. What I wouldn't give to be in your shoes this week."

Which in retrospect just goes to show that a pretty face can inspire even a bodiless spirit of intellect to dizzying heights of idiocy.

Chapter Six

My cat walked on my face just after dawn. My body thought I should have been getting a couple more hours of shut-eye at the least. Instead I shambled to the door to let Mister outside. Before the cat left, he bobbed his head at me, and his eyes glittered with nearly invisible flickers of orange light. Bob had taken temporary possession of Mister's body. (Actually, I suspected that Mister tolerated Bob's control only because he got to go see new things when I sent Bob out on a mission.)

Bob was a being of spirit, and was too fragile to go drifting around in sunlight. It could burn his usual form to vapor in a few seconds. The spirit needed some form of protection during full daylight, and Mister was it. I had my usual flash of concern and mumbled, "Be careful with my cat."

The cat rolled his eyes and gave me a contemptuous-sounding feline *mrowl*. Then Mister hurled himself against my legs in a gesture that had nothing to do with Bob, before bounding up the steps and out of sight.

I showered, got dressed, and got enough of a fire going in my kitchen stove to scramble some eggs and toast some bread. There was a scratching sound from the open trapdoor to my lab. Then I heard a series of thumps. A moment later the scratching came again, and I peered down the stepladder.

The little grey puppy had escaped the box, and was attempting to climb the stepladder. He made it up five or six steps, slipped, and thumped back down to the stone floor at the bottom of the ladder—evidently for at least the second time. He didn't whimper when he fell. He just sprawled, wiggled to get his paws back under him, then started up the stepladder again full of, well, dogged determination.

"Hell's bells, dog. You're insane. Did you know that? Certifiable."

The puppy climbed to the next step and paused to look at me, mouth dropping open in a doggie grin. He wagged his tail so hard he nearly fell off again. I went down and scooped him up, put him on the love seat, and sat down with him to eat breakfast. I shared, and made sure he got a bit of water to drink. Just because I wasn't keeping him didn't excuse me from showing a guest some measure of hospitality. Even if the guest was fuzzy.

While I ate, I mapped out my plan for the day. I'd have to spend most of it at Genosa's studio, if I was going to be able to protect anyone from incoming curses.

But ultimately that was a losing strategy. Sooner or later I would be in the wrong place, or else the curse might come in too hard or fast for me to stop. The smart plan was to find out where these curses were coming from. Someone had to be sending them. What I really had to do was find that person and push their face in a little. Problem solved.

What's more, I was pretty confident that whoever was behind these curses was close to Genosa's social circle. While not as invasive or vicious as magic that directly attacked a person's physical body, this curse was still plenty potent. For magic to work, you have to believe in it. Really believe, without any doubts or reservations. It isn't all that common for someone to have that much conviction directed toward murderous ends. It's even less common to have that kind of rancor for a complete stranger.

All of which meant that the killer was probably someone close to Genosa's crowd.

Or in it.

Which meant that there was at least a chance that I would come face-to-face with the killer at work today. Best pack for trouble.

Speaking of which, I wouldn't have to worry much about the Black Court making a move on me in daylight, but it didn't mean I could afford to let my guard down for long. Vampires had a general habit of recruiting surrogate thugs for wetwork in broad daylight, and a bullet between the eyes would kill me just as well as some vampire ripping my lower jaw off. In fact, it would be a lot better, because then the vamp could order the flunky to give himself up or suicide, and the mortal authorities who might otherwise cause trouble would become a nonissue.

I was better than most at maintaining a high alert, but even so I couldn't be sharp on my guard forever. I'd get tired, bored, make mistakes. To say nothing of how grumpy it would make me, generally speaking. The longer I waited to solve the vampire problem, the more likely I'd be to get dead. So I had to move fast. Which meant that I'd need to round up some help fast. It took me about ten seconds to figure out who I wanted to call. I even had time enough to go see one of them before work.

We finished breakfast, and I let the puppy handle the prewash. I got out my Rolodex, got on the phone, and left two messages with two answering machines. Then I pulled on my heavy black mantled duster, dropped the pup into one of its huge pockets, fetched my staff and rod along with a backpack full of various gadgets for on-the-fly spellwork, and went out to face the day.

My first destination, Dough Joe's Hurricane Gym, resided on the first floor of an old office building not far from the headquarters of Chicago PD. The place had once been a tragically if predictably short-lived country-and-western bar. When Joe moved in, he tore down every wall that wasn't a load-bearing section, ripped out the cheap ceiling tiles, peeled the floor down to smooth, naked concrete, and installed a lot of lights. To my right lay a couple of bathrooms large enough to do double duty as locker rooms. A large square of safety carpet boasted about thirty well-used pieces of weight-training equipment and several racks of weights and dumbbells that made my muscles ache just looking at them. In front of me was an honest-to-goodness boxing ring, though it wasn't raised. On the other side of the ring, a raised platform boasted a long row of boxing targets—heavy bags, speed bags, and a couple of flicker bags that I could rarely hit more than once in a row.

The last area was covered with a thick impact mat and was the largest in the gym. Several people in judo pajamas were already working through various grappling techniques. I recognized most of the pajama people on sight as members of Chicago's finest.

One of the men, a large and brawny rookie, let out a sharp shout, and then he and another man closed in to attack a single opponent. They were quick, and worked well together. If it had been anyone but Murphy up against them, they probably would have been successful.

Lt. Karrin Murphy, the woman in charge of the Special Investigations division of Chicago PD, stood an even five feet. Her blond hair had been tied back into a tail, and she wore white pajamas with a faded belt that was more grey than black. She was attractive in a pleasantly wholesome kind of way—crystal blue eyes, clear skin, an upturned nose.

And she'd been a student of aikido since she was eleven.

The brawny rookie underestimated her speed, and she had slipped aside from his kick before he realized his mistake. She caught him by an ankle, twisted with her whole frame, and sent him stumbling away for a second or two—time enough for her to handle the second attacker. He struck more cautiously, and Murphy let out an abrupt shout of her own, faked a jab, and drove a front kick into his belt. It wasn't at full strength, and he'd taken the blow correctly, but he fell back a couple of steps, hands lifted in acknowledgment. If Murphy had been in earnest, she'd have put him down, hard.

The rookie came back in, but he hadn't really gotten up to speed. Murphy blocked a jab and a slow reverse punch, got the rookie by the wrist, and sent him smashing down on the impact mat, one hand twisted to the breaking point and held firm at the small of his back. The rookie grimaced and slapped the mat three times. Murphy released him.

"Hey, Stallings," she said, loudly enough to be heard by the whole gym. "What just happened here?"

The older opponent grinned and said, "O'Toole just got beat up by a girl, Lieutenant."

There was a general round of applause and good-natured jeers from the other cops in the gym, including several calls of "Pay up!" and "Told you so!"

O'Toole shook his head ruefully. "What did I do wrong?"

"Telegraphed the kick," Murphy said. "You're a moose, O'Toole. Even a light kick from you will do the job. Don't sacrifice speed to get more power. Keep it quick and simple."

O'Toole nodded, and walked over to an open corner of the mat with his partner.

"Hey, Murphy," I called. "When are you gonna stop picking on little kids and fight someone your own size?"

Murphy flicked her tail over her shoulder, her eyes shining. "Come say that to my face, Dresden."

"Give me a minute to amputate my legs and I will," I responded. I took my shoes off and set them against the wall, along with my duster. Murphy got a smooth wooden staff about five feet long from a rack on the wall. I took my staff into a square marked in tape on the mat, and we bowed to each other.

We warmed up with a simple sequence, alternating strikes in a steady, working rhythm, wooden staves clacking solidly. Murphy didn't start pushing for more speed. "Haven't seen you for almost two weeks. You flaking out on this self-defense notion?"

"No," I said, keeping my voice down. "Been on a job. Finished it up last night." I lost focus, slipped up in the sequence, and Murphy's staff banged down hard on the fingers of my left hand. "Hell's bells, *ow!*"

"Concentrate, wimp." Murphy gave me a second to shake my fingers, and then she started again from the beginning. "You've got something on your mind."

"Something off the record," I said, lowering my voice.

She looked around. No one was close enough to listen in. "Okay."

"I need a thug. You available?"

Murphy arched a brow. "You need manpower?"

"Thugpower," I said.

Murphy frowned. "What do you have in mind?"

"Black Court," I said. "At least two in town, probably more."

"Hitters?"

I nodded. "One of them came pretty close to taking me last night."

"You okay?"

"Yeah. But we have to shut these guys down, and fast. They aren't gentle and fun-loving like the Reds."

"Meaning?"

"Meaning that when they feed, their victims don't usually survive. They don't feed as often, but the longer they stay, the more people are going to get killed."

Murphy's eyes glittered with a sudden, angry fire. "What's the plan?"

"Find them. Kill them."

Her brows shot up. "Just like that? No formal balls, no masquerades, no clandestine meetings as preliminaries?"

"Nah. I thought it might be nice to get the drop on the bad guys for a change."

"I like that plan."

"It's simple," I agreed.

"Like you," Murphy said.

"Just like me."

"When?"

I shook my head. "As soon as I find where they're holed up during daylight. I can probably do it in a day or three."

"How's Saturday?"

"Uh. Why?"

She rolled her eyes. "Murphy annual family reunion is this weekend. I try to be working on reunion weekend."

"Oh," I said. "Why don't you just, you know . . . not show up."

"I need a good excuse not to show up, or my mother won't let me hear the end of it."

"So lie."

Murphy shook her head. "She'd know. She's psychic or something."

I felt my eyebrows go up. "Well, gee, Murph. I guess I'll just try to arrange things so that the deadly monster threat will be convenient to ducking your annual family fun-fest. Your sense of priorities once more astounds me."

She grimaced. "Sorry. I spend time dreading this every year. Things are sort of hard between me and my mother. Family skews your sanity. I don't expect you to under—"

She broke off abruptly, and a little pang of hurt went through me. She didn't expect me to understand. I didn't have a mother. I didn't have a family. I never had. Even my dim memories of my father had all but vanished. I'd been only six years old when he died.

"God, Harry," Murph said. "I wasn't thinking. I'm sorry."

I coughed and focused on the sequence. "It shouldn't be a long job. I find the vamps. We go in, pound in some stakes, cut some heads, toss some holy water, and we're gone."

She began to speed the pace, evidently as glad as I to leave that comment unremarked. The strength of her swings made my hands buzz when her staff hit mine. "You mean we get to live the cliché?" she asked. "Stakes and crosses and garlic?"

"Yeah. Cakewalk."

Murphy snorted. "Then why do you need thugs?"

"In case they have goons. I need thugpower with countergoon capability."

Murphy nodded. "A few extra hands wouldn't be a bad idea." She sped up again, her staff a blur. I had to struggle to keep up. "Why don't you ask the holy knight guy?"

"No," I said.

"What if we need him?"

"Michael would come in a hot second if I asked him. But I'm tired of seeing him get hurt because of me." I frowned, almost lost the rhythm, then found it again. "God or someone like Him does Michael's event scheduling, and I get the feeling that Michael's a lot less invincible when he isn't officially on the clock."

"But he's a big boy. I mean, he knows the risks. He has brains."

"He also has kids."

Murphy faltered this time, and I hit one of her thumbs. She winced and nodded toward the rookie cop she'd humbled. "O'Toole there is Mickey Malone's nephew. He'd jump through fire for you, if I asked him along."

"God, no. No newbies on this run. A stupid mistake could be fatal."

"I could talk to Stallings."

I shook my head. "Murph, the boys in SI are a lot better at handling supernatural weirdness than the average bear—but a lot of them still don't really believe what they're dealing with. I want someone smart and tough, and who won't freeze or freak out, and that's you."

"They're better than that."

"What happens to them if something goes wrong? If I make a mistake. Or you do. Even if they got out in one piece, how do you think they would handle the backlash when they got back to the real world? Where people don't believe in vampires, and there are bodies to explain?"

Murphy frowned. "The same thing that would happen to me, I guess."

"Yeah. But you're their leader. You want to be responsible for sending them into that kind of mess? Expose them to that?"

Murphy looked at several of the men around the gym and grimaced. "You know I don't want that. But my point is that I'm as vulnerable as they are."

"Maybe. But you know the score. They don't. Not really. You know enough to be careful and smart."

"What about the White Council?" Murphy asked. "Shouldn't they be willing to help you? I mean, you're one of their own."

I shrugged. "By and large they don't like me. I need their help like I need a sword in the neck."

"Gee. Someone actually resisted your charm and finesse."

"What can I say. They have no taste."

Murphy nodded. "So who else are you going to get?"

"You and one more will do for coffin patrol," I said. "I know a guy who is good with vampires. And I'm going to have a driver standing by when it goes down."

"How many laws are you planning on breaking?"

"None," I said. "If I can help it."

"What if these vampires have human goons?"

"We disable them. I'm only gunning for Black Court. But if you want to pull double duty as conscience officer, that's fine by me."

We finished the sequence, backed a step away, and bowed to each other. Murphy walked with me to the edge of the mat, frowning and mulling things over. "I don't want to sidestep any laws. Vampire hunting is one thing. Going vigilante is another."

"Done," I said.

She frowned. "And I'd really, really like it if we did it on Saturday."

I snorted. "If we go early, maybe you can get laid up in the hospital or something, at least."

"Ha-ha," Murphy said.

"Do me a favor and keep an eye on missing persons for a few days. It might help tip us off to their location. I want every bit of information I can get."

"Gotcha," Murphy said. "You want to work on some hand-to-hand?"

I picked up my duster. "Can't. Got to be on the new job in half an hour."

"Harry, aikido is a demanding discipline. If you don't practice every day, you're going to lose what you've learned."

"I know, I know. But it isn't like I can depend on a routine from day to day."

"A little knowledge is a dangerous thing," Murphy said. She held my staff for me while I put on my coat and abruptly frowned as she handed it back.

"What?" I asked her.

Her mouth twisted into the shape it got when she tried to hold back laughter. "Is that a puppy in your pocket, or are you just glad to see me?"

I looked down. The puppy had woken from his nap and poked its head out of my duster's pocket, and was panting happily. "Oh. Right."

Murphy plucked the puppy out of my pocket, turned him belly up, and started rubbing his tummy. "What's his name?"

"No name. I'm not keeping him."

"Ah," Murphy said.

"Want a dog?"

She shook her head. "They take too much attention, and I'm gone at all hours."

"Tell me about it. Know anyone who does?"

"Not really."

"Do me a favor. Keep him for a day."

Murphy blinked. "Why me?"

"Because I have to go on a new job this morning and I haven't had time to get him settled with someone. Come on, Murph. He's friendly. He's quiet. You'll never know he's there. Just for the day."

Murphy glowered at me. "I'm not keeping him."

"I know, I know."

"I'm not keeping him."

"You just said that, Murph."

"Just so long as you understand that I'm not keeping him."

"I get it already."

She nodded. "Just this once, then. I'm doing paperwork at my desk today. But you'd better be there to pick him up by five."

"You're an angel, Murph. Thank you."

She rolled her eyes and settled the pup in the curl of her arm. "Yeah, yeah. What's the new job?"

I sighed and told her.

Murphy burst out laughing. "You're a pig, Dresden."

"I didn't know," I protested.

"Oink. Oink, oink."

I glowered at her. "Don't you have some paperwork to do?"

"Get there by five, pig."

"By five." I sighed. I grumbled to myself as I walked out to my car and left for my first day on the set.

Chapter Seven

Chicago is a business town. Entrepreneurs of every stripe duke it out ferociously in pursuit of the American dream, discarding the carcasses of fallen ventures along the way. The town is full of old business headquarters, most of them held by the long-term commercial giants. When a new business sets its sights on Second City, it's cheaper for them to settle in one of the newer industrial parks littered around the city's suburbs. They all look more or less alike—a grid of plain, blocky, readily adaptable buildings two or three stories high with no windows, no landscaping, and gravel parking lots. They look like enormous, ugly concrete bricks, but they're cheap.

Arturo had acquired a short-term lease on such a building in such an industrial complex twenty minutes west of town. There were three other cars parked in its lot by the time I got there. I had a nylon backpack full of various magical tools I might need to ward off malevolent energies: salt, a bunch of white candles, holy water, a ring of keys, a small silver bell, and chocolate.

Yeah, chocolate. Chocolate fends off all kinds of nasty stuff. And if you get hungry while warding off evil, you have a snack. It's multipurpose equipment.

One end of my carved wooden blasting rod protruded from the backpack in case I needed to make a fast draw. I was also wearing my shield bracelet, my mother's pentacle amulet, my force ring, and a new gizmo I'd been working with—a silver belt buckle carved into the shape of a standing bear. Better to have the magical arsenal and not need it, than to not have it and get killed to death.

I got out of the car. I had on a pair of slacks and a polo shirt, since I had no idea of what a production assistant on an adult film set was supposed to wear. The client would have to be happy with business casual. I slung the backpack over one shoulder and locked up the car. A second car pulled up as I did, a shiny green rental number, and parked next to the Blue Beetle.

Two men got out. The driver was a fit-looking man, maybe in his late thirties. He was a little taller than average and had the build of someone who works out in a nonfanatic kind of way. His medium-brown hair was long enough to look a little disheveled. He wore round-rimmed spectacles, a Nike T-shirt, and Levi's, and his cross-trainers probably cost him upwards of a hundred bucks. He nodded at me and said, "Good morning," in a tone of genuine cheer.

"Hi," I responded.

"New guy?" he asked.

"New guy."

"Cameraman?"

"Stunt double."

"Cool." He grinned, pulled a designer-label gym bag out of the back of the rental car, and slung it over his shoulder. He approached, offering his hand. "I'm Jake."

I traded grips with him. His hands had the calluses of someone who worked with them, and he had a confidence that conveyed strength without attempting to crush my fingers. I liked him. "Harry," I responded.

The second man who got out of the rental car looked like a weight-lifting commercial. He was tall and built like a statue of Hercules beneath tight leather pants and a sleeveless workout shirt. He had a high-tech tan, coal-black hair, and wasn't old enough to qualify for decent rates on his auto insurance. His face didn't match the Olympian body. His features rated on the western slope of the bell curve of physical appeal. Though to be fair he was staring at me with a murderous scowl, which probably biased my opinion.

"Who the hell are you?" he growled.

"I the hell am Harry," I said.

He pulled out his own gym bag and slammed the car door closed. "You always a wiseass?"

"No. Sometimes I'm asleep."

He took a pair of hard steps toward me and thrust the heel of one hand at my shoulder in a belligerent push. Classic macho-jitsu. I could have done a bunch of fairly violent things in response, but I try not to get into fights in a gravel parking lot if I can help it. I took the push without yielding and grunted.

"Wrist is a little limp," I said. "If you like I can show you an exercise or something, help you out."

His face twisted with abrupt heat. "Son of a bitch," the man swore, and dropped his bag so he could ball his huge hands into huge fists.

"Whoa," Jake said, and stepped between us, facing the big guy. "Hey, come on, Bobby. It's too early for this crap."

Bobby got a lot more aggressive once Jake was there to hold him back, snarling and cussing. I'd faced too many literal ogres to be too terribly impressed by a metaphorical one, but I was just as glad that it hadn't gone any farther. The kid was a hell of a lot stronger than me, and if he knew more than nothing about how to handle himself, he could ruin my whole day.

The kid subsided after a minute, picked up his stuff again, and scowled at me. "I know what you're thinking, and you can forget it."

I lifted my eyebrows. "So you're psychic too?"

"Wiseass stunt double," he snarled. "It happened *once*. You aren't going to make a name for yourself. You might as well just leave now."

Jake sighed. "Bobby, he's not a stunt double."

"But he said—"

"He was *joking*," Jake said. "Christ, he's newer at this than you. Look, just go inside. Get some coffee or springwater or something. You don't need this on a shooting day."

The kid glared at me again and jabbed his index finger at me. "I'm warning you, asshole. Stay out of my way if you don't want to get hurt."

I tried to keep all the panic and terror he'd inspired off of my face. "Okeydoke."

The kid snarled, spat on the ground in my direction, and then stormed inside.

"Someone woke up with his testosterone in a knot today," I said.

Jake watched Bobby go and nodded. "He's under pressure. Try not to take it personal, man."

"That's tough," I said. "What with the insults and violent posturing and such."

Jake grimaced. "Nothing to do with you personally, man. He's worried."

"About being replaced by a stunt double?"

"Yeah."

"Are you serious? What the hell does a stunt double do in a porno flick?"

Jake waved a hand vagucly toward his belt. "Extreme close-ups."

"Uh. What?"

"Historically speaking, it doesn't happen often. Especially what with Viagra now. But it isn't unknown for a director to bring in a double for the close of a scene, if the actor is having trouble finishing."

I blinked. "He thought I was a *stunt penis?*"

Jake laughed at my reaction. "Man. You *are* new."

"You been doing this work long?"

"Awhile," he said.

"Guess it's a dream job, eh? Gorgeous women and all."

He shrugged. "Not as much as you'd think. After a while anyway."

"Then why do you do it?"

"Habit?" he asked with an easy grin. "Plus lack of options. I thought about doing the family thing once, but it didn't work out." He fell silent for a second, his expression touched with faint grief. He shook his head to come out of it and said, "Look, don't worry about Bobby. He'll calm down once he figures out his stage name."

"Stage name?"

"Yeah. I think that's what has got him all nervous. This is only his second shoot. First one is in the can, but it'll be a bit before they do final edits and such. He's got until next week to figure out his performing name."

"Performing name, huh."

"Don't make fun of it," he said, expression serious. "Names have power, man."

"Do they. Really."

Jake nodded. "A good name inspires confidence. It's important for a young guy."

"Like Dumbo's magic feather," I said.

"Right, exactly."

"So what name do you go by?" I asked.

"Jack Rockhardt," Jake replied promptly. He eyed me for a moment, his expression assessing.

"What?" I asked.

"You mean you don't recognize the name? Or me?"

I shrugged. "I don't have a TV. Don't go to those theaters, either."

His eyebrows shot up. "Really? Are you Amish or something?"

"Yeah, that's it. I'm Amish."

He grinned. "Maybe you'd better come inside with me. I'll introduce you around."

"Thanks."

"No problem," Jake said.

We went on into the building, a place with sterile beige walls and invincible medium-brown carpeting. Jake led me to a door with a computer-printed sign that read, GREEN ROOM, and went inside.

A long conference table ran down the center of a comfortably sized room. Doughnuts, drinks, fruits, bagels, and other foods of every description were laid out on trays down its length. The room smelled like fresh coffee, and I promptly homed in on the coffee machine for a cup.

A plain-faced woman in her mid-forties entered, wearing jeans, a black tee, and a red-and-white flannel shirt. Her hair was tied back under a red bandanna. She seized a paper plate and dumped food on it at random. "Good morning, Guffie."

"Joan," Jake responded easily. "Have you met Harry?"

"Not yet." She glanced over her shoulder at me and nodded. "Wow. You are very tall."

"I'm actually a midget. The haircut makes me look taller."

Joan laughed and popped a doughnut hole in her mouth. "You're the production assistant, eh?"

"Yes."

She nodded. "So let's produce."

"I thought that was Arturo's bag."

"He's the director and executive producer. I'm the actual producer. Makeup, cameras, lighting, sets, you name it. I handle the crew and the details." She turned to me and offered her hand, shaking off sugary doughnut goodness as she did. "Joan Dallas."

"Pleasure," I said. "Harry Dresden."

Joan nodded. "Come on then. There's still a lot to do before we can shoot. Guffie, get to the dressing room and clean yourself up."

Jake nodded. "Are they here yet?"

Her tone of voice became annoyed. "Giselle and Emma are."

There was a moment of silent, pregnant tension. Jake winced and headed for the door. "Harry, nice to meet you. Joan's okay, but she'll work you to death."

Joan threw an apple at him. Jake caught it when it bounced off his chest, crunched into it with his teeth, and held it in his mouth so that he could wave as he left the room.

"Grab yourself some food, Stilts," Joan said. "You can help me put cameras together."

"I was hoping to talk to Arturo before we got going," I said.

She turned around with two plates loaded with breakfast pastries. She hadn't bothered getting any fruit. "You're a funny guy. He's probably not out of bed yet. Bring that box of cookies. If my blood sugar drops too low I might take your head off."

She led me down a short hallway to a cavernous room—a shooting studio. A slightly raised stage held an unlit set, which looked like a lavishly appointed bedroom. Arrayed in a line in front of it were several black plastic crates and a freestanding shop light. Joan flicked it on and started opening crates, popping a bit of food into her mouth every third or fourth movement.

"Nice place," I said.

"Been a bitch," Joan said between bites. "Last company here was supposed to be some kind of computer production deal, but they had to be lying. They redid all the wiring in here, routed in way heavier than they were supposed to have. Took me a week to get things working, and then I had to turn their old gym into something like a dressing room, but this place still isn't up to code."

"Ye canna change the laws of physics," I said.

She laughed. "Amen."

"Engineer then?" I asked.

"By way of necessity," she answered. "I've done sets, lighting, power. Even some plumbing. And," she said, opening boxes, "cameras. Gather 'round, gofer boy; you can help."

I settled down while she laid out parts from heavy plastic crates. She assembled them, several professional cameras and tripods, with the surety of long practice. She gave me instructions as she did, and I did my best to help her out.

There was a pleasant, quiet rhythm to the work, something that I hadn't really felt since the last time I'd been on a farm in Hog Hollow, Missouri. And it was interesting—technology was unfamiliar territory for me.

See, those who wield the primordial forces of creation have a long-running grudge with physics. Electronic equipment in particular tends to behave unpredictably—right up until it shuts down and stops working altogether. Old technologies seemed more stable, which was one reason I drove around town in a Volkswagen Beetle that had been built before the end of the Vietnam War. But newer products—videocameras, televisions, cell phones, computers—would die a horrible fizzling death after any extended time in my presence.

There was a sense of order to what we were doing that appealed to me on some level. Putting parts together, locking them into place, lining up plugs into their corresponding sockets, taping groups of wires together so that they wouldn't get tangled. I did well enough that Joan sat back and watched me work on the last camera on my own.

"So how is this supposed to work?" I said. "What happens next?"

"The lights." She sighed. "The damned lights are the most annoying part. We have to set them up so that no one looks too shiny or too wrinkly. Once that's done, I'll let the technical manager handle sound, and go ride herd on the actors."

"Metaphorically, I hope."

She snorted. "Yes. Some of them are decent enough— like that blockhead Guffie. But if you don't push them into getting things done, they'll never be ready for the set on time. Makeup, costume, that sort of thing."

"Aha. And some of them are late?" I asked.

"Scrump will be," she said. It almost came out a growl.

I pushed. "Who?"

"Tricia Scrump. Actress."

"You don't like her?" I asked.

"I despise that self-absorbed, egotistical little bitch," Joan said cheerfully. "She'll play the princess and everyone else in the cast will know that they don't have to show up on time, or be ready to go on time, or be entirely sober, since Her Lascivious Highness Trixie Vixen will be showing up late to everything anyway, high as a kite and doing exactly as she pleases. I long to slap her silly."

"You shouldn't repress your emotions like that," I said.

She let out a belly laugh. "Sorry. No reason to drag a newbie into old politics. Guess I'm just upset to be working with her again. I didn't expect it."

Aha. Hostility for the porn starlet. That's what we in the business call "motive." Joan did not strike a creepy, murderous *strega* vibe with me, but I'd learned the hard way that a skilled liar can look innocent right up until she stabs you in the back. I dug for more information like a good investigator. "Why not?"

She shook her head. "When Arturo left Silverlight Studios to start his own company, he made a lot of people angry."

"What do you think about that? The move, I mean."

She sighed. "Arturo is an idiot. He's a kind man, and he means well. But he's an idiot. Anyone who works with him now risks getting blacklisted by Silverlight."

"Even Trixie? I mean, if she's a big star, won't the studio kind of kowtow to her?"

Joan leaned down to check a connection I'd made, shoving the plug in. "Are you on drugs or something? She's a big star with a limited shelf life. They'd replace her without blinking."

"She sounds gutsy."

Joan shook her head. "Don't confuse courage with stupidity. I think she's vapid enough to actually believe she's too important to lose."

"If I didn't know better, I'd say you don't like her much."

"Doesn't matter whether or not I like her," Joan said. "It's my job to work with her."

I watched her set her mouth in a firm line as she started closing cases and stacking them up. I was willing to bet that Tricia Scrump, a/k/a Trixie Vixen, didn't have the same kind of professional resolve.

I helped Joan pick up the crates and tools and stack them against the far wall of the dim studio. She moved briskly, tension and distaste simmering under the surface of her determined expression. I studied her as covertly as I could. She clearly wasn't happy to be here. Could she be gunning for Arturo with some kind of heavy-duty entropy curse?

It didn't track. There hadn't been any hostility when she spoke about Arturo. And if she were a strong enough practitioner to throw out deadly spells, she wouldn't be able to keep up a career amidst so much technology. If she was harboring vengeful feelings toward Arturo, she was the best actress I'd ever seen.

I suppose that could have been possible. But my instincts were sending me mixed messages. On the one hand, they told me that Joan was on the level. On the other, they also told me there was more to the woman than met the eye. Something told me that things were more serious than they appeared—that this situation was even more dangerous than I had originally believed.

It bothered me. It bothered me a lot.

Joan shut the last case and interrupted my train of thought. "Okay then," she said. "Let's get the studio powered up."

"Um," I said. "Maybe I shouldn't be here when you do."

She lifted her eyebrows, evidently waiting for an explanation.

"Uh," I said. "I have a plate in my head. It's a little twitchy around electric fields. High-voltage equipment, that kind of thing. I'd rather come in when it was already up and running, so I can back off if there's a problem."

Joan stared at me with a lot of skepticism. "Is that so?"

"Yeah."

She frowned. "How did you *get* this job?"

Christ, I'm a terrible liar. I tried to think of an answer that didn't begin with, "Um."

But I was interrupted.

A surge of silent, invisible energy swept through the room, cold and foul. My stomach twisted with abrupt nausea, and my skin erupted in gooseflesh. Dark, dangerous magic swirled by, drawing my attention to the studio's exit. It was the kind of magic that destroys, warps, rots, and corrupts.

The kind of magic you'd need to feed a deadly entropy curse.

"What's wrong?" Joan shook me with one hand. "Harry? You're shaking. Are you all right?"

I managed to choke out, "Who else is in the building?"

"Jake, Bobby, Emma, and Giselle. No one else."

I stumbled to my pack and picked it up. If Joan hadn't helped me balance, I might have fallen down. "Show me where."

Joan blinked in confusion. "What?"

I shoved the sensation of the dark magic away as best I could and snarled, "They're in danger. Show me where! Now!"

My tone might have alarmed her, but her expression became more worried than frightened. Joan nodded and half ran out of the studio, leading me out a side door, up a flight of metal spiral stairs, and into another hallway. We sprinted down it to a room with a sign on it that said, DRESSING ROOM.

"Get back," I said, and stepped in front of her.

I hadn't yet touched the doorknob when a woman began to scream.

Chapter Eight

I tore the door open onto a room the size of my apartment, lined with freestanding mirrors, folding tables, and chairs. A cloud of foul energies slapped me in the face. Bobby stood off to my right, his expression registering surprise and confusion. To my left stood a woman in the corner of my vision, mostly naked. I didn't stop to goggle, but ran through the room to a second door. It was partly open and swinging closed again.

I slammed through it into a bathroom as big as my bedroom, which I suppose isn't all that unusual. The air was hot, humid, and smelled like fresh soap. The shower was running, its glass door broken into jagged teeth. The floor was covered in more broken glass, a little water, and a lot of blood. Two rigid, motionless bodies lay on the floor.

My instincts screamed a warning, and just before I stepped into the pool of bloodstained water, I threw myself into a jump. My shins hit heavily on the counter of the sink and I started to fall. I grabbed on to the faucet and hauled myself up. My shins hurt like hell, but I'd kept my feet off the floor. My brain caught up to my instincts, and I saw what was going on. The two people on the floor weren't motionless—they were locked into positions of rigid agony.

Sparks leapt up in the back corner of the room. A heavy, high-voltage light fixture had broken loose from the ceiling and fallen, hauling exposed wiring to lie in the thin sheet of scarlet liquid on the floor.

Like I said, I don't get along with technology when I'm trying to use it. But when I actually *want* to bust it up, I'm hell on wheels. I extended my right hand at the light fixture, snarled incoherently, and willed raw power over the electric menace like an invisible wrecking ball. The hex rippled through the air, and the live wires exploded into wild blue arcs of electricity for maybe two seconds.

And then the lights went out.

In the whole damn building.

Whoops.

I heard a pair of gasps from whoever was on the floor, presumably Jake and someone named Giselle. I got out my pentacle amulet.

"What's happening?" Bobby's voice sounded suspicious. Stars, what a dolt. "Hey, prick, what do you think you're doing?"

"Where are the damned emergency lights?" said an annoyed female voice. A light flicked on in the dressing room, and Joan appeared at the bathroom door holding a pocket flashlight on her key chain. "What's going on?"

"Call nine-one-one," I snapped. "Hurry, there's bleeding."

"You need a light," Joan said.

"Got one." I willed energy through the silver pentacle. It flickered and began to brighten with a steady blue glow that made the blood on the floor look black. "Hurry, and bring all the ice you can find with you when you come back."

Joan vanished from the door. She snarled, "Get out of the way, you blockhead," and her footsteps retreated back down the hall. I got off the sink, splashed into the water, and knelt beside the downed people.

Jake, naked from the waist up, stirred as I did. "Ow," he said in a rough voice. "Ow."

"Are you all right?" I asked.

He sat up, wobbling a little. "Never mind. Giselle, she must have slipped in the shower. I came in to help her."

I turned my attention to the girl. She was young and a little scrawny for my tastes, all long limbs and long hair. I rolled her onto her back. She had a cut running the length of her neck, curving from the base of her ear to above her collarbone. Blood shone on her skin, her mouth was partly open, and her dark eyes were glassy.

"Crap," I said. I seized a towel from a large shelf of them and pressed it down hard on the girl's wound. "Jake, I need you."

He looked up a little blearily. "Is she dead?"

"She will be if you don't help. Hold this down hard. Keep pressure on the wound."

"Okay." He didn't look steady, but he clenched his jaw and did as I instructed. While I elevated her feet with a rolled towel, Jake said, "I can't feel a pulse. She isn't breathing."

"Dammit." I tilted the girl's head back and made sure her mouth was clear. I sealed my mouth to hers and blew in hard. Then I drew back and put the heels of my hands near her sternum. I wasn't sure how hard to push. The practice dummy in the CPR class didn't have ribs to break. I guessed and hoped I got it right. Five pushes, then another breath. Five more, then another breath. The blue light from my amulet bobbed and waved about, making shadows lurch and shift.

For the record, CPR is hard to do for very long. I made it for maybe six or seven minutes, and was getting too dizzy to see when Jake told me to switch off with him. We swapped jobs. Joan returned with a big steel bowl of shaved ice, and I had her fold it into another towel, which I then pressed down over the wound.

"What are you doing?" Joan asked.

"She's cut bad. If we get her heart started, she'll bleed out," I panted. "The cold will make the blood vessels constrict, slow down the bleeding. It might buy her some time."

"Oh, God," Joan muttered. "Poor thing."

I leaned down to peer at her face. The skin on the left side of her features and on her throat was covered in blotches of dark, angry red. "Look. Burns."

"From the electricity?" Joan asked.

"Her face wasn't in the water," I said. I squinted between the girl and the shower. "The water," I said. "It turned hot on her. She got scalded and fell right through the damned glass."

Joan flinched as if she'd been stabbed with a knife, and her face turned grey. "Oh, my God. This is my fault. I hooked up the water heater myself."

"Jinxed," said Bobby from the dressing room. "This whole shoot is jinxed. We're screwed."

Joan was holding herself steady, but tears fell from off her chin onto the naked girl. I kept pressure on the injury. "I don't think this was your fault. I want you to get out front and show the paramedics in when they arrive."

Her face still ashen, she rose and took off without looking back. Jake kept up the mouth-to-mouth like he knew what he was doing. I was panting and holding the towel and ice against the wound when the paramedics finally showed up, carrying heavy-duty flashlights and rolling a wheeled stretcher between them.

I told them what had happened to the girl and got out of their way, taking a seat on the corner of a counter that ran along a wall of makeup mirrors. Jake joined me a minute later. "Thought I felt her breathe," he panted, his tone subdued. We watched the paramedics work. "God, this is really terrible. What are the odds of all that happening? You know?"

I frowned and closed my eyes, extending my senses into the room around me. Somewhere in the furor and panic, the choking cloud of destructive magic had dissipated. Barely a trace remained. With the crisis over and no action to occupy my mind, my hands started shaking and I saw a few stars in the corners of my vision. A phantom surge of panic sent my heart and breathing racing. I bowed my head and rubbed at the back of my neck, waiting for it to pass. The paramedics had some big old flashlights, so I put my amulet away, letting the blue light die out.

"You all right?" Jake asked.

"Will be in a minute. I hope she'll be okay."

Jake nodded, frowning. "Maybe Bobby's right."

"About a jinx?"

"Maybe." He studied me for a second, expression guarded. "How did you know?"

"Know what?"

"That we were in trouble. I mean, I thought you were in the studio. I ran in a couple of seconds after I heard her fall, and I was only a few feet away. You must have come through the door a couple of seconds after I did. How did you know?"

"Just lucky. We finished the cameras and Joan took me up there to introduce me or something."

"What was that light you had?"

I shrugged. "Present from a friend's kid. Some kind of fancy new thing the kids have. Light up jewelry for dance clubs and keggers."

"They call them raves now."

"Raves. Right."

Jake watched me for a moment and then slowly nodded his head. "Sorry. I'm being paranoid, I think."

"Been there. No problem."

He nodded and slumped down tiredly. "I thought I was a dead man in there. Thank you."

It seemed smart to keep the wizard thing as low-key as possible. Someone was flinging some nasty energy around. No sense in advertising my identity as a wizard of the White Council. "I didn't do much but run in," I said. "We're just lucky the power went out."

"Yeah."

The paramedics stood up, loaded Giselle onto the

stretcher, and picked it up. Jake and I both came to our feet as they did. "Is she going be okay?" he asked.

The paramedics didn't slow down, but one of them said, "She's got a chance." The man nodded to me. "Without the ice she wouldn't have had that."

Jake frowned and chewed on his lip, clearly upset. "Take care of her."

The paramedics started moving out with quick, steady steps. "Sir, you'd better come along with us to the hospital so that the doctors can check you out."

"I feel fine," Jake said.

The paramedics went around the corner, but the second one called back, "Electricity can do some nasty damage you might not feel. Come on."

But Jake stayed where he was. The paramedics took their lights with them, leaving the dressing room in darkness for a moment, until Joan returned with her little flashlight. "Guffie, get your Bowflexed ass into that ambulance."

He looked up at his reflection in the mirrored wall. His hair was sticking up every which way. "Though I apparently see the same stylist as Einstein, the Bride of Frankenstein, and Don King, I feel fine. Don't worry about me."

"I thought you'd say that," she said. "Fine, I'll drive you there myself. Everyone else needs to leave until I can make sure the power lines aren't going to kill anyone. Bobby and Emma are already outside. Harry, be back here by three, all right?"

"Why?" I asked.

"To start shooting."

"Shooting," Jake blurted. "After *that?*"

She grimaced. "The show must go on. Everyone out so I can lock up. Guffie, get in my car and don't argue with me. Arturo is meeting us at the hospital."

"Okay," Jake said. He didn't sound like he minded agreeing. "What about Bobby and Emma? They have a car?"

"Don't think so."

Jake picked up his sports bag, dug in it, and tossed me a set of keys. "Here. Give those to Emma for me?"

I caught them, and we all started out of the building. "Gotcha."

Joan sighed. "Maybe we are jinxed. It's like someone said *Macbeth*."

"What are the odds," Jake agreed.

Bubble, bubble, toil and trouble, fire burn and cauldron bubble. I didn't say anything to them, but I was pretty sure things would get worse before they got better.

A whole lot worse.

Chapter Nine

We went outside. Joan and Jake spoke briefly with Bobby and the woman I presumed to be Emma. Then Joan chivvied Jake into a car and drove out in a hurry, leaving the stage open for me to do some more snooping. There wasn't any time to waste with lethal magic like that on the loose, and the keys gave me a good excuse to do some more sniffing around.

I didn't hold out much hope that anything in Bobby the Bully's head would be important, so I focused on the woman and walked over to them. "Heya. I'm Harry. Production assistant."

"Emma," the woman said. She was actually very pretty. She had the kind of beauty that seemed to convey a sense of personal warmth, of kindness—a face best suited to smiling. Her eyes were shamrock green, her skin pale, her hair long and red, highlighted with streaks of sunny gold. She wore jeans with a black sweater, and made both of them look inviting—but she wasn't smiling. She offered me her hand. "I'm pleased to meet you. I'm glad you were there to help them."

"Anyone would have," I said.

"Come on, Emma," Bobby said, his expression sullen. "Let's call a cab and go."

She ignored him. "I don't think I've seen you around before."

"No, I'm local. A friend introduced me to Arturo, told him I needed a job."

Emma pursed her lips and nodded. "He's a softie," she said. "In case no one's told you, this isn't an average day on the set."

"I'd hope not. I'm sorry about your friend."

Emma nodded. "Poor Giselle. I hope she'll be all right. She's from France—doesn't have any family. I couldn't see her from where I was standing. Was it her throat that was hurt?"

"Yeah."

"Where? I mean, where was she hurt?"

I drew a line on my own face, starting at the back corner of my jaw and curving around to beside my Adam's apple. "There. Back to front."

Emma shuddered visibly. "God, the scars."

"If she lives, I doubt she'll mind them."

"Like hell she won't," Emma said. "They'll show. No one will cast her."

"Could have been worse."

She eyed me. "You don't approve of her profession?"

"I didn't say that."

"What, are you a religious type or something?"

"No. I just—"

"Because if you are, I'd like to tell you right now that I'm not, and I don't appreciate it when people pass judgment on my line of work."

"I'm not religious. I, uh—"

"I get so tired of hypocritical bastards who . . ." She started to say something else, then made a visible effort and shut her mouth. "I'm sorry. I'm not usually oversensitive. Sometimes I just get sick of people telling me how bad my work is for me. How it corrupts my soul. That I should abandon it and give my life to God."

"You're not going to believe me," I said. "But I know exactly what you mean."

"You're right," she said. "I don't believe you."

Her belt chirped, and she drew a cell phone from its clip. "Yes?" She paused for a moment. "No. No, sweetheart. Mommy already told you before I left. If Gracie says you get one cookie, then you only get one cookie. She's the boss until Mommy comes home." She listened for a moment, and then sighed. "I know, sweetie. I'm sorry. I'll be home soon. Okay? I love you too, sweetie. Kisses. Bye-bye."

"Kid?" I asked.

She gave me half of a smile as she put the phone back onto her belt. "Two. Their grandmother is with them."

I frowned. "Wow. I never really thought about, uh, actresses with children."

"Not many do," she said.

"Does, uh . . . does their father mind your career?"

Her eyes flashed hotly. "He isn't involved with them. Or me."

"Oh," I said. I offered her the keys. "From Jake, for the car. Sorry if I offended you. I didn't mean to."

She exhaled, and it seemed let out the pressure of her anger. She accepted them. "Not your fault. I'm tense."

"Everyone around here seems to be," I said.

"Yeah. It's this film. If it doesn't do well we're all going to be looking for work."

"Why?"

She shrugged a shoulder. "It's complicated. But we're all on contract with Silverlight. Arturo left them, but he had managed to slip something into his own contract with the studio that would let him continue hiring cast from Silverlight for three months after his departure."

"Oh," I said. "Jake said something about another movie."

She nodded. "Arturo wanted to do three of them. This is the second. If the movies go over well, Arturo will have a name for himself, and we'll have leverage to either quit contract with Silverlight or renegotiate better terms."

"I see," I said. "And if the movies crash, Silverlight will never pick up your contracts."

"Exactly." She frowned. "And we've had so many problems. Now this."

"Come *on,* Emma," Bobby called. "I'm starving. Let's go find something."

"You should start practicing some self-restraint for a change." The woman's green eyes flashed with irritated anger, but she smoothed it away from her face and said, "I'll see you here this afternoon then, Harry. Nice to meet you."

"Likewise."

She turned and glowered at Bobby as she walked to the car. They got in without speaking, Emma driving, and left the lot. I walked over to my car, pensive. Thomas and Arturo had been right. Someone had whipped out one hell of a nasty entropy curse—assuming that this wasn't a coincidental focus of destructive energy—the mystical equivalent of being struck with a bolt of lightning.

Sometimes energy can build up due to any number of causes—massive amounts of emotion, traumatic events, even simple geography. That energy influences the world around us. It's what gives the Cubbies the home-field advantage (though that whole billy goat thing sort of cancels it out), leaves an intangible aura of dread around sights of tragic and violent events, and causes places to get a bad reputation for strange occurrences.

I hadn't sensed any particular confluence of energies until just before the curse happened to Giselle and Jake, but that didn't entirely rule out coincidence. There is a whole spectrum of magical energies that are difficult to define or understand. There are thousands of names for them, in every culture—mana, psychic energy, totem, juju, chi, bioethereal power, the Force, the soul. It's an incredibly complex system of interweaving energy that influences good old Mother Earth around us, but it all boils down to a fairly simple concept: Shit happens.

But then again, other people around Arturo had been hurt. I could buy that lightning could strike once—but if I hadn't interfered, it would have hit four times. Not much chance for coincidence there.

No matter how much I might have wished it, the energy that had caused Giselle to slip into the glass door, the glass to break and cut her, and the lights to fall down and electrify the floor was not one of those natural hot spots of power. It had swirled past me like some vast and purposeful serpent, and it hadn't gone after the first person to cross its path. It had ignored me, Joan, Jake, Bobby, and Emma and gone into the shower after the girl.

So Arturo was wrong about at least one thing. He wasn't the target of the *malocchio*.

The women around him were.

And that pissed me off. Call me a Neanderthal if you like, but I get real irrational about bad things happening to women. Human violence was at its most hideous when a woman was on the receiving end, and supernatural predators were even worse. That was why seeing Thomas entrance Justine had set me off. I knew the girl was willing, sure. I was pretty sure Thomas didn't want any harm to come to her. But the more primitive instincts in me only saw that she was a woman and Thomas had been preying upon her.

No matter what the rational part of my head thinks, when I see someone hurt a woman my inner gigantopithicus wants to reach for the nearest bone and go Kubrickian on someone's head.

I got into the car, frowning more deeply, and forced myself to calm down and think. I took deep breaths until I relaxed enough to start analyzing what I knew. The attacks had the feeling of vendetta to it. Someone had a grudge against Arturo and was deliberately striking women near him. Who would hold a grudge that vicious?

A jealous woman, maybe. Especially since he was a man with three ex-wives.

Madge was in business with Arturo, though. She didn't seem to me the sort who would jeopardize her fortunes with something so primitive and intangible as vengeful hatred. The most recent wife, Tricia, was in the same situation, though I hadn't yet met her. The other ex-wife, Lucille maybe, was not supposed to be in the picture. Could she be using magic to get a little payback?

I shook my head and started my car. I'd been briefly exposed to an entropy curse once. It had been a lot more powerful than the *malocchio* that had nearly killed Jake and Giselle. I barely survived it—even with a hefty arsenal of magic and the sacrifice of a good man's life to divert the curse from me.

I'd saved Jake and Giselle, but I'd been lucky. It could as easily have been me getting electrocuted in a pool of my own blood. I'd managed to mitigate the *malocchio,* barely, but there was nothing to say that it couldn't happen again. And it was more than possible that next time the lance of vicious magic would be aimed right at me.

I started up the Blue Beetle and headed for my office, pondering on the road.

I didn't have enough information to make a solid guess on a perpetrator. Maybe it would make more sense to examine the murder weapon, as it were, and determine how it was being used.

Curses had the same sorts of limitation as any other spell, after all. Which meant that whoever was sending the Evil Eye had to have some sort of means of directing the magic at a target. Body parts worked best—a lock of hair, nail clippings, and fresh blood were the most common items used, but they weren't the only ones. A poppet, a little dolly dressed up like the intended victim, could also be used to aim a malevolent spell. I've heard you can even employ a good photo.

But targeting the spell was only one part of the process. Before the killer could send it anywhere, he had to gather up the energy to make it happen. A curse that strong would require a whole lot of work, gathering and focusing raw magic in one place. And after *that*, the energy would have to be molded, shaped into its desired result. Even among the magically gifted, that kind of discipline was rare. Sure, any of the White Council could do that as a matter of routine, but the White Council didn't include everyone with magical skill. Most weren't talented enough to apply for an apprenticeship. And there were plenty of people who washed out and never made it through their schooling.

Magic this powerful would be a dangerous business for someone new to the use of magic. Odds were good that this wasn't some petty, jealous whim of an arcane dabbler. Someone with a disturbing amount of ability was methodically committing murder.

But why? Why kill women working for Arturo? What effect would it have? The people involved in his films were clearly very nervous. Maybe someone was attempting to spread terror, to cause Arturo's business venture to implode.

Vengeance of some kind could be a motive, but after a moment's thought, I decided that greed opened up the field to more possibilities. Greed is a nice, sterile motivation. If the money's right, you don't need to know someone to take advantage of them. You don't have to hate them, or love them, or be related to them. You don't even have to know who they are. You just have to want money more than you want them to keep on breathing, and if history is any indicator, that isn't a terribly uncommon frame of mind.

I parked in my building's lot and stomped up the stairway to my office. Who would gain by Arturo's ruin? Silverlight Studios. I nodded. That line of thought fit a lot better than some sort of demented vengeance kick. It was a good place to get started, and I had a couple of hours to put to use. With luck, I could dig up the information I would need to support (or demolish) the idea of a bad guy with dollar signs where his conscience should be.

I opened my office door, but before I could go inside

I felt something cold and hard press against the back of my neck: the barrel of a gun. My heart fluttered into sudden, startled panic.

"Go into the office," said a quiet, rough voice, relaxed and masculine. "Don't make this any louder than it has to be."

Chapter Ten

Apparently a gun held to the back of my head engenders a sense of fellowship and goodwill in the depths of my soul. I cooperated.

I unlocked the door to the office, and the gunman followed me in. My office isn't big, but it's on the corner, and has windows on two walls. There's a table, a counter with my old coffee machine on it, some metal filing cabinets, and a table holding a display of pamphlets meant to help public relations with the normals. My desk sat in the corner between the windows, two comfy chairs for clients facing it.

The gunman walked me to one of my comfy chairs and said, "Sit."

I sat. "Hey, man, look—"

The gun pressed harder. "Hush."

I hushed. A second later something slapped my shoulder.

"Take it," the gunman said. "Put it on."

I reached back and found a heavy cloth sleeping mask with an elastic head strap. "Why?"

The gunman must have thumbed back the hammer of his weapon, because it clicked. I put the stupid mask on. "You might not know this, but I don't function all that well as an investigator when blinded."

"That's the idea," the gunman drawled. The gun left my neck. "Try not to make me feel threatened," he said through a yawn. "I'm all spooked and jittery. If you make any noise or start to get up, I'll probably twitch, and this trigger is pretty sensitive. My gun is pointed at your nose. The ensuing cause-and-effect chain could be inconvenient for you."

"Maybe next time you could just say 'freeze,'" I said. "No need to walk me through it step by step."

His tone sounded like he'd colored it with a faint smile. "Just want to make sure you understand the situation. If I blew your head off over a stupid misunderstanding, gosh, would our faces be red." He paused, then added, "Well, mine, anyway."

He didn't sound jumpy to me. He sounded bored. I heard him moving around for a minute, and then there was a sudden vibration in the air. I felt as if the skin of my face had suddenly dried into leather and tightened over my cheekbones.

"Okay," he said. "That'll do. Take it off."

I took the mask off and found the gunman sitting on the edge of my desk, a compact semiautomatic in his hand. He had it pointed at me in a casual way. He was a big guy, almost my own height, with dark golden hair just long enough to look a little exotic. He had grey-blue eyes that stayed steady and missed nothing. He wore casual black pants and a black sports jacket over a grey T-shirt. He was built more like a swimmer than a weight lifter, all leonine power and lazy grace taken completely for granted.

I looked around and saw a circle of salt as wide as two of my fingers poured around the chair. A Morton's salt cylinder sat on the floor nearby. A bit of scarlet stained some of the salt circle; blood. He'd used it to power up the circle, and I could feel its energy trapping all the magic in it, including my own.

The circle had formed a barrier that would stop magical energy cold. I'd have to physically break the circle of salt and disrupt that barrier before I could send any magic at the gunman. Which was probably the point.

I eyed him and said, "Kincaid. I didn't expect to hear from you until tomorrow at least."

"Rolling stones and moss, baby," the mercenary responded. "I was going through Atlanta when I got your message. Wasn't hard to get a direct flight here."

"What's with the Gestapo treatment?"

He shrugged. "You're a pretty unpredictable guy, Dresden. I don't mind making a social call, but I needed assurance that you were really you."

"I assure you that I'm me."

"That's nice."

"Now what?"

He rolled one shoulder in a shrug. "Now we have a nice talk."

"While you point a gun at me?" I asked.

"I just want a friendly chat without either of us getting his brain redecorated with magic."

"I can't do that," I said.

He shook a finger at me in a negative gesture. "The Council will burn anyone who gets caught doing it. That's different." He nodded at the circle. "But from in there, you literally can't. I'm here to talk business, not to die of stupidity. If you like, think of the precautions as a compliment."

I folded my arms. "Because nothing says flattery like a gun to the head."

"Ain't that God's own truth," Kincaid said. He set the gun down on my desk, put left his hand on it. "Dresden, I'm just plain folks. I'm still alive because I don't take stupid chances or walk into things blindly."

I tried to ditch the stubborn anger and nodded. "Okay, then. No harm, no foul."

"Good." He checked a nylon-strap watch on his left wrist. "I haven't got all day. You wanted to talk to me. So talk."

I felt annoyed enough to start screaming, but forced myself to rein it in. "There's a scourge of vampires in town."

"Black Court?"

"Yeah," I said.

"Whose scourge?"

"Mavra."

Kincaid pursed his lips. "Cagey old hag. I hear she heads up a pretty big crew."

"Yeah. I'm going to downsize them."

Kincaid's index finger tapped on his gun. "Black Court are tough to take down."

"Unless you get them in their coffins," I said. "I can find them."

"You want me to bodyguard you until then?"

"No. I want you to go there with me and help me kill them all."

A smile parted his lips from white teeth. "Going on an offensive would be nice. I'm getting bored on defense. What's the play?"

"Find 'em. Kill 'em."

Kincaid nodded. "Simple enough."

"Yeah, that's the idea. What are you going to cost me?"

He told me.

I choked. "Do you offer coupons or anything?"

Kincaid rolled his eyes and stood up. "Christ. Why did you waste my time, Dresden?"

"Wait," I said. "Look, I'll figure out a way to pay you."

He arched an eyebrow.

"I'm good for it."

"Maybe," he said. "But it's funny how a spending a lifetime as a hired gun makes you a little cynical."

"Take a chance," I said. "I'll get the money to you. And I'll owe you one."

His eyes glittered, flickers of malice and amusement sharing space in them. "Owed a favor by the infamous Dresden. I guess it might be worth enough of my time to give you a chance."

"Great."

"Two conditions," he said.

"Like?"

"I want at least one more set of eyes along," he said. "Someone good in a fight."

"Why?"

"Because if someone gets hurt, it takes two people to get him out alive. One to carry him and one to lay down cover fire."

"I didn't think you cared."

"Of course I do," he said. "The wounded guy might be me."

"Fine," I said. "What's the second condition?"

"You need to understand that if you try to stiff me, I'll have to protect my interests." He lifted a hand. "Don't get me wrong. It's just business. Nothing personal."

"It won't be an issue," I said. "Besides, you wouldn't want to eat my death curse, would you?"

"No. So I'd use a rifle at a thousand yards. The bullet outruns its own sonic boom, and you'd never even hear the shot. You'd be dead before you realized what happened."

That scared me. I've faced more than a few gruesome or nightmarish creatures, but none of them had been that calm and practical. Kincaid believed that he could kill me, if it came to that.

And thinking about it, I believed him too.

He watched my face for a minute, and his smile turned a shade wolfish. "You sure you want me on board?"

There was a pregnant half second of silence. "Yeah."

"All right." Kincaid stepped forward and brushed the salt circle with his toe. The tension of the circle's barrier vanished. "But I'm on the clock. I've got to get back to Ivy's place before Sunday."

"Understood," I said. "How do I get in touch?"

He slipped his gun into his jacket pocket and drew out a grey business card. He put the card on my desk and said, "Pager."

He turned to leave. I stood up and said, "Hey, Kincaid."

He glanced back at me. I tossed the sleep mask to him. He caught it.

"Just plain folk?" I asked.

"Yeah."

"Not supernatural?"

"I wish," he said. "Vanilla mortal."

"You're a liar."

His features smoothed into a neutral mask. "Excuse me?"

"I said you're a liar. I saw you during the fight at Wrigley, Kincaid. You fired a dozen shots, on the move and dodging bad guys the whole time."

"What's so supernatural about that?"

"In a fight, just plain folks miss sometimes. Maybe most times. You didn't miss once."

"What's the point of shooting if you're just going to miss?" He smiled, made a mime-gun of his thumb and index finger, and aimed at me. His thumb fell forward and he said, "I'm as human as you are, Dresden. I'll see you later."

Then he left.

I didn't know whether to feel better or worse. On one hand, he was an experienced gunman, and absolutely deadly in a fight. Human or not, I might need someone like that with me when I confronted Mavra.

On the other hand, I had no idea how I would be able to pay him, and I believed him when he said he'd assassinate me. The entire concept was scary as hell. The threat of a death curse that could be levied against a wizard's slayer was a major asset. It meant that anyone or anything that tried to attack a member of the White Council would hesitate, unwilling to risk the burst of destructive power a wizard could release in the last instants of his life.

But those instants would be too slow against a high-powered sniper round fired from ambush. I could imagine it, a flash and a thump on the back of my head, a split second of surprise, and then blackness before I could even realize the need to pronounce my curse.

Kincaid was right: It could work. The tactical doctrine of the powers-that-be in the magical communities of the world tended to run along a couple of centuries behind the rest of the planet. It was entirely possible that the seniormost wizards of the White Council had never even considered the possibility. Ditto for the vampires. But it could work.

The future abruptly seemed like a fairly unpleasant place for professional wizards.

I set about cleaning up the salt and settled down at my little desk, putting my thoughts in order. I had to find out more about the circumstances around the victims of the *malocchio*. I had to go digging for more information on Arturo Genosa's venture into the world of erotic film.

And if that wasn't enough, while I did all of that, I *also* had to figure out how to get enough money to keep my own hired thug from putting holes in my skull.

For most people it would be a desperate situation. But most people hadn't been through them as many times as I had. My worry and tension slowly grew, and as they did I took a perverse comfort in the familiar emotions. It actually felt *good* to feel my survival instincts put me on guard against premature mortality.

Hell's bells. Is that insane or what?

Chapter Eleven

I ran up a long-distance bill while I did my digging on Genosa. I called a dozen different organizations and business entities around Los Angeles, but computers answered almost every phone, and everyone I talked to referred me to their home page on the Internet. Evidently conversation with an actual human being had become passé. Stupid Internet.

I hit some walls, slammed my head against some closed doors, got a little information, and ran out of time. I wrote down Internet addresses, picked up some food, and went to see Murphy.

Special Investigations has its office in one of the clump of mismatched buildings comprising Chicago Police Headquarters. I checked in with the desk sergeant and showed him the consultant's ID card Murphy had given me. The man made me sign in and waved me through. I marched up the stairs and came out on the level housing holding cells and Special Investigations.

I opened the door to SI and stepped inside. The main room was maybe fifty feet long and twenty wide, and desks were packed into it like sardines. The only cubicle walls in the room were around a small waiting area with a couple of worn old couches and a table with some magazines for bored adults and some toys for bored children. One of them, a plush Snoopy doll spotted with old, dark stains, lay on the floor.

The puppy stood over it, tiny teeth sunk into one of the doll's ears. He shook his head, his own torn ear flapping, and dragged Snoopy in a little circle while letting out small, squeaky growls. The puppy looked up at me. His tail wagged furiously, and he savaged the doll with even more enthusiasm.

"Hey," I told him. "Murphy's supposed to be watching you. What are you doing?"

The puppy growled and shook Snoopy harder.

"I can see that." I sighed. "Some babysitter she is."

A tall man, going bald by degrees and dressed in a rumpled brown suit, looked up from his desk. "Hey, there, Harry."

"Sergeant Stallings," I responded. "Nice moves on Murphy today. The way you slammed her foot with your stomach was inspiring."

He grinned. "I was expecting her to go for a lock. Woman is a nasty infighter. Everyone tried to tell O'Toole, but he's still young enough to think he's invincible."

"I think she made her point," I said. "She around?"

Stallings glanced down the long room at the closed door to Murphy's cheap, tiny office. "Yeah, but you know how she is with paperwork. She's ready to tear someone's head off."

"Don't blame her," I said, and scooped up the puppy. "You get a dog?"

"Nah, charity case. Murphy was supposed to be keeping an eye on him. Buzz her for me?"

Stallings shook his head and turned his phone around to face me. "I plan to retire. You do it."

I grinned and went on down to Murphy's office, nodding to a couple other guys with SI along the way. I knocked on the door.

"God dammit!" Murphy swore from the other side. "I said not now!"

"It's Harry," I said. "Just stopping by to get the dog."

"Oh, God," she snarled. "Back away from the door."

I did.

A second later the door opened and Murphy glared up at me, blue eyes bright and cold. "Get more away. I've been fighting this computer all day long. I swear, if you blow out my hard drive again, I'm taking it out of your ass."

"Why would your hard drive be in my ass?" I said.

Murphy's eyes narrowed.

"Ah, hah, hah, heh. Yeah, okay. I'll be going, then."

"Whatever," she said, and shut her office door hard.

I frowned. Murphy wasn't really a "whatever" sort of person. I tried to remember the last time I had seen Murphy that short and abrupt. When she'd been in the midst of post-traumatic stress, she'd been remote but not angry. When she was keyed up for a fight or feeling threatened, she'd be furious but she didn't draw away from her friends.

The only thing that had come close to this was when she thought I was involved in a string of supernatural killings. From where she'd been standing, it looked like I had betrayed her trust, and she had expressed her anger with a right cross that had chipped one of my teeth.

Something was upsetting her. A lot.

"Murph?" I asked through the door. "Where did the aliens hide your pod?"

She opened the door enough to scowl at me. "What's that supposed to mean?"

"No pod, huh. Maybe you're an evil twin from another dimension or something."

The muscles along her jaw clenched, and her expression promised murder.

I sighed. "You don't seem to be your usual self. I'm not an analyst or anything, but you kinda look like something is bothering you. Just maybe."

She waved a hand. "It's this paperwork—"

"No, it isn't," I said. "Come on, Murphy. It's me."

"I don't want to talk about it."

I shrugged. "Maybe you need to. You're about two steps shy of psychotic right now."

She reached for her door again, but didn't close it. "Just a bad day."

I didn't believe her, but I said, "Sure, okay. I'm sorry if the dog added to it."

Her expression became tired. She leaned against the doorway. "No. No, he was great. Barely made a sound. Quiet as a mouse all day long. Even used the papers I put down."

I nodded. "You sure you don't want to talk?"

She grimaced and glanced around the office. "Maybe not here. Walk with me."

We left and headed down the hall to the vending machines. Murphy didn't say anything until she bought a Snickers bar. "My mom called," she said.

"Bad news?" I asked.

"Yeah." She closed her eyes and bit off a third of the candy bar. "Sort of. Not really."

"Oh," I said, as if her answer made some kind of sense. "What happened?"

She ate more chocolate and said, "My sister, Lisa, is engaged."

"Oh," I said. When in doubt, be noncommittal. "I didn't know you had a sister."

"She's my baby sister."

"Um. My condolences?" I guessed.

She glowered at me. "She did this on purpose. With the reunion this weekend. She knew exactly what she was doing."

"Well, it's a good thing someone knew, 'cause so far I have no freaking clue."

Murphy finished the candy bar. "My baby sister is engaged. She's going to be showing up this weekend with her fiancé, and I am going to be there without a fiancé or a husband. Or even a boyfriend. My mother will never let me hear the end of it."

"Well, uh, you had a husband, right? Two of them, even."

She glared. "The Murphys are Irish Catholic," she said. "My not one but *two,* count them, *two* divorces won't exactly wash clean the stigma."

"Oh. Well, I'm sure whoever you're dating would show up with you, right?"

She glanced back toward the SI offices. If looks could kill, hers would have blown that section of the building into Lake Michigan. "Are you kidding? I don't have time. I haven't been on a date in two years."

Maybe I should have gone for the ultimate inept remark, and started singing about how short people got nobody to love. I decided to sting her pride a little instead. She'd reacted well to it before. "The mighty Murphy. Slayer of various and sundry nasty monsters, vampires, and so on—"

"And trolls," Murphy said. "Two more when you were out of town last summer."

"Uh-huh. And you're letting a little family shindig get you down like this?"

She shook her head. "Look. It's a personal thing. Between me and my mom."

"And your mom is going to think less of you for being single? A career woman?" I regarded her skeptically. "Murphy, don't tell me you're a mama's girl under all the tough-chick persona."

She stared at me for a moment, exasperation and sadness sharing space on her features. "I'm the oldest daughter," she said. "And . . . well, the whole time I was growing up, I just assumed that I'd be . . . her successor, I guess. That I'd follow her example. We both did. It's one of the things that made us close. The whole family knew it."

"And if your baby sister is all of a sudden more like your mom than you are, what? It threatens your relationship with her?"

"No," she said, annoyance in her tone. "Not like that. Not really. And sort of. It's complicated."

"I can see that," I said.

She slumped against the vending machine. "My mom is pretty cool," Murphy said. "But it's been hard to stay close to her the past few years. I mean, the job keeps me busy. She doesn't think I should have divorced my second husband, and that's been between us a little. And I've changed. The past couple of years have been scary. I learned more than I wanted to know."

I winced. "Yeah. Well. I tried to warn you about that."

"You did," she said. "I made my choice. I can handle living with it. But I can't exactly sit down and chat with her about it. So it's one more thing that I can't talk about with my mother. Little things, you know? A lot of them. Pushing us apart."

"So talk to her," I said. "Tell her there's stuff you can't talk about. Doesn't mean you don't want to be around her."

"I can't do that."

I blinked. "Why not?"

"Because I *can't*," she said. "It just doesn't work like that."

Murphy had genuine worry on her face and actual tears in her eyes, and I started feeling out of my depth. Maybe because it was a family thing. It seemed like something completely alien, and I didn't get it.

Murphy was worried about being close to her mom.

Murphy should just go talk to her mom, right? Bite the bullet and clear the air. With anyone else she'd have handled the problem exactly that way.

But I've noticed that people got the most irrational whenever family was around—while simultaneously losing their ability to distinguish reason from insanity. I call it familial dementia.

I may not have understood the problem, but Murphy was my friend. She was obviously hurting, and that's all I really needed to know. "Look, Murph, maybe you're making more of it than you need to. I mean, seems to me that if your mom cares about you, she'd be as willing as you are to talk."

"She doesn't approve of my career," Murphy said tiredly. "Or my decision to live alone, once I was divorced. We've already done all the talking on those subjects and neither one of us is going to budge."

Now *that* I could understand. I'd been on the receiving end of Murphy's stubborn streak before, and I had a chipped tooth to show for it. "So you haven't shown up at the reunion, where you'd see her and have to avoid all kinds of awkward topics, for the past two years."

"Something like that," Murphy said. "People are talking. And we're all Murphys, so sooner or later someone is going to start giving unasked-for advice, and then it will be a mess. But I don't know what to do. My sister getting engaged is going to get everyone talking about subjects I'd rather slash my wrists than discuss with my uncles and cousins."

"So don't go," I said.

"And hurt my mom's feelings a little more," she said. "Hell, probably make people talk even more than if I was there."

I shook my head. "Well. You're right about one thing. I don't understand it, Murph."

" 'S okay," she said.

"But I wish I did," I said. "I wish I worried about my uncle's opinions, and had problems to work out with my mom. Hell, I'd settle for knowing what her voice sounded like." I put a hand on her shoulder. "Trite but true—you don't know what you have until it's gone. People change. The world changes. And sooner or later you lose people you care about. If you don't mind some advice from someone who doesn't know much about families, I can tell you this: Don't take yours for granted. It might feel like all of them will always be there. But they won't."

She looked down, so that I wouldn't see a tear fall, I guess.

"Talk to her, Karrin."

"You're probably right," she said, nodding. "So I'm not going to kill you for shoving your well-intentioned opinion down my throat in a vulnerable moment. Just this once."

"That's decent of you," I said.

She took a deep breath, flicked a hand at her eyes, and looked up with a more businesslike face. "You're a good friend, putting up with this crap. I'll make it up to you sometime."

"Funny you should say that," I said.

"Why?"

"I'm scouting out a money trail, but the information I'm after is apparently on the Internet. Could you hit a few sites for me, help me get my hands on it?"

"Yes."

"*Gracias.*" I passed her the addresses and gave her a brief rundown of what I was looking for. "I'm going to be out and about. I'll call you in an hour or two?"

She sighed and nodded. "Did you find the vampires?"

"Not yet, but I got some backup."

"Who?" she asked.

"Guy named Kincaid. He's tough."

"A wizard?"

"No. One of those soldier of fortune types. Pretty good vampire slayer."

Murphy arched a brow. "Is he clean?"

"As far as I know," I said. "I should hear from our wheelman tonight. With luck, I'll find the lair and we'll hit them."

"Hey, if it just so happens that we have to go after them on—"

"Saturday," I finished for her. "I know."

I left, and told the pup my theory about familial dementia on the way down the stairs. "It's just a theory, mind you. But it's got the support of a ton of empirical evidence." I felt a quiet pang of sadness as I spoke. Family troubles were something I hadn't ever had. Wouldn't ever have. Murphy's problems with family might have been complicated and unpleasant, but at least they existed.

Every time I thought I had gotten through my orphan baggage, something like this came up. Maybe I didn't want to admit how much it still hurt. Not even to myself.

I scratched the pup's notched ear as I walked out to the Beetle. "My theory is just theoretical," I told him. "Because how the hell should I know?"

Chapter Twelve

I swung past my apartment to grab lunch, a shower, and some clothes without so much blood on them. A beaten-up old Rabbit had lost a game of bumper tag with a Suburban, and traffic was backed up for a mile. As a result, I got back to the set a few minutes late.

A vaguely familiar girl with a clipboard met me at the door. She wasn't old enough to drink, but made up for a lack of maturity with what I could only describe as a gratuitous amount of perkiness. She was pretty, more awkwardly skinny than sleek, and had skin the color of cream. Her dark hair was done up in Princess Leia cinnamon rolls, and she wore jeans, a peasant-style blouse, and clunky-looking sandals. "Hi!" she said.

"Hi, yourself."

She checked her clipboard. "You must be Harry, then. You're the only one left, and you're late."

"I was on time this morning."

"That makes you half as good as a broken watch. You should be proud." She smiled again to let me know she was teasing. "Didn't I see you talking to Justine at Arturo's party?"

"Yeah, I was there. Had to leave before I turned into a pumpkin."

She laughed and stuck out her hand. "I'm Inari. I'm an associate production assistant."

I shook her hand. She wore some light, sweet scent that I liked, something that reminded me of buzzing locusts and lazy summer nights. "Nice to meet you—unless you're stealing my job. You're not a scab, are you?"

Inari grinned, and it transformed her face from moderately attractive to lovely. She had great dimples. "No. As an associate gofer, I'm down the ladder from you. I think your job is safe." She checked a plastic wristwatch. "Oh, God, we need to get moving. Arturo asked me to take you to his office as soon as you got here. This way."

"What's he want?"

"Beats me," Inari said. She started a brisk walk, and I had to lengthen my steps to keep up with her as she led me deeper into the building. She flipped to a second page and took a pen from behind one hair-bun. "Oh, what would you like on your vegetarian pizza?"

"Dead pigs and cows," I said.

She glanced up at me and wrinkled her nose.

"They're vegetarians," I said defensively.

She looked skeptical. "With all the hormones and things they put in meats, you know that they're having a number of very bad effects on you. Right? Do you know the kind of long-term damage fatty meats can do to your intestinal tract?"

"I choose to exercise my status as an apex predator. And I laugh in the face of cholesterol."

"With an attitude like that, you're going to wind up with bulletproof arteries."

"Bring it."

Inari shook her head, her expression pleasant and un-yielding. "Everyone decided they wanted to stick with veggies when I order. If someone has meat, the grease will get all over the rest of the pizza, so they settled on veggies."

"Then I guess I will too."

"But what do you want on yours? I mean, I'm sup-posed to make everyone happy here."

"Kill me some animals, then," I said. "It's a protein thing."

"Oh, you should have said," Inari replied, smiling at me. We stopped in front of a door and she scribbled on her clipboard. "Some extra cheese, maybe some beans and corn. Or wait. Tofu. Protein. I'll fix you up."

Bean-curd pizza, good grief. I should raise my rates. "You do that." The puppy stirred in my pocket and I stopped. "Here, there's something you could help me with."

She tilted her head at me. "Oh?"

I reached into my pocket and drew the pup out. He was sleeping, every inch of him completely limp. "Could you keep my friend company while I talk to Arturo?"

The girl melted with adoration the way only girls can, and took the pup, cradling him in the crook of her arm and crooning to him. "Oh, he's so sweet. What's his name?"

"No name," I said. "Just watching him for a day or three. He might be hungry or thirsty when he wakes up."

"I love dogs," she replied. "I'll take good care of him."

"Appreciate it."

She started to walk away. "Oh, Harry, I almost forgot. What do you want to drink? Is Coke okay?"

I eyed her suspiciously. "It isn't noncaffeinated, is it?"

She arched a brow. "I'm health-conscious, not insane."

"Dear child," I said. She gave me another sunny smile and jounced off down the hall, holding the pup as if he were made of glass. I went into the office.

Arturo Genosa was inside, sitting on the corner of a desk. His silver hair looked rumpled, and a half-smoked cigar smoldered in a thick ashtray beside him. He summoned up a tired smile for me as I came in. "Hey, Harry." He came over and gave me one of those manly Mediterranean hugs, the kind that leave bruises. "God bless you, Mister Dresden. Without you there, I think we would have lost them both. Thank you."

He kissed me on either cheek. I'm not a kissy-huggy type, really, but I figured it was another manly European affection thing. Either that or he'd just marked me for death. I stepped back and said, "The girl going to be all right?"

Arturo nodded. "Going to live. All right? That I don't know." He waved a hand at his neck. "The scars. They will be very bad."

"Tough on an actress."

He nodded. "In the phone book, your ad says you give advice."

"Technically I sell it," I said. "But that's really more for—"

"I need to know," he said. "Need to know whether I should stop the project."

I arched an eyebrow. "You think that's why these people have been attacked?"

He picked up his cigar, fiddling around with it. "I don't know what to think. But I was nowhere nearby. This could not have been an attack on me."

"I agree," I said. "And it was the Evil Eye. I'm sure of it."

"Mister Dresden, if a man threatens me, then it is nothing to face it. But this person, whoever he is, is hurting the people near me. I no longer choose only for myself."

"Why would someone want to stop your film, Mr. Genosa?" I asked. "I mean, pardon me if this insults you, but it's a skin flick. There are lots of them."

"I don't know. Maybe it is the business end," he said. "Small entrepreneur, maybe could be a threat to more entrenched businessmen. So they lean. Apply pressure. Quietly, you understand."

"If I didn't know better, I'd swear you just told me

that you think you're being persecuted by a covert pornography syndicate."

Genosa put the cigar in his mouth, rolling it around. He drummed his fingers on the desk and lowered his voice. "You joke, but in the past few years someone has been buying the studios a little at a time."

"Who?"

He shook his head. "It is hard to say. I have investigated, but I am not a detective. Is there any way you could—"

"I'm already on it. I'll tell you if I turn up anything."

"Thank you," he said. "But what should I do today? I can't allow any of these people to be harmed."

"You're racing the clock, right? If you don't finish the film, your business is kaput."

"Yes."

"How long do you have?"

"Today and tomorrow," he said.

"Then you should ask yourself how willing you are to let ambition get someone killed. Then weigh it against how willing you are to let someone scare you out of living your life." I frowned. "Or maybe lives, plural. You're right when you say you aren't choosing only for yourself."

"How can I make that choice?" he asked.

I shrugged. "Look, Arturo. You need to decide if you are protecting these people or leading them. There's a difference."

He rolled the cigar back and forth between his fingers, and then nodded slowly. "They are adults. I am not their father. But I cannot ask them to risk themselves if they do not wish to. I will tell them they are free to leave should they choose, with no ill will."

"But you will stay?"

He nodded firmly.

"Leader, then," I said. "Next thing you know, Arturo, I'll be buying you a big round table."

It took him a second, but he laughed. "I see. Arthur and Merlin."

"Yeah," I said.

He regarded me thoughtfully "Your advice is good. For a young man, you have good judgment."

"You haven't seen my car."

Arturo laughed. He offered me a cigar, but I turned him down with a smile. "No, thank you."

"You look troubled."

"Yeah. Something about your situation doesn't sit right with me. This whole thing is hinky."

Genosa blinked. "It is what?"

"Hinky," I said. "Uh, it's sort of a Chicago word. I mean that there's something not right about what's going on."

"Yes," he agreed. "People are getting hurt."

"That's not it," I said. "The attacks have been brutal. That means that the intentions of whoever is behind them are equally brutal. You can't sling around magic that you don't really believe in. That isn't something a simple business competitor would come up with—even assuming some hardball corporate types decided to start trying a supernatural angle instead of hiring fifty-dollar bruisers to lean on you."

"You think it is personal?" he asked.

"I don't think anything yet," I said. "I need to do more digging."

He nodded, expression sober. "If you stay here, you can keep protecting my people?"

"I think so."

He pressed his lips together, expression resolved. "Then I will tell th—"

The door flew open and a living goddess of a woman stormed into the office. She was maybe five-foot-four and had brilliant, lush blond-highlighted red hair that fell to the small of her back. She wore only high-heeled pumps and a matching dark green two-piece set of expensive-looking designer lingerie, translucent enough to defeat the purpose of wearing clothing at all. It ably displayed all kinds of pleasant proportions of tanned, athletic female.

"Arturo, you Eurotrash pig," she snarled. "What do you think you are doing, bringing that woman here?"

Genosa flinched at the tone, and did not look at the woman. "Hello, Trish."

"Do *not* call me that, Arturo. I've told you over and over."

Genosa sighed. "Harry, this my newest ex-wife, Tricia Scrump."

And he let this gem slip out of his fingers? Shocking.

The woman's eyes narrowed. "Trixie. Vixen. It's been legally changed."

"Okay," Arturo said mildly. "Now what are you talking about?"

"You know full well what I'm talking about." She spat the words. "If you think you are going to split this feature between two stars, you are sadly mistaken."

"That isn't going to happen at all," he said. "But with Giselle hurt, I had to find someone else, and on such short notice . . ."

"Don't patronize me." Tricia ground her teeth. "Lara is retired. Re. Tie. Urd. This film is mine. I am *not* going to let you use my drawing power to fuel a comeback appearance for that . . . that *bitch.*"

I thought about pots and kettles.

"It won't be an issue," Genosa said. "She has agreed to a mask and a pseudonym. You are the star, Tricia. That has not changed."

Trixie Vixen folded her arms, geometrically increasing her cleavage. "Fine, then," she snapped. "As long as we understand each other."

"We do," Arturo said.

She threw her hair back over her shoulder, a gesture filled with arrogance, and glared at me. "And who is this?"

"Harry," I provided. "Production assistant."

"Well then, Larry. Where the hell is my latte? I sent you for it an hour ago."

Evidently, reality did not often intrude on Tricia Scrump's life. It was probably shacked up with courtesy somewhere. I prepared to return verbal fire, but a panicked look from Arturo stopped the first reply that sprang to mind. "Sorry. I'll take care of it."

"See that you do," she said. She spun on one high heel, displaying her G-string and an ass that probably deserved its own billing in the credits, and stalked out.

At least she started to.

She abruptly stopped, frozen, her body tightening with tension.

A woman that made Trixie Vixen look like the ugly stepsister appeared in the door and blocked the starlet's exit. I had to force myself not to stare.

Tricia "Trixie" Scrump née Genosa née Vixen's beauty was up to code. You could run a checklist from it: lovely mouth, deep eyes, full breasts, slender waist, flared hips, long and shapely legs. Check, check, check. She looked like she'd been ordered from a catalog and assembled from a kit. She was a vision of a woman—but a prefabricated one, painted by numbers.

The newcomer was the real thing. She was grace. Beauty. Art. As such, she was not so easily quantified.

She would have been tall, even without the heeled faux-Victorian boots of Italian leather. Her hair was so dark that its highlights were nearly blue, a torrent of glossy curls held partially in check with a pair of milky ivory combs. She had eyes of dark grey with hints of violet twilight at their centers. Her clothes were all effortless style: natural fabrics, black skirt and jacket embroidered with abstract dark crimson roses with a white blouse.

Thinking back later, I couldn't clearly remember her facial features or her body, beyond a notion that they were superb. Her looks were almost extraneous. They weren't any more important to her appeal than a glass was to wine. It was at its best when invisible and showing the spirit contained within. Beyond mere physical presence, I could sense the nature of the woman—strength of will, intelligence, blended with a sardonic wit and edged with a lazy, sensuous hunger.

Or maybe the hunger was mine. In the space of five seconds, my attention to detail fractured, and I wanted her. I wanted her in the most primal sense, in every way I could conceive. Whatever gentle and chivalrous tendencies my soul harbored suddenly evaporated. Images swarmed over me—images of unleashing the fires burning in me upon willing flesh. Conscience withered a heartbeat later. Something hungry, confident, and unrepentant took its place.

I realized, on some distant level, that something was wrong, but there was no tangible, tactile sense of truth to the thought. Instincts ruled me, and only the most feral, vicious drives remained.

I liked it.

A lot.

While my inner Neanderthal was pounding his chest, Trixie Vixen took a step back from the dark-haired woman. I couldn't see her face, but her voice crackled with too much anger. She was afraid. "Hello, Lara."

"Trish," the woman said, with faint contemptuous emphasis on the name. Her voice smoldered, so low and delicious that my toes started to curl up. "You look lovely."

"I'm surprised to see you here," Tricia said. "There aren't any whips or chains on the set."

Lara shrugged, perfectly relaxed. "I've always felt that the best whips and chains are in the mind. With a little creativity, the physical ones are hardly necessary." Lara stared down at Tricia for a moment and then asked, "Have you given any more thought to my offer?"

"I don't do bondage films," Tricia said. A sneer colored the words. "They're for wrinkled old has-beens." She started forward with a determined stride.

Lara didn't move. Tricia stopped a bare inch from her and they met gazes again. The redheaded film star started trembling.

"Perhaps you're right," Lara said. She smiled and stepped clear of the doorway. "Keep in touch, Trish."

Trixie Vixen fled—at least as much as someone wobbling away on six-inch heels can flee. The dark-haired woman watched her with a smug smile on her mouth and then said, "Exit scene. It must be difficult to be the center of the universe. Good afternoon, Arturo."

"Lara," Arturo said. His tone was that of an uncle chiding his favorite niece. He came around his desk and walked over to the woman, offering both hands. "You shouldn't tease her like that."

"Arturo," she said warmly. She took his hands, and they did more social cheek kissing. I shook my head while they did, and managed to shove my libido out of the driver's seat of my brain. Captain of my own soul (even if my pants were considering mutiny), I began focusing my thoughts, building up a barrier to shield them.

"You are an angel," Arturo said to her. His voice was steady and kind and not at all that of a man having most of his blood channeled south of his belly button. How the hell could he not have reacted to her presence? "An angel to come here so quickly. To help me."

She waved a hand in a lazy motion. Her fingernails weren't terribly long, and didn't have any polish. "I'm always glad to help a friend, Arturo. Are you all right?" she asked. "Joan said you'd forgotten to refill your prescription."

He sighed. "I'm fine. Lowering my blood pressure would not have helped Giselle."

Lara nodded. "It's horrible, what happened. I'm so sorry."

"Thank you," he said. "I am not sure I am comfortable to have Inari here. She's a child."

"That's arguable," Lara said. "After all, she's old enough to perform now, if she wishes."

Arturo looked startled and a little sick. "*Lara.*"

She laughed. "I'm not saying she *should,* dear fool. Only that my baby sister makes her own choices now."

"They grow," Arturo said. His voice was a little sad.

"They do." Lara's eyes moved over to me. "And who is this? Tall, dark, and silent. I like him already."

"Harry," Arturo replied. He beckoned me over. "Lara Romany, meet Harry, our new production assistant. He just started today, so be kind to him."

"That shouldn't be too hard," she said, and slipped

her arm through Genosa's. "Joan wanted me to tell you that your prescription came in, and that she needs your help on the set."

Arturo nodded with a strained but genuine smile. "And you are to escort me down to take my medicine, eh?"

"Via my feminine wiles," Lara confirmed.

"Harry," Arturo said.

"I need to make a quick call," I answered. "I'll be right behind you."

The two of them left. Lara threw another look at me over her shoulder, her expression speculative. And hot. I mean, wow. If she'd crooked her finger, I think I would have been in danger of floating off the floor and drifting along behind her on a cloud of her perfume. Me and Pepé le Pew.

It took me maybe half a minute after they walked away before I was able to reboot my brain. After that, I ran a quick review of what had just happened through the old grey matter.

Pretty, pale, supernaturally sexy, and just a little scary. I could do the math. And I was willing to bet that Romany wasn't Lara's last name.

She looked a hell of a lot more like a Raith.

Son of a bitch. The White Court was here.

A succubus on the set. Strike that, the health-conscious kid sister made it two . . . succubuses. Succubusees? Succubi? Stupid Latin correspondence course. Or maybe she wasn't one, because I hadn't felt a thing like the attraction Lara Romany exuded when I was near little Inari.

It really hit me, then, that I'd wandered into a mess that might get me killed, regardless of how silly and embarrassing it sounded. Now I had to contend not only with pornography-syndicate conspiracies, but also a succubus of the White Court. Or maybe more than one, which for grammatical reasons I hoped was not the case.

So in addition to a feisty new Black Court partner in the war dance between the Council and the Vampire Courts, I also got angry lust bunny movie stars, deadly curses, and a thoroughly embarrassing job as my investigative cover.

Oh, and bean-curd pizza, which is just wrong.

What a mess.

I made a mental note: The next time I saw Thomas, I was going to punch him right in the nose.

Chapter Thirteen

After two or three tries, I got Genosa's phone to dial out to Murphy. "It's me, Murph. You get that information off the Internet?"

"Yeah. And then I talked to some people I know out there. I dug up some goodies for you."

"Peachy. Like what?"

"Nothing that will stand up in a court, but it might help you figure out what's going on."

"Wow, Murph. It's as if you're a detective."

"Bite me, Dresden. Here's the deal on Genosa. He's a dual citizen of the States and Greece. He's the last son of a big money family that fell on hard times. Rumor has it he left Greece to avoid his parents' debts."

"Uh-huh," I said. I continued searching through Genosa's desk and found a big old leather-bound photo album. "I'm listening."

"He wound up making and directing sex films. Did well investing the money, and he's worth a little more than four million, personally."

"Sex sells." I frowned, flipping through the photo album. It was neatly packed with excerpts from newspapers, transcripts, and photos of Genosa on the set of a number of national talk shows. There was another of him standing beside Hugh Hefner and surrounded by a number of lovely young women. "That's a lot of money. Is that all?"

"No," Murphy said. "He's paying alimony to three ex-wives out of some kind of fund set up to provide it. He's got almost all of what's left tied up in starting his own studio."

I grunted. "Genosa's under some serious pressure, then."

"How so?"

"He's only got about thirty-six hours to finish his movie," I said. "He's got one project done, but if he doesn't get a pair of profitable films, he'll lose the studio."

"You figure someone is trying to run him out of business?"

"Occam thinks so." I turned another page and blinked at the article there. "Damn."

"What?"

"He's a revolutionary."

"He's what?" Murphy asked.

I repeated myself redundantly again. "Apparently Arturo Genosa is considered a revolutionary in his field."

I could almost hear Murphy lift a skeptical eyebrow. "A revolutionary boink czar?"

"So it would seem."

She snorted. "How exactly do you get to become a porn revolutionary?"

"Practice, practice, practice?" I guessed.

"Wiseass."

I kept flipping pages, skimming the album. "He's been interviewed in about thirty magazines."

"Yeah," Murphy said. "Probably with illustrious names like . . . like *Jugs-A-Poppin* and *Barely Legal Lolita Schoolgirls.*"

I thumbed through pages. "And *People, Time, Entertainment Weekly,* and *USA Today.* He's also been on *Larry King* and *Oprah.*"

"You're kidding," she said. "*Oprah?* Why?"

"Hang on; I'm reading. It looks like he's got this crazy

notion that everyone should be able to enjoy themselves in bed without going insane trying to meet an impossible standard. He thinks that sex is natural."

"Sex is natural," Murphy said. "Sex is good. Not everybody does it, but everybody should."

"I'm the wiseass. You're the cop. Respect my boundaries." I kept reading. "Genosa also casts people of a lot of different ages instead of using only twenty-year-old dancers. According to a transcript of *Larry King,* he avoids gynecological close-ups and picks people based on the genuine sensuality of their performance rather than purely on appearance. And he doesn't believe in using surgically altered . . . uh . . ."

My face heated up. Murphy was probably my best friend, but she was still a girl, and a gentleman just doesn't say some words in front of a lady. I held the phone with my shoulder and made a cupping motion in front of my chest with both hands. "You know."

"Boobs?" Murphy said brightly. "Jugs? Hooters? Ya-yas?"

"I guess."

She continued as if I hadn't said anything. "Melons? Torpedoes? Tits? Gazongas? Knockers? Ta-tas?"

"Hell's bells, Murph!"

She laughed at me. "You're cute when you're embarrassed. I thought breast implants were required industry equipment. Like hard hats and steel-toed boots for construction workers."

"Not according to Genosa," I said. "He's quoted here saying that natural beauty and genuine desire make for better sex than all the silicone in California."

"I'm not sure whether I should be impressed or a little nauseous," Murphy said.

"Six of one and half dozen of another," I said. "Bottom line is that he's not your average pornographic artist."

"I'm not sure that's saying much, Harry."

"If you'd said that before I met him, I'd probably have agreed. But I'm not so sure now. I don't get any nasty vibe off him. He seems like a decent guy. Taking some measure of responsibility. Challenging the status quo, even if it hurts his profits.''

"I'm pretty sure there's no Nobel prize for pornography.''

"My point is that he's applying some measure of integrity to it. And people are responding well to him.''

"Except for the ones trying to kill him," Murphy said. "Harry, this is cynical, but people who choose a life like that draw problems down onto themselves sooner or later.''

"You're right. That is cynical.''

"You can't help everyone. You'll go insane if you try.''

"Look, the guy is in trouble and he's a fellow human being. I don't have to love his lifestyle to want to keep bad things from happening to him.''

"Yeah." Murphy sighed. "I guess I know this tune.''

"Do you think I could convince you to—''

The skin on the back of my neck went cold and clammy, tingling. I turned to the office doorway in time to see the lights in the hall flick out. My heart pounded in sudden apprehension. A shadowy figure appeared in the office door.

I picked up the first thing my hand found, Genosa's heavy glass ashtray, and flung it hard at the figure. The ashtray rebounded off the inner edge of the door and struck whoever it was. I heard a voiceless gasp of air. At the same time something hissed past my ear. A sharp thumping sound came from the wall behind me.

I shouted at the top of my lungs and ran forward, but my foot tangled in the phone cord. It didn't tug me into a pratfall, but I stumbled, and it gave the shadowy figure time to run. By the time I'd recovered my balance and gotten to the hallway, I couldn't see or hear anyone.

The hall itself was dark, and I couldn't remember the locations of either light switches or doors, which made a headlong pursuit less than advisable. It occurred to me that I made a wonderful target, leaning out of the door of the dimly lit office, and I slipped back inside, shutting and locking the door behind me as I went.

I looked at whatever had thumped into the wall behind me, and found, of all the stupid things, a small dart fixed with exotic-looking yellow feathers fringed with a tinge of pink. I tugged the dart out of the wall. It was tipped with what appeared to be bone instead of metal, and the bone was stained with something dark red or dark brown. I had the feeling it wasn't Turtle Wax.

A poisoned blowgun dart. I'd been ambushed before, but that was pretty exotic, even for me. Almost silly, really. Who the hell got killed with poison blowgun darts these days?

A buzz of noise came from the dropped receiver of the phone. I picked up an empty plastic cigar tube from next to Genosa's humidor and slipped the dart into it, then capped it before I picked up the phone.

"Harry?" Murphy was demanding. "Harry, are you all right?"

"Fine," I said. "And it looks like I'm on the right track."

"What happened?"

I held up the cigar tube and peered at the dart. The poisoned tip gleamed with its semi-gelatinous stain. "It was pretty clumsy, but I think someone just tried to kill me."

Chapter Fourteen

"Get out of there, Harry."

"No, Murph," I said. "Look, I think it was just someone trying to scare me, or they'd have used a gun. Can you get to those records today?"

"If they're matters of public record," she said. "We've

got the time difference on our side. What are you hoping to find?"

"More," I said. "This whole thing stinks. Hard to put a puzzle together when you're missing pieces."

"Get in touch if you learn something," Murphy said. "Magic or not, attempted murder is police business. It's my business."

"This time for sure," I said.

"Watch your ass, Bullwinkle."

"Always. Thanks again, Murph."

I hung up and flipped through the next several pages of Genosa's scrapbook, expecting nothing but more articles. I got lucky on the last few pages. He had big, glossy color photos there—three women, and I recognized two of them.

A subtitle beneath the first picture read, *Elizabeth Guns.* The photo was of Madge, Genosa's first wife. She looked like she'd been in her mid-twenties in the picture and she was more or less nude. Her hair was enormous and stiff-looking, an artificial shade of deep scarlet. She probably had to take off her makeup with a Zamboni machine.

The next photo read, *Raven Velvet,* beneath a picture of a nearly Amazonian brunette I didn't recognize. She had the kind of build that fairly serious female athletes can get, where the muscles are present, defined with obvious strength, but softened and rounded enough to look more pretty than formidable. Her hair was cut in a short pageboy, and at first I thought her features were really quite sweet, almost kind. But her expression was an unsmiling, haughty stare at the camera. Ex-Genosa two, I supposed. He'd called her Lucille.

The last picture was of the third former Mrs. Genosa. It was subtitled, *Trixie Vixen,* but someone had written across it in black permanent marker, *ROT IN HELL, YOU PIG.* There was no signature to tell who was responsible. Gee. I wonder.

I flipped through the album once more but didn't see anything new. At some point I realized that I was delaying going down to the set. I mean, yeah, there were probably going to be naked girls doing a variety of interesting things. And I hadn't gotten laid in a depressing number of months, which probably made it sound a little more interesting. But there's a time and a place to enjoy that kind of thing, and for me in front of a bunch of people and cameras was not it.

But I was a professional, dammit. And this was the job. I couldn't bodyguard anyone if I wasn't close enough to them to act. I couldn't figure out the source of the dark mojo without figuring out what was going on. And to do that, I needed to observe and ask questions—preferably without anyone knowing that's what I was doing. That was the smart thing, the professional thing. Conduct covert interviews while icons of sensual beauty got it on under stage lights.

Onward. I screwed up my courage, so to speak, and slipped warily out of the office and down the dimly lit hall to the studio.

There were a surprising number of people there. It was an enormous room, but it still looked busy. There were a couple of guys on each of four cameras, and there were a few more on hanging scaffolds that supported the stage lighting. A crew was working on the lighted set, which consisted of a bunch of panels made to look like an old brick wall, a couple of garbage cans, a trash bin, some loading pallets, and random bits of litter. Arturo and the beflanneled Joan were at the center of the activity, speaking to each other as they moved around placing cameras to their liking. Colt-legged Inari drifted along behind them marking positions on a chart. The notch-eared puppy followed her clumsily around, a piece of pink yarn tied around his neck and one of the loops of Inari's jeans. The puppy's tail wagged happily.

I was supposed to be doing the assistant thing after all, so I walked over to Genosa. The puppy saw me and galloped headlong into my shoe. I leaned down and scratched his ears. "What should I do to help, Arturo?"

He nodded at Joan. "Stick with her. She can show you the ropes as well as anyone. Watch, ask questions."

"Okeydoky," I said.

"You've met Inari?" Arturo asked.

"Bumped into her already," I said.

The girl smiled and nodded. "I like him. He's funny."

"Looks aren't everything," I said.

Inari's laugh was interrupted when her pants beeped. She reached into them and drew out an expensive cell phone the size of a couple of postage stamps. I scooped up the puppy and held him in the crook of one arm, and Inari untied his makeshift lead and handed it to me before walking a few steps away, phone to her ear.

A harried-looking woman in sweeping skirts and a peasant blouse came half running across the studio floor, straight to Joan and Arturo. "Mr. Genosa, I think you'd better come to the dressing room. Right now."

Genosa's eyes widened and his face went pale. He shot me a questioning glance. I shook my head at him and gave him a thumbs-up. He let out a slow breath, and then said, "What is happening?"

Joan, behind him, checked her watch, rolled her eyes, and said, "It's Trixie."

The woman nodded with a sigh. "She says she's leaving."

Arturo sighed. "Of course she'd say that. Shall we, Marion?"

They left, and Joan scowled. "There's no time for that prima donna."

"Is there ever?"

Her frown faded, replaced by simple weariness. "I suppose not. I just don't understand the woman. This project means as much to her future as to everyone else's."

"Being the center of the universe is a big job. Maybe it's weighing on her nerves."

Joan threw her head back and laughed. "That must be it. Let's get moving."

"What's first?"

We went to one of the other sets, this one dressed up like a cheap bar, and started going through boxes of random bottles and mugs for a more detailed appearance. I set the puppy down on the bar, and he waddled up and down the length of it, nose down to the surface and sniffing. After a few moments I asked, "How long have you known Arturo?"

Joan hesitated for a second, then continued dressing up the set. "Eighteen or nineteen years, I think."

"He seems like a nice man."

She smiled again. "He isn't," she said. "He's a nice boy."

I lifted my eyebrows. "How so?"

She rolled one shoulder in a shrug. "He lives on the outside of his skin. He's impulsive, more passionate than he can afford to be, and he'll fall in love at the drop of a hat."

"And that's bad?"

"Sometimes," she said. "But he makes up for it. He cares about people. Here, you get that top shelf. You don't need a stepladder."

I complied. "Soon I'll move up to putting stars and angels on the tops of Christmas trees. Me and that yeti in *Rudolph the Red-Nosed Reindeer.*"

Joan laughed again and answered me. Her words became indistinct and toneless, like the teacher in the Peanuts cartoons. My heart began to race, and a stab of both food hunger and lust went through my stomach on its way to the base of my spine. My head turned of its own volition, and I saw Lara Romany enter the studio.

She'd done her hair up in a style belonging to ancient Greece or Rome. She wore a short black silk robe with matching heels and stockings. She slid over the floor with a kind of fascinating, serpentine grace. I wanted to watch without moving. But some stubborn part of me shoved my brain into an intellectual cold shower. She was a life-draining vampire. I'd be stupid to let myself keep on reacting that way.

I tore my eyes off of her, and realized that the puppy had come to the edge of the bar near me. He was crouched, his eyes on Lara, and was growling his squeaky little growl again.

I looked around, and kept my eyes from moving back to her only by an effort of will. Every man in the room had become still, eyes locked onto Lara as she walked.

"The woman is Viagra with legs," Joan muttered. "Though I've got to admit, she knows how to make an entrance."

"Um. Yeah."

Lara took a seat in a folding chair, and Inari hurried over to kneel beside it in conversation. The electric sense of desire and compulsion faded a little, and people started moving about their tasks again. I helped Joan out, and kept the puppy near me, and in half an hour the first scene started shooting with Jake Guffie and a somewhat sullen-looking Trixie Vixen on the alley set.

Okay, let me tell you something. Porno sex is only loosely related to actual sex. The actors are constantly getting interrupted. They have to keep their faces turned in the right direction, and the body angling they have to do for the camera would make a contortionist beg for mercy. Every once in a while someone has to touch up their makeup, and it isn't only on their faces. You wouldn't believe where all it goes. There are lights shining in their eyes, people with cameras moving all around, and on top of all that, Arturo was giving them directions from behind the cameras.

Granted, my own sexual experience is somewhat limited, but I had never found any of that necessary. It was embarrassing for me to watch. Maybe in the editing room the scene would turn into something sensual and alluring, but on the set it mostly looked awkward and uncomfortable. I found excuses to look at other things, working hard to make sure one of them wasn't the lovely vampire. And I kept my eyes peeled for more deadly magic.

Maybe an hour into the shoot, I glanced aside and saw Inari pacing back and forth, a phone at her ear, speaking quietly. I closed my eyes, concentrated, and started Listening to her.

"Yes, Papa," she said. "Yes, I know. I will. I won't." She paused. "Yes, he's here." Her cheeks suddenly flushed pink. "What a terrible thing to say!" she protested. "I thought you were supposed to chase the boys off with a shotgun." She laughed, glanced across the studio and started walking away. "Bobby, Papa. His name is Bobby."

Aha. The plot thickens. I followed Inari's glance across the studio and saw Bobby the Sullen sitting in a folding chair near Lara, wearing a bathrobe. His impressive arms were folded over his chest, and he looked pensive and withdrawn. He paid no attention whatsoever to the shoot—or to Lara, for that matter. Inari, meanwhile, had moved a little beyond the range of my focused sense of hearing.

I frowned, pondered, and kept on the lookout for incoming black magic. Nothing untoward happened, beyond an audio monitor spitting sparks and dying when I walked too close to it. They shot three other scenes after that one, and I made sure not to notice much. They involved three, uh, performers I didn't recognize, two women and another man. They must have been the crew Joan said would follow Trixie's example by showing up late.

Of course, one of the people who *had* been on time was now in an ICU, and lucky to be there instead of the morgue. Punctuality was no protection against black magic.

Sometime a bit before midnight, the puppy was asleep in a bed I'd made him out of my duster. Most of the food (without meat, it seemed blasphemous to call it pizza) had been devoured. Trixie had flown into a tantrum an hour before, ranting at one of the cameramen and at Inari, and then stormed out of the studio wearing nothing but her shoes, and everyone was tired. The crew was setting up for a last scene—consisting of Emma, Bobby the Buff, and Lara Romany. I felt myself growing tense as Lara rose, and I withdrew to the back of the studio to get my thoughts together.

There was a movement from the darkness at the rear of the studio, only a few feet away, and I hopped back in a reflex born of surprise and fear. A shadowy figure darted out of a corner and headed for the nearest exit. My shock became a realization of a sudden opportunity, and I didn't stop to think before I went racing after the figure.

It hit the door and darted off into the Chicago night. I snatched my blasting rod from my backpack as I ran by and sprinted into pursuit, bolstered by anger and adrenaline, determined to catch the mysterious lurker before any more of the crew could be attacked.

Chases down dark Chicago alleys were getting to be old hat for me. Though technically, I suppose, we weren't in Chicago proper, and the broader, more generous spaces between the buildings of the industrial park could hardly qualify as alleys. Foot chases still happened often enough that I had taken up running for practice and exercise. Admittedly, I was usually on the other end of a foot chase, mostly due to my personal policies on hand-to-hand combat with anything that weighed more than a small car or could be described with the word *chitinous*.

Whoever I was after was not overly large. But he was fast, someone who had also practiced running. The industrial park was lit only sporadically, and my quarry was running west, away from the front of the park and into, of course, totally unlit areas.

With each step I got farther from possible help, and stood a higher chance of running into something I couldn't handle alone. I had to balance that against the possibility that I could stop whoever had been attacking Genosa's people before they could hurt anyone else. Maybe if it hadn't been mostly women who were hurt, and maybe if I didn't harbor this buried streak of chivalry, and if I were a little smarter, it wouldn't have been such an easy choice.

The shadowy object of my pursuit reached the back of the industrial lot and sprinted across twenty feet of almost pitch-black blacktop toward a twelve-foot fence. I caught up to him about halfway across, just managing to kick at one heel. He was running all out, and the impact fouled his legs and threw him down. I dropped my weight onto his back and rode him down into the asphalt.

The impact nearly knocked the wind out of me, and I imagine it did worse to him. The grunt as he hit came out in a masculine baritone, much to my relief. I'd been thinking in terms of "him" because if I'd been thinking "her" I don't think I could have kept myself from holding back in the violence department, and that's the kind of thing that can get you hurt, fast.

The guy tried to get up, but I slammed my forearm into the back of his head a few times, bouncing his face against the asphalt. He was tough. The blows slowed him down, but he started moving again and suddenly twisted with the sinuous strength of a serpent. I went to one side; he got out from under me and immediately leapt for the fence.

He jumped four or five feet up and started climbing. I pointed my blasting rod at the top of the fence, drew in my will and snarled, *"Fuego."*

Fire lashed across the top of the fence, bright and hot enough that the suddenly expanding air roared like a crack of thunder. Metal near the top of the fence glowed red, running into liquid a few feet above the man's head. Droplets pattered down like Hell's own rain.

The man cried out in shock or pain and let go of the fence. I beat him about the head and shoulders with my blasting rod when he did, the heavy wood serving admirably as a baton. The second or third blow stunned him, and I got the blasting rod across his neck in a choke, locked one of his arms behind him with a move Murphy had taught me, and pinned his face against the fence with my full weight.

"Hold still," I snarled. Bits of molten wire slithered down the chain link fence toward the ground. "Hold still or I'll hold your face there until it melts off."

He tried to struggle free. He was strong, but I had all the leverage, so that didn't mean much. Thank you, Murphy. I wrenched his trapped arm up until he gasped with pain. I snarled, "Hold. Still."

"Jesus Christ," Thomas stammered, his voice pained.

He ceased struggling and lifted his other hand in surrender. Recognizing the voice, I could place his profile too. "Harry, it's me."

I scowled at him and pulled harder on his arm.

"*Ow*," he gasped. "Dresden, what are you doing? Let go. It's *me*."

I growled at him and did, shoving him hard against the fence and standing up.

Thomas rose slowly, turning to me with his hands lifted. "Thanks, man. I didn't mean to surprise you like—"

I hit him solidly in the nose with my right fist.

I think it was the surprise as much as the blow that knocked him onto his ass. He sat there with his hands covering his face and stared up at me.

I drew up my blasting rod and readied another lash of flame. The tip of the rod glowed with a cinder-red glow of light barely a foot from Thomas's face. His normally pale face was ashen, his expression was startled, and his mouth was stained with blood. "Harry—" he began.

"Shut up," I said. I used a very quiet voice. Quiet voices are more frightening than screams. "You're using me, Thomas."

"I don't know what you're talking abou—"

I leaned forward, the blazing end of the blasting rod making him squirm backward. "I told you to shut up," I said in the same quiet voice. "There's someone I think you know on the set, and you didn't tell me about that. I think you've lied to me about other things too, and it's put me in mortal peril at least one and a half times today already. Now give me one good reason I shouldn't blast your lying mouth off your face right now."

The hair on the back of my neck suddenly tried to crawl away from my skin. I heard two distinct clicks behind me, the hammers being drawn back on a pair of guns, and Lara's maddeningly alluring voice murmured, "I'll give you two."

Chapter Fifteen

The first thought that went through my mind was something like, *Wow her voice is hot.* The second was, *How the hell did she catch up to us so quickly?*

Oh, and somewhere in there the practical side of me chimed in with, *It would be bad to get shot.*

What came out of my mouth was, "Is your last name really Romany?"

I didn't hear any footsteps, but her voice came from closer when she answered. "It was my married name. Briefly. Now please step away from my little brother."

Hell's bells, she was his *sister*? Familial dementia. She might not react rationally to a threat. I took a deep breath and reminded myself that under the circumstances, I'd be an idiot to push Lara Raith. "I assume that when I do, you'll lower the guns?"

"Assume instead that if you don't, I'll shoot you dead."

"Oh, for the love of God." Thomas sighed. "Lara, would you relax? We were just talking."

She clucked her teeth, a sound of almost maternal disapproval. "Tommy, Tommy. When you say ridiculous things like that, I have to keep reminding myself that my baby brother isn't as large an idiot as you would like us all to believe."

"Oh, come on," Thomas said. "This is a waste of time."

"Shut up," I said with an ungracious waggle of the blasting rod. I looked over my shoulder at Lara. She was wearing black lacy things with stockings and heels—

(How the hell had she caught up to us in the freaking heels? Even for a wizard, some things are simply beyond belief.)

—and she held a pair of pretty little guns in her hands. They probably weren't packing the high-caliber ammunition of heavier weapons, but even baby bullets could kill me just fine. She held them like she knew what she was doing, and sauntered closer through the heavy shadows, her skin luminous. And showing. And really gorgeous.

I gritted my teeth and beat back the sudden urge to taste-test the curvy dents in her stomach and thighs, and kept the blasting rod lit and pointing at Thomas. "Back off, toots. Put the guns down, stop with the come-hither whammy, and we can talk."

She stopped between one step and the next, a faintly troubled expression on her face. She narrowed her eyes, and her voice slid through the air like honey and heroin. "What did you say?"

I fought off the pressure of that voice and growled, "Back. Off." My inner Quixote was not to be entirely denied though, and I added, "Please."

She stared at me for a moment, and then blinked her eyes slowly, as if seeing me for the first time. "Empty night," she murmured, her tone one of someone speaking an oath. "You're Harry Dresden."

"Don't feel bad. I cleverly concealed my identity as Harry the Production Assistant."

She pursed her lips (which also looked delicious) and said, "Why are you threatening my brother?"

"It was a slow night and everyone else was busy."

There wasn't even the hint of a warning. One of the little guns barked, there was a flash of scarlet pain in my head, and I collapsed to one knee.

I kept the blasting rod trained on Thomas and lifted my hand to my ear. It came away wet with droplets of blood, but the pain had begun to recede. Lara arched a delicate eyebrow at me. Hell's bells. She'd grazed my ear with a bullet. With that kind of skill, between the eyes would be no trick at all.

"Normally I would admire that kind of piquant retort," she said in a silken, quiet voice. Probably because she thought it sounded scarier than if she'd said it loudly. "But where my little brother is concerned, I am in no mood to play games."

"Point taken," I said. My voice sounded shaky. I lowered the blasting rod until it wasn't pointing at Thomas, and eased away the power held ready in it. The sullen fire at the tip of the rod went out.

"Lovely," she said, but she didn't lower the twin pistols. The autumn's evening breeze blew her dark, glossy hair around her head, and her grey eyes shone silver in the half-light.

"Harry," Thomas said. "This is my oldest sister, Lara. Lara, Harry Dresden."

"A pleasure," she said. "Thomas, step out from behind the wizard. I don't want one of these rounds to take you if they go through."

My guts turned to water. I still had my blasting rod in hand, but Lara could pull the trigger quicker than I could aim and loose a strike at her.

"Wait," Thomas said. He pushed himself up to one knee and put himself between me and the other White vampire. "Don't kill him."

That earned Thomas an arched eyebrow, but a smile haunted her mouth. "And why not?"

"There's the chance that he'd be able to level his death curse, for one."

"True. And?"

Thomas shrugged. "And I have personal reasons. I'd take it as a favor if we could discuss the matter first."

"So would I," I added.

Lara let the ghostly smile remain. "I find myself liking you, wizard, but . . ." She sighed. "There is little room for negotiation, Thomas. Dresden's presence here is unacceptable. Arturo's independent streak is an internal matter of the White Court."

"I didn't come here to interfere with the White Court," I said. "It wasn't my intention at all."

She regarded me. "We all know what intentions are worth. Why then, wizard?"

"That's a good question," I said, turning my head deliberately to Thomas. "I'd love to hear the answer."

Thomas's expression become apprehensive. His gaze flicked to Lara, and I had the sudden impression that he was preparing to move against her.

Lara frowned and said, "Thomas? What is he talking about?"

"This is a tempest in a teapot, Lara," Thomas said. "It's nothing. Really."

Lara's eyes widened. "You brought him into this?"

"Um," Thomas began.

"You're damn right he did," I said. "You think I'd be here for the fun of it?"

Lara's mouth dropped open. "Thomas. You've entered the game *now?*"

Thomas pressed his lips together for a few seconds, then rose slowly to his feet. He winced and put one hand to the small of his back. "Looks that way."

"He'll kill you," Lara said. "He'll kill you and worse. You haven't got a fraction of the strength you'd need to threaten him."

"That all depends," Thomas said.

"On what?" she asked.

"On where the other members of the House decide to place their support."

She let out a short laugh of disbelief. "You think any of us would take your side over his?"

"Why not," Thomas said calmly. "Think about it. Father is strong, but he isn't invincible. If he's taken down by my influence, it leaves me in charge, and I'd be a hell of a lot easier to depose than he would. But if I lose, you can blame me for putting the psychic wristlock on you. Instant scapegoat. Life goes on and the only one to pay for it is me."

She narrowed her eyes. "You've been reading Machiavelli again."

"To Justine at bedtime."

Lara became quiet for a moment, her expression pensive. Then she said, "This is ill-advised, Thomas."

"But—"

"Your timing is horrible. Raith's position is already precarious among the Houses. Internal instability now could leave us vulnerable to Skavis or Malvora or those like them. If they sense weakness they won't hesitate to destroy us."

"Dad's losing it," Thomas countered. "He hasn't been right for years, and we all know it. He's getting old. It's only a matter of time before the other Lords decide to take him—and when that happens, all of us will go down with him."

She shook her head. "Do you know how many brothers and sisters have said such words to me over the years? He has destroyed them all."

"They went up against him alone. I'm talking about all of us working together. We can do it."

"Why now, of all times?"

"Why not now?"

She frowned at Thomas, and stared intently at him for better than sixty seconds. Then she shivered, took a deep breath, and pointed one gun at my head. And the other at Thomas.

"Lara," he protested.

"Take your hand out from your back. Now."

Thomas stiffened, but he moved his hand from his back slowly, fingers empty. I looked up and saw a bulge that brushed his shirt at the belt line.

Lara nodded. "I'm sorry, Tommy. I really am quite fond of you, but you do not know Father the way I do. You aren't the only Raith who takes advantage of being underestimated. He already suspects you have something afoot, and if he thinks for a moment I'm working with you, he'll kill me. Without hesitation."

Thomas's voice grew desperate. "Lara, if we act together—"

"We will die together. If not at his hands than at Malvora's and his like. I don't have a choice. It gives me no pleasure to kill you."

"Then don't do it!" he said.

"And leave you to Father's mercies? Even I have a few principles. I love you as much as anyone in the world, little brother, but I did not survive as long as I have by taking unnecessary risks."

Thomas swallowed. He didn't look at me, but his balance shifted a little, and his shirt rode up enough to show me the handle of a gun he had tucked into the back of his jeans. I didn't stare at it. I wouldn't have time to grab it and shoot before Lara could gun me down, but if Thomas could distract her for a beat or two, there might be a chance.

Thomas took a deep breath and said, "Lara."

Something in his voice had changed. The tone of it sounded the same, on the surface, but there was something beneath it that made the air sing with quiet, seductive power. It commanded attention. Hell, it commanded a lot of things, and it was creepy to hear it coming from him. I was glad that Thomas wasn't addressing me, because it would have been damned confusing.

"Lara," he said again. I saw her sway a little as he spoke. "Let me talk to you."

Evidently the sway was induced more by the evening breeze and those high heels than it was by Thomas's voice. "I'm afraid all you need say is good-bye, little brother." Lara thumbed back the hammer on both guns, her features calm and remote. "And you'd best say it for wizard as well."

Chapter Sixteen

I'd been in hairier situations than this one. Actually, it's sort of depressing, thinking how many times I'd been in them. But if experience had taught me anything, it was this:

No matter how screwed up things are, they can get a whole lot worse.

Case in point: our little standoff with Supertart.

Thomas shouted and darted to his left, across my view of Lara. As he went, I reached for the pistol tucked into the back of his jeans. Judging by the grip, it was a semiautomatic, maybe one of those fancy German models that are as tiny as they are deadly. I grabbed it, and felt pretty slick to be doing the teamwork thing—but Thomas's damned jeans were so tight that the gun didn't come loose. I leaned too far in the effort and wound up sprawling on my side. All I got for my oh-so-clever maneuver was scraped fingertips and a good view of Lara Raith in gunfighting mode.

I heard a shot go past, a kind of humming buzz in the air that provided an accent to the mild, barking report of the pistol. There were several shots in the space of a second or three. Two of them hit Thomas with ugly sounds of impact, one in the leg, and a second in the chest.

At the same time he hurled a small ring of keys at Lara, and it probably saved my life. She swatted them aside with the gun that had been trained on me. It gave me a precious second or two, and it was time enough to bring up my blasting rod and loose a panicked strike at her. It was sloppy as hell, even with the blasting rod to help me focus my will, and instead of a wrist-thick beam of semicoherent flame, it came out in a cone of fire maybe thirty feet across.

That made big noise—a thunderous thumping explosion as the heat displaced cool night air. Lara Raith had the reflexes that were depressingly common in all of those vampire types, and she darted out of the way of the flames. She leveled both guns at me as she did, blazing away like in those Hong Kong action movies. But evidently even Lara's superhuman skill wasn't enough to overcome surprise, lateral movement, a firestorm, *and* the spike heels. God bless the fashion industry and the blind luck that protects fools and wizards; she missed.

I shook out my shield bracelet and hardened my will into a wall of unseen but solid force in front of me. The last few shots from Lara's guns actually struck the shield, illuminating it in a flash of blue-and-white energy. I held the shield firmly in place and readied the blasting rod again, and faced Lara squarely.

The vampire slipped into the shadows between the

nearest building and a pair of huge industrial tanks and vanished from sight.

I padded forward to Thomas, keeping the shield up and in the general direction of where Lara had disappeared. "Thomas," I hissed. "Thomas, are you all right?"

It was a long beat before he replied, his voice weak and shaking. "I don't know. It hurts."

"You've been shot. It's supposed to hurt." I kept my eyes on the shadows, warily extending my senses as much as I could. "Can you walk?"

"Don't know," he panted. "Can't get my breath. Can't feel my leg."

I flicked my eyes down to him and back out again. Thomas's black T-shirt, was plastered to his chest on one side. He'd taken a hit in the lung, at least. If a major blood vessel had been struck, he was in trouble, vampire or not. The White Court were a resilient bunch, but in some ways they were just as fragile as the human beings they fed upon. He could heal up fast—I'd seen Thomas recover from broken ribs in a matter of hours—but if he bled out from a severed artery, he'd die like anyone else.

"Just hold still," I said. "Don't try to move until we know where she is."

"That'll get her," Thomas panted. "The old sitting-duck ploy."

"Give me your gun," I said.

"Why?"

"So that the next time you start talking I can shoot your wise ass."

He started to laugh, but it broke into agonized, wet coughing.

"Dammit," I muttered, and crouched down beside him. I set my blasting rod aside and slipped my right arm and one knee behind his back, trying to hold him vertical from the waist up.

"You'd better get moving. I'll manage."

"Would you shut up?" I demanded. I tried to ascertain the extent of his injuries with my free hand, but I'm no doctor. I found the hole in his chest, felt the blood coming out. The edges of the wound puckered and gripped at my hand. "Well," I told him. "Your wound sucks. Here." I took his right hand and pressed it hard against the hole. "Keep your hand there, man. Keep the pressure on. I can't hold it and carry you out too."

"Forget carrying me," he rasped. "Don't be an idiot. She'll kill us both."

"I can hold the shield," I said.

"If you can't return fire, it won't do you much good. Get clear, call the cops, then come back for me."

"You're delirious," I said. If I left him there alone, Lara would finish him. I got my right shoulder under his left arm and hauled him to his feet. He wasn't as heavy as I would have expected, but dragging him up like that had to have hurt him. The pain locked the breath in his throat. "Come on," I growled. "You've got a good leg. Help me."

His voice had become hollow, somehow ghostly, barely more than a whisper. "Just go. I can't."

"You *can*. Shut up and *help* me."

I started walking as fast as I could back toward the street end of the industrial park. I kept my shield bracelet up, focusing my will into a barrier all around us. It wasn't as strong as a more limited directional shield, but my eyes couldn't be everywhere, and a smart opponent would shoot me in the back.

Thomas would have been screaming if he could have gotten his breath. Over the next minute or two, his face went white—I mean, even more so than usual. He'd always been pale, but his skin took on the grey tone of a corpse, sooty hollows forming under his eyes. Even so, he managed to help me. Not much, but enough that I could keep us both moving without stumbling.

I started to think that we were going to make it back safely, when I heard running footsteps and a woman rounded the corner ahead of us, her pale skin glowing in the dimness.

I cursed, pushing more will into the shield, and crouched down, letting Thomas collapse ungraciously onto the gravel parking lot. I fumbled for his gun, found it, and whipped the weapon up. I flicked off the safety with my thumb, took a half second to aim, and pulled the trigger.

"No," Thomas gasped at the last possible instant. He leaned hard against me just as the gun went off, the barrel wavered, and the shot kicked up sparks on a concrete retaining wall fifty feet away. Panicked, I lined up the weapon again, though I knew it would be a useless gesture. I might have taken her out with a surprise shot, but there was no chance at all that I could outshoot Lara Raith in a direct confrontation.

But it wasn't Lara. I couldn't see very far in the dimness, but Inari stumbled to a halt only a few feet shy of me, her eyes wide and her mouth open. "Oh, my God," she cried. "Thomas! What happened? What have you done to him?"

"Nothing!" I said. "He's been hurt. For the love of Pete, *help* me."

She hesitated for a second, her eyes wide, and then rushed forward to Thomas. "Oh, my God. There's blood! He's b-bleeding!"

I shoved my blasting rod at her. "Hold this," I snapped.

"What did you do to him?" she demanded. She had begun weeping. "Oh, Thomas."

I felt like screaming in frustration, and I tried to look at every possible place Lara might be, all at the same time. My instincts screamed that she was getting closer, and I wanted nothing more than to run away. "I told you, nothing! Just get moving and open the doors for me. We have to get back inside and call nine-one-one."

I bent down to pick up Thomas again.

Inari Raith screamed in grief and rage. Then she used my blasting rod with both hands to clout me on the back of the neck with so much force that it snapped in half. Stars exploded over my vision and I didn't even feel it when my face hit the gravel.

Everything got real confused for a minute or two, and when I finally started stirring I heard Inari crying. "Lara,

I don't know what happened. He tried to shoot me, and Thomas isn't awake. He might be dead."

I heard footsteps on the gravel, and Lara said, "Give me the gun."

"What do we do?" Inari said. She was still crying.

Lara worked the slide on the gun with a couple of quiet clicks, checking the chamber. "Get inside," she said, her tone firm and confident. "Call emergency services and the police. *Now.*"

Inari got up and started to run off, leaving Thomas and me alone with the woman who had already half killed him. I tried to get up, but it was difficult. Everything kept spinning around.

I managed to get to one knee just as a cold, slithery feeling washed down my spine.

The three vampires of the Black Court did not announce their presence. They simply appeared as though formed from the shadows.

One of them was the one-eared vamp I had smacked with the holy-water balloon. On either side of him stood two more Black Court vamps, both male, both dressed in funeral finery, and both of teenage proportions. They hadn't been living corpses for very long—there were lividity marks on the arms and fingers of the first, and their faces hardly looked skeletal at all. Like the maimed vampire, they had long, dirty fingernails. Dried blood stained their faces and throats. And their eyes were filmy, stagnant pools.

Inari screamed a horror-movie scream and stumbled back to Lara. Lara sucked in a sharp breath, bringing the gun into point-down firing stance, spinning in a slow circle to watch each of the Black Court vamps in turn.

"Well, well," rasped the maimed vampire. "What luck. The wizard and three Whites to boot. This will be entertaining."

At which point I felt another, stronger slither of vile and deadly magical energy.

The *malocchio*. It was forming again, more powerfully than before—and I sensed that the deadly spell was already near and gathering more vicious power as it headed my way. Still dazed, I couldn't do a damned thing about it.

"Kill them," the Black Court vampire whispered. "Kill them all."

See what I mean? It's just like I said.

Things can *always* get worse.

Chapter Seventeen

I'm not hopeless at hand-to-hand, but I'm not particularly talented, either. I've been beaten senseless once or twice. Well. A lot. It isn't as unlikely as it sounds—a lot of the things that started pummeling me could bench-press a professional basketball team, whereas I was only human. In my neck of the woods, that meant that I was slightly tougher than a ceramic teacup.

I'd managed to survive the beatings thanks to good luck, determined friends, and an evil faerie godmother, but I figured that sooner or later my luck would run out, and I'd find myself alone, in danger, and at the limits of my endurance. Tonight had proved me right.

So it was a good thing I'd planned ahead.

I reached for my new belt buckle, with its carved design of a bear. The buckle was cast from silver, and the bear design was my own hand-carved work. It took me months to make it, though it wasn't particularly beautiful or inspirational, but I hadn't been trying for artistic accomplishment when I'd been creating it.

I'd been trying to prepare myself for, in the words of Foghorn Leghorn, just such an emergency.

I touched my left hand to my belt buckle and whispered, "*Fortius.*"

Power rushed into the pit of my stomach, a sudden tide of hot, living energy, nitrous for the body, mind, and soul. Raw life radiated out into my bones, running riot through my limbs. My confusion and weariness and pain vanished as swiftly as darkness before the sunrise.

This was no simple adrenaline boost, either, though that was a part of it. Call it *chi* or *mana* or one of thousand other names for it—it was pure magic, the very essence of life energy itself. It poured into me from the reservoir I'd created in the silver of the buckle. My heart suddenly overflowed with excitement, my thoughts with hope, confidence, and eager anticipation, and if I had a personal soundtrack to my life it would have been playing Ode to Joy while a stadium of Harry fans did the wave. It was all I could do to stop myself from bursting into laughter or song. The pain was still there, but I shrugged off the recent blows and exertions and suddenly felt ready to fight.

Even when magic is involved, there ain't no free lunch. I knew that the pain would catch up to me. But I had to focus. Survive now; worry about the backlash later.

"Lara," I said. "I realize that you're kind of invested in killing me, but from where I'm standing the situation has changed."

The succubus shot a glance at the vampires and then at Inari. "I concur, Dresden."

"Rearrange teams and get the girl out?"

"Can you move?"

I pushed myself up, feeling pretty peppy, all things considered. Lara had her back more or less to me, and was trying to keep her eyes on all three Black Courters. The vampires, in turn, simply stood there with only the flicker of something hungry stirring in their dead, eyes to proclaim them something other than lifeless corpses.

"Yeah, I'm good to go."

Lara shot a glance over her shoulder, her expression flickering with disbelief. "Impressive. *Pax,* then?"

I jerked my chin in a nod. "Twenty-four hours?"

"Done."

"Groovy."

"Their faces," Inari wailed. "Their *faces!* My God, what *are* they?"

I blinked at the terrified girl and shot a glance at Lara. "She doesn't know? You don't *tell* her these things?"

The succubus shrugged a shoulder, keeping most of her attention on the nearest vampire and said, "It's my father's policy."

"Your family is twisted, Lara. It really is." I picked up the shattered halves of my blasting rod. The carvings and spells laid on the wood were difficult, time-consuming, and expensive to make. I'd had to replace maybe half a dozen rods over the years, and it was the labor of better than a fortnight to create a new one. The girl had broken mine, which annoyed the hell out of me, but the drought of positive energy still zinging through me pointed out the upside: I now had two handy shafts of wood with jagged, pointy ends. I stepped between Inari and the nearest vampire and passed her one broken half of the rod. "Here," I said. "If you get the chance, make like Buffy."

Inari blinked at me. "What? Is this a joke?"

"Do it," said Lara. Her voice was laced with iron. "No questions, Inari."

The steel in the succubus's voice galvanized the young woman. She took the shard of wood without further hesitation, though her expression grew no less terrified.

Overhead, the dark energy of the curse swirled around and around, a constant, intimidating pressure on my scalp. I tried to block out all the distractions, focusing on the curse and on where it was going. I needed to know who its target was—not only for the sake of my investigation, but for my immediate survival.

That curse was several kinds of nasty. And as it happened, I had a constructive, life-affirming purpose for a boatload of nasty juju. I drew my silver pentacle from my neck and spoke a troubling thought aloud. "Why are they just standing there?"

"They're communing with their master," Lara stated.

"I hate getting put on call waiting," I said, wrapping

the chain of my pentacle around my fist. "Shouldn't we hit them now?"

"No," Lara said sharply. "They're aware of us. Don't move. It will only set them off, and time is our ally."

A sudden wash of almost physical cold set the hairs on the back of my neck on end. The curse was about to land, and I still wasn't sure who it was coming for. I glanced upward, hoping for a physical cue. "I wouldn't be so sure about that, Miss Raith."

One of the vampires, the smallest of the pair who had showed up with One-ear, suddenly shuddered. Its dead eyes flickered around until they landed on me, and then it spoke. You wouldn't think there would be a whole lot of difference between the rasp of one dry, leathery dead larynx and another, but there was. *This* voice flowed out and it wasn't the voice of the vampire whose lips were moving. It was an older voice. Older and colder and vicious, but somehow tinged with something feminine. "Dresden," that voice said. "And Raith's right hand. Raith's bastard son. And the darling of his eye. This *is* a fortunate night."

"Evening, Mavra," I said. "If it's all the same to you, can you stop playing sock puppet with the omega Nosferatu and move this along? I've got a big day tomorrow and I want to get to bed for it."

"Christ, Harry," came a choking voice. I looked back and saw Thomas on the ground, his eyes open. He looked like death, and he had trouble focusing on me, but at least he was lucid. "Are you drunk all of a sudden?"

I winked at him. "It's the power of positive thinking."

The puppet vampire hissed with Mavra's anger, and its voice took on a quavering, modulated, half-echoing quality. "Tonight will balance many scales. Take them, my children. Kill them all."

And a lot of things went down.

The vampires came for us. One-ear rushed at Lara. The sock puppet went for me, and the third one headed for Inari. It happened fast. My attacker may have been new to the game and clumsy, yet it moved at such a speed that it barely registered on my thoughts—but my body was still singing with the infusion of positive energy, and I reacted to the attack as if it had been the opening steps of a dance I already knew. I sidestepped the vampire's rush and drove my half of the former blasting rod down at its back, Buffy-like.

Maybe it works better on television. The wood gouged the vampire, but I don't think much of it got past its suit coat, much less pierced its heart. But the blow did manage to throw the thing off balance and send it stumbling past me. Maybe it actually hurt the vampire—the creature let out an earsplitting, creaking shriek of rage and surprise.

Inari screamed and swung her stake, but her Buffy impersonation wasn't any better than mine. The vampire caught her arm, twisted its wrist, and broke bones with a snap, crackle, pop. She gasped and fell to her knees. The vampire shoved her over and leaned down, baring its teeth (not fangs, I noticed, just yellow corpse-teeth) and spreading its jaws to tear out her throat and bathe in the flood of blood.

And as if that weren't enough, the curse suddenly coalesced and came shrieking out of the night to end Inari's life.

I had scant seconds to act. I charged the vampire, leaned back, pictured an invisible beer can beginning an inch above the vampire's teeth, and stomp-kicked the creature in the chin with my heel. It wasn't a question of Harry-strength versus undead superstrength. I'd gotten the chump shot in, and while the vampire might have been able to rip through a brick wall, it only weighed as much as a dried corpse and it didn't have enough experience to have anticipated the attack. I drove the kick home, hard. Physics took over from there, and the vampire fell back with a surprised hiss.

I seized Inari's right arm with my left. Energy flows out of the body from the right side. The left side absorbs energy. I stretched out my senses and felt the dark energy of the curse rushing down at Inari. It hit her a second later, but I was ready for it, and with an effort of will I caught the dark power coursing down into the girl before it could do her harm.

Pain erupted in my left palm. The power was cold—and not mountain-breeze cold, either. It was slimy and nauseating, like something that had come slinking out from the depths of some enormous subterranean sea. In that instant of contact, my head exploded with terror. This power, this black magic, was *wrong*. Fundamentally, nightmarishly, intensely *wrong*.

Since I'd begun my career as a wizard, I'd always believed that magic came from life, but that it was only potential energy, like electricity or natural gas or uranium. And while it may have come from positive origins, only its application would prove it good or evil. That there was no such thing as truly evil, malevolent, black magic.

I'd been wrong.

Maybe my own magic worked like that, but *this* power was something different. It had only one purpose—to destroy. To inflict horror, pain, and death. I felt that power writhe into me through my contact with the girl, and it hurt me on a level so deep that I could not find a specific word, even a specific *thought* to describe it. It ripped at me within, as though it had found a weakened place in my defenses, and started gouging out a larger opening, struggling to force itself inside me.

I fought it. The struggle happened all within an instant, and it hurt still more to tear that darkness loose, to force it to flow on through me and out of me again. I won the fight. But I felt a sudden terror that something had been torn away from me; that in simple contact with that dark energy, I had been scarred somehow, marked.

Or changed.

I heard myself scream, not in fear or challenge, but in agony. I extended my right hand and the black magic flowed out of it in an invisible torrent, fastening onto the vampire as it gained its feet again and reached out to grab me. The vampire's expression didn't even flicker, so I was sure it did not feel the curse coming.

Which made it a complete surprise when something

slammed into the vampire from directly overhead, too quickly to be seen. There was a sound of impact, a raspy, dry scream, and the vampire went down hard.

It lay on the ground like a butterfly pinned to a card, arms and legs thrashing uselessly. Its chest and collarbone had been crushed.

By an entire frozen turkey. A twenty-pounder.

The plucked bird must have fallen from an airplane overhead, doubtlessly manipulated by the curse. By the time it got to the ground, the turkey had already reached its terminal velocity, and was still hard as a brick. The drumsticks poked up above the vampire's crushed chest, their ends wrapped in red tinfoil.

The vampire gasped and writhed a little more.

The timer popped out of the turkey.

Everyone stopped to blink at *that* for a second. I mean, come on. Impaled by a guided frozen turkey missile. Even by the standards of the quasi-immortal creatures of the night, that ain't something you see twice.

"For my next trick," I panted into the startled silence, "anvils."

And then the fight was on again.

Inari screamed in pain from her knees on the ground. Lara Raith lifted Thomas's little gun, and tongues of flame licked from it as she shot at One-ear. She was aiming for his legs. I started to help her, but I'd been playing long odds, mixing it up in hand-to-hand with the Black Court, and they caught up to me.

The vampire I'd dodged in the opening seconds of the fight slammed its arm into my shoulders. The blow was broad and clumsy but viciously strong. I managed to roll with it a little, but it still sent me straight down onto the gravel and knocked the wind from my chest. I felt the edges of rock cut me in a dozen places at once, but the pain didn't bother me. Yet. Nonetheless, it took me a second to get my body moving again.

The vampire stepped right over me and closed in on the fallen girl. With a simple, brutal motion, it seized her hair and shoved her facedown onto the parking lot, baring the back of her neck. It bent forward.

Thomas snarled, "Get away from her!" He hauled himself forward using his unwounded leg and one arm, and he got the other around the vampire's leg. Thomas heaved, and the creature fell, then twisted like an arthritic serpent to grapple with him.

Thomas went mano a mano, no tricks, no subtlety. The living corpse got a hand on Thomas's throat and tried to tear his head off. Thomas writhed sinuously away from the full power of the creature, and then rolled over a couple of times. Thomas got hold of the thing's wrists and tried to force them away from his neck.

And then Thomas changed.

It wasn't anything so dramatic as the vampires of the Red Court, whose demonic forms lurked beneath a masquerade of seemingly normal human flesh. It was far subtler. A cold wind seemed to gather around him. His features stretched, changing, his cheekbones starker, his eyes more sunken, his face more gaunt. His skin took on a shining, almost luminescent luster, like a fine pearl under moonlight. And his eyes changed as well. His irises flickered to a shade of chrome-colored silver, then bleached out to white altogether.

He snarled a string of curses as he fought, and the sound of his voice changed as well—again, a subtle thing. It was more feral, more vicious, and its tone was not even remotely human. Thomas, despite his deathly injuries, went up against the Black Court killing machine in a contest of main strength and won. He forced the vampire's hands from his throat, rolled so that his good leg came up beneath the vampire, and, with the combined strength of his arms, Thomas threw the vampire into the brick wall of the nearest building.

Bricks shattered, and bits and pieces of them flew outward in a cloud of stinging shrapnel. The vampire collapsed to the ground for a moment, stunned. A heartbeat later, it stirred and began to rise again. Thomas's shoulders heaved, as though to push himself up and continue the fight, but whatever fuel had driven his transformation and sudden strength had been expended.

He fell limp and loose to the gravel, gaunt face empty

of expression. His all-white eyes went out of focus, staring, and he did not move.

Lara Raith wasn't doing badly for herself. The wind was blowing the short little black silk robe back off of her, so it was all black lace and pale flesh that somehow did not present a contrast to the gun. One-ear had fallen on his side. Shards of brittle bone protruded from both thighs and both knees, where Lara Raith had exercised her marksmanship. One-ear pushed himself up, and Lara put a shot in the arm supporting the vampire's weight. One-ear's elbow exploded in a cloud of ruined cloth, moldy flesh, and bone splinters, and the creature fell back to the ground.

Lara put a bullet through One-ear's left eye. The smell was indescribably nauseating. Lara aimed at the vampire's other eye.

"This won't kill me," the creature snarled.

"I don't need to," Lara responded. "Just to slow you down."

"I'll be after you in hours," One-ear-one-eye said.

"Look somewhere sunny," she responded. "*Au revoir,* darling."

The gun's hammer clicked down and silence ensued.

Lara had time to blink in disbelief at the gun. Then the vampire Thomas had stunned rushed at Lara's back. The creature wasn't quite a blur, but it was fast as hell. I tried to shout a warning at her, but it came out more of a croak than anything.

Lara shot a glance over her shoulder and started to move, but my warning had come too late. The vampire seized her by her dark hair and spun her around. Then it hit her with a broad swing of its arm and literally knocked her out of her high-heeled shoes. She flew at the nearest wall, half spinning in the air, and hit hard. The gun tumbled from her fingers and she fell, her eyes wide and frightened, her expression stunned. Her face had been cut on the cheek, at the corner of her mouth, and on her forehead. She was bleeding odd, pale blood in thick, trickling lines.

The vampire shuddered and leapt after her, landing

on all fours. It was graceful, but alien, far more arachnid than feline. The corpse prowled over to her, seized her throat, and shoved her shoulders against the wall. Then it thrust out a long, leathery tongue and started licking her blood, hissing in mounting pleasure.

One-ear slithered over to her as well, using his un-wounded arm and a serpentine writhing of the rest of his body. "Raith's second in command," the vampire rasped. "As well as the White who betrayed us. Now you're both mine."

Lara tried to push the vampire licking her blood away, but she wasn't strong enough, and she still looked dazed. "Get away from me."

"Mine," One-ear repeated. It drew Lara's hair back away from her throat. The other vampire took her hands and pinned them against the wall above her head.

One-ear touched its tongue to Lara's mouth and shivered. "I'll show you what real vampires are like. You'll see things differently soon. And you'll be lovely, still. For a little while. I'll enjoy that."

Lara struggled, but the haze of confusion over her eyes did not clear, and her motions had a dreamlike lack of coordination. Her face took on an expression of horror as both vampires leaned into her, their withered teeth settling onto her flesh. They bit her, and she bucked in terror and agony. There were ugly, slurping sounds beneath Lara Raith's screams.

Which was what I'd been waiting for. Once they had bitten down, I gathered up momentum as quietly as I could, closed the last few yards in the springing strides I would have used on a fencing strip, and drove the six-inch heel of one of Lara's black pumps as hard as I could into the space between the unwounded vampire's shoulder blades. I had the heel of my hand and the full weight of my body behind the blow, and I hit square and hard, so that the heel drove into its back, just left of its spine, directly at the vampire's withered heart.

I didn't get the response I would have liked best. The vampire didn't disintegrate or explode into dust. But it did convulse with a sudden scream, its body going into almost the same kind of spastic seizure the other one had displayed on having a turkey rammed through its chest. It staggered and fell to the ground, its dead face locked into a grimace of surprise and helpless pain.

One-ear was slow to react. By the time it tore its mouth from the gnawed and bleeding slope of Lara Raith's left breast, I had my mother's pentacle out and had focused all of my attention on it.

Now I've heard that the power of faith is simply another aspect of the magic I used all the time. I've also heard that it is a completely different kind of energy, totally unrelated to the living power I felt all around me. Certainly it garnered a very different reaction from various supernatural entities than my everyday wizardry did, so maybe they weren't related at all.

But that didn't matter. I wasn't holding a crucifix in the thing's face. I was holding the symbol of what *I* believed in. The five-pointed star of the pentacle represented the five forces of the universe, those of air, fire, water, earth, and of spiritual energy, laid into patterns of order and life and bound within a circle of human thought, human will. I believed that magic was fundamentally a force of life, of good, something meant to protect and preserve. I believed that those who wielded it therefore had a responsibility to use that power in the way it was meant to be used—and that was belief enough to tap into the vast power of faith, and to direct it against One-ear.

The pentacle burst into silver and blue light, a blaze as bright as an airborne flare. One-ear's stretched facial skin began to peel away, and the thick fluids oozing from its ruined eye socket burst into silver flame. The vampire screamed and threw itself away from that silver fire. If he'd had a crony left, they could have come at me from opposite directions, so that the blazing light from the pentacle could sear only one. But he didn't, and I followed after One-ear, keeping the pentacle held before me, my concentration locked upon it.

One-ear scrambled over the writhing vampire with the turkey-crushed chest, and the creature, maybe younger or more vulnerable than its leader, simply burst into flame as the pentacle glared down upon it. I had to skip back a step from that sudden heat, and the fallen vampire was consumed by blinding fire until nothing was left of it.

By the time my eyes had adjusted to the comparative darkness of the parking lot again, One-ear was nowhere to be seen. I checked over my shoulder and saw the transformed Lara Raith straddle the staked vampire, her eyes blazing silver and bright, her skin shining as Thomas's had. She drove blows down at its face, crushing it with the first few, then driving *into* its skull with sickening squelching sounds during subsequent blows. She continued, screaming at the top of her lungs the whole while, until she'd crushed its face and moved onto its neck, beating it into shapeless pulp.

And then she tore the vampire's head off its shoulders, killing it.

She rose slowly, pale eyes distant and inhuman. Her white skin was streaked with ichor of black, brown, and dark green, mingling with the pale, pinkish blood around her cuts and the bite wounds. Her dark hair had fallen from its mostly up style, and hung around her in a wild tangle. She looked terrified and furious and sexy as hell.

The succubus turned hungry eyes on me, and began a slow stalk forward. I let the gathered light ease out of my pentacle. It wouldn't do me any good against Lara. "We have a truce," I said. My voice sounded harsh, cold, though I hadn't tried to make it that way. "Don't make me destroy you too."

She stopped in her stockinged tracks. Her expression flickered with uncertainty and fear, and she looked a hell of a lot shorter without the do-me pumps. She shuddered and folded her arms over her stomach, closing her eyes for a moment. The luminous, compelling glow faded from her skin, her features becoming less unreal, if no less lovely. When she opened her eyes again, they were almost human. "My family," she said. "I have to get them out of here. Our truce stands. Will you help me?"

I looked at Inari, on the ground and paralyzed with pain. Thomas wasn't moving. He might have been dead.

Lara took a deep breath and said, "Mister Dresden, I can't protect them. I need your help to get them to safety. Please."

The last word had cost her something. Somehow, I held back from agreeing to help her on pure reflex. *That is a monumentally bad idea, Harry,* I cautioned myself. I shoved the knee-jerk chivalry aside and scowled at Lara.

She stood facing me, her chin lifted proudly. Her injuries looked vicious, and she had to be in pain, but she refused to let it show on her face—except for one moment, when she glanced at Thomas and Inari, and her eyes suddenly glistened. The tears fell, but she did not allow herself to blink.

"Dammit." I let out my breath in disgust at myself and said, "I'll get my car."

Chapter Eighteen

I debated talking to Arturo before I left but decided against it. Thomas and Inari were hurt, and the sooner they got medical care, the better. Additionally, One-ear the vampire had consciously gotten his own flunky immolated in order to escape. If he had some mystical method of communicating with Mama Mavra—or a cell phone—she might already be on the way with reinforcements.

One-ear was still pretty new to the vampire game, and his pair of followers had been virtual infants, and they had almost been more than all of us could handle. Mavra was in a different league entirely. She had been killing for centuries, and the near-extermination of the Black

Court had meant that only the smartest, strongest, and most deadly of its members had survived. One-ear was dangerous enough, but if Mavra caught us in the open, she would take us apart.

So I ran to get the Blue Beetle from the row of parking spaces near the building Arturo was using. It was a quick run, a couple of plots up and one over from where Thomas and Inari lay. I slipped into the building. Only a couple of people saw me, and I ignored them as I ducked into the studio doors, seized my backpack, my coat, and the sleeping puppy, and fumbled in the coat until I found my car keys. I carried the whole kit and caboodle out to the car.

I coaxed the Beetle to life and tore down the gravel lanes with all the speed its little engine could manage. The Beetle's single headlight glared over Lara, who had Thomas in a fireman's carry. She'd taken off the short black robe and had tied it into an improvised sling for Inari, who stumbled along behind her older sister.

I opened the doors and helped her lower Thomas into the back of the Beetle. Lara stared for a second at my car's interior. It didn't look like she approved of the stripped and improvised quality of it. "There's no seat in back," she said.

"That's why there's a blanket," I answered her. "Get in. How is he?"

"Alive, for now," Lara said. "He's breathing, but he's emptied his reserves. He'll need to refresh them."

I paused and stared at her. "You mean he needs to feed on someone."

Her eyes slid aside to Inari, but the girl had her hands full simply staying vertical through the pain, and probably wouldn't have heard the space shuttle lifting off. Nonetheless, Lara lowered her voice. "Yes. Deeply."

"Hell's bells," I said. I got the door for Inari and helped her into the passenger-side seat, buckled her in, and dropped the puppy in her lap. She clutched at him with her unwounded arm, whimpering.

I got the Beetle the hell away from the little industrial park. After several moments of hurried driving, I started to relax. I kept checking, but I saw no one following me. I played a few trail-shaking tricks, just in case, and finally felt able to speak. "I'll get you to my place," I told Lara.

"You can't possibly think that the basement of a boardinghouse will be secure."

"How do you know where I live?" I demanded.

"I've read the Court's defensive assessment of your home," she said with an absent wave of her hand.

Which was scary as hell, that someone had assessed my freaking apartment. But I wasn't going to show her that. "It's kept me alive pretty well. Once we get there we can fort up under my heavy defenses. We'll be stuck inside, but safe until morning."

"If you wish. But if he does not feed, Thomas will be dead within the hour."

I spat an oath.

"Mavra knows where you live, in any case, Dresden. She will doubtless have some of her personnel waiting near your apartment."

"True," I said. "Where else could we go?"

"My family's house."

"You all live in Chicago?"

"Of course not," Lara said, her voice tired. "But we keep houses in several cities around the world. Thomas has been in and out of Chicago for the past two or three years, between resort vacations. Justine is at the house, waiting for him."

"Inari will need a doctor."

"I have one," she said. Then added, "On retainer."

I stared at her in my rearview mirror for a moment (in which she appeared like anyone else) and then shrugged. "Which way?"

"North along the lake," she said. "I'm sorry. I don't know the street names. Turn right at the light ahead."

She gave directions and I followed them, and I reminded myself that it would be a bad habit to form. It took us better than half an hour to get up to one of the wealthy lakeside developments that just about any large body of water makes inevitable. I'd seen several such developments during the course of my investigations, but the area Lara directed me to was as elaborate and expensive-looking as any I had ever seen.

The house we finally pulled up to had multiple wings, multiple stories, and a couple of faux-castle turrets. It had cost someone eight digits, and could have doubled as the headquarters of the villain in a James Bond movie. Old timber had grown up around it, and was manicured into an idyllic forest of rolling, grass-green hummocks and beautiful, shapely trees wreathed in ivy and autumn leaves. Small lit pools were dotted here and there, each shrouded with its own low cloud of evening mist.

The drive rolled through Little Sherwood for better than half a mile, and I started feeling nervous. If anything tried to kill me, I was too far away from the road to run for help. Or even to scream for it. I shook my wrist to hear the jangle of the little silver shields on my bracelet, and made sure it was ready to go at an instant's notice.

Lara's pale grey eyes regarded me in the rearview mirror for a moment, and then she said, "Dresden, you and my brother have nothing further to fear from me this night. I will respect our truce, and extend guest rights to you while you are in my family's home. And I do so swear it."

I frowned and didn't chance a look at her eyes, even in the mirror. I didn't have to. There was something in her voice that I recognized. Call it the ring of truth.

The one advantage to dealing with supernatural foes was that the code of honor of the Old World was accepted and expected when we negotiated with one another. A sworn oath and the obligations of hospitality were more binding in those circles than the threat of physical force. What Lara had offered me meant that not only would she not attempt to do me harm—she would be obligated to protect me should anyone else attempt to do so. If she failed in her duties as a host, it would represent a major loss of face, should word of it get around.

But from what I'd gathered, Lara wasn't the one mak-

ing all the calls in the Raith household. If someone up
the family food chain—for example, Daddy Raith—
thought he could get away with it without word leaking
out, he might decide to subtract me from the old equation of life. It was a real risk, and I didn't want to take it.

The last vampire who had offered me the hospitality
of her home, Bianca, had drugged me, nearly killed me,
manipulated me into starting a war (which incidentally
forced me into a stupidly dangerous investigation with
the Queens of Faerie), and tried to feed me to her most
recent vampire "recruit," my former lover, Susan. There
was no reason to think that Lara wasn't capable of the
same treachery.

Unfortunately, my back wasn't exactly breaking under
the weight of all my options. I had no idea of how to
help Thomas, and my apartment was the only place in
town I would be safe. If I cut and ran Thomas wouldn't
survive it. I didn't have anything but a strong intuition
that Lara would hold to the letter of our truce. Two
seconds after it was over she'd finish what she started,
sure, but in the meantime we might be okay.

A paranoid little voice inside reminded me that Lara
seemed like she was more or less on the level, and that
it should make me nervous. Their near-humanity was
what made the White Court so dangerous. I'd never
come close to thinking that maybe Bianca was an okay
person underneath the blood-craving monster. I'd known
that she wasn't human, and I'd been wary every single
time I'd interacted with her.

I didn't get any more of a creature-feature vibe from
Lara than I did from Thomas. But I had to figure they
were cut from a similar mold. There would be lies under
lies. I had to be paranoid, which in this instance was
another word for *smart*. I couldn't afford to extend Lara
much trust if I wanted to avoid a rerun of the *Harry
Nearly Dies Because of His Stupid Chivalry Show*.

I promised myself that the second anything got dicey
I would blast my way out of that house through the
nearest wall, incinerating first and asking questions later.
It wouldn't be the subtlest escape in the whole world,

but I was pretty sure the Raiths could afford to repair the damages. I wondered if vampires had any trouble getting homeowner's insurance.

I pulled the Blue Beetle around the circular drive in front of Château Raith. Its engine shuddered, coughed, and finally died before I could shut it down. A sidewalk swept between a pair of vicious-looking stone gargoyles four feet high, and led through a rose garden bedded with pure white gravel.

The rose vines were old ones, some of them as thick as my thumb. Their spreading tendrils twined all around the entirety of the garden and over the feet of the crouching gargoyles. The lighting was all arranged in soft blues and greens, and it made the roses on the vines look black. Thick leaves grew all over the vines, but here and there I could see the wicked needle tips of larger-than-average thorns. The air was filled with their light, heady scent.

"Help Inari," Lara said. "I will carry Thomas."

"Considering that you're the one who shot him in the first place, *I'll* carry Thomas," I said. "*You* help Inari."

Her lips compressed slightly, but she nodded. "As you wish."

Damn straight, as I wish.

Lara leaned over to pull Inari from the car, but before she could touch the girl the notch-eared puppy sprang up out of his sleep, barking and snarling at Lara in squeaky fury. Lara jerked her hand back, brows lowering in consternation. "What's wrong with your animal?"

I sighed and slid into my leather duster, then came around to the passenger door. "I keep telling everyone he's not mine." I scooped up the little psychopath and deposited him in one of my coat pockets. He scrambled around in there for a minute, and then he managed to poke his head out. The puppy kept his eyes on Lara and kept growling. "There. Now the beast cannot harm you."

Lara gave me a cool look and coaxed Inari to her feet. Then she helped me draw Thomas out of the car as gently as possible. He was flaccid and cold, his eyes entirely white, but I could hear his labored breathing.

Without knowing the extent of the injuries to his upper body, I didn't dare risk a fireman's carry, so I got an arm under his shoulder blades and hamstrings, and lifted him like a child. He was heavy. My shoulders screamed, and my ears started ringing with a quiet, shrill tone.

I felt dizzy for a second, and shrugged it off with an effort of will. I couldn't afford to show any weakness now.

I followed Lara and Inari up the sidewalk to the house. Lara pushed a button on a small plastic panel beside the door and said, "Lara Raith." There was a heavy metallic *click-clack,* and one of the doors drifted slowly in.

Just then the lights of another car swept across us. A white limo pulled in beside the Blue Beetle on the circular drive and came to a halt. A moment later a white sedan pulled in behind the limo.

The limo's driver was woman over six feet tall wearing a grey uniform. Her hair was pulled back in a severe braid, and she wore dark red lipstick. A tall, strong-looking man in a grey silk suit got out on the passenger side of the limo. I caught sight of a shoulder rig while he was settling his jacket. His eyes swept around, taking in everything, including us at the door, the drive, the grounds, the trees, and the roof of the house. He was checking possible lines of fire. A bodyguard.

Simultaneously, another man and woman got out of the white sedan. At first I thought that they were the same two people. I blinked. The man looked the same, but the second woman was wearing a grey suit a lot like the one of the man with her. Then I got it—two sets of identical twins. They all looked wary, competent, and dangerous. They fanned out around the limo in silent coordination, like they'd done it a jillion times.

Then the driver opened the back door of the limo.

The air grew suddenly colder, as if the Almighty had flicked on the air-conditioning. A man slid out of the car. He was about six feet tall, dark of hair and pale of flesh. He was dressed in a white linen suit with a silver-grey silk shirt and Italian leather shoes. There was a scarlet gem of some kind fixed to his left earlobe, though his fine, straight hair hid it until a breeze briefly tossed the dark strands to one side. He had long, spatulate fingers, broad shoulders, the eyes of a drowsy jaguar, and he was better-looking than Thomas.

Beside me, Lara shuddered, and I heard her whisper, "Dammit, no."

The newcomer walked over to us, very slowly and deliberately. The doubles fell into position to his sides and behind him, and I couldn't help but think they looked like toys—two matched sets of Bodyguard Barbie and Bodyguard Ken. The pale man paused beside one of the gargoyles and plucked a stem and a rose from one of the plants there. Then he approached again, in no hurry whatsoever, plucking off leaves and thorns from the flower one by one.

When he was about four feet away he stopped, finally looking up from the rose. "Ah, dearest Lara," he murmured. His voice was deep, quiet, and as smooth as warm honey. "What a pleasant surprise to find you here."

Lara's expression slipped into a neutral mask, veiling the anxiety I could feel in the tension of her body. She inclined her head in a courtly nod, and left her eyes on the sidewalk.

The man smiled. His eyes swept over the rest of us meanwhile, distant and alien. "Have you been well?"

"Yes, my Lord."

His lips pursed into a pout. "This is hardly a formal occasion, little Lara. I've missed you."

Lara sighed. She met my eyes for a second, her expression one of warning. Then she turned to step closer to the man. She kissed his cheek without lifting her eyes and whispered, "And I you, Father."

Oh, crap.

Chapter Nineteen

Lord Raith looked Lara up and down. "That's . . . quite a novel ensemble you're wearing."

"It's been a busy night."

Raith nodded and went to Inari, gently touching her shoulder, peering at her arm in the makeshift sling. "What happened to you, daughter mine?"

Inari lifted eyes dull with pain and fatigue and said, "We were mugged. Or something. I think it must have been a gang. That makes sense, doesn't it?"

Raith didn't hesitate a beat. "Of course it does, dearest." He fixed his eyes on Lara and said, "How could you let something like this happen to your baby sister?"

"Forgive me, Father," Lara said.

Raith waved a generous hand. "She needs medical attention, Lara. I believe hospitals provide such a thing."

"Bruce is here," Lara said. "I'm sure he can take care of it."

"Which is Bruce?"

I would have expected her tone to hold annoyance, but if so I didn't hear it. "The doctor."

"He came with you from California? How fortuitous."

I couldn't take it anymore. "Hey, people. Chat time is over. The girl's about to pass out on her feet. Thomas is dying. So both of you shut your mouth and help them."

Raith whipped his head around to stare daggers at me. His voice was cold enough to merit the use of a Kelvin scale. "I do not respond well to demands."

I ground my teeth and said, "Both of you shut your mouth and help them. Please."

And they say I can't be diplomatic.

Raith flicked an irritated hand at the bookend brigade.

Bodyguard Kens and Barbies drew their guns in precise unison and raised them to shoot.

"No!" Lara said. She stepped in front of me and Thomas. "You can't."

"Can't?" Raith said. His voice was dangerously mild.

"They might hit Thomas."

"I am confident in their marksmanship. They will not hit him," Raith said, in a tone that suggested he wouldn't lose any sleep if they did.

"I've invited him," Lara said.

Raith stared at her for a moment, and then in that same soft voice asked, "Why?"

"Because we declared a twenty-four-hour truce while he assisted us," Lara answered. "If not for his help, we might all be dead."

Raith's head tilted to one side. He regarded me for a long moment, and then smiled. He didn't have Thomas beat when it came to smiles. Thomas's grin had so much life to it that it was practically sentient. Lord Raith's smile made me think of sharks and skulls. "I suppose it would be churlish to ignore my debt to you, young man. I will honor the truce and respect my daughter's invitation and hospitality. Thank you for your assistance."

"Whatever," I said. "Would you both shut your mouths and help them *now*. Pretty please. With sugar on top."

"I used to admire that kind of monolithic determination." Raith waved his hand again, though his eyes looked no less cold. The thugs put their guns away. One man and one woman went to Inari, supporting her and helping her into the house. "Lara, bring your physician to her quarters, if you would. Assuming he has mind enough left to treat her."

She bowed her head again, and something told me she resented doing it.

"I'll expect you and Thomas in my chambers at dawn so that we can discuss what happened. Oh, and if you would, Wizard Dresden—"

The King of the White Court knew me on sight. This just kept getting better and better.

"—Lara can show you where Thomas's chambers are. That girl of his is there, I think." Lord Raith drifted into the house, paced by his retainers.

By my count, there were still two whole goons available for Thomas toting, but I grunted like a big tough guy and set out to do it myself. We started walking into the house. "Nice guy," I commented to Lara. I was a little short of breath. "And I was all worried about meeting him."

"I know," Lara murmured. "He was really quite pleasant."

"Except for the eyes," I said.

She glanced at me again, something like approval in her features. "You saw that."

"That's what I do."

She nodded. "Then please believe me when I say that deception is what *we* do, wizard. My father does not like you. I suspect he wishes to kill you."

"I get that a lot."

She smiled at me, and I got hit with another surge of lust—maybe one that wasn't entirely inspired by her come-hither mojo. She was a smart, tough lady, and had plenty of courage. I had to respect that. And she was gliding along beside me dressed in skimpy black lingerie. Admittedly, the blood and ichor detracted from the overall look, but it gave me a good excuse to see the rest of her while making my assessment.

We went up a shallow, curving stairwell and down a long hall. I tried to stick mental landmarks into my memory so that I'd be able to leave in a hurry if I needed to. My vision blurred for a moment, and the high-pitched buzzing in my ears increased in volume. I took a breath and steadied myself against the wall.

"Here," Lara said. She turned to me and took Thomas. Either she was stronger than me or she was good at acting like it was no big deal. Probably both.

I rolled my aching shoulders in relief. "Thanks. How is he?"

"The bullets aren't going to kill him," she said. "He'd have died already. The Hunger may finish him, though."

I arched an eyebrow at her in question.

"The Hunger," she repeated. "Our need to feed. The angel of our darker natures. We can draw upon it to give us a kind of strength, but it's like fire. It can turn on you if you don't keep it under control. Right now Thomas is so hungry that he can't think. Can't move. He'll be all right once he feeds."

I felt an itch on the back of my neck and checked over my shoulder. "Your father's driver is tailing us."

Lara nodded. "She'll dispose of the body."

I blinked. "I thought you said he was going to be all right."

"He will be," Lara said, her tone carefully neutral. "Justine won't."

"What?"

"He's too hungry," Lara said. "He won't be able to control himself."

"Fuck that," I said. "That isn't going to happen."

"Then he'll die," Lara said tiredly. "This is the door to his suite."

She stopped at a door, and with my reflexes on automatic pilot I opened it for her. We went into a rather large room dominated by a sunken pit in the floor. The carpet was lush, a dark crimson, pillows were all over, and a smoking brazier rested in the center of the pit. The air was heavy with sweet incense. Quiet jazz drifted through the room from speakers I couldn't see.

On the opposite side of the room, a curtain twitched and then the girl appeared from what was evidently a room beyond. Justine's shoulder-length dark hair had been striped with trendy strands of dark blue and deep purple. She wore a white bathrobe several sizes too large for her and looked rumpled from sleep. She blinked dark, sleepy eyes and then gasped and rushed toward us. "Thomas? My God!"

I looked back over my shoulder. The driver stood just outside the doorway, speaking quietly into a cellular phone.

Lara carried Thomas down into the pit and carefully laid him upon the pillows and cushions, Justine at her side. The girl's face was twisted in anxiety. "Harry? What happened to him?"

Lara glanced up and me and said, "I need to make sure Inari is cared for. If you will excuse me." I didn't, but she left the room anyway.

Justine stared up at me, fear and confusion on her face. "I don't understand."

"Lara shot him," I said quietly. "And then some Black Court gorillas jumped us."

"Lara?"

"Didn't seem like she liked the idea, but she sure as hell gave it a whirl. Lara said he'd spent his reserves fighting, and that he would die if he didn't feed."

Justine's eyes flicked up to the doorway. She saw the driver standing outside. Justine's face blanched.

"Oh," she whispered.

Tears formed in her eyes.

"Oh, no. No, no," she said. "My poor Thomas."

I stepped forward. "You don't have to do this."

"But he'll die."

"Do you think he'd want it to be you instead?"

Her lips trembled and she closed her eyes for a moment. "I don't know. I've seen him. I know there's a part of him that wants to."

"And there's another part that doesn't," I said. "That would want you to be alive and happy."

She settled on her knees beside Thomas, staring down at him. She put her fingers on his cheek, and he moved for the first time since the fight with One-ear. He turned his head and placed a soft kiss on Justine's hand.

The girl shivered. "He might not take too much. He tries so hard not to take too much. Not to hurt me. He might stop himself."

"Do you really believe that?"

She was silent for a long moment, and then said, "It doesn't matter. I can't stand by and let him die when I can help him."

"Why not?"

She looked up at me, her eyes steady. "I love him."

"You're addicted to him," I said.

"That too," she agreed. "But it doesn't change anything. I love him."

"Even if it kills you?" I asked.

She bowed her head, gently stroking Thomas's cheek. "Of course."

I started to refute her, but just then the rush of energy from the silver belt buckle petered out. I started trembling violently. The pain of my injuries rushed back over me. Fatigue settled onto me like a backpack full of lead. My thoughts turned to exhausted sludge.

I vaguely remember Justine cajoling me to my feet and guiding me back through one of the curtains to a lavish bedroom. She helped me onto the bed and said, "You'll tell him for me, won't you?" She was crying through a small smile. "You'll tell him what I said? That I love him?"

The room was spinning, but I promised her that I would.

She kissed my forehead and gave me a sad smile. "Thank you, Harry. You've always helped us."

My vision narrowed to a grey tunnel. I tried to get back up again, but I could barely manage to turn my head.

So all I could do was watch Justine slide out of the bathrobe and leave the room to go to Thomas.

And to her death.

Chapter Twenty

Sometimes you wake up and there's a little voice inside your head that tells you that today is a special day. For a lot of kids, it sometimes happens on their birthdays and always on Christmas morning. I remember exactly one of those Christmases, when I was little and my dad was still alive. I felt it again eight or nine years later, the morning that Justin DuMorne came to pick me up from the orphanage. I felt it one more time, the morning Justin brought Elaine home from whatever orphanage she had been in.

And now the little voice was telling me to wake up. That it was a special day.

My little voice is some kind of psycho.

I opened my eyes and found myself on a bed the size of a small aircraft carrier. There was light coming into the room from beneath a curtain, but it wasn't enough to see more than vague outlines. I ached from almost a dozen minor cuts and abrasions. My throat burned with thirst, and my belly with hunger. My clothes were spattered in blood (and worse), my face was rough with the shadow of a beard, my hair was so mussed that it was approaching trendy, and I can't even imagine what I would have smelled like to anyone walking in. I needed a shower.

I slipped out into the entrance room, around the passion pit and its pillows. There wasn't a corpse lying in the pit or anything, but then that's what the driver had been for. The pale light of predawn colored the sky deep blue through a nearby window. I'd been down for only a few hours. Time to get into the car and get gone.

I opened the door to leave Thomas's chambers, but it was locked. I checked, but it was using at least a pair of key-only padlocks and maybe some kind of emergency bolt as well. There was no way I could open it.

"Fine. We do this Hulk style." I took a few steps back, focused on the wall I thought closest to the outside, and began to draw in my will. I took it slow, concentrating, so that I would have the best chance of keeping the spell under control. "Mister McGee, don't make me angry," I muttered at the wall. "You wouldn't like me when I'm angry."

I was about to huff and puff and blow the wall down when the door rattled, clicked, and opened. Thomas entered, looking as he always did, though this time he wore khakis and a white cotton turtleneck. He had a long coat of brown leather draped over his shoulders, and a gym bag in his hand. He froze when he saw me. His expression showed something I didn't think I'd ever seen in him before—shame. He looked down, avoiding my eyes.

"Harry," he said quietly. "Sorry about the door. Had to make sure you got left alone until you woke up."

I didn't say anything. But I remembered my last sight of Justine. Fury, pure and simple, flooded through me.

"I brought you some clothes, some towels." Thomas tossed the gym bag underhand. It landed on my foot. "There's a guest room two doors down on your left. You can use the shower in there."

"How's Justine?" I asked. My voice was flat and hard.

He stood there without lifting his eyes.

I felt my hands clench into angry fists. I realized that I was barely a breath away from attacking Thomas with my bare hands. "That's what I thought," I said. I walked past him to the door. "I'll clean up at home."

"Harry."

I stopped. His voice was raw with emotion, and sounded like he was trying to speak through a throat full of bitter mud. "I wanted you to know. Justine . . . I tried to stop in time. I didn't want to hurt her. Never."

"Yeah," I said. "You had good intentions. That makes it all right."

He folded his arms over his stomach, as if nauseous, and bowed his head. His long hair veiled his face. "I never pretended I wasn't . . . a predator, Harry. I never claimed she was anything but what she was. Food. You knew it. She knew it. I didn't lie to anyone."

I had a bunch of vicious answers I could have used, but I went with, "Before she went to you last night, Justine asked me to tell you that she loved you."

Short of shoving a running chain saw into Thomas's guts, I don't think I could have hurt him any more. He didn't look up when I spoke, and he started trembling with rapid breaths. "Don't go yet. I need to talk to you. Please. There are things happening that—"

I started walking out, and heard myself put every bit

of caustic contempt I could into the words: "Make an appointment at my office."

He took a step after me. "Dresden, Mavra knows about this house. For your own sake, at least wait for sunrise."

He had a point. Dammit. Sunrise would send the Black Court back to their hidey holes, and if they had any mortal accomplices, it would at least mean that I would only be up against run of the mill weapons and tactics. Arturo probably wouldn't be awake at the moment, and Murphy would just now be getting dressed and heading for the gym. Bob would stay out until the last minute he possibly could, so I'd have to wait for sunrise to talk to him anyway. I had a little time to kill.

"All right," I said.

"Do you mind if tell you a few things?"

"Yes," I said. "I mind."

His voice broke. "Dammit, do you think I wanted this?"

"I think you hurt and used someone who loved you. A woman. As far as I'm concerned, you don't exist. You look like a person, but you aren't. I should have remembered that from the beginning."

"Harry—"

Anger flared up in me like a wall of red flame behind my eyes. I shot a look at Thomas over my shoulder that made him flinch. "Be satisfied with nonexistence, Thomas," I said. "You're lucky you have it. It's the only thing keeping you alive."

I slammed the door behind me as I left his chambers. I slammed open the door to the guest room he'd mentioned. And then slammed it behind me, which was starting to seem a little childish, even through a haze of bitter anger. I tried to take deep breaths and got the shower going.

Hot water. Ye gods. There are no words to describe how good a hot shower feels after several years of living with no water heater of your own. I broiled myself for a while, and found soap, shampoo, shaving cream, and a razor waiting on a shelf inside the shower. I availed myself of them and began to calm down. I figured that once I got some coffee I might be almost stable again.

I guess if Lord Raith could afford a house that size, he could afford a water heater to match it, because I ran the shower as hot as I could stand for almost half an hour and it never got cold. When I got out, the bathroom mirror was steamed up and the air was thick and wet enough to suffocate me. I slapped my towel over all the wet bits, tied it to my waist, and left the bathroom for the guest bedroom. The air was cooler and drier and it made it a pleasure to simply inhale.

I opened the sports bag Thomas had thrown me. It held a pair of blue jeans that looked more or less my size and a pair of plain grey athletic socks. Then I found what I thought at first was a circus tent, but it turned out to be an enormous Hawaiian shirt with lots of blue and orange in its flowered pattern.

I looked at the thing skeptically while I put on the jeans. They fit pretty well. Thomas hadn't included any clean underwear, which was likely just as well. I'd rather go commando than wear undies that may have outlived their previous owner. I zipped up the jeans with considerable caution. A nearby dresser had a mirror on it, and I went to it to comb my hair while working up the nerve to put on the shirt.

Inari's image stood in the mirror, staring at my back. My heart flew up into my throat, then past it into my brain and out the top of my skull. "Holy crap!" I sputtered.

I turned to face her. She was wearing a cute little pink sleep shirt with prints of Winnie the Pooh all over it. The shirt would have fallen to midthigh on a shorter or younger girl, but on Inari it barely managed to escape indecency. Her right arm was wrapped to the elbow in a black plaster cast. Her left was cradled against her body, and she held the notch-eared puppy in it. He looked restless and unhappy.

"Hello," Inari said. Her voice was very soft and her eyes were distant and unfocused. Alarm bells started going off in my head. "Your pet got out into the manor last night," she went on. "Father asked me to find him and bring him back to you."

"Oh," I said. "Uh. Thank you, I guess. Don't let me keep you waiting. Just put him on the bed."

Instead of doing so, she stared at me—specifically, at my chest. "You have more muscle than I would have thought. And scars." Her eyes flicked down to the puppy. When she looked back at me, they had turned a pale shade of grey, and over the next several seconds that color gained a metallic sheen. "I came to thank you. You saved my life last night."

"Welcome," I said. "Puppy on the bed, please?"

She slid forward and lowered the little dog to the bed. He looked tired, but he started a quiet little warning growl, his eyes on Inari. After she put the dog down, she kept taking slow, sinuous steps toward me. "I don't know what it is about you. You're fascinating. I've been wanting the chance to speak with you all night."

I did my best not to notice the almost serpentine grace of her movements. If I noticed them too hard, I'd start ignoring everything else.

"I've never felt this before," Inari continued, almost to herself. Her eyes stayed locked on my bare chest. "About anyone."

She got close enough that I could smell her perfume, a scent that made my knees wobble for a second. Her eyes had become a shade of brightest silver, inhumanly intense, and I shivered as a spasm of raw physical need shot through me—different from when Lara had hit me with the come-hither, but just as potent. I had a flash image of pressing Inari down onto the bed and tearing the sweet little nightshirt off of her, and I closed my eyes to shove it away.

It must have taken longer than it seemed, because the next thing I knew, Inari pressed herself to me. She shivered and ran her tongue over my collarbone. I nearly jumped out of my borrowed jeans. I blinked my eyes open, lifted a hand, and opened my mouth to protest, but Inari pressed her mouth to mine and guided my hand down to brush against something naked and smooth and delicious. There was a panicked second in which some part of me realized that my caution hadn't been enough—that I'd been compromised and taken. But that part quickly shut up, because Inari's mouth on mine was the sweetest thing I'd ever tasted. The puppy continued growling his little warning, but it didn't matter, either.

We'd gotten to some seriously heavy breathing when Inari tore her lips from my mouth, panting, her mouth swollen with the heated kisses. Her eyes flashed pure and empty white, and her skin began to grow luminous and pearlescent. I tried to fumble some words out of my mouth, to tell her to stop. They didn't get past my tingling lips. She hooked one long leg behind one of mine and pressed in with a sudden and inhuman strength to slather a line of licking, wet kisses across my throat. Cold started spreading through me—delicious, sweet cold that stole warmth and strength even as the pleasure began.

And then the damnedest thing happened.

Inari let out a panicked shriek and staggered back from me. She fell to the floor on the other side of the guest room, gasping. She lifted her head a moment later to look at me, her eyes hazed with confusion and their original color again.

Her mouth had been burned. I saw blisters rising around her lips. "What?" she stammered. "What happened? Harry? What are you doing here?"

"Leaving," I said. I still felt short of breath, as if I'd been sprinting rather than doing energetic kissing. I turned from her, stuffed the dirty clothes in my pack, and pulled my duster on. I plopped the puppy down in his usual pocket and said, "I've got to get out of here."

Just then Thomas slammed the door open, his eyes wild. He looked from Inari to me and back, and exhaled, evidently trying to relax. "Thank God. Are you both all right?"

"My mouth," Inari said, her tone still sleepy and bewildered. "It hurts. Thomas? What happened to me?"

She started hyperventilating. "What's happening? Those *things* last night, and you were hurt, and your eyes were *white*, Thomas. I . . . what . . . ?"

Ow. It was painful to watch her. I'd seen people who had suddenly been shocked out of their innocence to the existence of the supernatural before, but it had rarely been something this sudden and terrifying. I mean, my God. The girl's family wasn't what she thought they were. They were also a part of this nightmarish new reality, and they had done nothing to prepare her for it.

"Inari," Thomas said gently. "You need to rest. You've barely slept and your arm needs time to heal. You should get to bed."

"How can I?" she said. Her voice started shaking and cracking, as if she were weeping, but no tears fell. "How can I? I don't know who you are. I don't know who I am. I've never *felt* anything like that. What's happening to me?"

Thomas sighed and kissed her forehead. "We'll talk, soon. All right? I'll give you some answers. But first you have to rest."

She leaned against him and closed her eyes. "I felt so empty, Thomas. And my mouth hurts."

He picked her up like a child and said, "Shhhh. We'll take care of it. You can sleep in my room for now. All right?"

"All right," she said. She closed her eyes and leaned her head against his shoulder.

Still damp from the shower, I grew cold enough to bite the bullet, take off my duster, and put on the Hawaiian shirt. The duster went on over it, which went a long way toward neutralizing the shirt's presence. I packed up everything to go and headed for the door. Thomas was just leaving his room again, locking it up behind him.

I stared at his profile. He cared for Inari. That much was obvious. And whether he wanted to admit it or not, he had cared for Justine as well. I felt cold, bitter anger run through me when I thought of Justine, who had risked her life for him on at least one other occasion. Who had given up her life for him last night. The sheer, vicious passion of my anger surprised me. And then I had another intuition.

He hadn't meant it to happen. Thomas may have hurt or killed the woman he loved, but the anger I felt wasn't solely a reaction to what he'd done. I was standing on the outside this time, but I'd seen this situation before, when the Red Court had destroyed Susan's life. I would never have wished harm on Susan, not in a thousand years, but the fact remained that if she hadn't been going out with me, she probably would still be in Chicago, writing her column for the *Midwest Arcane*. And she would still be human.

That's why I felt such anger and shame when I looked at Thomas. I was staring into a mirror, and I didn't like what I saw there.

I'd all but destroyed myself in the wake of Susan's transformation. For all I knew, right now Thomas was worse off than I'd been. At least I'd saved Susan's life. I'd lost her as a lover, but she was still a vital, strong-willed woman determined to forge a life for herself—just not with me. Thomas would not have even that much consolation. He'd been the one to pull the trigger, so to speak, and his remorse was tearing him apart.

I shouldn't have tried to hurt him more. I shouldn't have started chucking stones from within my own glass domicile.

"She knew what she was doing," I said into the silence. "She knew the risk. She wanted to help you."

Thomas's mouth twisted into a bitter smile. "Yeah."

"It wasn't your decision at that point, Thomas."

"I was the only one there. If it wasn't my call then whose was it?"

"Your dad and Lara knew Justine was important to you?"

He nodded.

"They set her up," I said. "They could have handed you anyone. But they knew Justine was here. Your father gave Lara specific instructions to take you to your room. And from what Lara said on the way here in the car, she knew what he was going to do."

Thomas lifted his eyes. He stared at his door for a moment and then said, "I see." He clenched a hand into a fist. "But it hardly matters now."

I couldn't refute that. "What I said was out of line."

He shook his head. "No. You were right."

"Right isn't the same thing as cruel. I'm sorry."

Thomas shrugged and we said nothing more on the matter.

"I've got places to go," I said, heading down the hall. "If you want to talk, walk me out."

"Not that way," Thomas said quietly. He stared at me for a minute and then nodded, some of the tension leaving him. "Come on. I'll take you around the guards and monitors. If my father sees you leaving, he might try to kill you again."

I turned around and fell into step beside Thomas. The puppy whimpered and I scratched him behind the ears. "What do you mean, again?"

He spoke quietly, his eyes flat. "Inari. He sent her to you when he saw that you left my chambers."

"If he wanted me dead, why didn't he just come and do it?"

"It isn't how the White Court fights, Harry. We use misdirection, seduction, manipulation. We use others as instruments."

"So your dad used Inari."

Thomas nodded. "He intended her to have you as her first."

"Um. First what?"

"First lover," Thomas said. "First kill."

I swallowed. "I don't think she knew what she was doing," I said.

"She didn't. In my family, we start off life like any other kid. Just . . . people. No Hunger. No feeding. No vampire stuff at all."

"I didn't know that."

"Not many do. But it comes on you eventually, and

she's about the right age. The panic and the trauma must have acted like a catalyst on her Hunger." He stopped by a panel in the wall and nudged it with his hip. It slid open, revealing a dim corridor between interior walls. He went down it. "Between that, the painkillers, and the exhaustion, she didn't know what was going on."

"Let me guess," I said. "The first feeding is lethal."

"Always," Thomas said.

"But she's young and could be forgiven a loss of control under the circumstances. So I end up dead and it's a believable accident. Raith is clear of any blame."

"Yeah."

"Why the hell hasn't anyone told her, Thomas? What she is? What the world is really like?"

"We're not allowed," Thomas said quietly. "We have to keep it from her. It's my father's standard procedure. I didn't know when I was her age, either."

"That's insane," I said.

Thomas shrugged. "He'd kill us if we disobeyed."

"What happened to her mouth? I mean, uh, I wasn't exactly feeling observant when it happened. I'm not sure what I saw."

Thomas frowned. We left the concealed passage for a dimly lit room halfway between a den and a library, thick with books and comfortable leather chairs and the scent of pipe smoke. "I don't want to get too personal," Thomas said. "But who was the last person you were with?"

"Uh, you. During this walk."

He rolled his eyes. "Not like that. In the biblical sense."

"Oh." The question made me feel uncomfortable, but I said, "Susan."

"Ah," Thomas said. "No wonder."

"No wonder what?"

Thomas stopped. His eyes were haunted, but he was clearly making an effort to focus on the answer. "Look. When we feed . . . we mingle our lives with the prey. Blend them together. Transform a portion of their life into ours and then pull it away with us. Got it?"

"Okay."

"It isn't all that different between human beings," he said. "Sex is more than just sensation. It's a union of the energy of two lives. And it's explosive. It's the process for creating *life*. For creating a new *soul*. *Think* about that. Power doesn't *get* more dangerous and volatile than that."

I nodded, frowning.

"Love is another kind of power, which shouldn't surprise you. Magic comes from emotions, among other things. And when two people are together, in that intimacy, when they really, selflessly love each other it changes them both. It lingers on in the energy of their lives, even when they are apart."

"And?"

"And it's deadly to us. We can inspire lust, but it's just a shadow. An illusion. Love is a dangerous force." He shook his head. "Love killed the dinosaurs, man."

"I'm pretty sure a meteor killed the dinosaurs, Thomas."

He shrugged. "There's a theory making the rounds now that when the meteor hit it only killed off the big stuff. That there were plenty of smaller reptiles running around, about the same size as all the mammals at the time. The reptiles should have regained their position eventually, but they didn't, because the mammals could feel love. They could be utterly, even irrationally devoted to their mates and their offspring. It made them more likely to survive. The lizards couldn't do that. The meteor hit gave the mammals their shot, but it was love that turned the tide."

"What the hell does that have to do with Inari getting burned?"

"Aren't you listening? Love is a primal energy, Harry. To actually touch that kind of power hurts us. It burns. We can't take any energy that's been touched by love. It dampens our ability to cause lust, as well. Even the trappings of love between two people can be dangerous. Lara's got a circular scar on the palm of her left hand where she picked up the wrong wedding ring. My cousin

Madeline picked up a röse that had been a gift between lovers, and the thorns poisoned her so badly she was in bed for a week.

"The last time you were with anyone, it was with Susan. You love each other. Her touch, her love is still upon you, and still protecting you."

"If that's true, then why I am still adjusting my pants every time Lara walks by?"

Thomas shrugged. "You're human. She's lovely and you haven't gotten any in a while. But trust me, Harry. None of the White Court could wholly control or feed from you now."

I frowned. "But it was a year ago."

Thomas shrugged. "If there hasn't been anyone else, then it's still the strongest touch of another life on your own."

"How are you defining love?"

"It isn't a simple formula, Harry. I'm not sure. I recognize it when I see it."

"So what's love look like?"

"You can have everything in the world, but if you don't have love, none of it means crap," he said promptly. "Love is patient. Love is kind. Love always forgives, trusts, supports, and endures. Love never fails. When every star in the heavens grows cold, and when silence lies once more on the face of the deep, three things will endure: faith, hope, and love."

"And the greatest of these is love," I finished. "That's from the Bible."

"First Corinthians, chapter thirteen," Thomas confirmed. "I paraphrased. Father makes all of us memorize that passage. Like when parents put those green yucky-face stickers on the poisonous cleaning products under the kitchen sink."

It made sense, I guess. "What do you want to talk to me about?"

Thomas opened a door on the far side of the library and slipped into a long, quiet room. He flipped on the lights. There was thick grey carpeting on the ground. The walls were grey as well, and track lighting overhead splashed warm light over a row of portraits hung across three walls of the room. "You're actually here. I mean, I never thought you would be in one of our homes— even this one, near Chicago. And I need you to see something," he said quietly.

I followed him in. "What?"

"Portraits," Thomas said. "Father always paints a portrait of the women who bear him children. Look at them."

"What am I looking for?"

"Just look."

I frowned at him but started on the left wall. Raith was no slouch as a painter. The first portrait was of a tall woman with Mediterranean coloring, dressed in clothes that suggested she had lived in the sixteenth or seventeenth century. A golden plate at the base of the portrait read, EMILIA ALEXANDRIA SALAZAR. I followed the paintings around the room. For someone who was supposedly feeding on people through sex, Raith had done comparatively little begetting. I was just guessing, but it didn't look like any two portraits happened within twenty or thirty years of each other. The costumes progressed through the history of fashion, steadily growing closer to the present day.

The next-to-last portrait was of a woman with dark hair, dark eyes, and sharp features. She wasn't precisely pretty, but she was definitely attractive in a striking, intriguing sense. She sat on a stone bench wearing a long, dark skirt and a deep crimson cotton blouse. Her head had an arrogant tilt to it, her mouth held a self-amused smile, and her arms rested on the back of the bench on either side of her, casually claiming the entire space as her own.

My heart started pounding. Hard. Stars went over my vision. I struggled to focus on the golden nameplate beneath the portrait.

It read, MARGARET GWENDOLYN LEFAY.

I recognized her. I had only one picture to remember her by, but I recognized her.

"My mother," I whispered.

Thomas shook his head. He slipped a few fingers under the turtleneck and drew out a silver chain. He passed it to me, and I saw that the chain held a silver pentacle much like my own.

In fact, *precisely* like my own.

"Not yours, Harry," Thomas said, his voice quiet and serious.

I stared at him.

"*Our* mother," he said.

Chapter Twenty-one

I stared at him hard, my heart lurching with shock, and my view narrowed down to a grey tunnel centered on Thomas. Silence filled the room.

"You're lying," I said.

"I'm not."

"You must be."

"Why?" he asked.

"Because that's what you do, Thomas. You lie. You use people and you lie."

"I'm not lying this time."

"Yeah, you are. And I don't have time to put up with this crap." I started for the door.

Thomas got in my way. "You can't ignore this, Harry."

"Move."

"But we—"

My vision went red with rage and I hit him in the face for the second time in six hours. He fell to the floor, twisted his hips, and swept my legs out from under me. I hit the ground, and Thomas piled onto me, going for an armlock. I got a leg underneath me and sank my teeth into his arm as he tried to get it around my neck. I pushed up and slammed him against a wall with my body, and we both staggered apart. Thomas got to his feet, scowling at his arm where I bit him. I leaned against the wall, panting.

"It's the truth," he said. He wasn't as winded as I was from the brief scuffle. "I swear it."

A half-hysterical chuckle slipped out of my mouth. "Wait, I've seen this one before. This is where you say, 'Search your feelings; you know it to be true.'"

Thomas shrugged. "You wanted to know why I'd been helping you. Why I risked myself for you. Now you know why."

"I don't believe you."

"Heh," Thomas said. "I told you that, too."

I shook my head. "You said it yourself: You use people. I think you're playing me against your father somehow."

"It might work out that way," he said. "But that's not why I asked you to help Arturo."

"Why then?"

"Because he's a decent man who doesn't deserve to get killed, and there's no way I could have done it on my own."

I thought that over for a moment and then said, "But that's not all of it."

"What do you mean?"

"Inari. You went nuts when that vamp was on her. Where does she fit in?"

Thomas leaned up against the wall beside my mother's portrait. He pushed his hair back from his face with one hand. "She hasn't been taken by her Hunger yet," he said. "Once she starts feeding it there's no going back. She'll be like the rest of us. My father is pushing her toward that point. I want to stop him."

"Why?"

"Because if . . . if she's in love, that first time, it could kill her Hunger. She'd be free. I think she's mature enough to be capable of that love now. There's a young man she's all twitterpated about."

"*Bobby*?" I blurted. "The macho violent kid?"

"Give him a break. How insecure would you be if you were planning on spending the day having sex on camera in front of the girl you'd like to ask to dinner?"

"This might shock you, but I've never really considered that question before."

Thomas pressed his lips together for a moment and then said, "If the kid loves her in return, then she could have a life. She could be free of the kinds of things that—" His voice broke. He had to cough before he continued. "Things like what happened to Justine. Like what my father has done to my other sisters."

"What do you mean, done to them?"

"He establishes that he is their superior. He overpowers them. Pits his Hunger against theirs."

My stomach twisted. "You mean he feeds on his own . . ." I couldn't finish the sentence.

"Do you need me to paint you a picture? It's the traditional way to settle family differences in all the Houses of the White Court."

I shuddered and looked up at my mother's portrait. "God. That's hideous."

Thomas nodded, his expression bleak and hard. "Lara is one of the most capable, intelligent people I've ever met. But around him, she turns into an obedient dog. He's broken her to his will. Forced her to crave what he does to her. I won't let that happen to Inari. Not when she could make her own life."

I frowned. "Won't that bring your dad down on you? Force him to try to make you like them?"

Thomas grimaced. "His tastes don't run that way."

"Small mercy, I guess."

"Not really. He doesn't want to keep me around. It's just a matter of time before he comes after me. His sons, every last one of them, died under suspicious circumstances that can't be traced back to him. I'm the first male to live as long as I have. Partly thanks to you." He closed his eyes. "And partly thanks to Justine."

"Hell's bells," I said quietly. The whole thing was almost ridiculous. "So let me get this straight. You want me to help save the girl, overthrow the dark lord, and defend the innocents terrorized by dark magic," I said. "And you want me to do it because you're my long-lost half brother, who needs someone noble to stand beside him in desperate battle for what's right."

He grimaced. "That phrasing has way more melodrama in it than I would have used."

"You've got to be kidding me. That's a really lame con."

"Give me *some* credit, Dresden." He sighed. "I know how to con. If you were really just another mark, I'd have come up with a better story."

"Forget it," I said. "If you'd been straight with me to begin with maybe I'd help. But this bullshit about my mother is over the line."

"She's my mother too," he said. "Harry, you knew she wasn't exactly white as the driven snow. I know you've learned a little over the years. She was one hell of a dangerous witch, and she kept some bad company. Some of it was with my father."

"You're lying," I growled. "What proof have you got?"

"Would anything satisfy you?" he demanded. "Proof is something you use with rational people, and right now you aren't."

The anger started fading a little. I hadn't gotten much rest, and was too tired to keep it up. I ached. I slid down the wall until I was sitting. I rubbed at my eyes. "It doesn't make any sense. What would she have been doing hanging around with your father?"

"God knows," Thomas said. "All I know is that there was some sort of business between them. It developed into something else. Father was trying to snare her permanently, but she wound up being too strong for him to completely enthrall. She escaped him when I was about five. From what I've been able to learn, she met your father the next year when she was on the run."

"Running from who?"

He shrugged. "Maybe my father. Maybe some people

in the Courts or on the Council. I don't know. She'd gotten into some bad business and she wanted out. Whoever she was in it with didn't want her gone. They wanted her dead." He spread his hands, palm up. "That's almost everything I know, Harry. I tried to learn all I could about her. But no one would talk to me."

My eyelids felt gummy. My chest hurt. I looked up at the portrait of my mother. She was a woman of evident vitality, life flowing from her and around her, even in the painting. But I'd never gotten the chance to know her. She died in the delivery room.

Damn it all, what if Thomas was playing it straight with me? It would mean that I knew a little more about why the White Council all watched me like I was Lucifer, the Next Generation. It would mean being forced to accept that my mother was involved in bad business. Scary, big, bad business of one kind or another.

And it would mean that maybe I wasn't entirely alone in this world. There might be family for me. Blood of my blood.

The thought made my chest hurt worse. As a child, I'd fantasized for hours at a time about having a family. Brothers and sisters, parents who cared, grandparents, cousins, aunts and uncles—just like everyone else. A group of people who would stick together through everything, because that's what families do. Someone who would accept me, welcome me, maybe even be proud of me and desire my company.

I never celebrated Christmas as a kid, after my dad died. It hurt too much. Hell, it still hurt too much.

But if I had a real family, then maybe things could change.

I looked up. Thomas's face had always been difficult to read, but I saw another mirror of myself there. He was having some of the same thoughts as me. I wondered if he'd been lonely, like I had. Maybe he'd daydreamed about a family who wouldn't be trying to manipulate him, control him, or simply kill him.

But I stopped myself before I could follow that line

of thought. Things were just too dangerous, and this issue too sensitive. I wanted, on some level, to believe Thomas. I wanted to believe him very much.

Which was why I couldn't afford to take any chances.

After a long moment, he said, "I'm not lying to you."

My voice came out soft, quiet, and calm. "Then prove it."

"How?" he asked. He sounded tired. "How the hell am I supposed to prove it to you?"

"Look at me."

He froze, his eyes still on the floor. "I don't . . . I don't think that would accomplish anything, Harry."

"Okay," I said. I started to rise. "Which way is my car?"

He lifted a hand. "Wait. All right," he said. He grimaced. "I was hoping to avoid this. I don't know what you're going to see if you look in there. I don't know if you'll still feel the same way about me."

"Ditto," I said. "We'd better sit down."

"How long will it take?" he asked.

"Seconds," I said. "Feels longer."

He nodded. We sat down about two feet from each other, cross-legged on the floor at the foot of my mother's portrait. Thomas took a deep breath and then lifted his grey eyes to mine.

The eyes are a window to the soul. Literally. Looking someone steadily in the eyes is an uncomfortable, intense experience for anyone. If you don't believe me, pick a stranger sometime, and just go up to them and stare them in the eye until that moment when there's a sudden acknowledgment of lowered barriers, that moment that inspires awkward silences and racing hearts. The eyes reveal a lot about a person. They express emotions and give clues to what thoughts are lurking behind them. One of the first things we all learn to recognize, as infants, are the eyes of whoever is taking care of us. We know from the cradle how important they are.

For wizards like me, that kind of eye contact is even more intense, and even more dangerous. Looking into someone's eyes shows me what they are. I see it in a light of elemental truth so clear and bright that it burns it into my head forever. I see the core of who and what they are during a soulgaze, and they see me in the same way. There's nothing hidden, no possibility of deception. I don't see absolutely every thought or memory that passes through their head—but I do get to see the naked, emotional heart of who and what they are. It isn't a precise research technique, but it would tell me if Thomas was playing it straight.

I met Thomas's grey eyes with my own dark gaze and the barriers between us fell.

I found myself standing in a stark chamber that looked like an abstract of Mount Olympus after its gods died. Everything was made of cold, beautiful marble, alternating between utter darkness and snowy light. The floor was laid out like a chessboard. Statuary stood here and there, all human figures carved in stone that matched the decor. Particolored marble pillars rose up into dimness overhead. There wasn't a ceiling. There weren't any walls. The light was silver and cold. Wind sighed mournfully through the columns. Thunder rumbled somewhere far away, and my nose filled with the sharp scent of ozone.

At the center of the forlorn ruin stood a mirror the size of a garage door. It was set in a silver frame that seemed to grow from the floor. A young man stood in front of it, one hand reaching out.

I walked a little closer. My steps echoed among the pillars. I drew closer to the young man and peered at him. It was Thomas. Not Thomas as I had seen him with my own eyes, but Thomas nonetheless. This version of him was not deadly-beautiful. His face seemed a little more plain. He looked like he might have been a little nearsighted. His expression was strained with pain, and his shoulders and back were thick with tension.

I looked past the young man into the mirror. There I saw one of those things that I would want to forget. But thanks to the Sight, I wouldn't. Ever.

The reflection room in the mirror looked like the one I stood in at first glance. But looking closer revealed that rather than black and white marble, the place was made from dark, dried blood and sun-bleached bone. A creature stood there at the mirror, directly in front of Thomas. It was humanoid, more or less Thomas's size, and its hide shone with a luminous silver glow. It crouched, hunched and grotesque, though at the same time there was an eerie beauty about the thing. Its shining white eyes burned with silent flame. Its bestial face stared eagerly at Thomas, burning with what seemed to be unsatiated appetite.

The creature's arm also extended to the mirror, and then with a shiver I realized that its limb was reaching a good foot past the mirror's surface. Its gleaming claws were sunk into Thomas's shaking forearm, and drops of dark blood had run from the punctures. Thomas's arm, meanwhile, had sunk into the mirror, and I saw his fingers digging in hard upon the flesh of the creature's forearm. Locked together, I sensed that the two were straining against each other. Thomas was trying to pull himself away from the thing. The creature was trying to drag him into the mirror, there among the dried blood and dead bones.

"He's tired," said a woman's voice.

My mother appeared in the mirror wearing a flowing dress of rich, royal blue. She watched the silent struggle while she drew closer. The portrait had not done her credit. She was a creature of life and vitality, and was more beautiful in motion than she could be in any frozen image. She was a tall woman, nearly six feet, and that was in flat sandals.

My throat tightened. I felt tears on my face. "Are you real?"

"Why should I not be?" she asked.

"You could just be a part of Thomas's mental landscape. No offense."

She smiled. "No, child. It's really me. In some measure, at least. I prepared you both for this day. I laid this working within each of you. A little portion of who and what I am. I wanted you to know who you were to each other."

I drew a shaking breath. "Is he really your son?"

My mother smiled, a sparkle in her dark eyes. "You have a perfectly serviceable sense of intuition, little one. What does it tell you?"

My vision blurred with tears. "That he is."

She nodded. "You must listen to me. I cannot be there to protect you, Harry. The two of you must take care of each other. Your brother will need your help, just as you will need his."

"I don't understand this," I said, gesturing at the mirror. "What do you mean, he's tired?"

My mother nodded at Thomas. "The girl he loved. She's gone. She was his strength. It knows that."

"It?" I asked.

She nodded at the mirror. "The Hunger. His demon."

I followed her nod with my gaze. The image-Thomas snarled something under his breath. The Hunger in the mirror answered in a slow, slithering tongue I did not understand. "Why didn't you help him?"

"I did what I could," my mother said. Her eyes flickered with something dark, an ancient spark of hatred. "I made sure that his father would endure a fitting punishment for what he did to us."

"You and Thomas?"

"And you, Harry. Raith yet lives. But he is weakened. Together you and your brother may have a chance against him. You will understand."

The Hunger hissed more words at Thomas. "What is it saying?" I asked.

"It's telling him to give up. That there's no point in fighting anymore. That it will never leave him in peace."

"Is it true?"

"Perhaps," she said.

"But he's fighting anyway," I said.

"Yes." Her eyes focused on mine, sad and proud. "It may destroy him, but he will not surrender himself to it. He is of my blood." She drifted to the very edge of the mirror and reached out a hand. It emerged from the mirror's surface as if from a motionless pool.

I stepped closer myself, reaching out to touch her

hand. Her fingers were soft and warm. She wrapped them around mine, and squeezed. Then she lifted her hand and touched my cheek. "As are you, Harry. So tall, like your father. And I think you have his heart as well."

I couldn't answer her. I just stood there, silently crying.

"I have something for you," she said. "If you are willing."

I opened my eyes. My mother stood before me holding what I thought was a small gem or a jewel between long fingers. It pulsed with a low, gentle light.

"What is it?" I asked her.

"Insight," she said.

"It's knowledge?" I asked.

"And the power that goes with it," she said. She gave me a half smile, touched with irony. It looked familiar. "Think of it as a mother's advice, if you like. It doesn't make up for my absence, child. But it's all that I have to give."

"I accept it," I whispered. Because it was the only thing I could give her in return.

She passed me the gem. There was a flash, a tingling pain in my head, and then a lingering, dull ache. For some reason that didn't surprise me. You don't gain knowledge without a little pain.

She touched my face again and said, "I was so arrogant. I laid too great a burden upon you to bear alone. I hope that one day you will forgive me my mistake. But know that I am proud of what you have become. I love you, child."

"I love you," I whispered.

"Give my love to Thomas," she said. She touched my face again, her smile loving and sad. Tears slid from her eyes as well. "Be well, my son."

Then she drew her arm back into the mirror and the soulgaze was over. I sat on the floor facing Thomas. There were tears on his face. Both of us looked at each other, and then up at my mother's portrait.

After a moment I offered Thomas his pentacle on its chain. He took it and put it on.

"Did you see her?" he asked. His voice was shaking.

"Yeah," I said. The aching, lonely old hurt was overflowing me. But I suddenly found myself laughing. I had seen my mother with my Sight. I had seen her smile, heard her voice, and it was something I could never lose. Something no one could ever take away from me. It couldn't wholly make up for a lifetime of loneliness and silent grief, but it was more than I ever thought I would have.

Thomas met my eyes, and then he started laughing too. The puppy wriggled his way from my duster's pocket and started bounding back and forth and in circles in sheer, joyous excitement. The little nut had no clue at all what we were happy about, but evidently he didn't feel he needed one to join in.

I scooped up the puppy and rose. "I'd never really seen her face," I said. "I'd never heard her voice."

"Maybe she knew you wouldn't have," Thomas replied. "Maybe she did it like that so you could."

"She told me to tell you that she loved you."

He smiled, though it was sad and bitter. "She told me the same thing."

"Well," I said. "This changes things some."

"Does it?" he asked. He looked uncertain as he said it, frail.

"Yeah," I said. "I'm not saying that we're going to start from a fresh slate. But things are different now."

"They aren't for me, Harry," Thomas said. He grimaced. "I mean . . . I knew this already. It's why I tried to help you wherever I could."

"I guess you did," I said quietly. "I thought you were just saving up for a favor. But you weren't. Thank you."

He shrugged. "What are you going to do about Arturo?"

I frowned. "Protect him and his people, of course. If I can. What did Lara mean when she said that Arturo's independent streak was a matter for the White Court?"

"Damned if I know." Thomas sighed. "I thought he was just someone Lara knew from the industry."

"Does your dad have any connection to him?"

"Dad doesn't advertise what he's doing, Harry. And I haven't spoken more than twenty words to him in the last ten years. I don't know."

"Would Lara?"

"Probably. But ever since Lara worked out that I wasn't just a dim-witted ambulatory penis, she's been on her guard when we've talked. I haven't been able to get much out of her. So now I mostly sit there and nod and look wise and make vague remarks. She assumes that I know something she doesn't, and then she thinks the vague remark is actually a cryptic remark. She wouldn't want to move on me until she's figured out what it is I'm hiding from her."

"That's a good tactic if people are paranoid enough."

"In the Raith household? Paranoia comes bottled, on tap and in hot and cold running neuroses."

"What about your dad? He know any magic?"

"Like maybe entropy curses?" Thomas shrugged. "I hear stories about things he's done in the past. Some of them must be close to true. Plus he's got a huge library he keeps locked up most of the time. But even without magic, he can just rip the life out of anyone who pisses him off."

"How?"

"It's like when we feed. It's usually slow, gradual. But he doesn't need that kind of time or intimacy. Just a touch, a kiss, and wham, they're dead. That whole kiss-of-death thing in *The Godfather*? He was where that phrase originated, only for him it was literal."

"Really?"

"Supposedly. I've never seen him do it myself, but Lara has, plenty of times. Madeline once told me once that he liked to open conversations that way, because it made sure he had the complete attention of everyone still breathing."

"Stories. Supposedly. For someone on the inside, your information isn't real helpful."

"I know," he said. "I'm not thinking clearly right now. I'm sorry."

I shook my head. "Can't throw stones."

"What do we do?" he asked. "I'm . . . I feel lost. I don't know what to do."

"I think I do," I said.

"What?"

Instead of answering him, I offered him my hand.

He took it, and I drew my brother to his feet.

Chapter Twenty-two

I waited until the predawn gloom had become full, dismal, rainy morning to leave Château Raith. Thomas helped me pull a few things together while I waited, and I borrowed a phone to make some calls.

After that, the puppy and I got back in the Beetle, hit the drive-through at McDonald's, and puttered back home to my apartment. I got out of the car and noticed a couple of blackened spots on the ground. I frowned and looked closer, discovering that they were in a methodical pattern. Someone had been trying to force their way past my wards, the magical protections I'd set up around the boardinghouse. They hadn't broken through them, but the fact that someone or something had tried made me more than a little uncomfortable. I got the shield bracelet ready to go as I went down the stairs, just in case, but nothing frustrated from fruitless attempts to break in was waiting for me. Mister appeared from under my landlady's car and followed me down the stairs.

I got into my apartment fast and shut the door behind me. I muttered a spell that lit half a dozen candles around the room, and braced myself for Mister's greeting. He made his usual attempt to bulldoze my legs out from under me with his shoulders. I put the puppy on the floor, where he panted happily at Mister, wagging his tail by way of friendly greeting. Mister did not look impressed.

I kept moving, trying to stay focused. I didn't think I had any time to waste. I shoved aside the rugs over the stepladder down to the lab, hauled the door open, and slid down into the lab. "Bob," I said. "What'd you find out?"

Mister padded over to the top of the stairs. A cloud of flickering orange lights arose from the cat and flowed down the stepladder to the lab. The lights streamed over to the skull on its shelf, and Bob's eye sockets flickered to life. "It was a long, cold night," he said. "Saw a place where a couple of ghouls set up shop, out by the airport."

"Did you find Mavra?"

"You know, Harry, the Black Court has become awfully cagey about picking a base of operations of late."

"Did you find Mavra?"

"They've had centuries of experience," Bob said. "And Chicago is huge. It's like trying to find a needle in a cliché."

I gave the skull a flat look and said in a flat voice, "Bob, you're the only one in a thousand miles who could have found them. You are an invaluable asset and ally whose knowledge is matched only by your willingness to give of yourself to others. There, ego stroked. Did you find Mavra?"

Bob scowled. "You take all the fun out of getting complimented. Did you know that?" He muttered something under his breath, mainly in Chinese, I think. "Not yet."

"What?" I demanded.

"I've narrowed it down," Bob said.

"How narrow?"

"Uh," the skull said. "It isn't in any of the strip clubs."

"Bob!" I demanded. "You were running around *strip* joints all day!?"

"I was only thinking of you, Harry," Bob said.

"What?"

"Well, a lot of the people on the set of that movie do some erotic dancing as a sideline, and I wanted to make sure that, you know, your bad guy wasn't going to take a night off to kill some locals as a warm-up." Bob coughed. "See?"

I narrowed my eyes and took deep breaths. It didn't really stop my anger from rising but it made it happen a little more smoothly.

"A-and you will be glad to know that every exotic dancer in Chicago is alive and well. Safeguarded by your friendly neighborhood air spirit," Bob said. "Um. Say, Harry, that is quite the homicidal gleam in your eye."

I took off my coat and looked around the lab until I located my clawhammer. I picked it up.

Bob's voice gained a hurried, stammering edge. "And while I know that wasn't exactly the mission you sent me out on, you have to admit that it was really quite a noble purpose that totally supported your quest to preserve life."

I took a practice swing with the hammer. I took my duster off, folded it, laid it over the table, and tried again. Much better. I fixed a murderous gaze on the skull on the shelf.

"Gee, uh, Harry," Bob said. "I was just doing the breast job I co—best, best! The best job I could!"

"Bob," I said, in a very reasonable tone of voice, "I don't need to know about strippers. I need to know about Mavra."

"Well. Yes, of course, boss. Um, so I noticed that you're holding that hammer. And that your knuckles are turning kind of white there. And that you look sort of tense."

"Don't worry," I said. "I'm going to feel a lot better in a minute."

"Ha," Bob said in a nervous false laugh. "Ha-ha. Ha. That's funny, Harry."

I raised the hammer. "Bob," I said, "get your ethereal ass out of that skull. And back into Mister. And you get out on the *street* and find Mavra before high noon or I'm going to smash your skull into freaking *powder!*"

"But I'm tired and it's raining and I don't know if—"

I raised the hammer and took a step forward.

"Ack!" Bob choked. The cloud of orange lights spilled out of the skull in a hurried rush and zipped back up the stairs. I followed them, and saw the last few sparkles around Mister's ears as Bob took possession of the cat again. I opened the door and the big tom bounded out into the morning.

I slammed the door, scowling. My thoughts were in a boiling turmoil beneath a fairly calm surface. I felt something I hadn't before—a sort of bitter taste in my mouth that took occasional side trips down to my stomach.

Anger and fear were things I knew. They were emotions that had often saved my life. But this sensation was different—something like my concern for Mister when I sent him out with Bob, but quieter, more haunting, and it didn't fade from one minute to the next.

I think maybe it was about Thomas. Before that morning there'd been no one in my life except a few truly hard-core friends, some familiar professional associates, my cat, and one or two dedicated enemies who visited at least as often as my friends. But now I had a brother. Kinfolk, as old Ebenezar would say. And it changed things.

I was used to watching out for myself—not that my friends never did anything for me, but with respect to the day-to-day problems of life, I operated solo, except for a herd of depressing thoughts for company. I thought about how I already had a grave, complete with a white marble headstone, waiting for me at Graceland Cemetery, courtesy of an enemy now dead, but no less ready to receive me. I thought about how my utter ineptitude at romance was probably going to preserve my bachelor status for the next several decades. I thought about how many bad guys out there would be glad to take me out, and how it might take people weeks to realize I'd vanished.

And I thought about growing old. Alone. It was not unusual for a wizard to live more than three centuries, but that wouldn't stop time from taking its toll. Sooner or later I'd be old and frail, maybe even tired of living. And dying. I would have no one to share it with me, or hold my hand when I was afraid.

In some simple, unexplainable, and utterly irrational way, Thomas's presence had altered that. His blood was in common with my own, and knowing it had created a strong emotional bond like nothing I had felt before. My heart sped a little bit out of sheer happiness at the thought.

But no matter how happy discovering a brother made me, I would be a fool if I didn't realize another, darker side to the situation.

After a lifetime alone, I had a brother.

And I could lose him.

The bitter sensation intensified at the thought, and I knew what it felt like to worry for family.

I shut the door to the lab and covered it with its rug. I fumbled through my little pantry until I found my bottle of aspirin. The puppy followed me closely, and attacked my shoelaces when I stopped. I opened the bottle, chewed three aspirin up, and swallowed them, no drink. I hear that's a bad sign, when you can do medication like that.

I grimaced, rubbing at my head again, and tried to quiet the tide of emotion running around my nervous system. There were things I had to do, and I would need my mind to be ordered if I wanted to survive them. First things first. I checked my problem inventory:

Multiple injuries, including a vicious headache from where Inari had socked me.

On one side of me lurked a mysterious wielder of a sloppy but lethal curse.

On the other side, a homicidal vampire and her crew of killers.

And, lest I forget, somewhere behind me was a cold, distant mercenary who was going to kill me if I didn't pay his fee—and I had no idea where I would come up with the cash.

What a mess. And it wasn't yet midmorning. And I was only growing more tired and beat up as the day went by. That meant that my smartest option was to attack the problem with a frontal assault with no delay, while my head was relatively clear.

I had to get moving before the bad guys got organized and came at me again.

Damn. If only I knew *where* I needed to move.

And if only I didn't have a sinking feeling that it might already be too late.

Chapter Twenty-three

I was waiting in the parking lot at Chicago PD headquarters when Murphy arrived from the gym. She was on her motorcycle, complete with heavy boots, a black helmet, and a dark leather jacket. She noted my car on the way in, and swung the bike into the parking space beside me. The bike's engine let out a relaxed, leonine growl, then died away.

Murphy swung off the bike and took off her helmet. She shook out her golden hair, which looked good when it was somewhat mussed. "Good morning, Harry."

At the sound of her voice, the puppy started thrashing around in my pocket until he managed to stick his head out, panting happily up at Murphy. "Morning," I said. "You sound pretty chipper."

"I am," she answered. She scratched the puppy's

head. "Sometimes I forget how much I like riding the bike."

"Most chicks do," I said. "Roar of the engine and so on."

Murphy's blue eyes glittered with annoyance and anticipation. "Pig. You really enjoy dropping all women together in the same demographic, don't you?"

"It's not my fault all women like motorcycles, Murph. They're basically huge vibrators. With wheels."

She tried for an angry expression, but part of a laugh escaped her throat, and she let it turn into a wide smile. "You're bent, Dresden." She frowned then, and looked at me a little closer. "What's wrong?"

"Took a bit of a beating yesterday," I said.

"I've seen you beaten before. It doesn't look like this."

Murph had known me for too long. "It's personal stuff," I said. "I can't talk about it yet."

She nodded and was silent.

The silent stretched until I said, "I found out I might have family."

"Oh." She frowned, but it was her concerned-friend frown instead of her impatient-cop frown. "I won't push. But if you ever want to talk about it . . ."

"When I want to," I told her. "Just not this morning. Have you got time to grab some breakfast with me?"

She checked her watch, and her eyes flicked toward a security camera and then to me, a warning. "Is this about that case we were discussing?"

Aha. The walls had ears, which meant that it was time for euphemisms. "Yeah. We'd be meeting with one other problem solver to discuss the situation."

She nodded. "You got the data?"

"Sorta," I said.

"Well. You know how much I'm looking forward to the family picnic today, but I might have a few minutes. Where did you want to eat?"

"IHOP."

Murphy sighed. "My hips hate you, Dresden."

"Just wait until they get to sit in my ritzy car."

We got in the car and I dropped the pup into the box I'd put in the backseat and lined with some laundry I'd had in the Beetle's trunk. He started wrestling with a sock. I think the sock was winning. Murphy watched him with a smile while I drove.

It was a Saturday morning, and I expected the International House of Pancakes to be packed. It wasn't. In fact, an entire corner had been sectioned off with an accordion-folded screen as reserved seating, and there still weren't enough customers to fill the remaining tables. The usual radio station wasn't on. The people eating breakfast seemed to be doing so in almost total silence, and the only sound was the clink of silverware on plates.

Murphy glanced up at me and then around the room, frowning. She folded her arms over her stomach, which left her right hand near the gun she kept in a shoulder rig. "What's wrong with this picture?" she asked.

Motion in the reserved area drew my eye, and Kincaid appeared and beckoned us. The lean mercenary was dressed in greys and dull blues, very nondescript, and had his hair pulled into a ponytail under a black baseball cap.

I nodded and went over to Kincaid, Murphy at my side. We stepped into the screened-off area. "Morning," I said.

"Dresden," Kincaid replied. His cool eyes slid over Murphy. "I hope you don't mind me asking the manager for a quiet section to sit in."

"It's fine. Kincaid, this is Murphy. Murph, Kincaid."

Kincaid didn't so much as glance at her. He drew the accordion curtains closed. "You said this was business. Why did you bring a date?"

Murphy clenched her jaw.

"She's not a date," I said. "She's going with us."

Kincaid stared at me for a second, all ice and stone. Then he barked out a throaty laugh. "I always heard you were a funny guy, Dresden. Seriously, what is she doing here?"

Murphy's eyes went flat with anger. "I don't think I like your attitude."

"Not now, kitten," Kincaid said. "I'm talking business with your boyfriend."

"He is *not* my boyfriend," Murphy growled.

Kincaid looked from Murphy to me and back again. "You're kidding me, Dresden. This isn't amateur hour. If we're playing with the Black Court, I don't have time to babysit little Pollyanna here, and neither do you."

I started to speak, and thought better of it. Murphy would have my head if I tried to protect her when she didn't think she needed it. I took a small but prudent step back from them.

Murphy eyed Kincaid and said, "Now I'm sure of it. I don't like your attitude."

Kincaid's lips lifted away from his teeth, and he moved his left arm, showing Murphy the gun rig under his jacket. "I'd love to chat with you over breakfast, cupcake. Why don't you run and find a high chair so that we can."

Murphy's gaze didn't waver. She looked from Kincaid's eyes to his gun and back. "Why don't we sit down. This doesn't·need to get ugly."

Kincaid's grin widened, and it wasn't a pleasant expression. He put a broad hand on her shoulder and said, "This is where the big boys play, princess. Why don't you be a good girl and go watch your *Xena* tapes or something."

Murphy eyed Kincaid's hand on her shoulder. Her voice became softer, but it sure as hell didn't sound weak. "That's assault. But I'll tell you this once. I won't repeat myself. Don't touch me."

Kincaid's face contorted with rage, and he gave her shoulder a shove. "Get out of here, whore."

Murphy didn't repeat herself. Her hands blurred as she caught Kincaid's wrist, broke his balance by half bending her knees, then twisted and threw him hard at a wall. Kincaid slammed over a table and into the wall, but rolled out of it almost instantly, his hand going for his gun.

Murphy trapped his gun arm between her arm and body as he drew, and her own gun appeared with nearly magical swiftness, pressed hard against the underside of Kincaid's chin. "Call me that again," she said in a quiet voice. "I dare you. I double-dog dare you."

Kincaid's angry expression vanished so swiftly that it could only have been artificial. Instead a faint grin made its way onto his mouth, even brushing at his eyes. "Oh, I like her," he said. "I'd heard about her but I wanted to see it myself. I like this one, Dresden."

I bet he always went for his gun when he liked a woman. "Maybe you should stop talking about her like she isn't standing there holding a gun under your chin."

"Maybe you're right," he said. Then he faced Murphy and lifted his empty hand, relaxing. She released his arm, lowered the gun, and stepped back, still scowling, but Kincaid put his gun down, then took a seat with his hands palm flat on the table beside the weapon. "Hope you won't remain offended, Lieutenant," he told her. "I needed to see if you measured up to your reputation before we went forward."

Murphy shot me her patented Harry-you-idiot glare and then focused an opaque expression on Kincaid. "Do you feel better now?"

"I feel satisfied," Kincaid replied. "It's a little easy to get you started, but at least you're competent. Is that a Beretta?"

"SIG," Murphy said. "Do you have a license and permit for your weapon?"

Kincaid smiled. "Naturally."

Murphy snorted. "Sure you do." She looked at Kincaid for a minute and then said, "Get this straight from the get-go. I'm still a cop. It means something to me."

He regarded her thoughtfully. "I heard that about you too."

"Murph," I said, sitting down at the table. "If you have something to say to him, say it to me. I'm his employer at the moment."

She arched an eyebrow. "And you can be sure that his actions are all going to be legal ones?"

"Kincaid," I said. "No felonies without checking with me first. Okay?"

"Yassuh," said Kincaid.

I spread out an open hand at Murphy. "See? Yassuh."

She regarded Kincaid without much in the way of approval but nodded and pulled out a chair. Kincaid rose as she started to sit down. Murphy glared at him. Kincaid sat down again. She pulled at the chair again and I rose. She put a hand on her hip and glared at me. "It doesn't count as chivalrous courtesy if you're only doing it to be a wiseass."

"She's right," Kincaid admitted. "Go ahead, Lieutenant. We won't be polite."

Murphy growled, and started to sit. I began to stand up again anyway, but she kicked me in the shins and plopped down. "All right," she said. "What do we know?"

"That I'm starving," I said. "Wait a second." I held off any business until after we'd ordered breakfast and the waitress brought it out to the reserved section. Once that was done and we were eating, we closed the screen again.

"All right," I said after a moment. It came out muffled by a mouthful of gastronomic nirvana. Say what you will about nutrition; IHOP knows good pancakes. "This meeting is to share some information I've gained in the last day and to go over our basic plan."

"Find them," said Murphy.

"Kill them," said Kincaid.

"Yeah, okay," I said. "But I thought we might flesh out that second one a little more."

"No need to," said Kincaid. "In my experience it's pretty much impossible to kill it if you don't know where it is." He lifted his brows, looking up from his food. "Do you know where it is?"

"Not yet," I said.

Kincaid glanced at his watch, and then went back to his food. "I'm on a schedule."

"I know that," I said. "I'll find them today."

"Before sundown," Kincaid said. "Suicide to go at them after dark."

Murphy scowled at Kincaid. "What kind of attitude is that?"

"A professional one. I have a midnight flight to my next contract."

"Let me get this straight," Murphy said. "You'd just walk away because these murdering creatures didn't fit into your schedule?"

"Yes." Kincaid kept eating.

"It doesn't bother you that innocent people might die because of them?"

"Not much," Kincaid said, and took a sip of coffee.

"How can you just say that?"

"Because it's the truth. Innocent people die all the time." Kincaid's fork and knife scraped on his plate as he sliced up some ham and eggs. "They're better at it than your average murdering monster."

"Jesus," Murphy said, and stared at me. "Harry, I don't want to work with this asshole."

"Easy, Murph," I said.

"I'm serious. You can't condone his attitude."

I rubbed at my eyebrow with a thumb. "Murph, the world is a cruel place. Kincaid didn't make it that way."

"He doesn't care," Murphy said. "Are you sure you want someone who doesn't care about what we're doing along when things go to hell?"

"He agreed to go and fight," Harry said. "I agreed to pay him. He's a professional. He'll fight."

Kincaid pointed a finger at me and nodded, chewing on another bite.

Murphy shook her head. "What about a driver?"

"He'll be here today," I said.

"Who is he?"

"You don't know him," I said. "I trust him."

Murphy looked at me for a second and then nodded. "What are we up against?"

"Black Court vampires," I said. "At least two, and maybe more."

"Plus any help they might have," Kincaid said.

"They can flip cars with one hand," I said. "They're fast. Like, Jackie Chan fast. We can't go toe-to-toe with them, so the plan is to hit them in daylight."

"They'll all be asleep," Murphy said.

"Maybe not," Kincaid said. "The old ones don't need to sometimes. Mavra could be functional."

"And what's more," I said, "she's a practitioner. A sorceress at least."

Kincaid inhaled and exhaled slowly through his nose. He finished the bite he was on, and then he said, "Shit," before taking another.

Murphy frowned. "What do you mean, a sorceress at least?"

"Kind of an industry term," I said. "Plenty of people can do a little magic. Small-time stuff. But sometimes the small-timers practice up, or tap into some kind of power source and get enough ability to be dangerous. A sorcerer is someone who can do some serious violence with magic."

"Like the Shadowman," Murphy said. "Or Kravos."

"Yeah."

"Good thing we got a wizard along then," Kincaid said.

Murphy looked at me.

"Wizard means that you can do sorcery if you need to," I said, "but it also means you can do a lot of other things too. A wizard's power isn't limited to blowing things up, or calling up demons. A good wizard can adapt his magic in almost any way he can imagine. Which is the problem."

"What do you mean?" Murphy said.

"Mavra is good at veils," I said, mostly to Kincaid. "Real good. She did some long range mental communications last night, too."

Kincaid stopped eating.

"You're saying that this vampire is a wizard?" Murphy asked.

Kincaid stared at me.

"It's possible," I said. "Maybe even likely. It would

go a long way toward explaining how Mavra survived all this time."

"This mission is heading for downtown FUBAR," Kincaid said.

"You want out?" I asked.

He was silent for a minute and then shook his head. "But if Mavra is awake and active, and if she's able to start tossing heavy magic around in closed quarters, we might as well drink some Bacardi-and-strychnine and save ourselves some walking."

"You're afraid of her," Murphy said.

"Damn right," Kincaid said.

She frowned. "Harry, can you shut down her magic? Like you did with Kravos?"

"Depends how strong she is," I said. "But a wizard could handle her. Probably."

Kincaid shook his head. "Magical lockdown. I've seen that work before," he said. "One time I saw it fail. Everybody died."

"Except you?" I asked.

"I was in back, covering our spellslinger when his head exploded. Barely made it out the door." Kincaid pushed a piece of sausage around his plate. "Even if you can shut her down, Mavra's still going to be real tough."

"That's why you get to charge so much," I said.

"True."

"We go in Stoker-standard," I said. "Garlic, crosses, holy water, the works."

"Hey," Murphy said. "What about that pocketful-of-sunshine thing you told me about? With the white handkerchief you used on Bianca a few years back?"

I grimaced. "Can't," I said.

"Why not?"

"It's impossible, Murph. It isn't important why." I hauled the conversation back on course. "We should be able to keep Mavra back until we deal with any goons. Then we can take her down. Any questions?"

Kincaid coughed significantly, and nodded at the table, where the waitress had, at some point, left us a bill. I frowned and fumbled through my pockets. I had enough to cover it, but only because I managed to find a couple of quarters in the various pockets of my duster. I left the money on the table. There wasn't enough for a tip.

Kincaid regarded my lump of wrinkled small bills and change, then studied me with a distant, calculating gaze that would have made some people very nervous. Like people who had agreed to pay a lot of money but didn't *have* any.

"That's it for now then," I said, rising. "Get anything you need ready, and we'll go later today. I want to hit them as soon as I find them."

Kincaid nodded and turned back to his plate. I left. My shoulder blades felt itchy when I turned my back to Kincaid. Murphy kept pace with me and we headed back to the Beetle.

Murphy and I didn't talk while I drove her back to CPDHQ. Once we got there, and the car had stopped, she looked around the inside of my car, frowning. "What happened to the Beetle?"

"Mold demons."

"Oh."

"Murph?"

"Hmm?"

"You okay?"

She pressed her lips into a line. "I'm trying to adjust. In my head, I think what we're doing is just about the only thing we responsibly can. But I've been a peace officer since before I could drink, and this kind of cowboy thing feels . . . wrong. It isn't what a good cop does."

"Depends on the cop, I think," I said. "Mavra and her scourge are above the law, Murph, in every sense that matters. The only way they're going to get stopped is if someone steps up and takes them down."

"I know that here," she said, and touched her own forehead with her finger. Then she clasped her hand into a fist and put it over her heart. "But I don't *feel* it here." She was quiet for a moment more and said, "The vampires aren't the problem. I can fight that. Glad to. But there are going to be people around them, too. I don't know if I can pull the trigger when there are going to be people around who could get hurt. I signed on to protect them, not to trap them in a cross fire."

Not much I could say to that.

"Can I ask you something?" she said after a minute.

"Sure."

She studied me with a faint, concerned frown. "Why can't you do the sunshine thing? Seems like it would be really handy about now. It isn't like you to call something impossible."

I shrugged. "I tried it a couple years back," I said. "After the war started. Turns out that you've got to be genuinely happy to be able to fold sunshine into a hankie. Otherwise it just doesn't work."

"Oh," said Murphy.

I shrugged.

"I guess I'll be in Wolf Lake Park, at the picnic, for a few hours at lunchtime. But I'll have my pager with me," she said.

"Okay. Sorry I didn't drag you into some horrifying, morally questionable, bloodthirsty carnage in time."

She smiled, more with her eyes than her mouth. "See you in a while, Harry." Murphy got out of the car. She checked her watch and sighed. "T minus two hours and counting down."

I blinked at her. "Whoa."

Murphy gave me a skeptical glance. "What?"

"Whoa," I said again. Thoughts were congealing in my brain, and I raked through my memory to see if the facts fit the idea. "Countdown. Son of a bitch."

"What are you talking about?"

"Do you have the police reports on the two women who died in California?"

Murphy lifted an eyebrow, but said, "In my car. Hang on a second." She jogged a couple of spaces down to her car. I heard her pop open the trunk and slam it again. She reappeared with a thick manila folder and passed it to me.

I found the reports inside and scanned over them in rising excitement. "Here it is," I said, jabbing a finger at the report. "I know how they're doing it. Damn, I should have guessed this sooner."

"How they're doing what?" Murphy asked.

"The Evil Eye," I said, the words hurrying together as I grew more excited. "The *malocchio*. The curse that's hitting Genosa's people. It's on a timer."

She tilted her head. "It's automated?"

"No, no," I said, waving my hands. "It's on a schedule. Both women who died were killed in the morning, a little bit before ten o'clock." I closed my eyes, trying to picture the reports Genosa had given me. "Right . . . nine forty-seven and nine forty-eight. They died at the same time."

"That's not the same time, Harry."

I waved a hand, impatient. "They are. I'll bet you anything. The recorded time gets written down by officers on the scene in their report, and who would worry about a minute either way?"

"Why is it significant?" Murphy said.

"Because the two curses that have struck here in Chicago arrived at eleven forty-seven in the morning, and damned close to that last night. Add two hours to the deaths in California to account for the difference in time zones. The curse was sent at the same time. Thirteen minutes before noon or midnight." I followed the logic chain forward from that one fact. "Hell's bells," I breathed.

"I'm not going to ask you to explain every time you pause, Harry, because you know damned well I don't have a clue about what you're saying or what it means."

"It means that the killer isn't doing the curse on his own," I said. "I mean, there's no *reason* to do it that way, unless it's because you don't have a choice. The killer is using ritual magic. They've got a sponsor."

"You don't mean a corporation," Murphy said.

"No," I answered. "What time is it?"

"Ten-thirty," Murphy said.

"*Yes,*" I hissed, and slammed the clutch into gear. "If I haul ass there's time."

"Time?"

"To protect Genosa and his people," I said. "That entropy curse is coming down on them in about an hour." I stomped on the gas and shouted out the window over my shoulder, "This time I'll be ready for it!"

Chapter Twenty-four

I expected Genosa to look awful the next morning, but evidently I had a temporary monopoly on rough nights in Chicago. He was waiting for me at the door when I got to the studio, dressed in slacks and a tennis shirt, perfectly coiffed and genial. I got another European-type hug before I'd gotten all the way out of the Beetle.

"The *malocchio,* it happened again," he said. "Didn't it. Last night when you ran out."

"Yeah," I said.

He licked his lips. "Who?"

"Inari. She's all right."

Arturo blinked several times. "Inari? That's insane. What possible threat could she be to anyone?"

Incipient succubus. No threat at all there. "There's got to be some reason she was targeted. We just don't know what it is yet."

"She's only a child," Genosa said, and for the first time I heard something like real anger in his voice. That was something to be noted. When kind men grow angry, things are about to change. "Have you any idea who is behind it?"

"Not yet," I said, and opened the storage compartment under the Beetle's hood. "But this is definitely more than business for somebody. For them it's personal. I think they're going to take another swing this morning, and I'm going to have a surprise for them when they do."

"How may I help?"

"Get the set moving like everything's normal. I need to get a spell of my own ready."

Arturo frowned at that, and it crinkled all the creases at the corners of his face into unfamiliar lines. "And that is all I can do?"

"For now."

He sighed. "All right. May fortune smile on your efforts, Mister Dresden."

"Don't know why she'd start now," I said, but gave him a quick smile by way of encouragement.

Genosa returned the smile and went back into the building. I followed him a couple of minutes later with my pack loaded with a fifty-foot retractable chalk line, a mirror, a box of tinfoil, and half a dozen candles. I hurried inside, and checked the greenroom and the dressing room before I found Jake Guffie loitering around the shooting studio in dark grey boxers and a loose silk robe. He had a paperback and a bottle of Gatorade, and was draped over his chair in a pose meant to convey calm and confidence. I'm not sure what made me think he was faking, but I knew it even before I spoke to him.

"Jake," I said. "Just the guy I need to see."

He jumped like a nervous cat and gave me a reproachful glance. "Oh. Good morning, Harry. What can I do for you?"

"I need your help with something for about ten minutes."

He tilted his head at me. "Yeah? What?"

I hesitated for a moment and then shrugged. "I'm setting up a spell to protect everyone from evil magic."

"Uh," Jake said, narrowing his eyes. "I don't want to disrespect your religion, man. But did someone spike your breakfast cereal with LSD or something?"

"What can I say, Jake. I'm insane but harmless. Come

with me and help me draw some lines on the floor with chalk, and after that I'll leave you alone." I drew an X over my chest with a fingertip. "Cross my heart."

He looked around, maybe for an excuse to leave, but then shook his head and stood up. "What the hell," he said. "Maybe I'll learn something."

He followed me up the stairs to the top floor of the building. I found the northmost hall, put down my backpack, and started rummaging through it. Jake watched me for a minute before he said, "Is this some kind of feng shui thing?"

"Uh. Actually, it is, now that I think about it," I said. "Feng shui is all about manipulating positive and negative energy around, right? Here, hold this. What I'm doing here is setting up a kind of . . . well, a lightning rod, for lack of a better analogy. I'm setting things up so that if that negative energy gathers again, it gets sent to the place I want it to go, rather than at a particular target. Like a person."

"Feng shui," he said. "Okay, I can buy that."

"Let me snap this," I said, and did, leaving a line of light blue chalk on the floor. "There. Come on." I started down the hall, and after a moment Jake came after me.

I really did need someone's help, and if I had to get someone to give me a hand on the set, I wanted either Jake or Joan, as the least disturbing—or at least the least threatening—folks I had met. And since Joan was a woman, and therefore more likely to become a target of the curse, I didn't want her running back and forth through this gathering spell. The point was to move the bad mojo away, after all. It would have been silly to leave her standing right there in the middle of it.

Even if Jake wasn't an overt believer in the supernatural scene, he was at least laid-back enough that he proved to be a capable helper. I had him follow me around the building with the end of the chalk line in hand. On each level of the building I tried to move around as much of the building's perimeter as I could, leaving chalk lines on the floors and walls. I would lay down the line, snapping it against the surface to leave a light dusting of blue chalk—and as I did I poured out a whisper of my will with it, leaving each of the chalk lines quivering with a small amount of energy. My goal was to lay enough of these spikes of directional energy to make sure that when the curse came in again, it would have to cross at least one of them.

If everything worked to plan, the curse would come flying toward its target, cross one or more of my spikes, and be redirected to follow the lines. Then, at the approximate center of the building, which turned out to be a darkened corner of the soundstage, I laid down my mirror, shiny side up, and set up my candles at the cardinal points of another circle centered around the it. The spikes of force led directly toward the mirror, and I took the time to mark out another circle and light the candles, leaving a subtle quiver of energy in the new circle, too.

"Oh, right," Jake said. "I read about this one. Mirror to pull the bad mojo away?"

"Sort of," I said, standing up and dusting off my hands. "If I've done it right, the curse comes flying in, hits the mirror, and bounces back at whoever threw it."

Jake lifted his eyebrows. "That's kind of hostile, man."

"No, it isn't," I said. "Someone tries to send good vibes at us, they'll get that bounced back at them. They go trying to pull off another killing . . . well. What goes around comes around."

"Hey, that's a fundamental core of many religions," Jake said. "Golden rule, man."

"Yeah, it is," I said. "Maybe a little more literal than usual, in this case."

"You really think this place is cursed?" Jake said. His expression was thoughtful.

"I think someone doesn't want Arturo's new company to succeed," I replied. "Among other things."

Jake frowned. "You think Silverlight Studios is behind it?"

"Possible," I said. "But things have been pretty nasty for someone with a money motivation."

"Materialism is not good for the soul," Jake said. "Those are the folks who can do the worst, when they're after money."

"Money's new," I answered. "Power's old. Power is the real deal. Money, voters, oil, SUVs—they're just stand-ins for power."

"For a feng shui artist, you're sort of intense, man."

I shrugged. "That's the first time anyone's ever told me that."

"You got a woman?"

I rolled up the chalk line. "Had one. Didn't work out."

"That could explain it," Jake said. "Arturo gets like you between wives. Thank God that's over."

I blinked and looked Jake. "Over?"

"Yeah," Jake said. "I mean, he hasn't sent out invitations or anything, but I know the guy. He's had hearts floating around his head for a couple of months, and he's in his days-before-wedding phase now."

That was important. That was really freaking important. "Are you sure?" I asked.

Jake shrugged, his expression puzzled. "I'm not gonna testify to it in federal court or anything, man. I mean, city court, sure."

Footsteps came around the corner, and Bully Bobby appeared, wearing shorts and a T-shirt and carrying a little notebook with a golf pencil. "Jake," he said. "Finally, man. Arturo says I have to tell him today. What do you think of Rocko Stone? Or maybe Rack McGranite?"

"Rocko is way overdone already," Jake said. "And racks are more of a girl thing."

"Oh, right."

"Go with something nonstandard, man. How about Gowan?"

"Gowan?" Bobby asked.

"Sure, he was a knight."

"Like those Round Table guys?"

"Yeah, like that," Jake said.

"Sounds kinda . . . soft, don't you think?"

"Maybe," Jake said. "Stiffen it up with a heavier last name. Like Commando."

Bobby frowned. "Gowan Commando," he said, and from his tone the kid just didn't get it. "I guess that might work. Thanks, man." He paused and noticed me for the first time. "Oh, hey. Uh, Harry, right?"

"Like yesterday," I said. I didn't use my happy voice. "Morning."

"Yeah, morning." Bobby coughed and glanced at Jake, who clenched a fist in an encouraging be-strong sort of gesture. "Harry," Bobby said, "I was kind of an asshole to you yesterday, man. Sorry."

It probably says something about me that I didn't even consider the possibility that he might be sincere until he coughed and shuffled over to offer me his hand. "We okay?" he asked.

I blinked at him. People didn't apologize to me much, as a rule, but I'd seen enough after-school specials to understand the theory. "What the hell." I traded grips with the kid and said, "It's nothing. Forget it."

He smiled a little and said, "Cool. So what are you guys doing?"

"Feng shui," Jake said.

"You know martial arts?" Bobby asked me.

Now that he wasn't threatening violence, I could see that this kid was a jewel. He could potentially provide some lucky wiseass with straight lines for the rest of his natural life, and you can't put a price on that. "A little."

"Cool."

Jake shook his head, and managed to keep from smiling. "Need anything else then, Harry?"

"Not right now."

He nodded. "Come on, Gowan. Let's go see if Joan needs help with anything."

"Hey," I said. "Jake."

"Yeah?"

"Is Lara here today?"

He arched an eyebrow. "Yeah. Why?"

"No reason," I said. "I'll catch up to you later."

They left, and I sat down in my dim, magically booby-trapped corner to think.

It was important that Arturo was in love. My gut told me it was important, but I couldn't kick my tired brain into telling me *why*. I rubbed at my eyes. I needed more sleep to do any thinking, so I went looking for the next best thing—coffee and a backup brain.

Murphy answered the phone and I greeted her through the coffee and most of a doughnut.

"You're mumbling, Harry," Murphy said. "Speak up."

I slurped coffee, scalded my mouth on the stuff, and set it aside to cool off a little. "Sorry, burned my tongue. Did you get any more information about Arturo Genosa?" I asked.

"Some," Murphy said. "I got in touch with a guy I know in LA. He came up with municipal records and even some files from Genosa's lawyer, but there's not much in the way of admissible."

"That's okay. Just trying to get a picture."

I heard her digging out a file and opening it. "Okay. He's got a will on file, leaves everything to a couple of charities and his next of kin, looks like his mother in Greece—but she died a couple of years ago, so I guess the money all goes to charity."

"What about his wives?" I asked.

"Control of their fund would have gone to his mother, but since she's dead they get to keep drawing from it indefinitely. It's in the prenuptial agreement for all three of them."

"Three?" I asked. Hell's bells, if the man was in love . . . "Does it mention a fourth wife?"

"Nope."

"What about a fourth marriage license?"

I heard her rustling around the file, and tested the coffee while she did. Ah, perfection. "Stupid fax machine paper," she growled. "It's floppy and the pages all stick together." Then she stopped for a second and said, "Son of a bitch, there is one."

"When?"

"Dated for next Thursday."

"To who?"

"I can't tell. There's a big blurry spot," Murphy said. "Fax machine must have messed it up. But it's definitely marriage license number four."

"But with no prenuptial number four," I said.

"No prenup number four."

"Hello, new next of kin," I said.

"Hello, motive," Murphy agreed. "Hello, suspects."

The greenroom door opened and I looked up in time to see a woman with a lingerie-model body under a flimsy robe enter the room, holding a big revolver. She pointed the gun at me, found the extension of the phone I was on and pulled it out of the wall, then said into a cell phone, "I've got him."

I sat there holding the dead phone and the warm coffee and said, "Hello, Trixie."

Chapter Twenty-five

Trixie Scrump-Genosa-Vixen-Expialidocius leaned against the door and said, "Don't get up, Barry. And don't move your hands." Her voice shook with nervous energy, and the barrel of the gun waved drunkenly back and forth. The knuckles of the hand holding the cell phone to her ear were white. "I don't want to shoot you."

"You know, people don't want to crash their cars either. But there is always some idiot who drives and talks on the cell phone at the same time, and crunch," I said. "Maybe you should put your phone down until we're done. Just to be safe."

"Don't give me orders," she snapped, pushing the gun

at me like it was some sort of sexual aid. She wobbled on her high heels when she did, but managed not to fall over. "Don't you dare give me orders!"

I shut up. She was already wound pretty tight. I have a bad habit of turning into a real wiseass when someone makes me nervous. It's just a reflex. But if I pushed Trixie too hard, her precarious self-control might snap, accidentally setting off the gun. I'd die of shame if she unintentionally shot me, so I resolved to keep my mouth shut. Mostly. "Okay."

"Keep your hands right there, and don't move."

"Can I sip some of my coffee at least?" I asked. "It just got to the right temperature."

She scowled. "No. You never got me my latte."

"Right," I said. "Good point."

We sat there for a couple of minutes while my arms started getting tired, holding coffee and a useless phone in place like that. "So what happens now, Ms. Vixen?"

"What do you mean?"

"Well, there's me and you here, and then there's that gun. Usually there's a specific purpose to using a gun as a negotiation tactic, but so far all you're doing is pointing it at me. I'm no expert, but as I understand it, you get to make demands or something."

"I know you're afraid," she spat. "That's why you're talking. You're nervous and talking because you're afraid of me."

"I am paralyzed at the thought of losing my senior division shuffleboard career," I said. "That's just how much you scare me. But I'm also curious about our next step."

"There is no next step," she said.

"Um. So we sit here for the rest of eternity?"

She sneered. "No. In a minute I'm going to leave."

I lifted my eyebrows. "Just like that?"

"Yeah."

"You . . . brilliant fiend," I said. "I wouldn't ever have guessed that your plan was to do nothing."

She smirked. "It's all I need to do."

"I thought you might be worried that I would tell the police about it afterward."

Trixie laughed and looked genuinely amused. "Oh? You're going to tell them what? That I held a gun on you for no reason, did nothing, and then left?"

"Well. Yeah."

"Which are they going to believe? That crappy story or that you confronted me when I was alone, made unwanted sexual advances, and that I had to pull the gun out of my purse to discourage you?"

I narrowed my eyes. Actually, that wasn't a stupid plan, which made me doubt Trixie had come up with it all on her own. But why hold me in place for only a few moments? I checked the room's clock. Eleven forty. Crap. "Oh," I said. "You want me sidelined for the next time you call up the curse."

Her eyes widened. "How did you know th—" She broke off abruptly, her head twitching, evidently listening to someone on the phone. "Oh. I know. I'm not telling him anything. I don't see why you . . ." She winced. "Oh. Oh. Yes, all *right*. Do *you* want to come down here to do this? Fine, then. Fine." Her face darkened into a vicious scowl, but most of her attention came back to me.

"Who's on the phone?" I asked her.

"None of your business."

"Actually it is. Literally. Since I'm being paid to find the identities of whoever is swinging that curse."

Trixie let out an ugly laugh. "What difference would it make if you did? It isn't as though the police are going to believe the use of a magic curse as a murder weapon."

"Maybe. But cops aren't the only authority in the universe. Anyone ever tell you about the White Council?"

She licked her lips, and her eyes flickered around the room. "Of course they did," she lied.

"So you know that employing magic to murder another human being carries the death penalty."

She stared at me. "What are you talking about?"

"The trial wouldn't be real long. Maybe ten or fifteen

minutes, tops. And once they find you guilty, you'll be executed on the spot. Beheaded. With a sword."

Her mouth worked uselessly for a second. "You're lying."

"I'm an honest guy. Maybe you're in denial and projecting."

"I am not," she snapped. "You're just trying to scare me. It's a lie."

"I wish," I said. "My life would have been simpler. Look, Trixie, you and whoever you're working with might get away with it if you back off right now. Leave off the curses and get out of town."

She lifted her chin defiantly. "And if we don't?"

"Bad things happen. You're already beaten, Ms. Vixen. You just don't know it. If you roll out that curse again, you're going to get a taste of it for yourself."

"Are you threatening me?"

"Not a threat," I said. "Just a fact. You and your ritual are done."

"Oh," she said, regaining her composure. "You underestimate my powers."

I snorted. "You haven't *got* any powers."

"Yes, I do. I've killed with them."

"You've killed with a *ritual*," I said.

"What's the difference?"

"The difference," I said, "is that if you have any skill of your own at magic, you don't need a ritual."

"Whatever. They're the same thing anyway. Magic. Power."

"No," I said. "Look, a ritual spell like that doesn't have anything to do with you. It's like a cosmic vending machine. You put two quarters in, push the right button, and the curse comes flying out, courtesy of some psychotic otherworldly force that enjoys that kind of thing. It doesn't take skill. It doesn't take talent. You could be a freaking monkey and invoke that curse just as well."

"There's no practical difference," she maintained.

"Yes, there is."

"What?" she asked.

"You're about to find out."

Instead of looking uncertain, she smiled. "You're talking about that sacred circle you had set up on the soundstage."

She'd recognized the circle? Oh, crap.

"We knew that you'd try something," she went on. "All I had to do was follow you when you came in. I don't know what you thought you were going to accomplish, but I'm pretty sure all of your squiggles and candles aren't going to do whatever you wanted them to, given that I broke your circle and smeared all your chalk lines."

And she was right. Double crap.

"Trixie," I said. "You can't possibly think that this is all right. Why are you doing this?"

"I'm protecting what's mine, Larry," she said. "It's business."

"Business?" I demanded. "Two people are dead already. Giselle and Jake were at death's door, and I don't even want to think about what would have happened to Inari if I weren't there. What the fuck do you think you're *doing?*"

"I don't feel any need to explain myself to you."

I blinked at her slowly and then said, "You don't know either. You don't know who he's marrying."

She didn't say anything, but her eyes blazed with scorn and fury.

I shook my head, continuing. "So you've just been eliminating all the women around Arturo Genosa. One at a time. You don't even know if you're killing the right person."

"There's only one little girl toy left pretty enough to suit his tastes," she said.

"Emma," I said.

"And once she's gone, I won't have to worry about her stealing what's mine."

I stared at her for a second. "Are you insane?" I said. "Do you think you'll get away with this?"

"I'd love to see some prosecutor try me for witchcraft," she responded.

Trixie was too stupid to believe me about the White

Council and too self-absorbed to keep my name straight, but for crying out loud, she had to be human. "Hell's bells, Trixie. Emma's got kids."

"So did Hitler," Trixie snapped.

"No, he didn't," I said. "He had *dogs*."

"Whatever," Trixie said.

I checked the clock. Eleven-forty-three. In four minutes, give or take, Emma would die.

Trixie's attention snapped to the phone and she listened for a moment, throwing out a terse, "Yes." Then the phone abruptly squealed with feedback, and Trixie flinched hard enough to make me worry that she'd lost control of her weapon. "Dammit," she said. "I hate these stupid cell phones."

Cell phones are the caged canaries in the coal mines of the supernatural. When a little magic gets moving, cell phones are some of the first pieces of equipment to be disrupted. Odds were good that someone on the other end of that phone was starting to move energy around.

Which meant that the *malocchio* was coming to kill Emma.

And so long as Trixie kept me in the greenroom, there wasn't a damned thing I could do to prevent it.

Chapter Twenty-six

If I didn't do something, another woman was going to die, and a couple of kids were going to become orphans. Of course, I also had a gun in my face. If I *did* do something, I would die. The smart thing would be to let Trixie finish delaying me and wait for her to leave. Emma would be dead, but I'd have at least twelve hours in which I could shut the Evil Eye franchise down. If I didn't cooperate, Emma and I would both die, and the bad guys would still be at large.

So the smart money was on staying put. Simple logic.

But there are things older than logic—like instinct. One of the most primal instincts in the human soul is the desire to protect children from harm. Even if the idea of Emma's death hadn't been motivation enough, the very *thought* of how savagely this stupid, venal, selfish harpy might scar Emma's children made me want to call down fire enough to roast Trixie Vixen and her sculpted ass to ash.

I found myself tensing to go after her, and damn the gun. It wasn't as brainless as you might think. Killing is not so easy as it seems. Most people are wired to be careful of their fellow human beings. Soldiers and cops both are specifically given training to overcome that instinct, and the criminals who fire at other people are usually driven to it by desperation.

And even trained soldiers and hardened criminals are often wildly inaccurate. Billy the Kid once emptied his Colt revolver at a bank teller from less than three feet away, and missed him six times. I'd seen a police reel of a cop who had been forced to draw and fire at a suspect, and he'd emptied a full clip at the man from less than twenty feet, missing him every time.

Trixie may have had the gun, but she didn't have experience, training, or much in the way of composure. If she hesitated, even for a fraction of a second, it would be possible for me to close on her. If she didn't hesitate, the odds against me were not unthinkably high. It was possible that she might miss me enough times to let me take the gun.

Of course, it was possible she'd put a bullet through my eye, too. Or through my throat. Or maybe my guts.

I felt a sudden, ethereal wind, cold and ugly. The curse was almost there, and it was deadlier, more potent than ever before. A bare second of concentration told me that I would have no prayer of blocking that much magic, and even redirecting so much raw power would be nearly impossible. I don't know what had happened to make the curse that much stronger, that much deadlier, and it scared me half out of my mind.

I had to do something, and I had to do it now.

I needed a distraction, but the best I could do was to abruptly whip my head toward the door, and to shift my weight as if I might stand up.

"Don't move," Trixie snarled.

I licked my lips, staring at the door.

I saw her expression become uncertain. She rubbernecked toward the door—only for a second, but it would have to do.

I threw my still-steaming coffee at her. It sloshed across her shoulder and neck. She screamed in surprise and sudden pain. I lunged at her, lifting the handset of the telephone to swing at her head.

She cried out and stared at me, her lovely face stunned, terrified.

The Quixote reflexes kicked in.

I hesitated.

The gun went off from two feet away.

I recovered before I could lose much momentum and slammed into her, a full-body impact that drove her shoulder blades up against the wall beside the door. The gun roared again, and the sharp, acrid tang of cordite and the syrupy smell of blood flooded over me. I got my fingers around the wrist of her gun hand and slammed it against the wall. The gun barked some more, but finally tumbled from her fingers to the floor.

I kicked it across the room. Trixie clawed at my eyes with the nails of her free hand. Pain jolted through me. I got an arm around her waist and threw her bodily away from me, opposite the way I had kicked the weapon. She hit the table and folded over it, scattering a box of doughnuts and a plate of various fruits.

Then she sank to the floor, sobbing. One of her stockings had been soaked in blood, from ankle to calf, and she curled up, clutching at her wounded leg. I recovered the gun without touching the handle, checked, and found it empty. I turned my eyes to Trixie Vixen.

She shrank away from me, weeping in pain and terror. She held up her other arm as a useless shield. "No. No, please. I didn't mean it. I didn't mean it."

The adrenaline rushed through me, wild and mindless. I wanted to kill her.

A lot.

I hadn't ever felt that before—a sudden surge of fury, contempt, and disdain mixed in with a physical excitement only a few degrees short of actual arousal. It wasn't an emotion. It was nothing that tame and limited. It was a force, a dark and vast tide that picked me up and swept me along like a Styrofoam packing peanut. And I liked it.

There was something in me that took a deep and gloating satisfaction in seeing my enemy on the floor and helpless. That part of me wanted to see her screaming. And then see her die screaming.

I'm not sure how I kept myself from acting on that flood of violence and lust. But instead of gut-shooting Trixie, I stared coldly at her for a second, studying her injuries. One of the shots must have either bounced into her calf or entered directly when the gun had gone off during the struggle. She bled, but not enough to kill her anytime soon, and the lines of her calf and foot seemed twisted, slightly misshapen. The bullet must have broken a bone.

"Please," she babbled, staring at the gun I now held. "I'll do whatever you want. Just say it. Oh, God, please don't kill me."

I stalked to the door. I noted a couple of bullet holes in it, and heard myself speak, my voice quiet and deadly cold. "Shut up."

She did, shuddering with sobs, hiding her face. The scent of urine joined the other smells in the room. I kept her revolver in hand and jerked the door open hard, to rush through it and back to the soundstage to deal with the curse.

I didn't have to bother.

Emma's corpse lay on its back in the hall outside. She had been wearing spandex biking shorts with a matching sports halter. There was blood forming a pool beneath her. A small, neat hole directly into her sternum accompanied the hole in her forehead, just over her right eyebrow. She lay with her knees bent beneath her, her arms spread a little. A prescription bottle lay on the ground, just barely touching one fingertip. She'd been dead before she fell, and her body had simply relaxed bonelessly to the ground.

The shots couldn't have been more perfect if they'd been delivered by a professional assassin. The odds against stray bullets randomly hitting where they had were inconceivably high. The *malocchio* had killed her. The stray bullets had simply been its instrument.

I heard Trixie gasp behind me, and turned to see her staring at the body. "No," she whispered, the timing of the words somehow disjointed and random. "That wasn't in the plan. This wasn't part of it. He *never* said that."

I heard running footsteps coming down the hall, and looked up in time to see a couple of the camera guys, Jake, and Arturo round the corner. They came to an abrupt stop, staring at the scene in shock. Someone— Jake, I thought—let out a high-pitched, squawking cry.

I suddenly realized that I was standing over a dead woman while another bled from a bullet wound ten feet away—and that I was holding the gun that did it to them both.

Trixie's eyes widened as if she recognized the opportunity. Her mouth twisted into a sudden, vindictive, mad-eyed rictus. She let out a scream, wailing, "Help me! Help me, oh, God, don't let him kill me too!"

I didn't have long to decide on a course of action, but I got the benefit of one of those crystallized moments, when nothing happens and it seems like you've got all the time in the world to think.

I'd been too slow and now Emma was dead. Worse yet, I looked guilty as hell, short-term. In the long term, forensics would show that Trixie had been holding the gun when it went off, but I had never been on good terms with the largest part of Chicago's legal system, either in the courts or law enforcement. At least one cop, now in Internal Affairs, would be glad to take this opportunity to crucify me, and if I took my chances with the law, the weapon plus the eyewitness testimony of a would-be victim could provide the state with a reasonable case. Even if they didn't win, I could still spend the duration in prison, months or possibly years, until the case was decided—but all it would really take was one or two days. By then Mavra and her scourge would find me and kill me. I knew from bloody experience that not even the strongest jail cell meant much to supernatural beings with murder in mind.

I still didn't know who was helping Trixie. If I didn't figure out who was behind this mess, they could keep going, keep on killing. If I was out of the picture, they'd get away with it, and the thought stirred up my rage once more. Emma's death had changed things. Before, there had been danger, but no one had died on my watch. Not for lack of trying, sure, but I'd been there in time to avert any deaths. But now Emma, whose worst crime probably had a lot to do with providing a decent living for her children, was lying there like so much meat, and her kids had no mommy.

I stared at Trixie for a hot, wild second, and the look choked her continued shrieks to whimpers. Trixie may have been female, but as of that moment she wasn't a woman anymore. She'd crossed a line. As far as I was concerned, she and her allies had forfeited their membership card to the humanity club when they killed Emma.

And I'd be damned if I was going to let them get away with it. But I couldn't do it from the inside of a cell.

I turned and hurried into an adjoining hall and toward the nearest door, but found it locked. I cursed and ran back, heading for the front door. Someone shouted but I ignored them. I sprinted the last twenty feet and was about to hit the door when it abruptly swung open.

Joan stepped in from the parking lot, panting. She wore old jeans and another flannel shirt over a tee. She had her keys in one hand, and a clawhammer in the other. She'd gone through the locked door and beaten me to the exit.

"What are you doing?" she demanded.

I checked over my shoulder. I heard more shouts and running footsteps, heavy and fast. Bobby was running after me. If he tried to stop me here in the hall, I didn't think I could get away from him without hurting him, maybe badly. But when I took another step toward Joan she swallowed, her face pale with fright but her eyes determined, and lifted the clawhammer.

"Joan," I panted. "I have to go."

"No," she said. "I don't know what's going on, but I can't let you leave. I heard gunshots. Emma and Trish are hurt."

I didn't have time to discuss it. I took a handkerchief from my pocket, wrapped it around the handle of Trixie's gun to maybe preserve any prints, and lifted it, not quite pointing it at Joan. "There's not time to explain, but if you don't let me go it's going to keep happening. Someone else on the crew will get hurt tonight."

Her expression became angry. "Don't you dare threaten these people."

"It isn't a threat," I half screamed. I hated to do it, but I pointed the gun at her. "Move."

She started shaking but adjusted her grip on the hammer and shook her head.

"I mean it," I said, and took a step forward, radiating as much menace as I knew how.

Joan stared at the gun for a moment. Then an expression of resolution took the fear from her face. She lowered the hammer and took a step toward me, putting the barrel of the gun about six inches from her sternum. "I can't let you hurt anyone else. If you want to leave," she said quietly, "you'll have to kill me too."

I stared at her for a moment. Then I gripped the gun's barrel with my left hand, left the handkerchief around the handle, and offered it to her.

She stared at me. "What are you doing?"

"Take it," I said. "Trixie's fingerprints are on the handle, so don't touch it. She was the shooter. She's working with someone and they're responsible for all the deaths and injuries lately. But when the cops show, she'll lie to them, and it looks bad for me. If the police arrest and hold me, I won't be able to help you when they strike again tonight. I have to go."

She shivered and took the gun. She held it like it might bite her. "I don't understand."

"Joan. If I was the one who shot them, I'd have shot you too. Would I give you the gun if I'd done it? Just leave the murder weapon here for the cops?"

She hesitated, uncertain.

"Help me," I told her. There was a tense note of fear in my voice. "I need to get back to my place, get a few things, and go before the cops start watching it. Try to delay them. Just for five minutes, please. My God, it's going to happen *again* if I don't stop it."

She glanced over her shoulder at the door.

"Please, Joan," I said quietly. "God, please help me." Silence fell heavily, except for more footsteps, coming closer.

"I must be insane," she said. "I must be insane."

She stepped aside.

I did the only thing I could under the circumstances. It made me look guilty as hell, but if I wanted to keep breathing I didn't have much choice.

I ran.

Chapter Twenty-seven

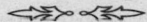

I hit the parking lot at a run, piled into the Blue Beetle, and started it up. Behind me I heard the building's fire alarm go off, a deafening ringing of emergency bells. In addition to the police, and probably an ambulance, a bunch of fire trucks were about to show up as well. It was going to be one hell of a mess to sort through, at least for the CPD. By the time they made sure the building had been evacuated, seen to Trixie's wound, and taken statements from everyone in the building I could probably walk to Havana. She'd bought me at least ten minutes and probably more.

"Bless you, Joan," I muttered. I slapped the old car into reverse and cleared out, heading for my apartment. I was on the highway and gone before any sirens started converging. I drove carefully and under the limit, since getting pulled over for a citation could be fatal, and tried to think unobtrusive thoughts. But I found myself mulling over the details of the *malocchio*.

Trixie Vixen had been in the room with me when the last curse came down, and while she was clearly involved, it hadn't come from her. She'd known about it in great detail, though, and she'd known enough about magic to screw up the hurried wards I'd raised around the studio. Couple that with bragging about her power, and I figured she'd been involved in the actual magic at some point—she probably had handled part of the ritual that brought the curse down.

It made sense. Trixie was a jumbo-sized self-obsessed drama queen, complete with melodramatic dialogue, tantrums, and smug confidence that she was the center of the universe. The deaths and near-deaths from the *malocchio* had given new depths to the term *freak accident*. Swarms of bees, bridge-jumping cars, and electrocution in a puddle of one's own blood were some pretty ridiculous ways to kill someone. And that frozen turkey thing had come straight out of a cartoon.

They would have been funny if it hadn't been for the deaths.

But the curse had been different today. No winding, slow buildup, no murder weapons manufactured by the Acme Corporation, and no spillover onto other people nearby. Unlike the others, Emma's death had been the result of a surgical strike of focused, violent energy. The earlier editions of the curse had been more like a stone-headed hatchet than a scalpel. Today's curse had been far stronger than the ones I'd felt before, too.

And Trixie was the lowest common denominator.

Any kind of magic spell requires certain things to happen. You have to gather in the energy for whatever it is you're trying to do. Then you have to shape it with your thoughts and feelings into what you want it to do. And finally you have to release it in the direction you want it to go. To use a rough metaphor, you have to load the gun, aim it, and pull the trigger.

The problem was that with a curse that powerful, you were talking about a very big gun. Even with a ritual supplying the power for it, controlling that power was a task that not just anybody could do. Aiming and pulling the trigger were easier, but handling them all at once would be very difficult even for some wizards. That's why for the big projects you need three people working together, and it's the basis for the stereotype of three cackling witches casting spells in concert over a cauldron.

Trixie stormed off the set before the curse had come at Inari last night, and she hadn't been in the studio when it happened twelve hours prior to that. But she *had* been there with me today. Trixie the Drama Queen's personality was stamped all over the near-insane deaths, but I was damned sure that she wasn't a wizard.

Therefore, she'd had help. Someone would need to manage the energy, while Trixie shaped the curse into some kind of ludicrous death scenario. And someone else had to pull the trigger, channeling the spell to its intended recipient—also something that required a little more skill and focus than I was willing to believe Trixie had. So it would take three of them.

Three *stregas*.

Three former Mrs. Arturo Genosas.

The curse that killed Emma had been different. It had been a hell of a lot stronger, for one thing, and it had come at her a hell of a lot faster. And the death it had brought down on her had been efficient and quick. If Trixie wasn't with them, then it meant that either one of the others had some serious skill, or they'd been able to find a replacement witch who had been content with making the murder swift, clean, and simple.

Four killers working together. I was the only one around who could get in their way, and they knew I was getting closer to them. Under the circumstances, they had only one logical target for the next iteration of the spell, twelve hours from now.

Me.

That was assuming, of course, that Mavra and the vampire scourge—or possibly the man I'd hired to help me kill them—didn't take me out first. Maybe they wouldn't get their chance. See? That's the power of positive thinking.

I got back to my apartment and got out of the car just in time to see Mister flying down the sidewalk as fast as he could run. He looked both ways before crossing the street, and we entered the apartment together. I started gathering things and shoving them into a nylon gym bag, then opened the door down to the lab. Bob flowed out of Mister, who promptly shuffled over to the fire and collapsed into sleep.

"Well?" I called down as I finished packing the bag. "Did you find her?"

"Yeah, I found her," Bob called.

"About time," I said. I went down the ladder in a hurry, and flicked several candles alight with a muttered word. I got out a roll of parchment about a foot and a half square. Then I spread it onto the worktable in the lab's center and set a fountain pen beside it. "Where?"

"Not far from Cabrini Green," Bob said. "I got a good look around the place."

"Good. You've got permission to come out long enough to show me what you found."

He made a sighing sound but didn't complain. The usual cloud of glowing orange motes of light slid out of the skull's eye sockets, though perhaps it was a little less bright and swirly than usual. The cloud of light surrounded the pen, and it rose up of its own accord, then began scratching a drawing of the lair on the parchment. Bob's voice, a little indistinct now, said, "You aren't going to like this."

"Why not?"

"It's a shelter."

"A homeless shelter?"

"Yeah," Bob said. "Does some rehab work with drug addicts, too."

"Stars and stones," I murmured. "How could vampires take something that public?"

"There's no real threshold on a public building, so they didn't need an invitation. I think they probably came in from Undertown, right into the shelter's basement."

"How many people have they hurt?"

Bob's pen flickered over the parchment. When I draw maps I usually end up with a series of lopsided squares and wavery lines and incomplete circles. Bob's drawing looked like it could have been done by da Vinci. "There were three bodies stacked up in a corner of the basement," Bob said. "A few of the shelter's staff had been made into rough thralls and are covering for them, them, sort of. Maybe half a dozen people hadn't been enthralled, but they were tied up and locked into a cedar closet."

"Any goons?"

"Big-time. Half a dozen Renfields, and each of them has a darkhound to boot."

"Renfields?" I asked.

"How in the world can you exist in this century and not know about Renfields?" Bob demanded. "You need a life, stat."

"I read the book. I know who Renfield was. I'm not familiar with the parlance for Renfield in the plural."

"Oh," Bob said. "What do you need to know?"

"Well. First off, what did they call them before Stoker published the book?" I asked.

"They didn't call them anything, Harry," Bob said in a tone of gentle patience. "That's *why* the White Court had Stoker publish the book. To tell people about them."

"Oh. Right." I rubbed at my eyes. "How do the vampires do their recruiting?"

"Mind-control magic," Bob said. "The usual."

"Always with the mental control," I muttered. "Let me make sure my facts are straight. Rough thralls just stand around looking blank until they get orders, right?"

"Yeah," Bob said, pen scratching. "Sort of like zombies, but they still have to go to the bathroom."

"So a Renfield is the fine version of thralldom?"

"No," Bob said. "A fine thrall is so controlled that they might not even *know* that they're a thrall at all, and it lasts long-term."

"Like what DuMorne did to Elaine."

"Uh, I guess so, yeah. Like that. That kind of thing takes a subtle hand, though. Enthralling someone also requires a lot of time and a certain amount of empathy, neither of which has been readily available to Mavra."

"So?" I said, getting impatient. "A Renfield is a . . .?"

Bob put the pen down. "It's the quick, dirty way for the Black Court to pick up some cheap muscle. Renfields have been crushed into total thralldom through brute psychic force."

"You're kidding," I said. "The kind of mental damage that would do to someone . . ."

"It destroys their sanity when it happens," Bob confirmed. "Makes them no good for anything but gibbering violence, but since that's pretty much what the vampires wanted to begin with it works out."

"How do you get them out of it?" I asked.

"You don't," Bob said. "The original Merlin couldn't undo it, and neither could any of the saints on record to have tried. A thrall can be freed, or recover over time. Renfields can't. From the moment their minds break they've got an expiration date."

"Ugh," I said. "What do you mean?"

"Renfields get more and more violent and deranged, and they self-destruct in a year or two. You can't fix them. For all practical purposes, they're already dead."

I went over the facts in my head, and admired how much uglier the situation had just become. Over the years I've learned that ignorance is more than just bliss. It's freaking orgasmic ecstasy. I glanced at Bob and said, "Are you sure about your facts?"

The cloud of orange light flowed tiredly back into the skull on its shelf. "Yes. DuMorne did quite a bit of research on the subject back in the day."

"Murphy isn't going to like this," I said. "Dismembering monsters with a chain saw is one thing. People are another."

"Yeah. People are easier."

"Bob," I growled. "They're *people*."

"Renfields aren't, Harry," Bob said. "They might still be moving around but they're pretty much gone."

"Boy, would it be fun to explain that to a courtroom," I said. I shuddered. "Or to the White Council, for that matter. If I take out the wrong person, I could wind up in jail—or in a White Council star chamber trial. Mavra's using the laws to protect herself against us. That's so backward."

"Screw the laws! Kill 'em all!" Bob said with weary cheer.

I sighed. "What about the dogs?"

"Your basic animal," Bob said. "But they've been infused with a portion of the same kind of dark power that the Black Court runs on. They're stronger, faster, and they don't feel pain. I once saw a darkhound rip its way through a brick wall."

"I bet they look like normal dogs afterward, huh?"

"And before-ward," Bob said.

"I guess if the cops are on my case when this is over, the SPCA can come along for the ride." I shook my head. "And on top of all that, Mavra is also keeping those hostages in the closet for food. She'll use them as human shields once fighting starts."

"Or as bait in a trap," Bob said.

"Yeah. Either way it makes things more complicated, even if we go in when Mavra and her scourge are sleeping." I looked at Bob's diagram of the lair. "Any security system?"

"Old electronic one," Bob said. "Nothing fancy. No problem for you to hex it down."

"Mavra will know that. She'll have sentries. We need to get past them."

"Forget it. Rough thralls and Renfields don't exactly make the most observant guardians in the world, but the darkhounds make up for them. If you want to sneak up, you'll have to be invisible, inaudible, and unsmellable. Don't count on a surprise attack."

"Dammit. What kind of weapons are they toting?"

"Uh, teeth. Mostly teeth, Harry."

I glared at him. "Not the dogs."

"Oh. The thralls have got some baseball bats. The Renfields have assault rifles, grenades, and body armor."

"Holy crap."

Bob leered at me from his shelf. "Awww. Izzums scared of the mean old machine guns?"

I glowered and flipped a pencil at the skull. "Maybe Murphy can figure out a way to do this without starting World War Three. Meanwhile, change of topic incoming. I need your opinion."

"Sure," Bob said. "Hit me."

I told him about the entropy curse and who I thought was behind it.

"Ritual magic," Bob confirmed. "More amateurs."

"Who sponsors ritual curses these days?" I asked.

"Well. In theory, a lot of Powers. In practice, though, the writings on most of them have been gathered up by the Council or the Venatori or someone else with some supernatural clout. Or else destroyed. It might take me some time to recall all the details."

"Why?" I asked.

"Because I've got about six hundred years' worth of memories to sort through, and I'm exhausted," Bob said, his voice softer, as though coming from far away. "But you can be pretty sure that whoever is backing a death curse isn't real friendly."

"Tell me something I don't know," I said. "Hey, Bob."

"Hmm?"

"Is it possible to work some kind of spell that would last, I dunno, maybe twenty or thirty years?"

"Sure, if you spend enough money," Bob said. "Or if you're some kind of sentimental family sap."

"Sentimental? How's that?"

"Well, you can anchor magic to certain materials, right? Most of them are very expensive. Or you do the cheap kind like you use on your blasting rod and such, refresh them once in a while." The skull's eyes were growing rapidly dimmer. "But there are times when you can anchor it to a person."

"That isn't doable," I said.

"Not for you," Bob said. "Gotta be a blood relation. Blood in common, that kind of thing. Maybe if you had a kid. But I guess you'd need a girlfriend for that, huh."

I raked my hand through my hair, thinking. "And if you do it that way, the spell lasts? Even for that long?"

"Oh, sure," Bob said. "As long as the person you anchor it to is alive. Takes a tiny bit of energy off them to keep the spell from slowing down. That's why all the really nasty curses you hear about usually involve some family somewhere."

"So for instance," I said, "my mother could have laid out a curse on someone. And as long as I was alive, it would still be viable."

"Exactly. Or like that loup-garou guy. His own bloodline keeps the curse fueled." The skull's mouth opened in a yawn. "Anything else?"

I picked up the map and tucked it into a pocket. Bob was at the end of his resources, and I had no time to lose. I'd have to finish out this one on my own. "Get some rest and see what you can remember," I said. "I've got to clear out before the cops get here." I started to get up off my stool, and every muscle in my body complained to be moving again. I winced and said, "Painkillers. Definitely need painkillers too."

"Luck, Harry," Bob mumbled, and the glittering orange lights in the skull's eye sockets dimmed completely.

My body ached as I climbed back out of the lab. It was getting to be pretty good at aching, actually, by virtue of all the practice. I could ignore pain. I had a talent for ignoring it. That talent had been refined by the harsh lessons of life and the even harsher lessons of Justin DuMorne. But even so, the discomfort took its toll. My bed wasn't particularly luxurious, but it looked that way when I passed it on my way to the door.

I had my keys in my hand and my bag over one shoulder when the there was a rattling from the dim corner by the door. I paused, and a moment later my wizard's staff twitched, rattling again. It shuddered and twitched, thumping against the wall and the floor in staccato fits, too much rhythm to the sounds for them to be meaningless.

"Well," I muttered. "It's about damn time."

I picked up my staff, rapped one end hard on the floor, and focused my attention on the length of wood. I reached down through it, into the steady, heavy power of the earth beneath it, and then beat out my own short rhythm on the stone. My staff went still, then quivered sharply twice in my hand. I set out water and food for Mister, left, and locked my apartment behind me, then sealed the wards of protective energy around it.

By the time I was up the stairs, a heavy old Ford truck, a battered and tough-looking survivor of the Great Depression, pulled into the gravel parking lot at the side of the boardinghouse and crunched to a halt. It had Missouri plates. A gun rack at the back of the cab held an old double-barreled shotgun in its top slot, and a thick, stumpy old wizard's staff in the one beneath it.

The driver set the brake and swung open the door without letting the engine die. He was old but hale, a short, stocky man in overalls, heavy working boots, and a flannel shirt. He had broad hands with scarred knuckles, and wore a plain steel ring on each index finger. A few white hairs drifted around his sun-toughened scalp. He had dark eyes, a severely annoyed expression, and he snorted upon seeing me. "Hey, there, Hoss. You look like ten miles of bad—"

"Clichés," I interjected, smiling. The old man puffed out a breath of quiet laughter and offered me his hand. I shook it, and found myself newly appreciative of the calloused strength that belied the man's evident age. "Good to see you, sir. I was starting to feel a little swamped."

Ebenezar McCoy, senior member of the White Council, a sometime mentor of mine, and by all accounts I'd heard one hell of a strong wizard, clapped me on my biceps with his free hand. "You, in over your head? It's as if you're too stubborn to know when to run."

"We'd best get moving," I told him. "The police will be along shortly."

His frown knitted his shaggy white eyebrows together, but he nodded and said, "Hop in."

I got in the truck and slid my staff into the gun rack with Ebenezar's. The old man's staff was shorter and thicker than mine, but the carved sigils and formulae on it were noticeably similar, and the texture and color of the wood was identical. They'd both come from the same lightning-wounded tree, back on Ebenezar's land in the Ozarks. I shut the door and closed my eyes for a moment, while Ebenezar got the truck rolling.

"Your Morse is rusty," he said a few minutes later. "On my staff it sounded like you spelled it 'blampires.' "

"I did," I said. "Black Court vampires. I just shortened it some."

Ebenezar *tsk*ed. "Blampires. That's the problem with you young people. Shortening all the words."

"Too many acronyms?" I asked.

"Ayuh."

"Well, then," I said. "I'm glad you took the time to RSVP me. I have a problem that needs to stay on the QT, but is rapidly going FUBAR. I'm sorry to call you LD through AT&T instead of using UPS, but I needed your help ASAP. I hope that's OK."

Ebenezar grunted, shot me a sidelong look, and said, "Don't make me kick your ass."

"No, sir," I said.

"Black Court," he said. "Who?"

"Mavra. You know her?"

"I know *it*," he said, the pronoun mildly emphasized. "Killed a friend of mine in the Venatori once. And she was in the Wardens' files. They suspect she's got a little skill at dark sorcery and consider her to be very dangerous."

"It's more than a little skill," I said.

The old man frowned. "Oh?"

"Yeah. I've seen her throw raw power around, and put up the best veil I've ever seen through. I also saw her using some long-range mental communications with her flunkies."

The old man frowned. "That's more than a little."

"Uh-huh. She's gunning for me. Only, you know, without the guns."

Ebenezar frowned, but nodded. "She holding that mess at the Velvet Room against you?"

"That's how it looks from here," I said. "She's taken two swings at me. But I found where she's laired, and I want to take her down before she gets to three."

"Makes sense," he said. "What's your plan?"

"I've got help. Murphy—"

"The police girl?" he interrupted.

"God, don't call her a girl," I said. "At least not to her face. Yeah, her, and a mercenary named Kincaid."

"Haven't heard of him," Ebenezar said.

"He works for the Archive," I said. "And he's good at killing vampires. I'm going in with those two, but we need someone standing by to get us out in a hurry."

"I'm your driver, eh?" he mused. "And I suppose you

want someone to lock down Mavra's power, if she's got access to that much magic."

"It hadn't occurred to me, really," I lied. "But hey, if you are bored and want to do that to pass the time while you keep the car running, I don't mind."

The old man's teeth flashed in a wolfish smile. "I'll keep that in mind, Hoss."

"I don't have anything to use as a channel, though," I said. "Are you going to be able to target her without hair or blood or something?"

"Yes," Ebenezar said. He didn't elaborate how he'd do it. "Though I doubt I can get her down to nothing. I can prevent her from working anything big, but she might have enough left in her to be annoying."

"I'll take what I can get," I said. "But we need to move right now. She's already taken several people."

"Vampires are that way," Ebenezar agreed in a casual tone, but I saw the way his eyes narrowed. He didn't care for monsters like Mavra any more than I did. I could have kissed him.

"Thank you."

He shook his head. "What about her death curse?"

I blinked.

"You'd thought of that, right?" he asked.

"What death curse?" I stammered.

"Use your head, boy," Ebenezar said. "If she's got a wizard's power, she might well be able to level a death curse at you when she goes down."

"Oh, come on," I muttered. "That's no fair. She's *already* dead."

"Hadn't thought of that, eh?" he asked.

"No," I said. "Though I should have. Been a busy couple of days, what with dodging all the certain death coming at me from every direction. Not a second to spare for thinking. We have precious little time."

He grunted. "So where we going?"

I checked the time at a passing bank billboard. "A picnic."

Chapter Twenty-eight

What looked like a small army had invaded a portion
of Wolf Lake Park and claimed it in the name of God
and Clan Murphy. Cars filled the little parking lot
nearby, and lined the nearest lane for a hundred yards
in either direction. Summer had been generous with the
rain for once, and all the trees in the park had put on
glorious autumn colors so bright that if I scrunched up
my eyes until my lashes blurred my vision they almost
seemed to be afire.

In the park, a couple of gazebos had been stockpiled
with tables and lots of food, and a pair of portable pavil-
ions flanked them, giving shade to maybe a dozen people
who had fired up their grills and were singeing meat.
Music was playing from several different locations, the
beats of the various songs stumbling into one another,
and evidently someone had brought a generator, because
there was an enormous TV set up out in the grass while
a dozen men crowded around it, talking loudly, laughing,
and arguing about what looked to be a college football
game.

There were also a pair of volleyball nets and a bad-
minton net, and enough Frisbees flying around to foul
up radar at the local airports. A giant, inflatable castle
wobbled dramatically as a dozen children bounced
around on the inside of it, caroming off the walls and
one another with equal amounts of enthusiasm. More
kids ran in packs all over the place, and there must have
been a dozen dogs gleefully racing one another and begging food from anyone who seemed to have some. The
air smelled like charcoal, mesquite, and insect repellent,
and buzzed with happy chatter.

I stood there for a minute, watching the festivities.
Spotting Murphy in a crowd of a couple of hundred peo-

ple wasn't easy. I tried to be methodical, sweeping the area with my gaze from left to right. I didn't spot Murphy, but as I stood there it occurred to me that a bruised and battered man better than six and a half feet tall in a black leather duster didn't exactly blend in with the crowd at the Murphy picnic. A couple of the men around the television had spotted me with the kind of attention that made me think that they were with the law.

Another man walking by with a white Styrofoam cooler on one shoulder noticed the men at the television and followed their gaze to me. He was in his mid-thirties and about an inch or two over average height. His brown hair was cut short, as was a neatly cropped goatee. He had the kind of build that dangerous men seem to develop—not enormous, pretty muscle, but the kind of lean sinew that indicated speed and endurance as well as strength. And he was a cop. Don't ask me how I could tell—it was just something about the way he held himself, the way he kept track of his surroundings.

He promptly changed course, walked up to me, and said, "Hey, there."

"Hey," I said.

His tone was overtly friendly, but I could taste the suspicion in it. "Mind if I ask what you're doing here?"

I didn't have time for this crap. "Yes."

He dropped the fake friendliness. "Listen, buddy. This is a family get-together. Maybe you could find another part of the park to stand around looking forboding."

"Free country," I said. "Public park."

"Which has been reserved by the Murphy family for the day," he said. "Look, buddy, you're scaring the kids. Walk."

"Or you'll call the cops?" I asked.

He set the cooler down and squared off facing me, just barely far enough away to avoid a sucker punch. He looked relaxed, too. He knew what he was doing. "I'll do you a favor and call the ambulance first."

By this time we were getting more attention from the football fans. I was frustrated enough to be tempted to

push him a little bit more, but there was no sense in it.
I assumed that the cops in the family were off today,
but if I got beaten up someone might call in and find
out about Emma's death. That was a good way to get
bogged down in a holding cell and dead.

The guy faced me with confidence, even though I had
a head and shoulders on him and outweighed him by
forty or fifty pounds. He knew if anything happened,
he'd have a ton of help.

Must be a nice feeling.

I lifted a hand by way of capitulation. "I'll go. I just
need to speak to Karrin Murphy for a moment.
Business."

His expression flickered with surprise that was quickly
hidden. "Oh." He looked around. "Over there," he said.
"She's reffing the soccer game."

"Thanks."

"Sure," the man said. "You know, it wouldn't kill you
to be a little more polite."

"Why take chances," I muttered, turning my back on
him and heading over to the makeshift soccer field.
There were a bunch of rugrats too big for playground
equipment and too young for pimples playing with what
could kindly be construed as abundant enthusiasm while
a few motherly types looked on. But I didn't see
Murphy.

I began to turn around and start another sweep. At
this rate I would have to ask someone for directions.

"Harry?" Murphy's voice called from behind me.

I turned around. My jaw dropped open. I was lucky
none of the kids kicked their soccer ball into my exposed
uvula. It took me a minute to stammer, "You're wearing
a dress."

She glowered up at me. Murphy wasn't going to qualify under anyone's definition of *willowy* or *svelte*, but she
had the build of a gymnast—tough, flexible, and strong.
Generally speaking, being five-nothing, a hundred and
nothing, and female had made her professional life less
than pleasant, including getting her landed in charge of
Special Investigations—a post that was the career equiv-

alent to being exiled to the Bastille, or maybe left out for the ants.

Murphy had excelled at her new job, much to the distress of the folks who had gotten her put there. Partly, to be sure, because she had engaged the services of the only professional wizard in Chicago. But also because she was damned good at her job. She'd been able to inspire loyalty, to judge and employ her detectives' skills effectively, and to keep everyone together through some fairly terrifying times—both in my company and outside of it. She was smart, tough, dedicated, and everything else an ideal leader of a police division should be.

Except male. In a profession that was still very much a boys' club.

As a result, Murphy had made a number of accommodations to the male ego. She was an award-winning marksman, she had taken more than her share of martial-arts tournaments, and she continued to train ferociously, most of it with, among, and around cops. There was no one in the department who had any questions about whether or not Murphy could introduce the baddest bad guys to new vistas of physical pain in hand-to-hand, and no one who had survived the battle with the loup-garou would ever doubt her skill with firearms or her courage again. But being Murphy, she went the extra mile. She wore her hair shorter than she liked it, and she went almost entirely without makeup or adornments. She dressed functionally—never scruffy, mind you, but almost always very subdued and practical—and never, ever wore a dress.

This one was long, full, and yellow. And it had flowers. It looked quite lovely and utterly . . . wrong. Just wrong. Murphy in a dress. My world felt askew.

"I hate these things," she complained. She looked down, brushing at the skirt, and swished it back and forth a little. "I always did."

"Wow. Uh, why are you wearing it, then?"

"My mom made it for me." Murphy sighed. "So, I thought, you know, maybe it would make her happy to see me in it." She took a whistle from around her neck,

promoted one of the kids to referee, and started walking.
I fell into pace beside her.

"You found them," she said.

"Yeah. Our driver is here, and I called Kincaid about
twenty minutes ago. He'll have the hardware nearby and
waiting for us." I took a deep breath. "And we need to
move in a hurry."

"Why?" she asked.

"I'm pretty sure your brothers and sisters in law enforcement are going to want to sit me down for a long
talk. I'd rather they didn't until I've closed a couple of
accounts." I gave her a brief rundown of Emma's
murder.

"Christ," she said. After a few steps she added, "At
least this time around I heard it from you first. I've got
a change of clothes in the car. What else do I need
to know?"

"Tell you on the way," I said.

"Right," she said. "Look, I promised my mom I'd
come see her before I left. My sister wanted to talk to
me about something. Two minutes."

"Sure," I said, and we veered toward one of the pavil-
ions. "You have a big family. How many?"

"Couple of hundred the last time I looked," she said.
"There, in the white blouse. That's mother. The girl in
the tight . . . everything is my baby sister, Lisa."

"Baby sister has pretty legs," I noted. "But those
shorts must be a little binding."

"The clothes keep the blood from reaching her brain,"
Murphy said. "At least that's my theory." She stepped
under the pavilion, smiling, and said, "Hi, Mom!"

Murphy's mom was taller than her daughter, but she
had that kind of matronly plumpness that comes with
age, pasta, and a comfortable life. Her hair was dark
blond, threaded through with grey that she had made no
effort at all to conceal, and it was held back off her face
with a jade comb. She was wearing a white blouse, a
floral print skirt, and tinted sunglasses. She turned
around to face Murphy as we walked up, and her face

lit for a moment. "Karrin," she said, her tone warm and wary.

Murphy held out her hands as she walked over to her mom, and the two clasped hands and hugged. There was a sort of stiffness to the gesture that suggested ritual, formality, and less-than-pleasant emotional undercurrents. They batted a few chatty words back and forth, and while they did I noted something odd. There had been at least a dozen people under the pavilion when we came in, but most of them had wandered away. In fact, there was a widening circle of open space clearing out around the pavilion.

Murphy didn't miss it, either. She glanced back at me, and I quirked an eyebrow at her. She twitched one shoulder in a minimal shrug, and went back to talking with her mom.

A minute later only five people were within twenty or thirty feet: me, Murphy, her mom, little sister, Lisa, and the man whose lap she was draped across. The guy with the cooler. They were behind Murphy and me, and I turned my body halfway so that I could look at them without totally ignoring Murphy and her mom.

Lisa reminded me a lot of Murphy, had Murphy been an estrogen princess rather than a warrior princess. Blond hair, fair skin, a pert nose, and cornflower blue eyes. She wore a scarlet baby-doll T-shirt with the Chicago Bulls' team logo stretched out over her chest. Her shorts had been blue jeans at some point, but they had come down with a bad case of spandex envy. She wore flip-flops and dangled them from her painted toes as she sat across the lap of the man I presumed to be the fiancé Murphy had mentioned.

He made quite a contrast with Lisa. He was a bit older than her, for one. Not double her age or anything, but definitely older. He was being careful not to let any expression show on his face, and it made me think that he was worried about something.

"Mom," Murphy was saying. "This is my friend Harry. Harry, this is my mother, Marion."

I put on my best smile for Mother Murphy and stepped forward, offering her my hand. "Charmed, ma'am."

She shook my hand and gave me a calculating look. Her grip reminded me of Murphy's—her hands were small, strong, and had been hardened by work. "Thank you, Harry."

"And this is my baby sister, Lisa," Murphy said, turning to face her for the first time. "Lisa, this is—" Murphy froze, her words dying into a choking gasp. "Rich," she said after a second, her voice shaking with a tide of emotion. "What are you doing here?"

He murmured something to Lisa. The girl slipped off his lap, and he stood slowly up. "Hello, Karrin. You're looking well."

"You miserable son of a bitch," Murphy spat. "What do you think you're doing?"

"Karrin," Murphy's mom snapped. "There is no place for that kind of language here."

"Oh, please!" Lisa cried.

"I don't have to put up with that, Karrin," Rich growled.

Murphy clenched her hands into fists.

"Whoa, whoa, people," I said. I must have been feeling suicidal, because I took a step forward and placed myself in the middle of the circle of angry stares. "Come on, guys. At least let me get introduced to everyone before the fighting starts, so I'll know who to duck."

There was a second of heavy silence, and then Rich snorted out a quiet laugh and subsided back into his chair. Lisa folded her arms. Murphy tensed up a little, but with her it was a good sign. She always got that deadly relaxed look to her stance when she was about to kick someone's ass.

"Thank you, Harry," Mama Murphy said in a loud tone. She stepped forward with a paper plate laden with a hamburger and passed it to me. "It's nice to know there is another adult present. Why don't we get everyone introduced, Karrin."

I checked the burger. It had everything on it but

cheese. Just the way I liked it. I was favorably impressed with Mama Murphy. And I was starving, too. More bonus points.

Murphy stepped up beside me. "Right. Introductions. Harry, this is my baby sister, Lisa." She glared daggers at the man. "And this is Rich. My second husband."

Oh, dear Lord.

Murphy stared from her mom to her sister to Rich. "I know we haven't talked in a while, Mother. So let's get caught up. Why don't we start with why Lisa is engaged to my ex-husband and none of you even bothered to *tell* me?"

Lisa lifted her chin. "It isn't my fault if you're too much of a bitch to get a man to stay with you. Rich wanted an actual woman, which is why you aren't involved with him anymore. And I didn't tell you because it was none of your damned business."

"Lisa," scolded Mama Murphy. "That is not the kind of language a lady uses."

"And those aren't the kind of clothes a lady wears," Murphy said, her voice tart. "She might as well talk like a whore, too."

"Karrin!" Mama Murphy protested, her voice shocked.

There wasn't time for this, either. I stepped up next to Murphy and gave Rich a half-desperate look.

"Ohhhhh-kay," Rich said. He stood up from his chair, slipping an arm around Lisa's shoulders. "This is no good. Come on, baby. Time for a walk until you cool off. Let's go find a beer."

"Murph," I said. I leaned down enough to mutter at her ear, "Remember. No time."

Murphy folded her arms, her expression unrepentant, but at least she turned away from her sister. Rich and Murphy Spice walked off toward the other pavilion.

Mother Murphy waited until they were gone before she faced us, her frown speaking volumes of disapproval. "For goodness' sake, Karrin. You aren't children anymore."

Explosion averted, at least for the moment. I seized the opportunity to eat the hamburger.

Oh. My. God. For food this good, I'd marry Murphy just for her mom's cooking on holidays.

"I can't believe it," Murphy said. "Rich. I thought he was working in New Orleans."

"He is," Mama Murphy said. "Lisa went down for Mardi Gras. Apparently he had to arrest her."

"Mother," Murphy protested. "You let her go to Mardi Gras? I had to sneak out of the house to go to the prom."

Mother Murphy sighed. "Karrin, you're the oldest child. She's the youngest. All parents get a little more relaxed along the way."

"Apparently," Murphy said, her voice bitter, "that includes tolerating felonies like providing alcohol to a minor. She's underage for beer until next month."

"It's always about work, isn't it," Mama Murphy said.

"This has nothing to do with work," Murphy shot back. "Mother, he's twice her age. How could you?"

I partook of near-divine hamburger and kept my head down, and felt wise for doing so.

"In the first place, dear, it isn't up to me. It's your sister's life. And he isn't twice her age. Worse things have happened." She sighed. "We all felt Lisa should be the one to talk to you, but you know how she hates confronting you."

"She's a gutless little harlot, you mean."

"That will be enough, young lady," Mama Murphy said, her voice crackling with heat and steel. "Your sister found a man who genuinely loves her. I might not be entirely confident about the notion, but she's old enough to make her own choices. And besides, you know how much I always liked Rich."

"Yes, I know," Murphy growled. "Can we talk about something else?"

"All right."

"Where are the boys?"

Mama Murphy rolled her eyes and nodded at the group around the big television out on the grass. "Somewhere in there. You can hear them yelling if you listen."

Murphy snorted. "I'm surprised Rich isn't watching the game, too."

"Karrin, I know you're still angry with him. But it's hardly the man's fault that he wanted to start a family."

"That was just a rationalization, Mother," Murphy said. "What he wanted was for me to stay home so that I wouldn't make him look bad at work."

"I'm sorry you still think that," Mama Murphy replied. "But you're cheapening him. It isn't as though he could start a family by himself. He wanted a woman willing to do that with him. You made it clear that you didn't."

"Because I didn't want to give up what I do."

"There are other people in the family who have taken up your father's duties," Mother Murphy said, her voice bitter. "There's no need for you to do it."

"That isn't why I became a cop."

Mother Murphy shook her head and sighed. "Karrin. Your brothers are all serving. They're taking their time in settling down. I don't want to tell you what to do with your life—"

Murphy snorted.

"—but I do want to have the chance to hold my grandchildren while I'm still young enough and strong enough to do it. Rich wants to settle down, and your sister wants to be the woman he does it with. Is that such a bad thing?"

"I just can't see you flying to New Orleans every month to visit them."

"Of course not, dear," Mama Murphy replied. "I don't have that kind of money. That's why they'll be settling down here."

Murphy's mouth dropped open.

"Rich has already put in for his transfer and had it approved. He'll be working for the FBI office here in Illinois."

"I don't *believe* this," Murphy grated. "My own sister. Here. With Rich. And you're just going to keep throwing this in my face."

"Not everything is about you, Karrin," her mother said, her voice prim. "I'm sure we can all be adults about this."

"But he's my ex-*husband*."

"Whom you *divorced*," Murphy's mother replied. But the harsh words were delivered in a gentle tone. "For goodness' sake, Karrin, you've already made it clear that you didn't want him. Why should you care if someone else does?"

"I don't," Murphy protested. She waved a vague hand. "But Lisa isn't just 'someone.' "

"Ah," said Mama Murphy.

Just then Murphy's cell phone chirped. She checked it, frowned, and said, "Excuse me." Then she walked twenty or thirty feet away from me, out into the sunshine, head bent to the phone.

"That will be work, I assume," Mama Murphy said to me. "You're the private investigator, aren't you?"

"Yes, ma'am."

"I saw you on *Larry Fowler*."

I sighed. "Yeah."

"Is it true that he's suing you for demolishing his studio?"

"Yeah. And his car. I had to get a lawyer and everything. The lawyer says that Fowler's guy won't have a case, even in civil court, but it's expensive and it's taking forever."

"The legal system can be that way," Mama Murphy agreed. "I'm sorry my daughter dragged you into our family squabble."

"I volunteered," I said.

"And now you regret it?"

I shook my head. "Hell—uh, heck, no. She's been there for me too many times, Mrs. Murphy. I don't know if you're aware of how dangerous her job can be. The kinds of things she faces in Special Investigations can be especially difficult. And disturbing. Your daughter saves lives. There are people who would be dead right now if she hadn't been there. I'm several of them."

Mama Murphy was quiet for a moment before she

said, "Before they established Special Investigations, the department routinely handed all those cases to senior detectives in the Thirteenth Precinct. The cases were referred to as black cat investigations. The detectives as black cats."

"I didn't know that," I said.

She nodded. "My husband was a black cat for twelve years."

I frowned. "Murphy never told me that."

"I never told her. And Karrin never knew her father very well," Mama Murphy said. "He was away so much of the time. And he died when she was only eleven."

"Line of duty?"

Momma Murphy shook her head. "The work got to him. He . . . he grew distant and started to drink too much. And one night at his desk he took his own life." She faced me and said, her voice tired and sad, "You see, Harry, my Collin never spoke of it, but I can read between lines as well as anyone. I know what my daughter is facing."

That hung in the air between us for a moment.

"She's good," I said. "Not just skilled. She's got a good heart, Mrs. Murphy. I'd sooner trust her with my life than anyone else in the world. It isn't fair for you to give her a hard time about her job."

Mama Murphy's eyes sparkled, though they were also a little sad. "She thinks she's protecting me from the awful truth, Harry, when I complain about her work and she keeps things secret in reply. It makes her happy to know that her mother is not even aware of such dangerous things. I could never take that away from her."

I arched an eyebrow at Mama Murphy. Then smiled.

"What?" she asked.

"I see where she gets it," I said.

Murphy turned back to me, her expression hard, and beckoned me. I went over to her.

"It's Kincaid," she said, her voice held tight and quiet. "He says to tell you he's at the shelter and the Red Cross has shown up."

"What? Hell's bells."

She nodded. "They do a blood drive every three months out of the shelter's basement."

Where the Black Court was. Where the coffins and Renfields and darkhounds were. Mavra and her brood would never allow themselves to be seen. The Red Cross volunteers were as good as dead if they went in the basement. "Oh, crap."

"I'm calling it in," she said.

"No," I said, alarmed. "You can't do that."

"Like hell I can't," she said. "People are in danger."

"And they're going to be in *more* danger if this escalates," I said. "Tell Kincaid to try to delay the Red Cross people. We'll get down there and hit Mavra right now, before the volunteers can put themselves in the line of fire."

Murphy scowled up at me, her voice rising a little. People started to give us surreptitious looks. "Don't tell me how to do my job."

"This *isn't* your job, Murph," I said. "Do you remember when I told you that I'd tell you everything? Do you remember that you agreed to trust my judgment? That you wouldn't go calling in the cavalry on these things?"

Her expression became even more furious. "Do you think that I'm too stupid to know how to handle this?"

"I think that you're way too worked up already. And that you can't let this family thing get in the way of making the right decision. Getting the mortal authorities involved would be bad for everyone, Murph. Bad for you. Bad for SI. You might win the day, but when these things hit back, your people are going to suffer."

For a second I thought she was going to strangle me. "What do you expect me to do?"

I got in her face, and I didn't care if she avoided my eyes or not. "I *expect* you to listen to the person who knows what he's talking about. I expect you to trust me, Murph, the way I trusted you. Get on the damn phone and tell Kincaid what I said and ask where to meet him. Then we take care of business."

The eye contact got more intense, but Murphy shivered and broke it off before it could go any deeper.

"Fine," she said. "I'll do it. But don't think I won't kick your ass over this later. Now back off before you blow up my phone."

I did, returning to the pavilion.

Mama Murphy regarded me speculatively. "Work?"

I nodded.

"That was quite an argument," she said.

I shrugged.

"It would seem that you won it."

I sighed and said wryly, "And I'll pay for it later."

"You'll both be leaving, then?"

"Yeah."

Mama Murphy looked back and forth between me and Murphy for a moment and then said, "Let me get you another burger before you go."

I blinked at her.

She assembled food, including a second burger for Murphy, and passed me the paper plates. She frowned at my hands, then up at my face, and asked, "Will you take care of my daughter?"

"Yes, ma'am. Of course I will."

Her blue eyes flashed fiercely, and she said, "Let me get you a piece of cake."

Chapter Twenty-nine

Murphy grabbed a gym bag out of her car and then followed me to Ebenezar's truck. She stopped about twenty feet short of it and said, "You're kidding me."

"Come on," I said. "You want to show up where there might be some trouble in your own car? That'd be nice for responding emergency units to see. So get in."

"What does it run on, coal?"

Ebenezar stuck his bald head out of the window, scowling. "No idea. Mostly I just turn it loose to hunt down dinner for itself."

"Murph," I said. "This is Ebenezar McCoy. Ebenezar, this is Karrin Murphy."

"You," Ebenezar said without approval. "I heard you've given the boy a hard time."

Murphy scowled. "Who the hell are you?"

"My teacher," I told her in a quieter voice. "A friend."

She glanced at me, then pursed her lips. She didn't miss the shotgun or the staff in the truck. "You're coming along to help?"

"As long as you don't think I'm too old, girlie," he drawled, heavy on the sarcasm.

"You got a driver's license? You driven Chicago streets lately?"

The old wizard scowled at her.

"Thought so," she said. "Move over."

He sputtered. "What?"

"I'm driving," she said. "So move."

I sighed. "Better move over, sir," I told Ebenezar. "We're in a hurry."

Murphy's gym bag thumped onto the ground and she stared at me with her mouth open.

"What?" I asked.

"*Sir?*" she said, her voice incredulous.

I scowled at her and ducked my head.

She picked up her bag, blinked a couple of times, and said, in her professionally politest tones, "If you don't mind, Mister McCoy, I know the streets better, and there are lives at stake."

Ebenezar's scowl had been half subverted by a small smile, but he said, "Bah. I'm too old to see the street signs anyway." He opened the door and started scooting. "Get in, get in. Come on, Hoss; we ain't got time to wait on you."

Murphy did not go so far as to slap her magnetic cop light on the top of the truck, but she got us to a parking garage near Mavra's lair in a big hurry. She knew the streets of the old town as well as anyone I'd ever seen, and she regarded niceties like red lights, one-way streets, and right-of-way with an almost magnificent lack of concern. Ebenezar's old truck kept up with her gamely enough, though I found my head bouncing off the roof a couple of times.

I told Murphy what I'd learned about the vampires' lair on the way.

Murphy shook her head. "Damn. This isn't what I expected. That they'd take something right in the middle of so many people."

"Me either," I said. "But that only means we need to move sooner instead of later. The longer the vamps are there, the more of those hostages they're going to bleed out, and the greater the risk of one of their Renfields snapping and opening up on pedestrians with an assault rifle."

"Assault rifles," Murphy said. "And hostages. Jesus, Harry, people could die."

"No *could* about it. They're already dying," I replied. "At least three bodies already. And the Renfields are just a matter of time."

"What if you're wrong?" Murphy said. "Do you really expect me to charge in guns blazing against people who might or might not already be dead? I have an obligation to protect citizens, not to sacrifice them."

My teeth clacked together as the truck went over a heavy bump. "These are the Black Court. They kill, and they do it frequently. Not only that, but they can propagate their kind more rapidly than any other vampire. If we let a nest of them go unmolested, we could potentially have dozens of them in a few days. In two weeks there could be hundreds. Something has to be done, and now."

Murphy shook her head. "But it doesn't mean it needs to be vigilante work. Harry, give me three hours to establish probable cause and I'll have every cop and every SWAT team in two hundred miles ready to take on that nest."

"And you'll tell them what, exactly?" I said. " 'Basement full of vampires' is not going to cut it, and you know it. And if they go in with blinders on, cops will get killed.''

"And if it's us?'' Murphy asked. "What then? We kick down the door, shoot anything standing, and then make like we're the Flying Van Helsings? A direct assault on a wary target is one of the best ways in the world to get killed.''

"So we figure something out," I said. "We get a plan.''

Murphy shot me a look past Ebenezar, who evidently had decided to stay out of it. "This isn't like the Wal-Mart plan with the marbles, is it?''

"I'll tell you when I know. Let's get there and see if we can find out first. Maybe Kincaid will have something.''

"Yeah," Murphy said without much hope. "Maybe. Here, this is where Kincaid is meeting us.''

It wasn't a pleasant neighborhood. The city had been working on urban renewal projects for decades, but the lion's share of the money had gone to restore higher-profile, more infamous neighborhoods, such as Cabrini Green. In that time, many neighborhoods that had been borderline steadily eroded, and had usurped the infamous-neighborhood crown. The slum is dead. Long live the slum.

I'd seen worse, but not many. Tall buildings and narrow alleys choked out a lot of the sunshine. Most windows below the third or fourth floor had been boarded up. Ground level commercial properties were largely vacant. The storm drains were clogged with litter and other urban detritus, most of the streetlights were out, and graffiti and gang signs had been spray-painted everywhere. The air smelled like mildew, garbage, and exhaust. The residents of the neighborhood moved with brisk purpose, confidence, and flat eyes as they walked, doing everything they could to indicate by body language that they were not good targets for assault or robbery.

I spotted a drug house in the first ten seconds of looking around. The burned-out hulk of an abandoned car had been stripped for parts before it had been set on fire, and I had a notion that Murphy was the first cop to visit in the past several weeks.

But there was something missing.

Bums. Transients. Homeless folk. Winos. Bag ladies. Even in broad daylight there should have been someone collecting cans, panhandling change, or shambling along drinking from a bottle still covered with a paper bag.

But there wasn't. Everyone moving was getting from one place to another, not eking out a living from the environment.

"Look kind of quiet to you here?" Murphy asked, voice tight.

"Yeah," I said.

"They've been killing," she said, almost spitting the words.

"Maybe. Maybe not," Ebenezar said.

I nodded. "There's dark power at work here. People sense that, even if they don't know what it is. You're feeling it now."

"What do you mean?"

I shrugged. "The presence of dark magic. It makes you feel nervous and angry. If you forced yourself to calm down and tried to sense it, you could feel it. It leaves a kind of stain around it."

"Stinks," rumbled Ebenezar.

"What does that have to do with missing street people?" Murphy asked.

"You've been here about three minutes, and the power bothers you already. Imagine living in it. Getting a little more afraid every day. Angrier. More demoralized. People get rattled enough to leave, even if they don't understand why. Over the long term this kind of power breeds its own wasteland."

"You mean that the vampires have been here for a while?" she asked.

"To have this much effect, it's been days at least," I said, nodding.

"More like two weeks." Ebenezar grunted with assurance. "Maybe three."

"God," Murphy said, shivering. "That's scary."

"Yeah. If they've been here that long, it means Mavra has something in mind."

She frowned. "You mean that this vampire came here and then chose when to make you aware of its presence? This could be a trap."

"It's possible. Paranoid, but possible."

Her mouth tightened into a line. "You didn't mention that at breakfast."

"We're doing battle with the living dead, Murph. Expect the occasional curveball."

"Are you patronizing me now?"

I shook my head. "No. Honest. Where's Kincaid?"

"Second level of this parking garage," Murphy said.

"Stop on the first level," I told her.

"Why?"

"He doesn't know about Ebenezar, and I don't want to spook him. We'll walk up and meet him."

Ebenezar nodded to us and said, "Good call, Hoss. Decent gunman can be twitchy. I'll give you a minute, then drive on up."

Murphy stopped the truck and we got out. I waited until we were several paces from the truck before I lowered my voice and said, "I know. You're afraid."

She glared at me, and started to deny it. But she knew better, and shrugged one shoulder instead. "Some."

"So am I. It's okay."

"I thought I was over this," she said. Her jaw tightened. "I mean, the night terrors are gone. I can sleep again. But it isn't like before, Harry. I used to get scared, but I'd be excited too. I would have wanted to do it. But I don't want this. I'm so afraid that I'm about to throw up. Which sucks."

"You're scared because you've learned things," I told her. "You know the kinds of things you're fighting," I said. "You know what could happen. You'd be an idiot if you *weren't* afraid. I wouldn't want someone with me who didn't have enough sense to be worried."

She nodded, but asked, "What if I freeze up on you again?"

"You won't."

"It could happen."

"It won't," I said.

"You sure?"

I winked at her and twirled my staff in one hand. "I wouldn't be betting my life on it otherwise. You've got my back, Murph. Shut up and dance."

She nodded, her expression remote. "There's nothing we can do to stop these things."

The *we* had changed. She meant the police. "No. Not without getting a lot of good cops killed."

"Those people with the vampires. These Renfields. We'll have to kill some of them. Won't we?"

"Probably," I said in a quiet voice.

"It isn't their fault they were taken."

"I know. We'll do whatever we can to avoid killing them. But from what I know about them, they're too far gone to leave us many options."

"Do you remember Agent Wilson?" Murphy asked.

"The Fed you shot off my back."

Murph's expression flickered, though it wasn't quite a flinch. "Yeah. He went outside the law to bring down the people he thought were beyond its reach, and now we're making that same choice."

"No, we aren't," I said.

"No? Why not?"

"Because they aren't people."

Murphy frowned.

I thought about it. "Even if they were, assuming they were still as dangerous and untouchable, would it change anything?"

"I don't know," she said. "That's what scares me."

For as long as I'd known her, Murphy had upheld the law. She had a good head on her shoulders when it came to the nature of good and evil and of right and wrong, but her first duty had been to the law. She'd believed in it, that it was the best way to help and protect her fellow man. She'd had faith that the power of the law, while imperfect, was absolute—almost holy. It was a rallying point in her soul, a foundation block of her strength.

But several years of staring out at the darkness had showed her that the law was both blind and deaf to some of the nastier parts of the world. She'd seen things that moved in the shadows, perverting the purpose of the law to use it as a weapon against the people she had sworn to defend. Her faith had taken a beating, or she wouldn't even have considered stepping outside the boundaries of her authority. And she knew it.

That knowledge cost her dearly. There weren't any tears in her eyes, but I knew that they were there, on the inside, while she mourned the death of her faith.

"I don't know the right thing to do," she said.

"Neither do I," I said. "But someone has to do something. And we're the only ones around. Either we choose to take a stand now or we choose to stand around at all the funerals regretting it later."

"Yeah," Murphy said. She took a deep, almost meditative breath. "I guess I needed to hear that said out loud." A small but violent light flared to life behind her eyes. "Let's go. I'm ready."

"Murph," I said.

She tilted her head and looked at me. My lips suddenly felt very dry.

"You look good in the dress."

Her eyes shone. "Really?"

"Oh, yeah."

The eye contact got dangerously intense and I shied off. Murphy let out a low, quiet laugh and touched the side of my face. Her fingers were warm, the touch light and delicate. "Thank you, Harry."

We came up to the second level of the garage together, walking with businesslike strides. The lights were out. In the depths of shadows I could see two vans parked side by side. The first one was a beat-up old fossil of a vehicle, born in an era when people would have thought it absurd to make a van "mini." A Red Cross decal on the driver's door proclaimed its identity.

The second was a white rental van. We approached, and Kincaid slid the side door open. I couldn't see him very well in the shadows. "Didn't take long," he commented. "You walk fast."

"Wheelman's here," I said. "He's coming up in an old Ford truck in a minute. Wanted to let you know first."

Kincaid glanced at the ramp and nodded. "Fine. What do we know?"

I told him. He took it all in without speaking, glanced once at the map Bob had drawn me, and said, "Suicide."

"Eh?" I said.

Kincaid shrugged. "We go in there guns blazing, we're going to get burned two feet from the door."

"I tried to tell him that," Murphy said.

"So we get a plan," I said. Any suggestions?"

"Blow up the building," Kincaid said without looking up. "That works good for vampires. Then soak what's left in gasoline. Set it on fire. Then blow it all up again."

"For future reference, I was sort of hoping for a suggestion that didn't sound like it came from that Bolshevik Muppet with all the dynamite."

"Check," Kincaid said.

I peered at the van. "Hey. Where are the Red Cross people?"

"I killed and dismembered them," Kincaid said.

I blinked.

Kincaid stared at me for a second. "That was a joke."

"Right," I said. "Sorry. Now where are they?"

"On their lunch break. They somehow got the idea that I was a cop and that they would interfere with a sting if they went into the shelter. I gave them a C-note and told them to go grab lunch."

"They believed you?" I asked.

"They somehow got the idea that I had a badge."

Murphy eyed Kincaid. "That's the kind of thing that's illegal to own."

Kincaid turned to dig in the white van. "Sorry if I came afoul of your sensibilities, Lieutenant. Next time I'll let them walk in and get killed. I added the hundred to your bill, Dresden." A dark jacket with the Red Cross logo on the shoulder flew out of the van and hit Murphy in the chest. She caught it, and a second later caught the matching baseball cap that followed. "Put them on," Kincaid said. "Our ticket to get close enough to get the drop on them. Maybe even get some walking targets out of the way."

"Where did you get those?" I asked.

Kincaid leaned out of the van enough to arch an eyebrow at me. "Found 'em."

"Kincaid," Murphy said, "Give me the keys to the Red Cross van."

"Why?"

"So I can change," Murphy said, her voice tight.

Kincaid shook his head. "You got nothing everyone here hasn't seen before, Lieutenant," he said. After a moment he glanced at me and said, "Unless . . ."

"Yes," I said through clenched teeth. "I've seen that sort of thing. It's been a while, but I dimly remember."

"Just checking," Kincaid said.

"Now give her the damned keys."

"Yassuh, Massah Dresden," he said laconically, and tossed a ring with only two keys at Murphy. She caught it, let out a growling sound, and stalked over to the Red Cross van. She opened it and climbed in.

"Not bad," Kincaid said, low enough that Murphy wouldn't have heard him. He kept rooting around in the minivan, evidently without feeling any need for a light. "Her in a dress, I mean. Makes you notice she's a woman."

"Shut up, Kincaid."

I could hear the wolfish smile, even if I couldn't see it. "Yassuh. Now don't look. I'm getting dressed and I blush easy."

"Blow me, Kincaid," I growled.

"Don't you owe me enough already?" I heard him moving around. "You give any more thought to shutting down Mavra's sorcery?"

"Yeah," I said. Ebenezar's truck growled as it changed gears. "Our wheelman is going to handle it."

"You sure he can?"

"Yeah," I said. "Here he comes."

Kincaid stepped out of the van with guns strapped all over attachment points on a suit of black ballistic body armor that looked a generation or two ahead of the latest police-issue. He had one set of big-ass revolvers, a couple of those tiny, deadly machine guns that shoot so fast they sound like a band saw, and a bunch of automatics. They all came in matching pairs, presumably because he had an audition for the lead in a John Woo movie later that day.

Kincaid donned a second Red Cross jacket to help hide all the weaponry, and added his own matching cap like Murphy's. He watched Ebenezar's truck coming, and said, "So who is this guy?"

Just then Ebenezar's truck rolled up, its headlights in our eyes until it had all but passed. "So, Hoss," Ebenezar was saying through the open window. "Who is this hired gun?"

The old man and the mercenary saw one another and stared at each other from maybe seven or eight feet apart. Time stopped for one of those frozen, crystallized instants.

And then both of them went for their guns.

Chapter Thirty

Kincaid was faster. One of the guns he'd had on him got to his hand so quick it might have been teleported there from under his coat. But even as he raised the gun toward the old wizard, there was a flash of emerald light from a plain steel ring on Ebenezar's right hand. I felt a low, harsh hum in the air and a surge of dizziness, and Kincaid's pistol ripped its way out of his fingers and shot away into the shadows of the parking garage.

I swayed on my feet. Kincaid recovered before I did and a second gun came out from under the Red Cross jacket. I looked up to see Ebenezar settle the old shotgun's stock against his shoulder, both barrels squarely on Kincaid's head.

"What the hell!" I blurted, and threw myself between them. It put Kincaid's pistol in line with my spine and Ebenezar's shotgun in line with my head, which seemed like a positive at the moment. As long as I was in front of the weapons, the two couldn't get a clean shot at each other. "What the hell do you think you're *doing?*" I demanded.

"Hoss," snarled Ebenezar, "you don't know what you're dealing with. Get down."

"Put the shotgun down," I said. "Kincaid, put the pistol away."

Kincaid's voice, behind me, sounded no different than it had at breakfast. "That sounds like a fairly low-percentage move for me, Dresden. No offense."

"I told you," Ebenezar said, his voice different—cold and terrible and hard. I'd never heard the old man speak that way before. "I told you if I ever saw you again, I'd kill you."

"Which is one reason you haven't seen me," Kincaid answered. "There's no point to this. If we start shooting, the kid's going to get hit. Neither of us has an interest in that."

"I'm supposed to believe you give a damn about him?" Ebenezar snarled.

"Half a damn, maybe," Kincaid said. "I sort of like him. But what I meant was there's no profit for either of us in killing him."

"Put the damned guns down!" I choked. "And stop talking about me like I'm a kid who isn't here."

"Why are you here?" Ebenezar demanded, ignoring me.

"I'm a hired gun," Kincaid said. "Dresden hired me. Do the math, Blackstaff. Of all people you should know how it goes." The tone of Kincaid's voice changed to something thoughtful. "But the kid doesn't know what we do. Does he?"

"Harry, get *down,*" Ebenezar said, speaking to me again.

"You want me down?" I said. I met Ebenezar's eyes and said, "Then I want your word you aren't going to open up on Kincaid until we've talked."

"Dammit, boy. I'm not giving my word to that—"

Anger made my voice lash out, hard and sharp. "Not him. Give me your word, sir. Now."

The old man's gaze wavered and he lifted his forward hand from the shotgun, fingers spread in a conciliatory gesture. He let the barrel ease down. "All right. My word to you, Hoss."

Kincaid exhaled slowly through his teeth. I felt his weight shift behind me.

I glanced back. His gun was half lowered. "Yours too, Kincaid."

"I'm working for you right now, Dresden," he said. "You already have it."

"Then put the gun away."

To my surprise, he did, though his empty eyes remained fastened on Ebenezar.

"What the hell was that about?" I demanded.

"Defending myself," Kincaid said.

"Don't give me that crap," I said.

Anger touched Kincaid's voice. It was a cold thing that lined his words with frost. "Self-defense. If I'd known your fucking wheelman was Blackstaff McCoy, I'd have been in another state by now, Dresden. I want nothing to do with him."

"It's a little late for that now," I told him. I glared at Ebenezar. "What are you doing?"

"Taking care of a problem," the old man said. He kept his eyes on Kincaid while he drew the gun back into the truck. "Harry, you don't know this"—his mouth twisted with bitter revulsion—"this thing. You don't know what it's done."

"You're one to talk," Kincaid replied. "Gorgeous

work at Casaverde, by the way. Russian satellite for a measured response to Archangel. Very nice."

I whirled on Kincaid. "Stop it."

Kincaid met my eyes, calm and defiant. "Permission to engage in philosophical debate with the hypocrite, sir?"

Anger hit me in a red wave, and before I realized what I was doing I was up in Kincaid's face, shoving my nose at his. "Shut your mouth. Now. This man took me in when no one else would, and it probably saved my life. He taught me that magic, that *life* was more than killing and power. You might be a badass, Kincaid, but you aren't worth the mud that falls off his goddamned boots. If it came to it, I'd trade your life for his without a second thought. And if I see you trying to provoke him again I'll kill you myself. Do you understand me?"

There was a second where I felt the beginnings of the almost violent psychic pressure that accompanies a soulgaze. Kincaid must have felt it coming on, too. He let his eyes slip out of focus, turned away from me, and started unpacking a box in the van. "I understand you," he said.

I clenched my hands as hard as I could and closed my eyes. I tried not to move my lips while I counted to ten and got the blaze of my temper under control. After a few seconds I took a couple of steps back from Kincaid and shook my head. I leaned against the fender of Ebenezar's old Ford and got myself under control.

Blazing anger had gotten me into way too many bad situations, historically speaking. I knew better than to indulge it like that—but at the same time it felt good to let off a little steam. And dammit, I'd had a good reason to slap Kincaid down. I couldn't believe that he would have the temerity to compare himself to my old teacher. In any sense.

Hell, from what Ebenezar had said, Kincaid wasn't even human.

"I'm sorry," I said a minute later. "That he was trying to push your buttons, sir."

There was a significant beat before Ebenezar answered.

"It's nothing, Hoss," he said. His voice was rough. "No need to apologize."

I looked up and stared at the old man. He wouldn't meet my eyes. Not because he was afraid of a soulgaze beginning, either. He'd insisted on it within an hour of meeting me. I still remembered it as sharply as every other time I'd looked on someone's soul. I still remembered the old man's oak-tree strength, his calm, his dedication to doing what he felt was right. And more than simply looking like a decent person, Ebenezar had lived an example for an angry and confused young wizard.

Justin DuMorne had taught me *how* to do magic. But it was Ebenezar who had taught me *why*. That magic came from the heart, from the essence of what the wizard believed—from who and what he chose to be. That the power born into any wizard carried with it the responsibility to use it to help his fellow man. That there were things worth protecting, defending, and that the world could be more than a jungle where the strong thrived and the weak were devoured.

Ebenezar was the only man on the planet to whom I regularly applied an honorific. As far as I was concerned, he was the only one who truly deserved it.

But a soulgaze wasn't a lie-detector test. It shows you the core of another person, but it doesn't shine lights into every shadowy corner of the human soul. It doesn't mean that they can't lie to you.

Ebenezar avoided my eyes. And he looked ashamed.

"There's work to be done, Ebenezar," I said in a measured tone. "I don't know what you know about Kincaid, but he knows his business. I asked him here. I need his help."

"Yes," Ebenezar agreed.

"I need yours too," I said. "Are you in?"

"Yes," he said. I thought I heard something like pain in his voice. "Of course."

"Then we move now. We talk later."

"Fine."

I nodded. Murphy had appeared at some point, now dressed in jeans, a dark shirt, and the Red Cross hat and jacket Kincaid had given her. She had her gun belt on, and she held herself a little differently, so I figured she had strapped on her Kevlar vest.

"All right," I said, stepping over to the van. "Ebenezar is going to shut down Mavra, or at least throw a wet blanket over anything she can do. You got everything you need, sir?"

Ebenezar grunted in the affirmative and patted a pair of old leather saddlebags he had tossed over his shoulder.

"Right," I said. "That means that our main problems should be the Renfields and their darkhounds. Guns and teeth. We'll want to get inside and down to the basement if we can. Then if bullets start flying, it should keep them from killing people upstairs and next door."

"What's the rest of the plan?" Kincaid asked.

"Kill the vampires, save the hostages," I said.

"For the record," Kincaid said, "I was hoping for an answer that vaguely hinted at a specific tactical doctrine rather than spouting off general campaign objectives."

I started to snap at him but reined in my temper. This wasn't the time for it. "You've done this the most," I said. "What do you suggest?"

Kincaid looked at me for a moment and then nodded. He glanced at Murphy and said, "Something in a Mossberg. Can you handle a shotgun?"

"Yeah," Murphy said. "These are close quarters, though. We'd need something heavy like that to stop a charge, but the barrel would need to be cut short."

Kincaid gave her a look, and said, "That would be an illegal weapon." Then he reached into the van and handed her a shotgun with a barrel that had been cut down to end just above the forward grip. Murphy snorted and checked out the shotgun while Kincaid rattled around in the white minivan again.

Instead of a second shotgun, though, he drew a weapon made of plain, nonreflective steel from the van. It was modeled after a boar spear of the Middle Ages, a shaft about five feet long with a cross-brace thrusting out on two sides at the base of the spear tip—a foot and a half of deadly, matte-black blade as wide as my hand at the base, and tapering down to a fine point at the tip. There was enough mass to the spear to make me think that he could as easily chop and slash with the edges of the spearhead as thrust with the tip. The butt end of the spear ended at some kind of bulbous-looking cap of metal, maybe just a counterweight. A similar double protrusion bulged out from the spear shaft at the base of the blade.

"Spear and magic helmet," I said in my best Elmer Fudd voice. "Be vewy, vewy quiet. We're hunting vampires."

Kincaid gave me the kind of smile that would make dogs break into nervous howls. "You got your stick ready there, Dresden?"

"You should go with a shotgun," Murphy told Kincaid.

Kincaid shook his head. "Can't shove the shotgun into a charging vampire or hellhound and hold them off with the cross-brace," he said. He settled the spear into his grip and did something to the handle. The beam of a flashlight clicked on from one side of the bulge at the base of the spearhead. He tapped the other one with a finger. "Besides, got incendiary rounds loaded zip-gun style in either end. If I need them, bang."

"In the butt end too?" I asked.

He reversed his grip on the spear and showed me the metal casing. "Pressure trigger on that one," he said. Kincaid dropped the spear's point down and held the haft close to his body, somehow managing to make the weapon look like a casual and appropriate accessory. "Shove it hard against the target and boom. Based it on the bang sticks those *National Geographic* guys made for diving with sharks."

I looked from the gadget-readied spear and body armor to my slender staff of plain old wood and leather duster.

"My dick is bigger than your dick," I said.

"Heh," Kincaid said. He draped a rope of garlic around his neck, then tossed another one to me, and a third to Murphy.

Murphy eyed the garlic. "I thought the vampires were going to be asleep. I mean, they staked Dracula in his coffin, right?"

"You're thinking of the movie," Kincaid said. He passed me a web belt with a canteen and a pouch on it. The pouch contained a medical kit, a roll of duct tape, a road flare, and a flashlight. The canteen had masking tape on the lid, and block letters in permanent marker identified it as holy water. "Read the book. Older or stronger members of the Black Court might not be totally incapacitated by sunlight."

"Might not even inconvenience Mavra," I said. "Stoker's *Dracula* ran around in broad daylight. But between daylight and Ebenezar, Mavra shouldn't have much in the way of powers. If there are any Black Court on their feet who want to come for us, they'll have to do it the dirty way."

"Which is why I got you a surprise, Dresden."

"Oh, good," I said. "A surprise. That's sure to be fun."

Kincaid reached into the van and presented me with a futuristic-looking weapon, a gun. It had a round tank the size of a gumball machine attached to its frame, and for a second I thought I'd been handed a pistol-sized flame thrower. Then I recognized it, cleared my throat, and said, "This is a paintball gun."

"It's a high-tech weapon," he said. "And it isn't loaded with paint. The ammunition is interspersed holy water and garlic loads. It'll hurt and frighten darkhounds and it will chew holes in any vamps that are moving around."

"While not putting any holes in us," Murphy chimed in. "Or in innocent bystanders."

"Okay," I said. "But this is a paintball gun."

"It's a weapon," Murphy said. "And a weapon that will do harm to the bad guys while not hurting your allies. That makes it a damned good one for you for such close quarters. You're good in a fight but you don't have close-quarters firearms or military training, Harry. Without ingrained fire discipline, you're as likely to kill one of us as the bad guys."

"She's right," Kincaid said. "Relax, Dresden. It's sound technology, and a good tool for teamwork. We do this simple. I'm on point. Then the shotgun. Then you, Dresden. I see a Renfield with a gun, and I'm going to drop flat. Murphy handles it from there. If we get a vampire or a darkhound, I'll crouch and hold it off with the spear. The two of you hit it with everything you can. Push it back until I can pin it on the spear. Then kill it."

"How?" Murphy asked. "Stakes?"

"Screw stakes," Kincaid said. He held out a heavy machete in an olive-drab sheath to Murphy. "Take off its head."

She clipped the machete onto her belt. "Gotcha."

"The three of us together should be able to take one vamp down the hard way if we're alert. But if one of them closes on us, we're probably going to die," Kincaid said. "The best way to stay alive is to hit them fast and stay on the offensive. Once we've put down any unfriendlies, you two can go save the hostages or take the Renfields to therapy or tap dance or whatever. If things go south, stay together and come straight back out. McCoy should have the truck out front and ready where he can see the door."

"I will," Ebenezar agreed.

"Okay," Kincaid said. "Anyone have any questions?"

"Why do they sell hot dogs in packages of ten but hot dog *buns* in packages of eight?" I said.

Everyone glared at me. I should probably leave off wizarding and chase my dream of becoming a stand-up comedian.

Instead, I put the toy gun in my right hand, my staff in my left, and said, "Let's go."

Chapter Thirty-one

I drove the Red Cross van up to the shelter. I pulled in right in front, put it in park, and said, "You two go in first. I'm sure whoever the vamps have working for them will recognize me, at least by description. Outside chance they'll know Murph, too, but the uniform might make them play along until you can get any bystanders out of the building."

"How should I do that?" Kincaid asked.

"Hell's bells, you're the big time mercenary. What am I paying you for?" I said, annoyed. "What's unit response time down here, Murphy?"

"This is gang country. Officially about six minutes. Reality is more like ten or fifteen. Maybe more."

"So we call it six or seven minutes to get clear after someone calls CPD screaming about rabid dogs and gunfire," I said. "The longer before that happens the better. So get it done calmly and quietly, Kincaid. Talk them out if you can."

"No problem," Kincaid said, and leaned his spear against the dashboard. "Let's go."

Murphy held her weapon down and close to her side and followed Kincaid into the building. I waited, but I had already planned to go on in if I didn't hear anything in the next minute or so. I started counting to sixty.

On forty-four, the door opened and a couple of bedraggled men and three or four raggedly dressed women, all of them more beaten down than actually aged, came shambling out.

"Like I said, it shouldn't take long," Kincaid was saying in a bluff, heavy, cheerful voice marked with the harder, shorter vowels of a Chicago accent. He came along behind the street folk, shepherding them out. "It's probably just a faulty detector. As soon as the guys from the gas company check out the basement and make sure it's safe, we'll get set up and get everyone paid. An hour, tops."

"Where is Bill?" demanded one of the women in a querulous voice. "Bill is the man from the Red Cross. You aren't Bill."

"Vacation," Kincaid said. His good-natured smile did not touch his eyes. They remained cold and uncaring as he reached through the van's window and picked up his spear. The woman took one look at his expression, another at the weapon, then ducked her head and scurried away from the shelter. The others followed suit, scattering like a covey of quail alerted to sudden danger.

I went inside, and Kincaid backed in after me, shutting the door. The reception area looked more like a security checkpoint—a small room, a couple of chairs, a heavy-duty security door, and a guard station behind a window of heavy bars. But the security door had been propped open with one of the chairs, and I could see Murphy standing in the room on the other side, her riot gun held level, her stance alert and ready.

I walked over to her. The room beyond the reception area was the size of a small cafeteria. Cubicle walls sprouted in one corner like some kind of crystalline growth. Half a dozen people dressed in business casual stood passively against the nearest cubicle wall, and Murphy had her gun leveled at them.

They should have been afraid. They weren't. They just stood there, eyes dull, faces set in vacant, bovine expressions. "Harry," she said. "Kincaid said we shouldn't let them out until you made sure they weren't dangerous."

"Yeah," I said. I hated to think of leaving simple thralls staring stupidly at nothing, given all the violence on the immediate agenda, but that would have been better than setting some bloodthirsty Renfield loose somewhere behind me. I closed my eyes for a moment, concentrating. There were a thousand other things I would rather do than examine victims of the Black Court with my Sight, but we didn't have time for anything else.

I opened my eyes along with my Sight, and focused on the people standing in line.

I don't know if you've ever seen a sheep slaughtered for mutton. The process isn't fast, even if it isn't really cruel. They make the sheep lie down on its side and cover its eyes. The sheep lies there without struggling, and the shepherd takes a sharp knife and draws a single, neat line across its throat. The sheep jerks in a sharp twitch of surprise, while the shepherd holds it gently down. It smells blood and stirs more. Then the animal quiets again under the shepherd's hand. It bleeds.

It doesn't look real, the first time you see it, because the blood is too bright and thick, and the animal isn't struggling. There's a lot of blood. It spreads out on the ground, soaking into dirt or sand. It dyes the wool of the sheep's chest, throat, and legs a dark, rusty red. Sometimes the blood gets into a puddle around its nose, and the animal's breaths make scarlet ripples.

Before the end, the sheep might twitch and jerk another time or two, but it's silent, and it doesn't really make an effort to fight. It lies there, becoming more still, and after several minutes that stroll past in no great hurry, it dies.

That's what they looked like to my Sight, those people the vampires had enthralled. They stood calmly, relaxed, thinking of nothing. Like sheep, they had been blindfolded to the truth somehow. Like sheep, they did not struggle or flee. Like sheep, they were being kept for whatever benefit their lives would provide—and like sheep they would eventually be taken for food. I saw them, defenseless and beaten, blood soaking into their clothing while they lay still under the hand of a being more powerful than they.

They stood quietly, dying like sheep. Or rather, five of them did.

The sixth was a Renfield.

For the briefest second, I saw the sixth victim, a burly man of middle years and wearing a blue oxford shirt, as a sheep like the rest of them. Then that image vanished, replaced by something inhuman. His face looked twisted and deformed, and his muscles swelled hideously, bulging with blackened veins and quivering with unnatural power. There was a band of shimmering, vile energy wreathing his throat in an animal's collar—the reflection of the dark magic that had enslaved him.

But worst of all were his eyes.

The man's eyes looked as if they had been clawed out by something with tiny, scalpel-sharp talons. I met his blind gaze, and there was nothing there. Nothing. Just an empty darkness so vast and terrible that my lungs froze and my breath locked in my throat.

By the time I realized what I was seeing, the man had already let out a feral shriek and charged me. I shouted in surprise and tried to back up, but he was simply too fast. He backhanded me. The enchantments on my duster diverted much of the power in it, so it didn't crack any of my ribs, but it was still strong enough to throw me from my feet and into a wall. I dropped to the floor, stunned.

An angel, blazing with fury and savage strength, spun toward the Renfield, her eyes shining with azure flame, a shaft of fire in her hands. The angel was dressed in soiled robes smudged with smoke and blood and filth, no longer white. She bled from half a dozen wounds, and moved as if in terrible pain.

Murphy.

There was a peal of thunder, and flame leapt from the shaft of light in her hands. The Renfield, now deformed with muscle like some kind of madman's gargoyle, accepted the blow, and batted the shaft of light from the angel's hands. She dove for the weapon. The Renfield followed, reaching for her neck.

Something hit it hard, a second shaft, though this one was made not of light but of what looked like solidified smog of black and deep purple. The blow drove the Renfield from its feet, and the angel recovered the fallen weapon. Another shaft of light thundered into the Renfield's head, and it collapsed abruptly to the ground.

I shook my head, trying to tear away from painful clarity of my Sight. I heard a footstep nearby. Still stunned, I looked behind me.

For just a second I saw something standing there. Something enormous, malformed, something silent and merciless and deadly. It had to crouch to keep from brushing the ceiling with the horns curling away from its head, and batlike wings spread from its shoulders to fall around it and behind it, to drag along the floor, and I thought I saw some kind of hideous double image lurking behind it like the corpse-specter of Death himself.

Then the second was past, I pushed my Sight away, and Kincaid stood frowning down at me. "I said, are you all right?"

"Yeah," I said. "Yeah, just clipped me."

Kincaid offered me his hand.

I didn't take it. I pushed myself to my feet instead.

His expression became opaque. It had an alien quality to it that made it more frightening than when it had been merely unreadable. He stepped over to the body of the middle-aged man in the blue oxford shirt, and jerked his spear out of the corpse. It was wet with blood all the way to the cross-brace.

I shuddered, but asked Murphy, "You okay?"

She still gripped the riot gun as she stood over the body, keeping her eyes on the five people remaining. There was a bloody, pulpy mess where the first shot had ripped open the man's leg, but it hadn't even slowed him down. It was messier where Murphy's second shot had torn into his head. Not that he would have been any better off if she'd hit him in the chest. People don't survive direct hits from shotguns delivered from a couple of steps away.

"Murph?" I asked.

"Fine," she said. Some of the Renfield's blood had sprayed onto her cheek, beading into red droplets below her distant eyes. "I'm fine. What now?"

Kincaid stepped up beside Murphy and put his hand on the end of the riot gun's barrel. He pushed gently, and she shot him a look before taking a steadying breath and lowering the weapon.

Kincaid nodded at the remaining thralls. "I'll get these

five out and meet you at the stairs. Don't go down without me."

"Don't worry," I said. "We won't."

He prodded the five thralls into motion and herded them out of the building. I oriented myself on the room's doors, remembering Bob's handy-dandy map, and headed for the door that led down to the basement. Murphy walked beside me. She said nothing, but fed two more shells into the riot gun. She reached for the doorknob.

I put mine there first. "Hold it, Murph," I said. "Let me check it for surprises."

She looked at me for a second and then nodded.

I closed my eyes and laid my hand on the door, gently pushing my awareness through the door, feeling silently for patterns of energy that might indicate magical wards like the ones protecting my apartment. My magical awareness was akin to the Sight, just as my sense of touch was akin to my sense of sight. It cost me less than opening the Sight, and was infinitely more gentle to my psyche.

I felt nothing, no waiting wards or prereadied traps of Mavra's deadly black magic. Generally speaking, the bad guys weren't terribly interested in learning defensive magic when they could be out blowing things up instead, but I was determined not to get sucker punched on something that basic.

"He was already gone," I told Murphy.

She said nothing.

"I saw him, Murph. I Saw him. There wasn't anything left inside him. He was . . . less than an animal. There was nothing else you could have done."

She spoke very quietly. "Shut the fuck up, Harry."

I did. I finished my check, felt around for the presence of any supernatural entities that might be right on the other side of the door, and Listened, to boot. Nothing. When I opened my eyes again, Kincaid was standing there with Murphy. I hadn't heard his approach. "Clear?" he asked.

I nodded. "The door isn't warded. I don't think there's anything waiting on the other side, but I can't be sure."

Kincaid grunted, glanced at Murphy, then leaned back and kicked the door open.

Murphy blinked at me. Kincaid was a big guy, sure, but it's tough to kick doors down on the first try. I'd seen men batter one with those same vicious kicks for fifteen minutes before the door gave way. Maybe he'd just gotten lucky.

Yeah, I believed that. The image of that enormous, demonic thing that had crouched in the mercenary's place loomed with a terrible clarity in my head.

Kincaid landed on balance, lifted the spear, and pointed the head and its attached flashlight down the closed, narrow stairway.

There was only silence.

And then the sound of a soft, mocking laugh from somewhere in the darkness below us.

Hell's bells. The back of my neck crawled up my scalp and into one ear.

"Form up," I murmured, because it sounded more military and tougher than saying, "You guys go first." Kincaid nodded and took a step down. Murphy readied the riot gun again and pressed in behind him. I picked up my air-powered popgun and followed her.

"Where are they keeping the hostages again?" Murphy asked.

"In a closet at the bottom of stairs, on the right."

"That was hours ago," Kincaid said quietly. "They could be anywhere now. Once we go down there, there's no room for playing around."

"The hostages are our first concern."

"Screw that. That's exactly *why* the vamps took hostages in the first place," Kincaid said. "If you let them dictate your tactics, they're going to use it to kill you."

"That isn't your concern," I said.

Kincaid's voice became quieter and harder. "It is when I'm standing this close to you. They might get me instead."

"That's why you get the big bucks."

He shook his head. "We don't even know if they're alive. Look, this is a basement. All we have to do is roll down the grenades and then go mop up whatever is left afterward. We're underground. The collateral damage will be minimal."

"That's not good enough," I said. "We save the hostages first. Once they're clear, *then* we take care of business with Mavra."

Kincaid glanced over his shoulder at me, his eyes narrow and cold. Defiance and contempt rang in every word. "It might be a little harder to rescue them if we're dead."

Murphy put the mouth of the riot gun against Kincaid's spine and said, "How good is that armor?"

Sometimes Murphy has a way with words.

We were all quiet for a couple of seconds. Then I said, "We might get killed trying to save the hostages. We *will* get killed if we don't stick together. Do the math, Kincaid. Or break your agreement and get out."

He stared at Murphy for a second and then relented, turning back to face the stairway. "Fine," he said. "We do it your way. It's amateur night."

We started down the first flight of stairs together, while whatever waited in the darkness below us laughed again.

Chapter Thirty-two

The basement in the shelter was unusually deep, especially for Chicago. The stairs went down about ten feet, and were only about two and a half feet wide. My imagination treated me to a brief vision of some grinning Renfield with a machine gun popping around the corner already shooting, bullets tearing all three of us to shreds in the space of a heartbeat. My stomach writhed in pure nervous fear, and I forced myself to put it aside and focus on my surroundings.

The walls had been mortared and painted white, but cracks and mineral stains from damp spots all but concealed the original color. At the bottom of the stairs was a landing maybe three feet square, and then a second set of stairs led farther down, the air getting more cramped and colder as they went.

The stale air smelled like mildew and rot. Our breathing and our movements sounded incredibly loud in the otherwise oppressive silence that followed, and I found myself pointing the paintball gun forward, over Murphy's head and Kincaid's shoulder, so that I could start shooting as soon as something bounded into view. For all the good it was likely to do. Against any normal thug, the weapon would do little but make them damp. Or vaguely aromatic.

The stairway ended at a half-open old door.

Kincaid nudged it slowly open with his spear, already crouched.

Murphy aimed her gun at the black doorway.

Me too. The end of my stupid paintball gun quivered involuntarily.

Nothing happened.

Silence reigned.

"Dammit," I muttered. "I don't have the nerves for this crap."

"Want me to find you a Valium?" Kincaid asked.

"Kiss my ass," I said.

He reached into his belt pouch and pulled out a couple of plastic tubes. He bent them sharply, shook them up, and they began to shine with chemical light. He edged up to the doorway and flicked one to the left, the other to the right, bouncing them off the walls so that he wouldn't expose himself to anyone in the hall beyond. Then he waited a beat and leaned out, peeking around. "Nothing moving," he reported. "No lights. But it looks like that map was pretty good. Hall on my right goes about ten feet, then ends at the door to that closet. Open hall on my left, twenty feet long, and opens into a room."

"Closet first," I said.

"Cover me."

Kincaid flowed down the last couple of stairs and through the door. Murphy kept within a foot of his back. Kincaid peeled off to the right. Murphy dropped into a crouch, shotgun aimed down the green-lit hall to the left. I wasn't as smooth, but I went after Kincaid, paintballs and staff ready.

The closet door was only five feet high and opened out, toward the hall. Kincaid listened at the door, then leaned aside to let me touch it first. I couldn't feel any enchantments on it, and nodded to him. He shifted his grip on the spear so that he'd be ready to drive the tip of it into anything that came at him from the closet, and drew the door open.

The light from his spear flickered around a dank little chamber that was too big to be a proper closet and too small to be a room. Patches of moisture and mildew blotted the damp stone walls, and the smell of unwashed bodies and waste rolled out of the door.

Half a dozen children, none of them older than nine or ten, huddled against the back wall of the closet. They were dressed in castoff clothing, most of it far too big, and they wore steel cuffs on their hands. The cuffs, in turn, were locked to a larger chain attached to a heavy steel ring bolted into the floor. The children reacted in silent terror, flinching away from the doorway and from the light.

Children.

Someone was going to regret this. If I had to take this building, hell, this *block* apart with nothing but raw will and my bare hands, someone was going to pay. Even the monsters should draw a line somewhere.

Then again, I guess that's why they call them monsters.

"Son of a bitch," I snarled, and ducked my head to step into the room.

Kincaid abruptly threw his weight against me, shoving me aside from the door. "No," he growled.

"Dammit, get out of my way," I said.

"It's a trap, Dresden," Kincaid said. "There's a trip wire. Go through that door and you'll kill all of us."

Murphy checked over her shoulder and returned to watching the darkness for trouble.

I frowned at Kincaid and picked up the plastic light stick, holding it out. "I don't see a wire."

"Not a literal wire," Kincaid. "It's a net of infrared beams."

"Infrared? How did you—"

"Dammit, Dresden, if you want to know about me, wait for the autobiography like everyone else."

He was right. It was a little late to be worrying about Kincaid's background now. "Hey, kids," I said. "Everybody stay really still and keep back, okay? We're going to get you out of here." I lowered my voice and said to Kincaid, "How do we get them out of there?"

"Not sure we can," Kincaid said. "The beam is rigged up to an antipersonnel mine."

"Well," I said. "Can't we just . . . can't you put a weight on a land mine and leave it there? So long as the weight holds the trigger down, it doesn't explode, right?"

"Right," Kincaid said. "But that's assuming we've gone back in time to World War Two." He shook his head. "Modern mines are pretty good at killing people, Dresden. This one's British, pretty recent."

"How can you tell?"

He tapped his nose. "The Brits use a different chemical priming charge than most. It's probably a bouncer, very nasty."

"Bouncer?"

"Yeah. If something interrupts the beam, the charge activates. Several individual submunitions get blown up into the air, or sideways, or however they want to set it up, in a pattern. Then they explode maybe five or six feet in the air. Sends a couple of thousand steel balls out in a big cloud. Kills everything in thirty, maybe forty meters if you're in the open, maybe a lot farther in a tight space like this. If it was me, I'd have set the charges up to get thrown straight down this hall. All these stone walls, the shrapnel would shred everything real good."

"I could hex down whatever is sending the beam," I said.

"Thus interrupting it," Kincaid said. "Thus kablowie. Thus death."

"Dammit." I swallowed and took a step back from the doorway, hoping the presence of my magic wouldn't screw up the device in a moment of monumentally bad timing. "I can shield us, if it's all coming in from one direction."

Kincaid arched an eyebrow. "Yeah?"

"Yeah."

"Damn. But it won't help those kids much. They're over there."

I scowled ferociously. "How do we disarm the device?"

"You still don't want the Bolshevik Muppet solution, right?"

"Right."

"Then someone has to crawl in there without setting it off, find the explosive, disable it and unhook it from the sensors."

"Right," I said. "Do it."

Kincaid nodded. "Can't."

"What?"

"I can't."

"Why *not?*"

He nodded at the doorway. "There are three beams set up in an asymmetrical crisscross over the doorway. There isn't enough room for me to get through the open spaces."

"I'm thinner than you," I said.

"Yeah, but longer and a hell of a lot gawkier. And I know what happens to tech when nervous wizards get close."

"Someone has to do it," I said. "Someone small enough to . . ."

We both looked down the hall at Murphy.

Murphy didn't look away from her vigil, and said, "How do I disarm it?"

"I'll talk you through," Kincaid said. "Dresden, better take her gun and cover us."

"Hey," I said. "I'm in charge here. Kincaid, talk her through it. Murphy, give me your gun so I can cover you."

I tied the handle of the paintball gun into my coat where my blasting rod usually went. I winked at Murphy, who saw the gesture and did not respond to it. She just passed me the gun and turned her baseball cap around. Then she walked down the hall, slipping out of her coat and gun belt on the way.

"Better lose the Kevlar too," Kincaid said. "I can pass it to you. Bottom left corner looks like the best bet. Stay as flat as you can and as much to the left as you can. I think you can get in."

"You think?" I asked. "What if you're wrong?"

He gave me an annoyed look. "You don't see me telling you how to watch that goddamned doorway in case all the vampires show up at any second to kill us, do you?" Kincaid asked.

I was going to scowl at him, but he had a point. I scowled at the darkness instead, gripping Murphy's gun. I fumbled for a second, because the riot gun must have been some kind of military-issue, and it took me a second to find the safety. I flicked it to reveal the red dot. Or at least I was thought it was red. The green chemical light made it look black.

"Stop," Kincaid said in a calm voice. "Unclench."

"Unclench what?" Murphy demanded.

"Unclench your ass."

"*Excuse* me?"

"You're going to trip the beam. You need another quarter inch. Relax."

"I am relaxed," Murphy growled.

"Oh," Kincaid said. "Damn, great ass then. Take off your pants."

I winced and checked over my shoulder Murphy was stretched out on the floor on her belly, her cheek on the cold floor, arms stretched above her. The small of her back was in the doorway. She managed to move her head just enough to eye Kincaid. "Once again?"

"Take off your pants," Kincaid said, smiling. "Think of the children."

She muttered something to herself and moved her arms, shifting slightly.

"No good," Kincaid said. "You're moving too far."

"Okay, genius," Murphy said. "What do I do?"

"Hold still," Kincaid said. "I'll do it."

There was silence for a second. Murphy hissed out a breath. Or maybe it was more of a gasp.

"I don't bite," he said. "Be still. I want to live through this."

"Okay," Murphy said in a small voice a moment later.

I scowled hard at the darkness and felt myself getting irrationally angry, and fast. I glanced back again. Murphy wriggled forward, all the way through the doorway. Her legs were pale, pretty, and strong. And I had to admit that Kincaid was completely correct about her posterior.

Kincaid was bracing her legs, hands on her calves and sliding down as she moved forward, helping her to keep them from accidentally moving too far. Or at least that damn well better have been what he was doing, because if it wasn't I would be forced to kill him.

I shook my head and returned to my vigil. *Get a grip, Harry,* I thought to myself. *It isn't like you and Murphy are an item. She isn't something you own. She's her own person. She does what she wants with who she wants. You're not even involved with her. You've got no say in it.*

I ran through those thoughts a couple of times, found them impeccably logical, morally unassailable, and still wanted to slug Kincaid. Which implied all kinds of things I didn't have time to think about.

I heard them speaking quietly to each other a moment later. Murphy was describing the explosive, and Kincaid was giving her instructions.

In the darkness beyond the last chemical light, I heard something move.

I shifted my weight, reaching into my belt pouch for my own chemical light sticks. I pressed them against the floor to break the layer separating the two chemicals and shook them until they started to emit their own soft green fire. I threw them down the hall, where they landed in the room beyond. The lights revealed little beyond more stone floor and some drywall. Bob had reported that the room was essentially a storage chamber, with several smaller chambers defined by recently installed drywall that could be used for storage, emergency shelters during the odd tornado warning, or additional rooms for those in need of a place to spend the night. But all I could see was half of a door, a couple of stacks of cardboard boxes, a dressmaker's dummy, and the glowing sticks of emerald light.

And then something large and four-legged moved in front of one of the lights for a second or two. The darkhound was a large and rangy animal, maybe a large Alsatian, and it deliberately stayed in place for a moment before vanishing into the shadows once more.

I kept the riot gun aimed down the hall and wished that Inari hadn't broken my damned blasting rod. I would far rather have had it than the gun. Without the blasting rod to help me focus and contain the destructive energies of flame I preferred, I didn't dare start blasting away at the bad guys with magic, especially in such tight quarters as the shelter. But then, maybe it was just as well. I had already met my quota for burning down public institutions this week.

I couldn't see anything else, but I knew there was something there. So I lowered my eyelids almost all the way and focused my attention, Listening. There was the faint sound of something breathing, but nothing more.

It wasn't enough. I lowered the gun a bit, relaxing my shoulders, and poured more of my focus into it, Listening more deeply than I ever had before. The sound of breathing became louder, and I picked out several other faint sources of it. A moment later I began to hear a dull throbbing, which I realized was a beating heart. More heartbeats joined it, a confused chorus of drumming beats, but I was able to identify individual rhythms into a pair of groups. One was a bit faster, lighter—smaller hearts, probably the darkhounds. There were four of them. The other group was human, and there were five hearts beating in an eager, savage cadence—pressed up against the walls on either side of the doorway, out of sight but less than twenty feet away.

And from the back of the room I heard footsteps, slow and deliberate. They slid quietly across the stone floor, and the wasted outline of an emaciated female form appeared in front of one of the glow sticks.

And no heartbeat accompanied it.

Mavra.

The darkhounds appeared, vague shapes, and paced restlessly through the shadows around the vampire. My heart lurched in sudden apprehension, and I released my attention from the Listening. I raised the gun, got to my feet, and backed away.

Again, that soft, mocking laugh drifted through the basement.

"Trouble," I said over my shoulder. "Five Renfields, four darkhounds at least, and Mavra's awake."

"Indeed," came Mavra's dry, dusty voice. "I've been waiting for you, Dresden. There's something I've been meaning to ask you."

"Oh?" I said. I looked over my shoulder at Kincaid and mouthed, *How long?*

Kincaid had crouched and taken up his spear again. He glanced back and said, "Thirty seconds."

"We take the kids and run," I whispered.

"I've been admiring you for some time now, Dresden," came Mavra's voice. "I've seen you stop bullets with your power. I've seen you stop knives and claws and fangs." She made a gesture with her hand. "And so I simply must know how well you will fare against your own weapon of choice."

And two Renfields stepped out into the doorway, blocking my view of Mavra. Each of them held a long metal device in their hands, and each of them wore something that bulged out above their shoulders, gleam-

ing shapes of rounded metal. A blue starter flame flickered at the end of the devices they held, and it hit me
all at once what was happening.

Both of the Renfields lifted their flamethrowers and
filled the cramped little hallway with fire.

Chapter Thirty-three

The riot gun went off, though I'm not sure if it was
because I'd instinctively decided to use the weapon or if
I'd just convulsed in surprise. The bad guys were twenty
feet away, which was plenty of distance for the shot from
the riot gun to spread. If I'd had it aimed well, it would
almost certainly have put one of them down. As it was,
the largest force of the blast went between them, though
from the way they jerked and twisted, either the sheer
roaring volume of the weapon was enough to intimidate
them or they'd caught a little shot as it went past. Fire
coughed uncertainly from the mouths of the flamethrowers, spattering the hall along the floors, walls, and
ceiling, where it clung in globs of what had to be a mix
of gasoline or some other accelerant, and petroleum
jelly—homemade napalm. The air went from cold to
roasting-hot, even from the aborted discharge of fire,
sucking the wind from my lungs.

Both men, unassuming-looking types in ragged clothing, their eyes wide and fanatical, hesitated for a second
before planting their feet again and taking aim once
more. It was only a second, but it was enough to save
my life. I dropped the gun, tossed my staff into my right
hand, and shook out my shield bracelet. I rammed panicked will into the focus and spread it in a wall of energy
before me.

The Renfields cut loose this time, flame as thick as spray from a breached hydrant roaring down the hall. I caught it on the shield, but I had never intended it to stop heat. It was primarily a defense against kinetic energy, and while I had used it to handle everything from bullets to runaway elevator cars in my career as a wizard, it just wasn't all that good at stopping the transfer of intense heat. The napalm-jelly splattered against the invisible shield, gallons of it, and the fire clung to it in white-hot glee. Its mindless fury seeped through the shield and flowed onto me.

It hurt. Oh, God, it *hurt*. The fingers of my left hand were the first to feel it, and then my palm and wrist, all in the space of a second. If you've never been burned, you can't imagine the pain. And my fingers, where millions of tactile nerves were able to send panicked damage-messages to my brain, felt as if they had simply exploded and been replaced with howling agony.

I jerked my hand back, and felt my focus waver, the shield start to fade. I gritted my teeth, and somehow managed to dig up the strength to extend my hand again, hardening the shield and my will. I backed away in shuffling half steps, my mind almost drowning in pain, desperately keeping the shield up.

"Ten seconds!" Kincaid shouted.

I saw blisters rising on my left hand. I felt my fingers curling into a claw. They looked thinner, as if made of melting wax, and I could see the shadows of my bones beneath the flesh. The shield grew weaker yet. The pain got worse. I stood now at the bottom of the stairs, and as the shield faltered, the empty space between me and the doorway behind me might as well have been a mile.

I didn't have ten seconds.

I reached into myself, into the horrible red pain, and drew forth more power yet. I focused it on my staff, and the sigils and runes carved along its surface became suddenly suffused with eye-searing scarlet light. My nose filled with the smell of charring wood, and as the shield wavered out of existence, I screamed, *"Ventas servitas!"*

The power I'd gathered in my staff shot out of it, an

invisible serpent of energy. The shield fell just as a shrieking gale of wind shot down the stairs. The column of air howled against me, throwing my duster forward around me like a flag, and caught the blazing napalm like a tub of Jell-O, hurling the fire back the way it had come and providing it with air enough to treble its size.

The fire went mad. It seared mortar from rough stone, and chewed cracks into the rock floor, the damp stone coughing and popping as water within expanded.

For an instant I could see the two Renfields, still spraying fire toward me. They started screaming, but they obeyed Mavra's raspy howls to stand fast, and it killed them. The napalm molded itself to them and the flame embraced them.

What hit the ground as they fell could not have been easily identified as human remains.

I kept my will on the wind, the carved runes on my staff blazing ember-orange, and it spread the flames into the far room in a deadly river of searing light and charred black ash. For agonized seconds I held the winds and spread the flames, and then my will faltered, the runes on the staff dimming. Pain overcame me for a second, and it hurt so much that I literally could not *see*.

"Wizard!" howled Mavra's voice, the words sounding like dusty scales and cold, reptilian fury. "Wizard! The wizard! Kill, kill, kill everything!"

"Get him!" Kincaid snarled. I felt Murphy get her arms under mine, and she started hauling me back with surprising power. I started seeing through the blinding agony in time to see a charred, inhuman-looking man wielding an ax leap at Kincaid. The mercenary rammed his spear full into the man's chest, stopping him in his tracks. A second man appeared from the smoke behind the first, this one holding a shotgun. There was a roaring sound, and fire tore through the impaled Renfield, then struck the second one full in the face with hideous, searing results. Kincaid jerked the spear clean of the corpse of the first Renfield, even as the second flailed around wildly, then pointed the shotgun in more or less the right direction.

Kincaid whirled the spear into a reverse grip, slammed it into the second Reinfield's chest and the second incendiary round blasted out from the housing at the butt end of the spear, and drove the remaining life from the man. A burning corpse hit the floor a second later.

A gun roared from the smoke. Kincaid grunted and staggered. The spear fell from his hands, but he didn't fall. He drew a gun in either hand and backed unsteadily away, the semiautomatic barking out shots as swiftly as he could send them into the choking smoke down the hall.

More Renfields, roasted but functional, came through the smoke, shooting. Darkhounds bounded around them, the naked and bloody shells of dogs, but filled with horrible rage. Behind them I saw Mavra's slender, deadly form, lit for the first time. She was wearing the same clothing I'd seen her in the last time—a tattered number from the Renaissance, all of black. Hamlet would have been happy to wear it. I saw her filmy dead eyes focus on me, and she lifted an ax in one hand.

The first two darkhounds reached Kincaid, and he went down under them before I could even cry out. One of the Renfields brought a sledgehammer down on him, while the other simply emptied a handgun into the pile as two more darkhounds threw themselves into it.

"No!" I shouted.

Murphy hauled me into the closet and out of the line of fire, just as Mavra threw. Her ax came tumbling end over end down the hall, and struck the stone wall at the back of the closet with such force that the head buried itself to the eye in the rock and the wooden handle shattered into splinters. Two of the children, still chained underneath where the ax hit, let out wails of pain and terror as splinters tore at them.

"Oh, God," Murphy said. "Your hand, oh, God." But she never stopped moving. She shoved me by main force into the back corner of the closet, picked up her gun, leaned into the doorway, and sent eight or nine measured shots down the hall, her face set in grim concentration. Her pale legs were a startling contrast against the black of her Kevlar vest. "Harry?" she shouted. "There's smoke, I can't see anything, but they're at the foot of the stairs. What do we do?"

I stared at a black box up on the wall, near the ceiling. Presumably Kincaid's antipersonnel mine. He'd been right. It was set up to open and spew its deadly projectiles diagonally down, so that they would bounce and fill both closet and hall with death.

"Harry!" Murphy shouted.

I barely had breath enough to answer. "Can you hook up the mine again?"

She looked over her shoulder at me, eyes wide. "You mean we can't get out?"

"Can you do it?" I barked.

She nodded, once.

"Wait for my signal, then arm it and get low."

She spun and leapt up onto a wooden chair near the mine, either something she had dragged there or something the bad guys had used too. She hooked up two alligator clips and held up a third, looking over her shoulder at me, her face pale. The children wept and screamed below her.

I dragged myself over to kneel in front of the children, facing down the hallway. I lifted my left hand, and stared at it in shock for a second. I always thought I looked good in red and black, but as a rule I preferred that to be my clothes. Not my limbs. My hand was a blackened, twisted claw of badly cooked meat, burned dark wherever it wasn't bloodred. My silver shield bracelet dangled beneath it, the charm-shields heat-warped, gleaming and bright.

I raised my other hand to signal Murphy, but then I heard a scream from down the hall, snarling and vicious and hardly human. The smoke swirled and cleared for a second, and I saw Kincaid, dragging one leg, his back against the wall. He had one hand clenched hard to his leg, and a gun in the other. He shot at a target I couldn't see until the gun started clicking.

"Now, Murphy!" I shouted. My voice thundered down the hall. "Kincaid! Bolshevik Muppet!"

The mercenary's head whipped around toward me. He moved like hamstrung lightning, swift and lurching and grotesque. He dropped the gun, released his leg, and threw himself straight at me with his three unwounded limbs.

Again I raised my shield, and prayed that the mine's infrared trip wire functioned.

Time slowed.

Kincaid flung himself through the doorway.

The mine beeped. There was a sharp, snapping click of metal.

Kincaid tumbled past me. I leaned aside to let him, and at the same instant brought every scrap of strength I had left to bear on the shield.

Lumpy metal spheres, maybe twenty or thirty of them, flew out into the air. I had angled my shield in a simple inclined plane, its base at the closet's doorway, its summit at the back wall of the closet, about four feet off the ground. Several of the spheres hit the shield, but the slope of it sent them rebounding out into the hall.

The submunitions exploded in a ripple of thunder and light. Steel balls flew in deadly sprays, rattling off stone walls and tearing into flesh with savage efficiency. The sloped shield flared into azure incandescence, energy from the shrapnel being absorbed and shed as flashbulb-bright bursts of light. The sound was indescribable, almost loud enough to kill all on its own.

And then it was over.

Silence fell, broken only by the crackling of flames. Nothing moved but drifting smoke.

Murphy, Kincaid, the captive children, and I were all huddled together in an unorganized pile of frightened humanity. We all sat there stunned for a moment. Then I said, "Come on. We have to get moving before the fire spreads." My voice sounded raw. "Let's get these kids out. I might be able to break these chains."

Kincaid reached up without speaking and took a key down from a high hook on the opposite wall. He settled back down to sit leaning against it, and tossed me the key.

"Or we could do that," I said, and passed the key to

Murphy. She started unlocking them. I was too tired to move. My hand didn't hurt, which was a very bad sign, I knew. But I was too tired to care. I just sat there and stared at Kincaid.

He had his hand clamped down on his leg again. He was bleeding from it. There was more blood on his belly, on one hand, and his face was positively smothered with it, as if he'd been bobbing for apples in a slaughterhouse.

"You're hurt," I said.

"Yep," he replied. "Dog."

"I saw you go down."

"It got nasty," he confirmed.

"What happened?" I asked.

"I lived."

"Your chest is bleeding," I said. "And there's blood on your hand."

"I know that."

"And your face is drenched in it."

He lifted an eyebrow and touched his free hand to his chin, then looked at the blood. "Oh. That isn't mine." He started fumbling at his belt.

I got enough energy together to go to him and help. He pulled a roll of black duct tape from a pouch on his belt and with sharp, jerking motions we wound the tape tightly around his wounded leg several times, layering the wound in adhesive, literally taping it closed. He used about a third of the roll, then grunted and tore it off. Then he said, "You're going to lose that hand."

"I was sending it back to the kitchen anyway. I ordered it medium well."

Kincaid stared at me for a second and then started letting out soft, wobbly-sounding laughter, as if it were something he didn't have a lot of practice at. He stood up, wheezing soft laughter, drew another gun and his own machete from his belt, and said, "Get them out. I'm going to dismember whatever is left."

"Groovy," I said.

"All that trouble we went to, and you just blew the place up. We could have done this to begin with, Dresden."

Murphy got the kids loose and they started getting

away from the wall. One of them, a girl no more than five years old, just collapsed against me crying. I held on to her for a moment, letting her cry, and said, "No, we couldn't have."

Kincaid regarded me, his expression unreadable. I thought I saw something wild and bloodthirsty and satisfied in his eyes for just a second. Then he said, "Maybe you're right."

He vanished into the smoke.

Murphy helped me to my feet. She had all the kids join hands, took the hand of the lead child herself, and led us all to the stairs. She bent and scooped up her jeans on the way. There wasn't enough denim left to avoid public indecency, and she dropped them with a sigh.

"Pink panties," I said, looking down. "With little white bows. I wouldn't have guessed that."

Murphy looked too tired to glare, but she tried.

"They really go with the Kevlar and the gun belt, Murph. Shows you're a woman with her priorities straight."

She stepped on my foot, smiling.

"Clear," said Kincaid's voice from the smoke. He appeared again, coughing a little. "Found four coffins occupied. One of them was that One-ear guy you told me about. Beheaded them. Vampires are history."

"Mavra?" I asked.

He shook his head. "That whole end of the hall looks like a chop shop for a black market organ bank. The vampire took that blast from the mine right in the kisser. You'd need her dental records and a jigsaw puzzle all-star to get a positive ID."

Kincaid didn't see Mavra flicker into sight. She rose out of the smoke behind him, horribly torn and mangled, badly burned, and angry as hell. She was missing her lower jaw, half of an arm, a basketball-sized section of lower abdomen, and one of her legs was attached by only a scrap of flesh and her black tights. For all of that, she moved no less swiftly, and her eyes burned with dead fire.

Kincaid saw the look on my face. He dropped flat.

I whipped the stupid little paintball gun out of my duster and emptied it at Mavra.

May lightning strike me dead if the damned thing didn't work like a charm. Hell, better than most charms, and I'm the guy who should know. The shots poured out almost as swiftly as from Kincaid's deadly little machine guns, and they splattered into Mavra, sizzling viciously. Silver fire immediately began chewing at her flesh wherever the paintballs struck and broke. It ripped into her and it happened *fast,* as if some hyperkinetic gourmet were taking a melon baller to her flesh.

Mavra let out a shocked and dusty shriek.

The holy water and garlic paintballs put a hole as wide as a three-liter bottle of Coke all the way through her. I could see the glow of fire in the pall of smoke behind her. She staggered and fell to her knees.

Murphy drew the machete from her belt and threw it underhand.

Kincaid caught it as he turned back to Mavra, and took her head off at the base of her neck. The head went one way. The body went straight down—there was no thrashing, no howling or spurting ichor, no gales of magical wind or sudden clouds of dust. Mavra's remains simply thumped to the ground, nothing but a withered cadaver once more.

I looked from Mavra's corpse to the paintball gun, impressed. "Kincaid. Can I keep this?"

"Sure," he said. "I'll add it to the bill." He stood up slowly, looking at the destruction. He shook his head. Then he joined us as we went up the stairs. "Even seeing it, it's tough to believe."

"What is?" I asked.

"Your shield. And that bit with all the wind and fire, especially with your hand like that." He glanced at me, something like caution in his expression. "I've never seen a wizard cut loose before."

What the hell. It wouldn't hurt to encourage the mercenary to be wary of me. I stopped and leaned on my staff. The runes still glowed with a sullen fire, though it was slowly fading. Tiny, white wisps of wood smoke curled up from it, sharp in my nose. It hadn't ever done *that* before, but there was no reason to mention that for the time being.

I looked straight at him until it was obvious that he was refusing to meet my eyes. Then I said in a quiet, gentle voice, "You still haven't."

I walked on out, leaving him to stare after me. I didn't think for a second that he would allow what he'd seen to scare him out of killing me if I didn't pay him. But it might scare him enough to make him more cautious about taking that option. Every little bit helps.

Before we got out of the shelter, I took off my duster and draped it onto Murphy's shoulders. It enveloped her entirely, its hem dragging the ground, covering her legs. She gave me a grateful look just as Ebenezar appeared in the doorway. The old man looked at the kids, then at my hand, and drew in a sharp breath.

"You all right to walk yourself out?" he asked.

"So far. We need to get these kids and ourselves the hell away from here."

"Fine," he said. "Where?"

"We'll take the kids to Father Forthill at Saint Mary of the Angels," I said. "He'll have a good idea of what can be done to help them."

Ebenezar nodded. "I know him by reputation. Good man."

We went outside and started loading kids into Ebenezar's old Ford truck. The old man had a gun rack at the back of the cab, his thick old staff in the bottom rack, his old Greener shotgun in the top one. He lifted the kids into the back one by one, where he had them lie down on a thick old thermal blanket and covered them with a second one.

Kincaid came out of the shelter carrying a contractor's heavy garbage bag, the smoke growing thicker behind him. The bag was half full. He threw it over one shoulder, then turned to me and said, "Taking care of details. As I see it, the contract is done. You satisfied with that?"

"Yeah," I said. "Nice working with you. Thank you."

Kincaid shook his head. "The *money* is how you thank me."

"Yeah, uh," I said, "about that. It's Saturday, and I'm going to have to talk to someone at the bank. . . ."

He stepped closer to me and handed me a white business card. It had a number printed on it in gold lettering. There was another number written in ink that made the balance currently in my checking account look extremely small. Nothing else.

"My Swiss account," he explained. "And I'm in no hurry. Have it there by Tuesday and we'll be square."

He got in the van and left.

Tuesday.

Crap.

Ebenezar watched the white van pull out, then helped Murphy get me into the truck. I sat in the middle, my legs over on Murphy's side of the cab. She had a first-aid kit in her hands, and as we rode along she covered my burned hand lightly with gauze, entirely silent. Ebenezar drove off cautiously. We heard sirens start up when we were a couple of blocks away. "The kids to the church," he said. "Then where?"

"My place," I said. "I'll get patched up for round two."

"Round two?" Ebenezar asked.

"Yeah," I said. "If I don't do something, a ritual entropy curse is gonna head my way before midnight."

"How can I help?" he asked.

I looked steadily at him. "We'll have to talk about it."

He squinted out ahead of us and kept his emotions off of his face. "Hoss. You're too involved. You do too much. You take on way too damned much."

"There's a bright side, though," I said.

"Oh?"

"Uh-huh. If I buy it tonight, at least I won't have to figure out how to pay Kincaid before he kills me."

Chapter Thirty-four

Ebenezar drove, and I felt myself float off into a pensive haze. Well, that wasn't exactly true. It was more of a pense-less haze, but I didn't complain about it. My mouth didn't want to work, and on some level I knew that numb, floating shock was better than searing agony. Somewhere in the background, Murphy and Ebenezar talked enough to work out details, and we must have dropped the kids off with Father Forthill, because when I finally got out of the truck, the back was empty of children.

"Murphy," I said, frowning. "I had a thought. If there's an APB out for me, maybe we shouldn't go back to my place."

"Harry," she said, "we've been here for two hours. You're sitting on your couch."

I looked around. She was right. The fireplace was going, with Mister in his favorite spot by the mantel, and the notch-eared puppy was lying on the couch next to me, using my leg as a pillow. I tasted Scotch in my mouth, one of Ebenezar's own brews, but I didn't remember drinking it. Man, I must have been in worse shape than I thought. "So I am," I said. "But that doesn't make my concerns any less valid."

Murphy had hung my coat up on its hook by the door and was wearing a pair of my knee-length knit shorts. They fell to halfway down her calf, and she'd had to tie a big knot in the front to keep them on, but at least she wasn't walking around in her panties. Dammit.

"I don't think so," she said. "I've talked to Stallings. He said there's an APB for someone matching your description, but your name isn't attached to it. Only that the suspect is wanted for questioning and may be using the alias Larry or Barry. There were no prints on the weapon, but it was registered to the witness." She shook her head. "I don't know how that happened. I'd say you got lucky, but I know better. And you'd make some wiseass remark about it."

I let out a broken little laugh. "Yeah," I said. "Hell's bells. Trixie Vixen has got to be the most vacuous, conceited, small-minded, petty, and self-absorbed baddie I've ever snooped out. That's what happened."

"What?" Murphy asked.

"My name," I said, still wheezing laughter. "She never got it straight. The woman got my freaking name wrong. I don't think she bothers to keep very close track of other people's existence if it doesn't profit her."

Murphy arched an eyebrow. "But there were other people there, weren't there? Someone must have known your name."

I nodded. "Arturo for sure. Probably Joan. But everyone else only knew my first name."

"And someone had to wipe any of your prints from the gun. They're covering for you," Murphy said.

I pursed my lips, surprised. Not so much that Arturo and his people had done it, but because of my reaction to the news—it made a warm spot somewhere inside me that felt almost completely unfamiliar. "They are," I said. "God knows why, but they are."

"Harry, you saved the lives of some of their people." She shook her head. "In the business they're in, I doubt Chicago's finest are exactly making them feel like valued members of the community. That kind of isolation brings people together—and you helped them. Makes you one of them when trouble comes."

"Makes me family," I said.

She smiled a little and nodded. "So you know who dunnit?"

"Trixie," I said. "Probably two others. My sense is that it's the Ex-Mr.-Genosa club, but that's just a hunch. And I think they had help."

"Why do you say that?"

"Because Trixie was getting instructions from someone on the phone when she was holding a gun on me,"

I said. "And they've been invoking that curse with a ritual. Unless someone's actually got some talent, it takes two or three people to raise the energy that's needed. And let's face it, three witches cackling over a cauldron somewhere is pretty much stereotyped into the public awareness."

"*Macbeth*," Murphy said.

"Yeah. And that movie with Jack Nicholson as the devil."

"Can I ask you something?"

"Sure."

"You told me about rituals once. The cosmic vending machine, right? An outside power offers to give you something if you fulfill a specific sequence of events."

"Yeah."

Murphy shook her head. "Scary. People can just do a dance and someone dies. Regular people, I mean. What happens if someone publishes a book?"

"Someone has," I said. "Plenty of times. The White Council has pushed it to happen a couple of times—like with the Necronomicon. It's a reasonably good way to make certain the ritual in question isn't going to work."

She frowned. "I don't get it. Why?"

"Supply and demand," I said. "There are limits to what outside forces can deliver to the mortal world. Think of the incoming power as water flowing through a pipeline. If a couple of people are using a rite once every couple of weeks, or every few years, there's no problem pumping in enough magic to make it work. But if fifty thousand people are trying to use the rite all at once, there isn't enough power in any one place to make it happen. It just comes out as a little dribble that tastes bad and smells funny."

Murphy nodded, following me. "So people who have access to rituals don't want to share them."

"Exactly."

"And a book of dark rituals is not something your average vacuous princess of porn picks up at the mall. So she had help."

"Yeah," I said, frowning. "And that last run on the curse had a professional behind it."

"Why do you say that?"

"It was a hell of a lot faster, for one thing, and deadlier. It hit so quick I didn't have time to redirect it away from the victim, even though I knew it was coming. It was stronger, too. A *lot* stronger, like someone who knew the business had taken the trouble to focus or amplify it somehow."

"What can do that?" Murphy asked.

"Coordination between talented wizards," I said. "Uh, sometimes you can use certain articles and materials to amplify magic. They're usually expensive as hell. Sometimes special locations can help, places like Stonehenge, or certain positions of stars on a given night of the year. Then there's the old standby."

"What's that?" Murphy asked.

"Blood," I said. "The destruction of life. The sacrifice of animals. Or people."

Murphy shivered. "And you think they're coming after you next?"

"Yeah," I said. "I'm in the way. They have to if they want to get away clean."

"Get away with their big old fund intact?"

"Yeah," I said.

"Seems pretty extreme for a greed killing," Murphy said. "I've got nothing against greed as a motivator, but damn. It's like some people just never grasp the idea that other people actually exist."

"Yeah," I said with a sigh. "I guess this time there just happened to be three of them standing in the same place."

"Heh," Murphy said. "God only knows what kind of unholy bad luck got three ex-wives together. I mean, what are the odds, you know?"

I sat up straight. Murphy had put her finger on it. "Stars and stones, you're right. How could I have missed that?"

"You've been a little busy?" Murphy guessed.

I felt my heart speed up. It beat with a dull pressure on

my hand. It wasn't pain yet, but it was coming. "Okay, let's think, here. Arturo didn't announce that he was getting married again. I mean, I only found out because someone who knows him made a sharp guess. And I doubt the ex-wives knew about it firsthand. In fact, I'd be willing to bet they were informed of the fact by a third party."

"Why?" Murphy asked.

"Because if you want to work magic on someone, you've got to believe in it. You've got to want it. Otherwise it just fizzles. That means that they *want* someone dead. Genuinely want it."

"Because when they found out it was a nasty surprise," Murphy said. "Maybe whoever told them tilted things even further before the ex-wives found out. Made it hit them really hard, make them really mad. I don't know, Harry. You'd need a fourth party to want Arturo's new squeeze nixed for that to hold water."

"Yeah," I agreed. Then I felt my eyes widen. "Unless that wasn't what they wanted at all. Murph, I don't think this is about money."

"I don't understand."

"Genosa's in *love*," I said. I felt myself rise to my feet. "Son of a bitch, it was right there in front of me the whole time."

Murphy frowned and rose with me, putting her hand on my good arm. "Harry, you need to sit back down. All right? You're hurt. You need to sit down until Ebenezar gets back."

"What?"

"Ebenezar. He thinks he can do something for your hand, but he had to pick up something first."

"Oh," I said. My head spun a little. She tugged at my arm and I sat back down. "But that's *it*."

"What's it?"

"Trixie and the other *stregas* are just weapons for someone else. *Genosa* is in *love*. That's why he didn't react to Lara like everyone else. They can't touch him. That's what this is all about."

Murphy frowned. "What do you mean? Who is using them as weapons?"

"The White Court," I said. "Lord Raith and the White Court. It's no coincidence that he *and* his second-in-command are in Chicago this weekend."

"What does Genosa's being in love have to do with anything?"

"The White Court can control people. I mean, they seduce them, get close, and before long they can sink in the psychic hooks. They can make slaves of the people they feed on, and make them *like* it to boot. That's the source of their power."

Murphy arched an eyebrow. "But not if someone is in love?"

I laughed weakly. "Yeah. They just said it out loud. It was an internal matter. Hell, it was practically the first thing she said about him. That Arturo was always falling in love."

"What who said?"

"Joan," I said. "Plain old practical, flannel-wearing, doughnut-scarfing Joan. And Lara the wonder slut. Not in that order. I'm sure of it."

Murphy scowled. "Egad, Holmes. You've got to provide me with some context if you want me to understand."

"Okay, okay," I said. "Here's the setup, all right? Raith is the leader of the White Court, but over the past several years he's been losing face. His personal power base is slowly eroding."

"Why?"

"Thomas, mainly," I said. "Raith apparently murders his sons before they start getting ideas of knocking him off and taking over the family business. He sent Thomas to get killed at the vampire masquerade ball, but Thomas hooked up with Michael and me and came out of it alive. Then Raith set Thomas up again last year, at the duel with Ortega, but Thomas got through that one, too. And from what I've deduced, Papa Raith isn't putting the fear of himself into his own children very well anymore."

"What's that got to do with Genosa?" she asked.

"Genosa publicly defied Raith's authority," I said.

"Arturo told me that someone had been slowly buying up the adult-movie companies, manipulating things from behind the scenes. Trace the money trail back and I'd bet you dollars to doughnuts that you'll find that it's Raith and that he owns Silverlight. By leaving Silverlight Studios and going off to break stereotypes by doing his own movies, Genosa was defying Raith's authority in a very public way."

"So you're saying that the White Court controls the erotica industry?"

"Or at least a bunch of it," I confirmed. "Think about it. They can influence people's opinions of all kinds of things—what physical beauty is, what sex is, how one should react to temptation, what is acceptable behavior in intimate relationships. My God, Murph, it's like training deer to come to a particular feeding point to make stalking and killing them easier."

Her mouth fell open for a moment. "God. That's . . . that's sort of terrifying. That's huge."

"And insidious," I said. "I never even thought about something like that happening. Or maybe it's fairer to say that it's *been* happening. Maybe Raith was just taking over the business from some other player in the White Court."

"So when Genosa thumbed his nose at Silverlight, it made Lord Raith look even weaker."

"Yeah," I said. "A mere human defying the White King. And Raith couldn't send Lara to control him, either, because Genosa is in love."

"Meaning?"

"The White Court can't touch someone who is in love," I said. "Real love. If they try to feed on them, it causes them physical agony. It's . . . their holy water, I guess you could say. Their silver bullet. They're terrified of it."

Murphy's eyes brightened and she nodded. "Raith wasn't able to control Genosa, so he had to find a way to torpedo the guy instead, or lose face."

"And be torn from his position of power. Exactly."

"Why not just kill Genosa?"

I shook my head. "The White Court seems to pride itself on elegance when it comes to power games. Thomas told me that when the Whites go to war with one another, they do it through indirect means. Cat's-paws. The more untraceable the better. They believe that intelligence and manipulation are more important than mere strength. If Raith just popped a cap in Arturo, it would have been still another loss of face. So . . ."

"So he finds someone he *can* control," Murphy said. "He sets them up to find out that the new wife is a danger to their positions, and he does it in the worst possible way, to make them readier to take action. He even hands them the murder weapon—a big, nasty dark ritual. He's not sure who it is, so he tells them to get rid of whoever Genosa is secretly engaged to. They've got a means, a motive, and an opportunity. Even in magical circles, I'll bet no one's going to be able to easily prove it was Raith who was responsible for the death of the woman Arturo was engaged to."

"And in love with," I said. "For Lord Raith it's a win-win situation. If they kill the fiancée, it will destabilize Genosa and hamper his ability to produce films. Hell, maybe Raith planned to wait until he fell into a depression afterward, and then send one of the ex-wives after a while to offer comfort, seduce him, and leave him vulnerable to Lara's control. If they *don't* manage to kill the fiancée, they might still create enough havoc and confusion to derail Genosa's work."

"And even if someone on the spooky end of the block figures out whodunit, Raith has it set it up so that they can't be traced back to him."

"Yeah," I said. "Meanwhile, Arturo is back in the fold and Raith has reconsolidated his power base. End of problem."

"But not if you interfere and stop him."

"Not if I interfere and stop him," I agreed. "So once Raith gets word that I'm sticking my nose into his business, he brings in Lara to keep an eye on me and take me out if she can."

"Or just take you," Murphy said. "If this guy is a

schemer, maybe he thought it would be great to have this Lara get hooks into you."

The puppy stirred, disturbed. I shivered and petted him. "Ugh," I said. "But it didn't work, and I'm close to blowing the whole thing wide open. Now he'll have to take a swing at me and get me out of the picture."

Murphy made a growling sound. "Gutless bastard. Going through other people like that."

"It's smart," I said. "If he really has been weakened, he wouldn't want to take on anyone from the White Council directly. Only a fool goes toe to toe with a stronger enemy. That's why Thomas did the same thing as his father—recruiting me to go up against him."

Murphy whistled. "You're right. How the hell did you get this bag of snakes?"

"Clean living," I said.

"You should tell Thomas to get lost," Murphy said.

"Can't."

"Why not?"

I looked at her in silence.

Her eyes widened. She understood. "It's him. He's family."

"Half brother," I said. "Our mother used to hang around with Lord Raith."

She nodded. "So what are you going to do?"

"Survive."

"I mean about Thomas."

"I'll burn that bridge when I come to it."

"Fair enough," Murphy said. "But what is your next move?"

"Go to Thomas," I said. "Make him help." I looked down at my bandaged hand. "I need a car. And a driver."

"Done," said Murphy.

I frowned, thinking. "And I might need something else from you tonight. Something tough."

"What?"

I told her.

She stared silently past me for a moment and then said, "God, Harry."

"I know. I hate to ask it. But it's our only shot. I don't think we can win this one with simple firepower."

She shivered. "Okay."

"You sure? You don't have to do it."

"I'm with you," she said.

"Thank you, Karrin."

She gave me a small smile. "At least this way I feel like I get to do *something* to help."

"Don't be silly," I said. "The image of you gunfighting in your panties is going to boost my morale for years."

She kicked my leg gently with hers, but her smile was somewhat wooden. She looked down to focus on the puppy, who promptly rolled over on his back, chewing at her fingers.

"You okay?" I asked. "You got kinda quiet."

"I'm fine," she said. "Mostly. It's just . . ."

"Just?"

She shook her head. "It's been sort of a stressful day for me, relationship-wise."

I know what you mean, I thought.

"I mean, first that asshole Rich and Lisa. And . . ." She glanced at me, her cheeks pink. "And this thing with Kincaid."

"You mean him taking your pants off?"

She rolled her eyes. "Yeah. It's been . . . well, it's been a really, really long time since a good-looking man took my pants off. I sort of forgot how much I enjoyed it. I mean, I know this is just a reaction to the danger and adrenaline and so on, but still. I've never reacted that strongly to a simple touch."

"Oh," I said.

She sighed. "Well, you asked. It's got me a little distracted. That's all."

"Just so you know," I said, "I don't think he's human. I think he's pretty major bad news."

"Yeah," Murphy said, her voice annoyed. "It's never the nice guys who get a girl worked up."

Apparently not. "Oh," I said again.

"I'll call a cab," Murphy said. "Get some clothes and my bike. The car's still back at the park, and there might still be family there. Give me about an hour, and I'll be ready to take you where you need to go, if you're able."

"I have to be," I said.

Murphy called the cab, and just as it got there Ebenezar opened the door, carrying a brown paper grocery sack. I looked up at him, feeling a sudden blend of emotions—relief, affection, suspicion, disappointment, betrayal. It was a mess.

He saw the look. He stopped in the doorway and said, "Hoss. How's the hand?"

"Starting to feel things again," I said. "But I figure I'll pass out before it comes all the way back."

"I might be able to help a little, if you want me to."

"Let's talk about that."

Murphy had pretty obviously picked up on the tension between us back at the shelter. She kept her tone and expression neutral and said, "My cab's here, Harry. See you in an hour."

"Thanks, Murph," I said.

"Pleasure to meet you, Miss Murphy," Ebenezar said. He corrected himself almost instantly. "Lieutenant Murphy."

She almost smiled. Then she gave me a look, as if to ask me if it was all right to leave me with the old man. I nodded and she left.

"Close the door," I told Ebenezar.

He did, and turned to face me. "So. What do you want me to tell you?"

"The truth," I said. "I want the truth."

"No, you don't," Ebenezar said. "Or at least not now. Harry, you have to trust me on this one."

"No. I don't," I responded. My voice sounded rough and raw. "I've trusted you for years. Completely. I've built up some credit. You owe me."

Ebenezar looked away.

"I want answers. I want the truth."

"It will hurt," he said.

"The truth does that sometimes. I don't care."

"I *do*," he said. "Boy, there is no one, *no one,* I would hate to hurt as much as you. And this is too much to lay on your shoulders, especially right now. It could get you killed, Harry."

"That isn't your decision to make," I said quietly. It surprised me how calm I sounded. "I want the truth. Give it to me. Or get out of my home and never come back."

Frustration, even true anger flickered across the old man's face. He took a deep breath, then nodded. He put the grocery sack down on my coffee table and folded his arms, facing my fireplace. The lines on his face looked deeper. His eyes focused into the fire, or through it, and they were hard, somehow frightening.

"All right," he said. "Ask. I'll answer. But this could change things for you, Harry. It could change the way you think and feel."

"About what?"

"About yourself. About me. About the White Council. About everything."

"I can take it."

Ebenezar nodded. "All right, Hoss. Don't say I didn't warn you.

Chapter Thirty-five

"Let's start simple," I said. "How do you know Kincaid?"

He blew out a breath, cheeks puffing out. "He's in the trade."

"The trade?"

"Yes." Ebenezar sat down on the other end of the couch. The puppy got up on wobbling legs and snuffled over to examine him. His tail started wagging. Ebenezar gave the little dog a brief smile and scratched his ears.

"Most of the major supernatural powers have someone for that kind of work. Ortega was the Red Court's, for example. Kincaid and I are contemporaries, of a sort."

"You're assassins," I said.

He didn't deny it.

"Didn't look like you liked him much," I said.

"There are proprieties between us," Ebenezar said. "A measure of professional courtesy and respect. Boundaries. Kincaid crossed them about a century ago in Istanbul."

"He's not human?"

Ebenezar shook his head.

"Then what is he?"

"There are people walking around who carry the blood of the Nevernever in them," Ebenezar said. "Changelings, for one, those who are half-Sidhe. The faeries aren't the only ones who can breed with humanity, though, and the scions of such unions can have a lot of power. Their offspring are usually malformed. Freakish. Often insane. But sometimes the child looks human."

"Like Kincaid."

Ebenezar nodded. "He's older than I am. When I met him, I still had hair and he had been serving the creature for centuries."

"What creature?" I asked.

"*The* creature," Ebenezar said. "Another half mortal like Kincaid. Vlad Drakul."

I blinked. "Vlad Tepesh? Dracula?"

Ebenezar shook his head. "Dracula was the son of Drakul, and pretty pale and skinny by comparison. Went to the Black Court as a kind of teenage rebellion. The original creature is . . . well. Formidable. Dangerous. Cruel. And Kincaid was his right arm for centuries. He was known as the Hound of Hell. Or just the Hellhound."

"And he's afraid of you," I said, my voice bitter. "Blackstaff McCoy. I guess that's your working name."

"Something like that. The name . . . is a long story."

"Get started, then," I said.

He nodded, absently rubbing the puppy behind the ears. "Ever since the founding of the White Council, ever since the first wizards gathered to lay down the Laws of Magic, there has been someone interested in tearing it apart," he said. "The vampires, for one. The faeries have all been at odds with us at one time or another. And there have always been wizards who thought the world would be a nicer place without the Council in it."

"Gee," I said. "I just can't figure why any wizard would think that."

Ebenezar's voice lashed out, harsh and cold. "You don't know what you're talking about, boy. You don't know what you're saying. Within my own lifetime, there have been times and places where even speaking those words could have been worth your life."

"Gosh, I'd hate to for my life to be in jeopardy. Why did he call you Blackstaff?" I asked, my voice hardening. An intuition hit me. "It's not a nickname," I said. "Is it. It's a title."

"A title," he said. "A solution. At times, the White Council found itself bound by its own laws while its enemies had no such constraints. So an office was created. A position within the Council. A mark of status. One wizard, and only one, was given the freedom to choose when the Laws had been perverted, and turned as weapons against us."

I stared at him for a moment and then said, "After all that you taught me about magic. That it came from life. That it was a force that came from the deepest desires of the heart. That we have a responsibility to use it wisely—hell, to *be* wise, and kind, and honorable, to make sure that the power gets used wisely. You taught me all of that. And now you're telling me that it doesn't mean anything. That the whole time you were standing there with a license to kill."

The lines in the old man's face looked hard and bitter. He nodded. "To kill. To enthrall. To invade the thoughts of another mortal. To seek knowledge and power from beyond the Outer Gates. To transform others. To reach beyond the borders of life. To swim against the currents of time."

"You're the White Council's wetworks man," I said. "For all their prattle about the just and wise use of magic, when the wisdom and justice of the Laws of Magic get inconvenient, they have an assassin. You do that for them."

He said nothing.

"You kill people."

"Yes." Ebenezar's face looked like something carved in stone, and his voice was quietly harsh. "When there is no choice. When lives are at stake. When the lack of action would mean—" He cut himself off, jaw working. "I didn't want it. I still don't. But when I have to, I act."

"Like at Casaverde," I said. "You hit Ortega's stronghold when he escaped our duel."

"Yes," he said, still remote. "Ortega killed more of the White Council than any enemy in our history during the attack at Archangel." His voice faltered for a moment. "He killed Simon. My friend. Then he came here and tried to kill you, Hoss. And he was coming back here to finish the job as soon as he recovered. So I hit Casaverde. Killed him and almost two hundred of his personal retainers. And I killed nearly a hundred people there in the house with them. Servants. Followers. Food."

I felt sick. "You told me it would be on the news. I thought maybe it was the Council. Or that you'd done it without killing anyone but vampires. I had time to think about it later, but . . . I wanted to believe you'd done what was right."

"There's what's right," the old man said, "and then there's what's necessary. They ain't always the same."

"Casaverde wasn't the only necessary thing you did," I said. "Was it."

"Casaverde," Ebenezar said, his voice shaking. "Tunguska. New Madrid. Krakatoa. A dozen more. God help me, a dozen more at least."

I stared at him for a long moment. Then I said, "You told me the Council assigned me to live with you because they wanted to annoy you. But that wasn't it. Because you don't send a potentially dangerous criminal element to live with your hatchet man if you want to rehabilitate him."

He nodded. "My orders were to observe you. And kill you if you showed the least bit of rebelliousness."

"Kill me." I rubbed at my eyes. The pounding in my hand grew worse. "As I remember, I got rebellious with you more than once."

"You did," he said.

"Then why didn't you kill me?"

"Jehoshaphat, boy. What's the point of having a license to ignore the will of the Council if you aren't going to use it?" He shook his head, a tired smile briefly appearing on his mouth. "It wasn't your fault you got raised by that son of a bitch DuMorne. You were a dumb kid, you were angry, and afraid, and your magic was strong as hell. But that didn't mean you needed killing. They gave the judgment to me. I used it. They aren't happy with how I used it, but I did."

I stared at him. "There's something else you aren't telling me."

He was silent for a minute. Then two. And a while later he said, "The Council knew that you were the son of Margaret LeFay. They knew that she was one of the wizards who had turned the Council's own laws against it. She was guilty of violating the First Law, among others, and she had . . . unsavory associations with various entities of dubious reputation. The Wardens were under orders to arrest her on sight. She'd have been tried and executed in moments when she was brought before the Council."

"I was told she died in childbirth," I said.

"She did," Ebenezar confirmed. "I don't know why, but for some reason she turned away from her previous associates—including Justin DuMorne. After that, nowhere was safe for her. She ran from her former allies and from the Wardens for perhaps two years. And she ran from me. I had my orders regarding her as well."

I stared at him in pained fascination. "What happened?"

"She met your father. A man. A mortal, without powers, without influence, without resources. But a man with a good soul, like few I have ever seen. I believe that she fell in love with him. But on the night you were born, one of her former allies found her and exacted his vengeance for her desertion." He looked up at me directly and said, "He used an entropy curse. A ritual entropy curse."

Shock paralyzed me for a moment. Then I said, "Lord Raith."

"Yes."

"He killed my mother."

"He did," Ebenezar confirmed.

"God. You're . . . you're sure?"

"He's a snake," Ebenezar said. "But I'm as sure as I can be."

The pounding spread up my arm, and the room pulsed brighter and dimmer in time with it. "My mother. He was standing three feet from me. He killed my mother." A child's pain—the emptiness in my life the shape of my unknown mother, my unfortunate father—swelled and screamed in rage. The source of that pain, or part of it, had finally been revealed to me. And in that moment, had I known where to strike, I would have eagerly embraced murder. Nothing mattered but exacting retribution. Nothing mattered but taking righteous vengeance for the death of a child's mother. *My* mother. I started shaking, and I knew that my sanity was buckling under the pressure.

"Hoss," Ebenezar said. "Easy, boy."

"Kill him," I whispered. "I'll kill him."

"No," Ebenezar said. "You've got to breathe, boy. Think."

I started gathering power. "Kill him. *Kill* him. Everything. All of it. Nothing left."

"Harry," Ebenezar snapped. "Harry, let go. You can't handle that kind of power. You'll kill yourself if you try."

I didn't care about that, either. The power felt too good—too strong. I wanted it. I wanted Raith to pay. I wanted him to suffer, screaming, and then die for what he had done to me. And I was strong enough to make it happen. I had the power and the resolve to bring such a tide of magic against him that he would be utterly destroyed. I would lay him low and make him howl for mercy before I tore him apart. He deserved nothing less.

And then fire blossomed in my hand again, so sudden and sharp that my back convulsed into an agonized arch, and I fell to the floor. I couldn't scream. The pain washed my fury away like dandelions before a flash flood. I looked around wildly and saw the old man's broad, calloused hand clamped down over my burned, lightly bandaged flesh with bruising strength. When he saw my eyes he released my hand, his expression sickened.

I curled up for a minute while my pounding heart telegraphed consecutive tidal waves of agony through me. It was several minutes before I could master the pain and sit slowly up again.

"I'm sorry," Ebenezar whispered. "Harry, I can't let you indulge your rage. You'll kill yourself."

"I'll take him with me," I got out between gritted teeth.

Ebenezar let out a bitter laugh. "No, you won't, Hoss."

"How do you know?"

"I've tried," he said. "Three times. And I didn't even get close. And you think your mother went without spending her death curse on her murderer? The creature who had enslaved her? Might as well ask if a fish remembered to swim."

I blinked at him. "What do you mean?"

"He's protected," he said quietly. "Magic just slides off him."

"Even a death curse?"

"Useless," he said bitterly. "Raith is protected by something big. Maybe a big damned demon. Maybe even some old god. He can't be touched with magic."

"Is that even possible?" I asked.

"Aye," the old man said. "I don't know how. But it is. Does a lot to explain how he got to become the White King."

"I don't believe it," I said quietly. "She'd been close to him. She must have known he was protected. She was strong enough to make the White Council afraid of her. She wouldn't have spent her curse for nothing."

"She threw it. She wasted it."

"So now my mother is incompetent as well as evil," I said.

"I never said that—"

"What do you know about her?" I said. I had my right hand clamped around my left wrist, hoping to distract myself from the pain. "How would you know? Did she tell you? Were you there with her?"

He looked down at the floor, his face pale. "No."

"Then how the hell do you know?" I demanded.

His words came out in a harsh croak. "Because I knew her, Hoss. I knew her almost better than she knew herself."

The fire crackled.

"How?" I whispered.

He drew his hand back from the puppy. "She was my apprentice. I was her teacher. Her mentor. She was my responsibility."

"You taught her?"

"I failed her." He chewed on his lip. "Harry . . . when Maggie was coming into her power, I made her life a living hell. She was barely more than a child, but I rode herd on her night and day. I pushed her to learn. To excel. But I was too close. Too involved. And she resented it. She ran off as soon as she could get away with it. Started taking up with bad sorts out of sheer rebellion. She made a couple of bad decisions, and . . . and then it was too late for her to go back."

He sighed. "You're so much like her. I knew it when they sent you to me. I knew it the minute I saw you. I didn't want to repeat my mistakes with you. I wanted you to have breathing space. To make up your own mind about what kind of person you would be." He shook his head. "The hardest lesson a wizard has to learn is that even with so much power, there are some things you can't control. No matter how much you want to."

I just stared at him. "You're an assassin. A murderer. You knew about what happened to my mother. You knew her and you never *told* me. Good God, Ebenezar. How could you do that to me? Why didn't you *tell* me?"

"I'm only human, Hoss. I did what I thought was best for you at the time."

"I *trusted* you," I said. "Do you know how much that *means* to me?"

"Yes," he said. "I never did it with the intention of hurting you. But it's done. And I wouldn't choose to do it any differently if it happened again."

He moved, got the sack, and hunkered down by me so that he could rest my forearm over one knee and examine the burned hand. Then he reached into the bag and drew out a long strand of string hung with some kind of white stone. "Let's see to your hand. I think I can get the circulation restored, at least a little. Maybe enough to save the hand. And I can stop the pain for a day or two. You'll still have to get to a doctor, but this should tide you over if you're expecting trouble tonight."

It didn't take him long, and I tried to sort through my thoughts. They were buried under a storm of raw emotions, all of them ugly. I lost track of time again for a minute. When I looked up, my hand didn't hurt and it seemed a little less withered beneath the white bandages. A string of white stones had been tied around my wrist. Even as I watched, one of them yellowed and began to slowly darken.

"The stones will absorb the pain for a while. They'll crumble one at a time, so you'll know when they stop working." He looked up to my face. "Do you want my help tonight?"

An hour ago it wouldn't even have been a question. I'd have been more than glad to have Ebenezar next to me in a fight. But the old man had been right. The truth hurt. The truth *burned*. My thoughts and feelings boiled in a blistering, dangerous tumult in my chest. I didn't want to admit what was at the core of that turmoil, but denying it wouldn't make it any less true.

Ebenezar had lied to me. From day one.

And if he'd been lying to me, what else had he lied about?

I'd built my whole stupid life on a few simple beliefs. That I had a responsibility to use my power to help people. That it was worth risking my own life and safety to defend others. Beliefs I'd taken as my own primarily because of the old man's influence.

But he hadn't been what I thought he was. Ebenezar wasn't a paragon of wizardly virtue. If anything he was a precautionary tale. He had seemed to talk a good game, but underneath that surface, he'd been as cold and as vicious as any of the cowardly bastards in the Council whom I despised.

Maybe he'd never claimed to be a shining example. Maybe I'd just needed someone to admire. To believe in. Maybe I'd been the stupid one, putting my faith in the wrong place.

But none of that changed the fact that Ebenezar had hidden things from me. That he'd lied.

That made it simple.

"No," I whispered. "I don't want you there. I don't know you. I never did."

"But you'd fight beside someone like the Hellhound."

"Kincaid's a killer for hire. He never pretended he was anything else."

The old man exhaled slowly and said, "I reckon that ain't unfair."

"Thank you for your help. But I've got things to do. You should go."

He rose, picked up the paper bag, and said, "I'm still there for you, Hoss, if you change your—"

I felt my teeth clench. "I said get out."

He blinked his eyes a few times and whispered, "A hard lesson. The hardest."

Then he left.

I refused to watch him go.

Chapter Thirty-six

I sat in the silence of the old man's departure and felt a lot of things. I felt tired. I felt afraid. And I felt alone. The puppy sat up and displayed some of the wisdom and compassion of his kind. He wobbled carefully over to me, scrambled up onto my lap, and started licking the bottom of my chin.

I petted his soft baby fur, and it gave me an unexpected sense of comfort. Sure, he was tiny, and sure, he was just a dog, but he was warm and loving and a brave little beast. And he liked me. He kept on giving me puppy kisses, tail wagging, until I finally smiled at him and roughed up his fur with one hand.

Mister wasn't about to let a mere dog outdo him. The hefty tom promptly descended from his perch on my bookshelf and started rubbing himself back and forth under my hand until I paid attention to him, too.

"I guess you aren't nothing but trouble," I told the dog. "But I already have a furry companion. Right, Mister?"

Mister blinked at me with an enigmatic cat expression, batted the puppy off the couch and onto the floor, and promptly lost interest in me. Mister flowed back down onto the floor, where the puppy rolled to his feet, tail wagging ferociously, and began to romp clumsily around the cat, thrilled with the game. Mister flicked his ears with disdain and went back up onto his bookshelf.

I laughed. I couldn't help it. The world might be vicious and treacherous and deadly, but it couldn't kill laughter. Laughter, like love, has power to survive the worst things life has to offer. And to do it with style.

It got me moving. I dressed for trouble—black fatigue pants, a heavy wool shirt of deep red, black combat boots. I put on my gun belt with one hand, clipped my sword cane to the belt, and covered it with my duster. I made sure I had my mother's amulet and my shield bracelet, sat down, and called Thomas's cell phone.

The phone got about half of a ring out before someone picked it up and a girl's frightened voice asked, "Tommy?"

"Inari?" I asked. "Is that you?"

"It's me," she confirmed. "This is Harry, isn't it."

"For another few hours anyway," I said. "May I speak to Thomas, please?"

"No," Inari said. It sounded like she had been crying. "I was hoping this was him. I think he's in trouble."

I frowned. "What kind of trouble?"

"I saw one of my father's men," she said. "I think he had a gun. He made Thomas drop his phone in the parking lot and get into the car. I didn't know what I should do."

"Easy, easy," I said. "Where was he taken from?"

"The studio," she said, her voice miserable. "He gave me a ride here when we heard about the shooting. I'm here now."

"Is Lara there?" I asked.

"Yes. She's right here."

"Put her on, please."

"Okay," Inari said.

The phone rustled. A moment later Lara's voice glided out of the phone and into my ear. "Hello, Harry."

"Lara. I know your father is behind the curse on Arturo, along with Arturo's wives. I know they've been gunning for his fiancée so that Raith can get Arturo back under his control. And I have a question for you."

"Oh?" she said.

"Yeah. Where is Thomas?"

"It excites me when a man is so subtle," she said. "So debonaire."

"Better brace yourself, then," I said. "I want him in one piece. I'm willing to kill anyone who gets in the way. And I'm willing to pay you to help me."

"Really?" Lara said. I heard her murmur something, presumably to Inari. She waited a moment, I heard a door close, and the tone of her voice changed subtly, becoming businesslike. "I am willing to hear you out."

"And I'm willing to give you House Raith. And the White Court with it."

Shocked silence followed. Then she said, "And how would you manage such a thing?"

"I remove your father from power. You take over."

"How vague. The situation isn't a simple one," she said, but I could hear a throbbing note of excitement in her voice. "The other Houses of the White Court follow House Raith because they fear and respect my father. It seems unlikely that they would transfer that respect to me."

"Unlikely. Not impossible. I think it can be done."

She made a slow, low purring sound. "Do you? And what would you expect from me in return? If my father has decided to remove Thomas, I am hardly capable of stopping him."

"You won't need to. Just take me to him. I'll get Thomas myself."

"After which, my father will be so impressed with your diplomatic skills that he cedes the House to me?"

"Something like that," I said. "Get me there. Then all you have to do is watch from the sidelines while Cat's-paw Dresden handles your father."

"Mmm," she said. "That would certainly raise my status among the Lords of the Court. To arrange for a usurpation isn't so unusual, but very few manage to have good seats to it as well. A firsthand view of it would be a grace note few have attained."

"Plus if you were standing right there and things went badly for me, you'd be in a good spot to backstab me and keep your father's goodwill."

"Of course," she said, without a trace of shame. "You understand me rather well, wizard."

"Oh, there's one other thing I want."

"Yes?" she asked.

"Leave the kid alone. Don't push her. Don't pressure her. You come clean with Inari. You tell her the deal with her bloodline and you let her make up her own mind when it comes to her future."

She waited for a beat and then said, "That's all?"

"That's all."

She purred again. "My. I am not yet sure if you are truly that formidable or simply a vast and mighty fool, but for the time being I am finding you an extremely exciting man."

"All the girls tell me that."

She laughed. "Let us assume for a moment that I find your proposal agreeable. I would need to know how you intend to overthrow my father. He's somewhat invincible, you see."

"No, he isn't," I said. "I'm going to show you how weak he really is."

"And how do you know this?"

I closed my eyes and said, "Insight."

Lara lapsed into a thoughtful silence for a moment. Then she said, "There is something else I must know, wizard. Why? Why do this?"

"I owe Thomas for favors past," I said. "He's been an ally, and if I leave him hanging out to dry it's going to be bad for me in the long term, when I need other allies. If the plan comes off, I also get someone in charge of things at the White Court who is more reasonable to work with."

Lara made a soft sound that was probably mostly pensive but that would have been a lot more interesting in the dark. Uh. I mean, in person.

"No," she said then. "That's not all of it."

"Why not?"

"That would be sufficient reason if it were me," she said. "But you aren't like me, wizard. You aren't like most of your own kind. I have no doubt that you have reasonable skill at the calculus of power, but calculation is not at the heart of your nature. You prepare to take a terrible risk, and I would know why your heart is set to it."

I chewed on my lip for a second, weighing my options

and the possible consequences. Then I said, "Do you know who Thomas's mother was?"

"Margaret LeFay," she said, puzzled. "But what does that—" She stopped abruptly. "Ah. Now I see. That explains a great deal about his involvement in political matters over the past few years." She let out a little laugh, but it was somehow sad. "You're much like him, you know. Thomas would sooner tear off his own arm than see one of his siblings hurt. He's quite irrational about it."

"Is that reason enough for you?" I asked.

"I am not yet entirely devoid of affection for my family, wizard. It satisfies me."

"Besides," I added, "I've just handed you a secret with the potential for some fairly good blackmail down the line."

She laughed. "Oh, you *do* understand me."

"Are you in?"

There was silence. When Lara finally spoke again, her voice was firmer, more eager. "I do not know precisely where my father would have had Thomas taken."

"Can you find out?"

Her voice took on a pensive tone. "In fact, I believe I can. Perhaps it was fate."

"What was fate?"

"You'll see," she said. "What sort of time frame did you have in mind?"

"An immediate one," I said. "The immediater the better."

"I'll need half an hour or a little more. Meet me at my family's home north of town."

"Half an hourish," I said. "Until then."

I hung up the phone just as a loud, low rumble approached my house. A moment later Murphy came back in. She was decked out in biker-grade denim and leather again. "I guess we're going somewhere."

"Rev up the Hog," I said. "You ready for another fight?"

Her teeth flashed. She tossed me a red motorcycle helmet and said, "Get on the bike, bitch."

Chapter Thirty-seven

Motorcycles aren't safe transport, as far as it goes. I mean, insurance statistics show that everyone in the country is going to wind up in a traffic accident of some kind and most of us are going to be involved in more than one. If you're driving around in a beat-up old Lincoln battleship and someone clips you at twenty miles an hour, it probably is going to frighten and annoy you. If you're sitting on a motorcycle when it happens, you'll be lucky to wind up in traction. Even if you aren't in an accident with another vehicle, it's way too easy to get yourself hurt or killed on a bike. Bikers don't wear all that leather around simply for the fashion value or possible felony assaults. It's handy for keeping the highway from ripping the skin from your flesh should you wind up losing control of the bike and sliding along the asphalt for a while.

All that said, riding a motorcyle is *fun*.

I put on the bulky, clunky red helmet, fairly certain that I had never before disguised myself as a kitchen matchstick. Murphy's black helmet, by comparison, looked like something imported from the twenty-fifth century. I sighed as the battered corpse of my dignity took yet another kick in the face and got on the bike behind Murphy. I gave her directions, and her old Harley growled as she unleashed it on the unsuspecting road.

I thought the bike was going to jump out from underneath me for a second, and my balance wobbled.

"Dresden!" Murphy shouted back to me, annoyed. "Hang on to my waist!"

"With what?" I shouted back. I waved my bandaged hand to one side of her field of vision and the hand holding the staff to the other.

In answer, Murphy took my staff and shoved the end

of it down into some kind of storage rack placed so conveniently close to the rider's right hand that it couldn't have been mistaken for anything but a holster for a rifle or baseball bat. My staff stuck up like the plastic flagpole on a golf cart, but at least I had a free hand. I slipped my arm around Murphy's waist, and I could feel the muscles over her stomach tensing as she accelerated or leaned into turns, cuing me to match her. When we got onto some open road and zoomed out of the city, the wind took the ends of my leather duster, throwing them back up into the air of the bike's passage, and I had to hold tight to Murphy or risk having my coat turn into a short-term parasail.

We rolled through Little Sherwood and up to the entrance of Château Raith. Murphy brought the Harley to a halt. It might have taken me a few extra seconds to take my arm from around her waist, but she didn't seem to mind. She had her bored-cop face on as she took in the house, the roses, and the grotesque gargoyles, but I could sense that underneath it she was as intimidated as I had been, and for the same reasons. The enormous old house reeked of the kind of power and wealth that disdains laws and societies. It loomed in traditional scary fashion, and it was a long way from help.

I got off the bike and she passed me my staff. The place was silent, except for the sound of wind slithering through the trees. There was a small flickering light at the door, another at the end of the walk up to it, and a couple of splotches of landscape lighting, but other than that, nothing.

"What's the plan?" Murphy asked. She kept her voice low. "Fight?"

"Not yet," I said, and gave her the short version of events. "Watch my back. Don't start anything unless one of the Raiths tries to physically touch you. If they can do that, there's a chance they could influence you in one way or another."

Murphy shivered. "Not an issue. If I could help it they weren't going to be touching me anyway."

An engine roared and a white sports car shot through

the last several hundred yards of Little Sherwood. It all but flew up the drive, narrowly missed Murphy's bike, spun, and screeched to a neat stop, parallel-parked in the opposite direction.

Murphy traded a glance with me. She looked impressed. I probably looked annoyed.

The door opened and Lara slid out, dressed in a long, loose red skirt and a white cotton blouse with embroidered scarlet roses. She walked purposefully toward us. Her feet were bare. Silver flashed on a toe and one ankle, and as she drew closer I heard the jingle of miniature bells. "Good evening, wizard."

"Lara," I said. "I like the skirt. Nice statement. Very *Carmen*."

She flashed me a pleased smile, then focused her pale grey gaze on Murphy and said, "And who is this?"

"Murphy," she said. "I'm a friend."

Lara smiled at Murphy. Very slowly. "I can never have too many friends."

Murph's cop face held, and she added a note of casual disdain to her voice. "I didn't say your friend," she said. "I'm with Dresden."

"What a shame," Lara said.

"I'm also with the police."

The succubus straightened her spine a little at the words, and studied Murphy again. Then she inclined her head with a little motion half suggesting a curtsy, a gesture of concession.

The other door of the white sports car opened and Reformed Bully Bobby got out, carsick and a little wobbly on his feet. Inari followed him a second later, slipping underneath one of his arms to help hold him steady despite her own broken arm and sling.

Lara raised her voice. "Inari? Be a darling and fetch her for me right away. Bobby, dear, if you could help her I would take it as a kindness."

"Yeah, sure," Bobby said. He looked a little green but was recovering as he hurried toward the house with Inari.

"We'll bring her right down," Inari said.

I waited until they had gone inside. "What the hell are they doing here?" I demanded of Lara.

She shrugged. "They insisted and there was little time for argument."

I scowled. "Next time you're practicing the sex appeal, maybe you should spend some time working up some 'go-thither' to go with all the 'come-hither.'"

"I'll take it under advisement," she said.

"Who are they bringing out?" I asked.

Lara arched a brow. "Don't you know?"

I gritted my teeth. "Obviously. Not."

"Patience then, darling," she said, and walked around to the back of the sports car, hips and dark hair swaying. She opened the trunk and drew out a sheathed rapier—a real one, not one of those skinny car-antenna swords most people think of when they hear the word. The blade alone was better than three feet long, as wide as a couple of my fingers at the base, tapering to a blade as wide as my pinkie nail and ending in a needle tip. It had a winding guard of silver and white-lacquered steel that covered most of the hand, adorned with single red rose made of tiny rubies. Lara drew out a scarlet sash, tied it on, and slipped the sheathed weapon through it. "There," she said, and sauntered over to me again. "Still *Carmen*?"

"Less *Carmen*. More *Pirates of Penzance*," I said.

She put the spread fingers of one hand over her heart. "Gilbert and Sullivan. I may never forgive you that."

"How will I find the will to go on?" I asked, and rolled my eyes at Murphy. "And hey, while we're on the subject of going on . . ."

Inari slammed the door of the house open and held it that way. Bobby came out a minute later, carrying an old woman in a white nightgown in his arms. The kid was big and strong, but he didn't look like he needed to be to carry her. There was an ephemeral quality to the woman. Her silver hair drifted on any wisp of air, her arms and legs hung weakly, and she was almost painfully thin.

The kid came to us, and I got a better look. It wasn't

an old woman. Her skin was unwrinkled, even if it had the pallor of those near death, and her arms and legs weren't wasted, but were simply slender with youth. Her hair, though, was indeed silver, white, and grey. The evening breeze blew her hair away from her face, and I knew it had gone grey literally overnight.

Because the girl was Justine.

"Hell's bells," I said quietly. "I thought she was dead."

Lara stepped up beside me, staring at the girl, her features hard. "She should be," she said.

Anger flickered in my chest. "That's a hell of a thing to say."

"It's a matter of perspective. I don't bear the girl any malice, but given the choice I would rather she died than Thomas. It's the way of things."

I shot her a look. "What?"

Lara moved a shoulder in a shrug. "Thomas pulled himself away from her at the last possible instant," she said. "Truth be told, it was *after* that instant. I don't know how he managed it."

"And that bothers you?" I demanded.

"It was an unwarranted risk," she said. "It was foolish. It should have killed him to draw away."

I gave her a look that managed to be both blank and impatient.

"It's the intensity of it," she said. "It's . . . a unification. Thomas's store of life energy was all but gone. Forcibly breaking away from a vessel—"

"From Justine," I interrupted.

Lara looked impatient now. "Forcibly breaking away from Justine was an enormous psychic trauma, and he was at his weakest. Taking only lightly and breaking the contact isn't difficult. In fact, it's normally the way of things. But he'd been feeding regularly from the girl for several years. He could draw energy from her with a simple caress. To take her fully . . ." Lara's eyes grew a shade paler, and the tips of her breasts tightened against her blouse. "There's no thought involved in it. No judgment. No hesitation. Only need."

"That's horrible," Murphy said, her voice a whisper. "To force that on her."

Lara's pale eyes drifted to Murphy. "Oh, no. It isn't coerced, dear officer. She was more than willing to give. When prey has been taken so many times, they stop caring about death. There's only the pleasure of being fed upon. They're eager to give more, and they care nothing about the danger."

Murphy sounded sickened. "Maybe she broke it off instead."

Lara's mouth curled into a smirk. "No. By the time my brother took enough to restore him to his senses, the girl was little more than an animal in season."

Murphy's eyes narrowed as she stared at Lara. "And talking about it excites you. That's sick."

"Have you never made yourself hungry by talking about food, Officer Murphy?" Lara asked.

Murphy scowled, but didn't answer.

"In any case," Lara said, "what Thomas did was cruel. Justine cared for him as much as any of our prey ever can. There was little left when he drew away, of her body or her mind. Strictly speaking, she is survived, Officer. But I'm not sure one could say that she is alive."

"I get it," I said. "She and Thomas had . . . made an impression on each other. A sort of psychic bond. And you think Justine might be able to tell us where he is."

Lara nodded. "It happens when we keep someone too long. Though I'm surprised you know of it."

"I didn't," I said. "But when Bianca took Justine from him, Thomas knew that she was being held in Bianca's manor. He wouldn't say how."

Lara nodded. "If there is enough of her mind left, she might be able to lead us to my brother. I do not think he will be far from here. Father does not often travel far outside the property he controls."

Bobby reached us with the girl, and Inari ducked into the house and came out with a wheelchair. She rushed it over to Justine, and Bobby settled her into it.

I knelt down by the wheelchair. Justine lay almost

bonelessly, barely holding her head up. Her dark eyes were heavy and unfocused. A small smile touched her mouth. Her eyes were sunken and her skin was almost translucent. She took slow, shallow breaths, and I heard her make a soft, pleased sound on each exhalation.

"Man," I breathed. "She looks out of it."

"Tick-tock," Murphy reminded me.

I nodded and waved my hand in front of Justine's eyes. No reaction. "Justine?" I said quietly. "Justine, it's Harry Dresden. Can you hear me?"

A faint line appeared on her forehead, though her expression did not quite become a frown. But it was something.

"Justine," I said. "Listen to me. Thomas is in trouble. Do you hear me? Thomas is in danger, and we need you to find him."

A slow shudder rolled through her. She blinked her eyes, and though they didn't quite focus, they stirred, looking around her.

"Thomas," I said again. "Come on, Justine. I need you to talk to me."

She took a deeper breath. The languid pleasure on her face faded, replaced with a portion of both sadness, and desire. "Thomas," she whispered.

"Yeah," I said. "Where is he? Can you tell me where he is?"

This time her eyes lost focus completely, then closed. Her lovely face smoothed into an almost meditative concentration. "Feel."

"Where?" Frustration threatened to overwhelm me. "What do you feel?"

She moved a hand and touched the opposite wrist. Then her knee. "Chains. Cold."

Lara leaned over her and asked, "Is he far away?"

Justine shivered. "Not far."

"Which direction?" I asked.

She made a feeble, vague motion with her hand, but frowned at the same time.

"I don't think she's strong enough to point," I said to Lara.

Lara nodded and told Inari, "Turn the chair around slowly, please."

"Justine," I said, "can you tell us when he's in front of you?"

The girl opened her eyes. They met mine for a heartbeat, and boy howdy did I chicken out and look away fast. No soulgaze, please. I'd had too many dying sheep tattooed into my memory for one day. But as Inari turned the chair, Justine suddenly lifted her head and her hand and pointed out into the darkness. The motion was weak, but in comparison to the others it was nearly forceful.

Lara stared out at the night for a moment and then said, "The Deeps. He's in the Deeps."

"What?" Murphy asked.

Lara frowned. "It's an old cave on the northern edge of the property. There's a shaft, a natural chasm, and no one is sure how far down it goes. We use it for . . ."

"Disposing of things," I said quietly. "Like corpses."

"Yes."

"How long will it take us to get there?"

"There's a service road to the groundskeeper's cottage," she said. "Go around the manor and head north. There's a white fence on the far side of the lawn. Look for the gate."

"I won't have to. You're coming with us," I said.

Lara didn't get to answer, because the night abruptly filled with deadly thunder, and a major-league pitcher planted a fastball directly between my shoulder blades. I went down hard, and concrete skinned my face. I heard Murphy grunt and hit the ground half of a heartbeat later.

I managed to move my head a second later, in time to see one of the Bodyguard Kens standing on the front porch of the manor. He worked the slide on a shotgun, the barrel tracking Lara. The succubus darted to her left, as swift and graceful as a deer, and the bodyguard followed her. The barrel of the gun found Inari before it caught up to Lara, and the girl stood frozen, her eyes as wide as teacups.

"Look out!" Bobby screamed. He hit Inari in a flying tackle that would have rattled the teeth of a professional fullback, and the gun went off. Blood scattered into the air in a heavy red mist.

Bodyguard Ken started pumping another round into the weapon, and the nearest target was Justine. The girl sat staring toward where she'd said Thomas was. I didn't think she could even hear the shots, much less move to avoid them, and I knew that she was going to die.

That is, until Murphy popped up into a kneeling firing stance, gun in hand. The gunman spun to aim at her and fired. He'd rushed himself, and the blast went wide of Murphy. It tore into the white sports car and shredded its left front tire.

Murphy didn't shoot back right away. She aimed her pistol for an endless half second while Bodyguard Ken ejected the previous shell and began to squeeze the trigger again. The spent shell hit the ground. Murphy's gun barked.

Bodyguard Ken's head jerked to one side, as if someone had just asked him a particularly startling question.

Murphy shot him three more times. The second shot made a fingertip-sized hole in the gunman's cheekbone. The third shattered against the brick of the house, and the fourth smacked into his chest. He must have been wearing armor, but the impact of the hit was enough to send him toppling limply backward. The shotgun went off as he fell, discharging into the air, but he was dead before the echoes faded away.

Murphy watched the gunman with flat, icy eyes for a second and then spun to me, setting her gun aside to reach under my coat.

"I'm okay," I wheezed. "I'm okay. The coat stopped it."

Murphy looked startled. "Since when has the duster been lined with Kevlar?"

"It isn't," I said. "It's magic. Hurts like hell but I'll be all right."

Murphy gripped my shoulder hard. "Thank God. I thought you were dead."

"Check the kid. I think he took a hit."

She went to over to Bobby and Inari, and was joined

by Lara. I followed a moment later. Inari was whimpering with pain. Bobby was in shock, lying there quietly while he bled from his shredded shoulder and arm. He'd been lucky as hell. Only part of the blast had taken him, and while the wound would leave him with some nasty scars, it hadn't torn open any arteries. He'd live. Murphy grabbed a first-aid kit off of her bike and got the wound site covered up and taped down with a pressure bandage. Then she moved on to the girl.

"Is he all right?" Inari's voice was panicky. "He was so brave. Is he all right?"

"He should be," Murphy said. "Where's it hurt?"

"It's my shoulder," Inari said. "Oh, God, it hurts."

Murphy tore open the girl's T-shirt with ruthless practicality and examined the injury. "Not shot," she said. "Looks like she did it when the kid pulled her out of the line of fire." Murphy moved her hand and Inari went breathless and pale with pain. "Crap, it's her collarbone, Harry. Maybe a dislocated shoulder too. She can't move herself. Both of them need an ambulance, and now." She looked over at the bodyguard and shook her head. "And there's a fatality on the scene. This is getting bad, Dresden. We have to put this fire out before it goes wild."

"We don't have time to wait around while the cops sort things out," I said.

"And if we don't report the shooting along with the gunshot wounds, we're going to have police crawling through every inch of our lives."

"It was an accident," Lara said. "The boy and Inari were looking at my father's collection of guns. She slipped and fell. The shotgun went off."

"What about the body?" Murphy demanded.

Lara shrugged. "What body?"

Murphy glared at Lara and cast me a glance of appeal. "Harry?"

"Hey, telling the truth keeps getting me put in jail. And the last time I tried to engineer a cover-up, I wound up cleverly running off with the murder weapon and covering it with my prints before handing it over to someone who thought I was a murderer at the time. So don't look at me."

"There's no time to argue about this," Lara said. "If one of my father's guards saw you, he'll have reported you. The others will be on their way, and will be more heavily armed." She focused on Murphy. "Officer, let me handle this quietly. It will only protect the mortal officers who might get involved. And, after all, only the man who died committed any crime."

Murphy narrowed her eyes.

"I will owe you a favor," Lara said. "If matters go well tonight, it could be a considerable asset to you in the future. Dealing with the Raiths is a dark business. Let it stay in the dark."

Murphy hesitated. Then her mouth firmed into a line and she nodded once. She changed out the clip in her pistol to a fresh one. "Come on," she said. "Let's move before I start thinking about this."

"Moving before I think is my specialty," I said.

"The road," Lara said. "Through the gate behind the house I'll meet you at the groundskeeper's cottage."

"Why not squeeze onto the bike?" I said.

Murphy gave me an arch look.

"I'm just being practical," I said defensively.

"Someone has to call the ambulance and move the body," Lara said. "And I'd get there faster on my own in any case. I'll catch up to you when I can."

Which I figured was as much assurance as I'd get from her. It wasn't encouraging, but time was short, my options few, and standing around outdoors was likely to get everyone a bad case of deaditis.

So I strode to Murphy's bike. "Let's go."

Murphy came over to me, eyes on Lara. "She'll turn on us," she said quietly.

"She'll back the winning horse. So it had better be you and me. Can you handle the vigilante thing?"

She smiled at me, nervous but game. "Get on the bike, bitch."

She got on, I got on behind her, and, rebels that we were, neither of us put on a helmet.

What can I say? I like to live dangerously.

Chapter Thirty-eight

Murphy zipped around the house, tearing up the lawn with her Harley. We were doing better than sixty by the time she cleared the smooth turf surrounding the manor and zipped through an open gate onto a long, narrow gravel lane lined with high hedges.

Ahead of us, headlights on high-beam flashed into our eyes and an engine roared.

Lara had been right. Raith's bodyguards knew we were coming.

The car surged toward us.

Murphy's head whipped left and right, but the hedges were old growth, impassable and unbroken. "Crap! No time to turn!"

Ahead of us, I saw the silhouette of the remaining Bodyguard Ken climb out of the car window to sit on it, and lift a gun to his shoulder.

I leaned forward into Murphy, and took my staff from the holster. "Murphy!" I shouted. "We need more speed! Go faster!"

She looked over her shoulder, blue eyes wide, blond hair lashing around her cheeks.

"Go!" I screamed.

I felt her shoulders set as she turned back to the front and stomped on gears with one foot, and the old Harley roared as it dug into the road with ferocious power and shot ahead at terrifying speed. Flame spat from the shape ahead of us, and bullets hit the road, kicking up sparks and bits of gravel with a series of whistling whip-lash sounds that beat the sound of exploding shots to us by almost a second.

I ignored the gunman, focusing on the staff. Of all my foci, the staff was the most versatile. Meant simply to assist with the redirection of forces I could use to call wind, to bend steel bars, and to channel lightning. I had used my staff to erect barriers of force, disrupt hostile magics, and in a pinch to beat bad guys about the head and shoulders.

I took the tool, the trademark and icon of a wizard, and couched it under my arm like a lance, the tip extending past Murphy's bike. I reached out for my will and gathered up power, feeding it into the rune-carved wood.

"What are you doing?" Murphy screamed.

"Faster!" I thundered. "Don't turn!"

Murphy had another gear, and that damned Harley had to have been built by demons, not engineers. No vehicle without a roll cage had any business going that fast.

But I needed it to have enough force to survive. Even wizards cannot escape the consequences of physics. You can call up a storm of fire, but it won't burn without fuel and air. Want to infuse yourself with superhuman strength? It's possible. But keep in mind that just because your muscles have gotten supercharged, it doesn't mean that your bones and joints can support the weight of a Volkswagen.

By the same line of reasoning, force still equals mass times acceleration no matter how big your magic wand might be. Me plus Murphy plus her Harley didn't mass anywhere near what the car and the people in it did. I could give us an advantage, but even with the staff I could stretch the rules only so far. Our mass wasn't going to change—and that meant that we needed all the acceleration we could get.

I started channeling our force into the staff, focusing it into a blunted wedge in front of us. All the extra power flooding ahead of us started heating the air, and flickers of blue and purple fire began streaking back around us in a corona, like one of the space shuttles on reentry.

"You have got to be kidding me!" Murphy screamed.

The oncoming car got closer. The bodyguard started shooting again, then dropped the gun and slid back into the car in a panic, strapping on his seat belt.

"This is insane!" Murphy yelled. But the Harley kept going faster.

The oncoming headlights loomed up in blinding brilliance. The other driver leaned on the horn.

Murphy screamed in terror and challenge in response.

I shouted, *"Forzare!"* and unleashed my will. It went rocketing down through the staff. Again its runes and sigils flared into hellish light, and the flickering corona of fire ahead of us blazed into an incandescent cloud.

Murphy's bike didn't waver.

Neither did the bodyguards' car.

There was a flash of light and thunder as the force lance struck the car, and between the reckless speed of Murphy's Hog and my will, physics landed firmly on our side. Our side of the equation was bigger than theirs.

The car's hood and front bumper crumpled as if they'd hit a telephone pole. The windows shattered inward as force I'd redirected lashed through the car. I screamed as glass and steel started flying, and with every scrap of strength that I had, I willed an angle into the lance, deflecting the car. Its front right wheel flew up off the ground, and the rest of the car followed, flipping up into the air and into a lateral roll.

I heard the bodyguards inside screaming.

There was an enormous crunch, totally drowning out Murphy's cry and my own howling, and then we were through it, continuing down the lane, shedding flames behind us like bits of wax melting from a candle, and we were suddenly screaming in triumph. We'd survived. The smoldering staff suddenly felt like it weighed a ton, and I almost dropped it. Exhaustion followed into the rest of my body a breath later, and I slumped against Murphy's back, looking behind us.

The car hadn't exploded, like they do on TV. But it had torn through ten or twelve feet of heavy hedge and slammed into a tree. The car lay on its side, steaming. Glass and broken bits of metal were spread on the ground around it in a field of debris at least fifty feet across. The air bags had deployed, and I could see a pair of crumpled forms inside. Neither of them was moving.

Murphy kept the Harley racing forward, and was casting laughter into the wind all the way down the road.

"What?" I called to her. "Why are you laughing?"

She half turned her head. Her face was flushed, her eyes sparkling. "I think you were right about the vibrator thing."

Half a mile later we rolled up to a house that could have handled a family of four without trouble. By the standards of the Raith estate, I guess that qualified it as a cottage. Murphy killed the bike's engine maybe two hundred yards out, and we coasted in the rest of the way, the only sound the crunching grind of gravel under the tires. She stopped the bike, and we both sat there in the silence for a minute.

"See a cave?" she asked me.

"Nope," I said. "But we can't wait for Lara to show up."

"Any ideas how to find it?" Murphy asked.

"Yeah," I said. "I've never heard of a ritual spell that didn't involve fire and some chanting and some smelly incense and stuff."

"Christ, Dresden. We don't have time to wander around the woods in the dark hoping to smell our way to the cave. Isn't there some way you could find it?"

"With magic? Iffy. I'm not sure what I would do to look for a cave."

Murphy frowned. "Then this is stupid," she said. "We'd be smarter to back off and come back with help and light. You could defend yourself against this curse, couldn't you?"

"Maybe," I said. "But that last one came in awfully strong and fast, and it changes everything. I can swing at a slow-pitch softball and hit it every time. Not even the best hitter can hit five hundred against major-league pitching."

"How did they do it?" she asked.

"Blood sacrifice," I said. "Has to be. Raith is involved

with the ritual now." My voice twisted with bitter anger. "He's got experience using it. He's got Thomas now, which means he isn't going to target him with the curse. Raith's going to bleed him to help kill me. The only chance Thomas has is for me to stop the curse."

Murphy sucked in a breath. She hopped off the bike and drew her gun, holding it down by her leg. "Oh. You circle left and I'll circle right and we'll sniff for the cave, then."

"Argh, I'm an idiot," I said. I leaned my still-glowing staff against the bike and jerked the silver amulet off my neck. "My mother left this to me. Thomas has one like it. She had forged a link between them so that when one of us was touching both of them we got a . . . sort of a psychic voice mail."

"Meaning what?" Murphy asked.

I twisted the chain around the index finger of my burned hand, letting it dangle. "Meaning I can use that link to find the other amulet again."

"If he has it," Murphy said.

"He will," I said. "After last night, he won't take it off."

"How do you know that?"

"Because I know it," I said. I held my right hand palm up and tried to focus upon it. I found the link, the channel through which my mother's latent enchantment had contacted Thomas and me, and I poured some of my will into it, trying to spread it out. "Because I believe it."

The amulet quivered on its string and then leaned out toward the night to our left.

"Stay close," I said, and turned in that direction. "Okay, Murph?"

There was no answer.

My instincts clamored in alarm. I dropped my concentration and looked around, but Murphy was nowhere in sight.

Directly behind me there was a muffled sound, and I turned to find Lord Raith standing there with an arm around Murphy's neck, covering her mouth and with a knife pressed up hard against her ribs. He was wearing all black this time, and in the autumn moonlight he looked like little more than a shadow, a pale and grinning skull, and a very large knife.

"Good evening, Mister Dresden."

"Raith," I said.

"Put the staff down. Amulet too. And the bracelet." He pressed the knife and Murphy sucked in a sharp breath through her nose. "Now."

Dammit. I dropped the bracelet, the staff, and my amulet to the grass.

"Excellent," Raith said. "You were right about Thomas keeping his amulet with him. I found it around his neck when I was cutting his shirt off to have him chained down. I was fairly certain that you would judge such an obviously linked item to be too hazardous to employ in any location magic, but on the off chance I was wrong, I kept my own location spell going. I've been watching you since you arrived."

"You must feel smug and self-satisfied. Are you getting to a point?" I asked.

"Absolutely," he said. "Kneel and place your hands behind your back."

The remaining Bodyguard Barbie appeared. She had a set of prisoner's shackles.

"What if I don't?" I asked.

Raith shrugged and shoved an inch of knife between Murphy's ribs. She bucked in sudden, startled pain.

"Wait!" I said. "Wait, wait! I'm doing it."

I knelt, put my hands behind my back, and Bodyguard Barbie hooked steel links to my wrists and ankles.

"That's better," Raith said. "To your feet, wizard. I'm going to show you the Deeps."

"Kill me with that entropy curse from point-blank range, eh?" I said.

"Precisely," Raith responded.

"Gaining you what?" I asked.

"Immense personal satisfaction," he said.

"Funny," I said. "For a guy warded against magic, you seemed to want to get rid of my gear pretty bad."

"This is a new shirt," he said with a smile. "And besides, can't have you killing the help—or Thomas—to spite me."

"Funny," I said. "You seem to be a lot of talk and not much do. I've heard about all kinds of things you are capable of. Enslaving women you feed on. Killing with a kiss. Superhuman badassedness. But you aren't doing any of it."

Raith's mouth set into a snarl.

"The White Council has taken a few shots at you, but when they quit you didn't go gunning for anyone," I continued. "And hey, what with you being invincible and all, there's got to be a reason for that. You must have been approached by others. I bet you got some pretty juicy offers. And I just can't square that with someone who allows a tart like Trixie Vixen to snap at him over the phone like she did to you today."

Raith's white face went whiter with rage. "I would not say such things were I in your position, wizard."

"You're going to kill me anyway," I said. "Hell, you've pretty much got to. I mean, we're at war, after all, and there you are all immune to magic. Must be a lot of pressure from the Reds for the White Court to get off its ass and do something. Makes you wonder why you didn't just wham, kiss-of-death me back there. Maybe get it on tape or something so you could show it off. Or hell, why you haven't socked the kiss of death on Murphy there just to shut me up."

"Is that what you want to see, wizard?" Raith said, his tone threatening.

I smiled at Raith's threat, and said, my tone a school-yard singsong, "Lord Raith and Murphy, sitting in a tree, *not* K-I-S-S-I-N-G."

Raith clutched harder at Murphy's throat, and she arched her back, gasping, "*Dresden.*"

I subsided with the chant, but I didn't let up. "See, immune to getting hurt is one thing," I said. "But I'm thinking my mother's death curse hit you where it hurt— a while later. There's a parasite called a tick. Lives in the Ozarks. And it is nigh invulnerable," I said. "But it isn't unkillable. Hard to squash, sure. But it can still be pierced with the right weapon. Or it can be smothered." I smiled at Raith. "And it can starve."

He stood as still as a statue, staring at me. His grip on Murphy's throat slackened.

"That's why you've been old news," I said quietly. "Mom said she arranged it so that you would suffer. And since the night you killed her, you haven't been able to feed. Have you. Haven't been able to top off the tank of vampire superpower gas. So no kisses of death. No assaults on wizards. No direct assaults on Thomas when a couple of deathplots failed. You even had to have willing help for this operation, 'cause there was no more enslaving women to your will. Though I take it from Inari being alive that the plumbing works. And after that, I take it from the fact that you haven't raped her into psychic slavery that you can't do that part. Must have made things hard for you, huh, Raith. Did you get the double entendre there, man? Made things hard?"

"Insolent," Raith said at last. "Utterly insolent. You *are* like her."

I let out a breath. It had been only a strong theory until his reaction had confirmed it. "Yeah. Thought so. You've been nothing but talk since my mom got finished with you. Living for years, talking a good game and hoping that no one noticed what you weren't doing. Hoping no one figured out that one of your broodmares gelded you. Bet that was terrifying. Living like that."

"Perhaps," he said in a low murmur.

"They're going to figure it out," I said quietly. "This is a pointless exercise. It will cost you to kill us, and you aren't getting any more. Ever. You'd be smarter to cut your losses and start running."

Raith's cold face again lifted into a smile. "No, boy. You aren't the only one who worked out what your mother did to me. And how. So instead, you and your brother are going to die tonight. Your deaths will end your mother's paltry little binding, along with her bloodline, of course." His eyes flashed to Murphy and he said with a slow smile, "And then perhaps something to eat. I am, after all, very hungry.

"You son of a bitch," I snarled.

Raith smiled at me again. Then told the Barbie, "Bring him."

And with that, Murphy still pinned on his knife—don't miss the symbolism there, Doc Freud—he led us through thirty yards of trees and down a rough slope into cold and darkness.

Chapter Thirty-nine

<⟨⟩⟨⟩>

Lord Raith led us into the cave he called the Deeps, and the Bodyguard Barbie kept her gun on me while simultaneously remaining well out of easy reach. She wasn't any Trixie Vixen anyway. If I jumped her, she'd shoot me, and that would be that. Not that I could have done much jumping, what with the leg irons and all. I had trouble just shuffling along while ducking my head low enough to keep from bumping into rocky protrusions from the cave's roof.

"Murph?" I said. "How are you doing?"

"I'm feeling a little repressed," she responded. There was tight pain in her voice. "I'm fulfilling this hostage stereotype, and it's pissing me off."

"That's good," Raith said. He still had her by the neck, with the knife he held actually pressed a tiny bit into the wound he'd already given. "Defiance adds a great deal of enjoyment to feeding, Ms. Murphy." He put a contemptuous emphasis on the honorific. "It is, after all, a great deal more pleasurable to conquer than to rule. And defiant women can be conquered again and again before they break."

I ignored Raith. "How's your side?"

Murphy shot a glare over her shoulder at her captor. "A little prick like this? It's nothing."

In answer, Raith threw Murphy against the wall. She caught herself and turned, her hand blurring in a short, vicious strike.

Raith wasn't human. He caught her hand without so much as looking at it. He drove her hand and wrist back against the wall, and brought the bloodied tip of his knife sharply up under her chin. Her lip twisted into a defiant snarl and her knee lashed up as she kicked. Raith blocked it with a sweep of his thigh and pressed in close to her, all sinuous, serpentine speed and strength, until he was pressed to her front, his face to hers, raven-black hair mingling with her dark gold.

"Warrior women are all the same," Raith said, his eyes on Murphy's. His voice was low, slow, lilting. "You all know your way around struggling with other bodies. But you know little about the needs of your own."

Murphy stared at him, shoulders twitching, and her lips slowly parted.

"It's bound into you," Raith whispered. "Deeper than muscle and bone. The need. The only way to escape the blackness of death. You cannot deny it. Cannot escape it. In joy, in despair, in darkness, in pain, mortalkind still feels desire." His hand slid down from her wrist, his fingertips lightly brushing the thick veins. A soft sound escaped from Murphy's throat.

Raith smiled. "There. You already feel yourself weakening. I've taken thousands like you, lovely child. Taken them and broken them. There was nothing they could do. There is nothing you can do. You were made to feel desire. I was made to use it against you. It is the natural cycle. Life and death. Mating and death. Predator and prey."

Raith leaned closer with each word, and brushed his lips against Murphy's throat as he spoke. "Born mortal. Born weak. And easily taken."

Murphy's eyes went wide. Her body arched in shock. She let out a low, sobbing sound, as she tried and failed to hold back her voice.

Raith drew his head slowly back, smiling down at Murphy. "And that's only a taste, child. When you know what it is to be truly taken later this night, you will understand that your life ended the moment I wanted you." His hand moved, sudden and hard, digging his thumb against the wound in her ribs. Her face went white, and another, similar cry escaped her. She crumpled, and Raith let her fall to the ground. He stood over her for a moment, and then said, "We'll have days, little one. Weeks. You can spend them in agony or in bliss. The important thing to realize is that I'll be the one who decides which. You are no longer in command of your body. Nor your mind. You no longer have a choice in the matter."

Murphy gathered herself together and managed to lift her eyes again. They were defiant, and blurred with tears, but I could see the terror in them as well—and a sort of sickened, hideous desire. "You're a liar," she whispered. "I am my own."

Raith said, quietly, "I can always tell when a woman feels desire, Ms. Murphy. I can feel yours. Part of you is so tired of being disciplined. Tired of being afraid. Tired of denying yourself for the good of others." He knelt down, and Murphy's eyes shied away from his. "That part of you is what wanted to feel the pleasure I just gave. And it is that part of you that will grow as it feels more. The defiant young woman is already dead. She is simply too afraid to admit it."

He seized her hair and started dragging her, careless and hard. I saw her face for a second, confusion and fear and anger warring for control of her expression. But I knew she'd taken a wound far more grievous than any physical injury I'd seen her sustain. Raith had forced her to feel something, and there had been nothing she could do to stop him. She'd done her best to tear into him, and he had slapped her down like a child. It wasn't Murphy's fault that she'd lost that fight. It wasn't her fault that he'd forced sensation upon her. I mean, hell, he was the lord of the freaking nation of sexual predators, and even weakened and hampered by my mother's curse, he had been able to take apart Murphy's psychic and emotional defenses.

If he got the full measure of his powers back, what he would do to Murphy in retaliation for what my mother had done to him would be worse than death.

The damnedest thing was that there wasn't much I could do about it. Not because I was chained up, held at gunpoint, and probably going to die—though I had to admit, that might make things somewhat difficult—but because this wasn't a fight that someone else could win for Murphy. The real battle was inside of her—her strength of will against her own well-founded fears. Even if I did ride in on a white horse to save her, it would mean only that she would be forced to question her own strength and integrity thereafter, and that would be nothing more than a slow death of her self-reliance and strength of will.

It was something I could not save her from.

And I had asked her to face it.

Raith hauled on her hair as if it had been a dog's lead. Murphy didn't fight back.

I clenched my hands into impotent fists. Murphy was in very real danger of dying that night, even if she kept on breathing and her heart kept on beating. But she would have to be the one to save herself.

The best thing I could do was nothing. The best thing I could say was nothing. I had some power, but it couldn't help Murphy now.

Hell's bells, irony blows.

Chapter Forty

I'd been in a few caves that were the headquarters for
dark magic and those who trafficked in it. None of them
had been warm. None of them had been pleasant. And
none of them had been professionally decorated.

Until now.

After a long, precipitous slope into the earth, the
Raith Deeps opened up into a cavern bigger than most
Paris cathedrals. To a degree, it resembled one. Lights
played in soft colors on the walls, mostly shifting rosy
hues. The cave was of living rock, and the walls had all
been shaped by water into nearly organic-looking curves
and swirls. The floor sloped very slightly up, to where a
shift in the rock gave rise to an enormous carved chair
of pure, bone-white stone. The chair had been decorated
with flares and flanges and every kind of carved frivolity
you could imagine, so that it sat at the center of all the
carving like a peacock poised in front of its tail. Water
fell in a fine mist from overhead, and more lights played
through it, broken by the droplets into myriad spectra.
To the right hand of the throne was a smaller carved
seat—almost a stool really, like the ones you'd imagine
lions or seals perching on during circus performances.
To the left was a jagged, broken gap in the rock, and
behind the throne, where more of the mist fell, was simply darkness.

Though the stone was smooth, it undulated in regular,
ripple-shaped rises toward the throne from where we
entered the Deeps. Here and there along the rippled
floor were groups of pillows and cushions, thick woven
carpets, low, narrow tables set with wine and the kinds
of finger foods that tended to get smeared about fairly
easily.

"Well, it's subtle," I said to no one in particular. "But

I like it. Sort of *The King and I* meets *Harem Honeys and Seraglio Sluts II*."

Raith strode past me and threw Murphy at a pile of pillows and cushions along one wall, the one farthest away from the entrance. She knew how to take a fall, and though the motion had been vicious and torn out some of her hair, she landed well, coming up to a shaky crouch. Bodyguard Barbie dragged my manacles and me over to the wall nearby and padlocked me to a steel ring in the wall. There was a whole row of such rings there. I tried to wiggle a little, testing the strength of the steel ring, but whoever built it knew what he was doing. No wiggle, no flexion of the ring where it joined the wall.

"Time?" Raith asked.

"Eleven-thirty-nine, my lord," the bodyguard reported.

"Ah, good. Still time." He walked over to a group of pillows in the far corner of the room, and I realized that they had been strewn around a little raised platform of stone. The platform was a circle perhaps ten feet across, and inside of it was a thaumaturgic triangle, an equilateral shape within the ring of the circle used in most ritual magic because it was easier for amateurs to draw a freaking triangle than a pentacle or a Star of Solomon. Thick incense wafted up from braziers around the circle, giving the cold air the sharp scent of cinnamon and some other, more acrid spice. "Wizard, I believe you have met my assistants."

Two women rose from the shadows within the circle and faced me. The first was Madge, Arturo's first wife, the disciplined businesswoman. She wore a white robe trimmed with scarlet cloth, and her hair was down. It made her look both younger and simultaneously lent her an overripe look, like fruit a day swollen and spoiled. Her eyes were no less calculating, but there was an edge of something there that I recognized—cruelty. The love of power, to the exclusion of the well-being of one's fellow beings.

The second woman, of course, was Trixie Vixen. She looked awful and she didn't get up. I could see the thick bandages over her wounded leg as she sat quietly on one hip, the silk of her own crimson-trimmed white robe spread out in such a way that it normally would have revealed enticing curves of calf and thigh. Her eyes had the heavy, flickering look of someone on far too many drugs, and used to it.

Thomas was chained to the floor in the center of the thaumaturgic triangle. He was naked, gagged, and his pale skin was covered with bruises and the stripes of being beaten with a slender cane. There was a low ridge of rock under his spine that arched his back off the floor, pinning his shoulders back and exposing his chest in such a fashion that he would be unable to move, even if someone should be leaning over him in order to cut out his heart.

"You're missing one," I said. "Where's wifey number two?"

"Dear Lucille." Raith sighed. "She was far too eager to please, and melodramatic about it to boot. I did not authorize her little attempt to poison you via blow dart, wizard, though I suppose I would not have been upset with her had she succeeded. But she was guiding the spell last night and had the incredibly bad taste to attempt to murder my daughter." Raith sighed. "I very nearly felt obligated to you for saving her, Dresden. Lucille assured me that she had only the best of intentions and wanted to do all that she could to continue helping me."

"So you sacrificed her for the curse this morning," I spat.

"No, he didn't," Madge said in a quiet, rather chillingly conversational tone. "I did. The little bitch. I'd been dreaming about something like that for years. They're wrong about revenge, you know. All the movies. I found it quite fulfilling and rewarding, from an emotional standpoint."

"I helped," Trixie protested. "I helped kill her."

"Bullshit," I said. "You were right there holding a *gun* on me when Lucille died, you . . . you self-deluded, half-witted schlong-jockey."

Trixie shrieked, lurched up, and started to throw herself at me. Madge and Raith caught her arms and let her thrash for a moment, until she was panting and drooping. They eased her back down. "Be still," Raith said. "That's quite enough from you."

Trixie hit him with a sullen scowl. "You don't tell me wh—"

Madge slapped her. Hard. One of her rings left a long line of fine red droplets on Trixie's cheek. "Idiot," she spat at Trixie. "If you'd told the police his *name* instead of forgetting it for your pills and needles, the wizard would be in a cell right now."

"What the fuck does it matter?" Trixie snarled, not looking up. "He's had it now. It didn't make any difference."

Madge tilted her head back and lifted her right hand, palm out and fingers spread, and said, "*Orbius*."

There was a surge of power that grated against my wizard's senses, and something wet and stinking that looked like a fusion of a fresh cow patty and a dew speckled cobweb came into being, slapping across Trixie's face. She fell back, clawing at it with her painted fingernails and screaming. Whatever the stuff was, it stuck like superglue, and it rendered her screams all but inaudible.

I shot a hard glance at Madge. She had power. Not necessarily a lot of it, but she had it. No wonder she'd made sure her hands were full when she first met me. The touch of one practitioner's hand against another's was electric and unmistakable. She'd dodged me neatly, which meant . . .

"You knew I was getting involved," I said.

"Of course," Raith confirmed. He added a pinch of something to one of the braziers and picked up a carved box. He drew black candles from it and placed them at each tip of the triangle. "Drawing you into a position of vulnerability was one of the points of the entire exercise. It was time to have flights of angels sing my dear son to his rest, and you and he had become entirely too friendly. I had assumed he was feeding from you and had you under his influence, but after I listened to the security tape from the portrait gallery I was delighted. Both of Margaret's sons. I finally will escape her ridiculous little binding, remove a troublesome thorn in my side—"

He kicked Thomas viciously in the ribs. Thomas jerked but made no sound, his eyes burning with impotent fury. Trixie Vixen fell over onto her side, back going into desperate arches.

"—slay the wizard that has a full quarter of the Red Court quaking in their fleshmasks, restore a rebellious employee to acceptable controls, and now, in addition to all of that, I have acquired someone with influence among the local authorities." His eyes lingered on the subdued Murphy for a moment, growing shades more pale.

Murphy didn't look up at him.

"Take off your shoes, little one," Raith said.

"What?" Murphy whispered.

"Take them off. Now."

She flinched at the harshness of his tone. She took her shoes off.

"Throw them over the edge. Socks too."

Murphy obeyed Raith without lifting her eyes.

The incubus made a pleased sound. "Good, little one. You please me." He walked in a circle around her as if she were a car he'd just purchased. "All in all, Dresden, a marked gain for the year. It bodes well for the future of House Raith, don't you think?"

Trixie Vixen's heels thumped on the floor.

Raith looked down at her and then at Madge. "Can you manage the ritual alone, dear?"

"Of course, my lord," Madge said calmly. She struck a match and lit one of the candles.

"Well, then," Raith said. He regarded Trixie with clinical detachment until her heels had stopped drumming on the stone floor. Then he seized her hair and dragged her to the left side of the enormous throne. She still moved weakly. He lifted her by the back of the neck and pitched her out into the darkness like a bag of garbage.

Trixie Vixen couldn't scream as she fell to her death. But she tried.

I couldn't stop myself from feeling protest and pain as I saw another human being killed. Even though I tried.

Raith dusted his hands against each another. "Where was I?"

"Taunting the wizard with how he has been manipulated from the beginning," Madge said. "But I would suggest that you let me begin the conjuring at this point. The timing should be just about right."

"Do it," Raith said. He walked around the circle, examining it carefully, and then walked over to me.

Madge picked up a curved ritual knife and a silver bowl and stepped into the circle. She pricked her finger with the knife and smeared blood upon the circle, closing it behind her. Then she knelt at Thomas's head, lifted her face with her eyes closed, and began a slow chant in a tongue whose words twisted and writhed through her lips.

Raith watched her for a long moment, and then his head abruptly snapped up toward the exit of the cave.

Bodyguard Barbie came to attention like a dog who has noticed its master taking a package of bacon out of the fridge.

"Sirens," Raith said, his voice harsh.

"Police?" asked Barbie.

"Ambulance. What happened? Who called them?"

Barbie shook her head. Maybe the questions were too complex for her to handle.

"Gee, Raith," I said. "I wonder why the EMTs have shown up. I wonder if the police are coming along, too. Don't you wonder that?"

The lord of the White Court glared at me, then turned to walk toward the ridiculously elaborate throne. "I suppose it doesn't matter one way or the other."

"Probably not," I agreed. "Unless Inari is involved."

He stopped, frozen in his tracks.

"But what are the chances?" I asked. "I mean, I'm sure the odds are way against her being hurt. Riding a long way in the back of the ambulance with some young med tech. I'm sure daddy's little girl is not going to vamp out for the very first time on an EMT or a doctor or a nurse or a cop, kill them in front of God and everybody, and start off her adult life with a trip to prison, where I'm sure lots of other unfortunate deaths would put her away for good."

Raith didn't turn. "What have you done to my child?"

"Did something happen to your child?" I asked. I probably said that in as insulting a fashion as I possibly could. "I hope everything is all right. But how will we know? You should just get on with the cursing, I guess."

Raith turned to Madge and said, "Continue. I'll be back in a moment." Then to the bodyguard he said, "Keep your gun aimed at Dresden. Shoot him if he tries to escape." The bodyguard drew her weapon. Raith turned and darted from the room, faster than humanly possible.

Madge continued her twisty chant.

"Heya, Thomas," I said.

"Mmmph," he said through the gag.

"I'm gonna get you out of here."

Thomas lifted his head from the ground and blinked at me.

"Don't space out on me, man. Stay with us here."

He stared at me for a second more and then groaned and dropped his head back onto the ground. I wasn't sure if that was an affirmative or not.

"Murph?" I called.

She looked up at me, then down again.

"Murph, don't fall apart on me. He's the bad guy and he's way sexy while he does it. That's his bag. He's supposed to be able to get to you."

"I couldn't stop him," she said in a numb voice.

"That's okay."

"I couldn't stop myself either." She met my eyes for a second and then slumped to the floor. "Leave me alone, Mister Dresden."

"Right," I muttered. I focused on the bodyguard. "Hey there. Look, uh. I don't know your name. . . ."

She just stared at me down the length of her gun.

"Yeah, okay, that's hostile," I said. "But look, you're a person. You're human. I'm human. We should be working together here against the vampires, right?"

Nothing. I get more conversation from Mister.

"Hey!" I shouted. "You! You demented U.S. Army surplus blow-up doll! I'm *talking* to you. So say something!"

She didn't, but her eyes glittered with annoyance, the first emotion I'd seen there. What can I say, inspiring anger is my gift. I have a responsibility to use it wisely.

"Excuse me!" I shouted as loudly as I could. "Did you hear me, *bitch?* At this rate I'm gonna have to blow you up too, just like I did the Bodyguard Kens and your twin."

Now real fury filled her eyes. She cocked her gun and opened her mouth as if she were going to actually speak to me, but I never got to hear what she was going to say.

Murphy made a soundless, barefooted run, leapt, and drove a flying side kick into the back of Bodyguard Barbie's neck. *Whiplash* was far too mild a word to describe what happened to the woman's head. Whiplash happens in friendly, healthy things like automobile accidents. Murphy meant the kick to be lethal, and that made it worse than just about any car wreck.

There was a crackling sound and Barbie dropped to the floor. The gun never went off.

Murphy knelt and searched the woman, taking her gun, a couple of extra clips, a knife, and a set of keys. She stood up and started trying keys on my manacles.

I looked up and watched Madge as she did. The sorceress remained on her knees in the circle, her chant flowing smoothly from her mouth in an unbroken stream. The ritual required it. Had she broken her chant, shouted a warning to the bodyguard, or moved outside the circle it would have disrupted the ritual—and that kind of thing can draw some awfully lethal feedback for showing disrespect to whatever power is behind the ritual. She was at least as trapped as I was.

"Took you long enough," I said to Murphy. "I was going to run out of actual sentences and just start screaming incoherently."

"That's what happens when your vocabulary count is lower than your bowling average."

"Me not like woman with smart mouth," I said. "Woman shut smart mouth and get me free or no wild monkey love for you." She found the right key and got the shackles off me. My wrists and ankles ached. "You had me scared," I said. "Until you called me Mister Dresden, I almost believed he'd gotten to you."

Murphy bit her lip. "Between you and me, I'm not sure he didn't." She shivered. "I wasn't doing much acting, Harry. You made a good call. He underestimated me. But it was too close. Let's leave."

"Steady. Just a little longer."

Murphy frowned, but she didn't run. "You want me to keep Madge covered? What if she does that magic-superglop thing on our faces too?"

I shook my head. "She can't. Not until the ritual is complete."

"Why not?"

"Because if she makes a mistake in the ritual there's going to be some backlash. Maybe it wouldn't touch us, or maybe it would—but it sure as hell would kill everyone in the circle."

"Thomas," Murphy breathed.

"Yeah."

"Can we mess up the rite?"

"Could. But to quote Kincaid, thus kablowie, thus death. If we interrupt the ritual or if she screws it up, things go south."

"But if we don't stop her, she kills Thomas."

"Well. Yeah."

"Then what do we do?" Murphy asked.

"We jump Raith," I said, and nodded back to the wall where she had crouched. "Get back to where he threw you. When he comes in again, we take him down and trade him for Thomas."

"Won't breaking the circle screw up the ritual?" Murphy asked.

"Not the outer circle," I said. "The circle is mostly there to help her have the juice for the ritual. Madge's got some talent. And a survival instinct. She can hold it together if we break it."

Murphy's eyes widened. "But breaking the triangle. *That* will screw up the ritual."

I regarded Madge steadily and said, loud enough to be sure she heard, "Yep. And kill her. But we aren't going to break the triangle yet."

"Why not?" Murphy demanded.

"Because we're going to offer Madge a chance to survive the evening. By letting her kill Raith in Thomas's place and let the curse go to waste. So long as someone dies on schedule, whatever is behind the ritual shouldn't mind." I walked over to stand directly outside the circle. "Otherwise, all I have to do is kick one of these candles over or smudge the lines of the triangle then back up to watch her die. And I think Madge is a survivor. She walks, Thomas is fine, and Raith isn't giving anyone any more trouble."

"She'll run," Murphy said.

"Let her. She can run from the Wardens, but she can't hide. The White Council is going to have some things to say to her about killing people with magic. Pointed things. Cutting things."

"Taunting the spellslinger must be a really fun game, since people like you and Raith keep playing it," Murphy said, "But don't you think he's going to notice that you aren't being held with a gun on you anymore?"

I looked down at the bodyguard's body and grimaced. "Yeah. The corpse is gonna be a giveaway, isn't it."

We looked at each other and then both bent down and grabbed an arm. We dragged the remains of the final Bodyguard Barbie over to the edge of the yawning chasm and dropped her in. After that I reached for my sword cane, still clipped to my belt, and loosened the blade in its sheath.

"Can't believe Raith let you keep that," Murphy said.

"The guard didn't seem to be very good at employing her initiative, and he didn't specifically mention my losing the cane. Don't think he noticed it. He was pretty busy gloating, and I was chained up and all."

"He's like a movie villain," Murphy said.

"No. Hollywood wouldn't allow that much cliché." I shook my head. "And I don't think he's thinking very clearly right now. He's pretty worked up about beating my mom's death curse."

"How tough is this guy?" Murphy asked.

"Very tough. Ebenezar says my magic can't touch him."

"How's about I shoot him?"

"Can't hurt," I said. "You might get lucky and solve our problem. But only a really critical shot will drop him, and even then it's iffy whether or not you'll get him. White Court vamps don't soak up gunshots as well as Red Court vampires do, or ignore them like the Black Court, but they can get over them in a hurry."

"How?"

"They have a kind of reserve of stolen life-energy. They tap into it to be stronger or faster, to recover from injuries, forcibly manipulate the sensations of police lieutenants, that kind of thing. They don't run around being as tough as the Black Court all the time, but they can rev the engine when they need to do it. It's probably safe to assume that Lord Raith has a great big honking tank of reserve energy."

"We'd have to run him out of gas in order to get to him long-term."

"Yep."

"Can we do that?"

"Don't think so," I said. "But we can force him to push himself pretty hard."

"So we almost beat him. *That's* the plan?"

"Yeah."

"That's not a very good plan, Harry," Murphy said.

"It's a wascally-wabbit plan," I said.

"Actually, it qualifies as a *crazy* plan."

"Crazy like a fox," I said. I put my hands on her shoulders. "There's no time to argue, Murph. Trust me?"

She flipped her hands up in a helpless little gesture

(slightly mitigated by the fact that she had a gun in one and a knife in the other) and turned to stalk back to the cushions where Raith had initially thrown her. "We're going to die."

I grinned and stepped back to the ring where Raith had me chained up. I stood there in the same pose as when I'd been prisoner, and held the shackles behind my back as if they might still be attached.

I had barely settled into position when there was the sound of one, two, three gazelle-like bounds on the sloped tunnel floor, and Raith shot into the cavern, scowling. "What idiocy!" he snarled toward Madge. "That stupid buck from Arturo's studio nearly slaughtered my daughter by sheer incompetence. The medical teams are taking them now."

He stopped talking abruptly. "Guard?" he snapped. "Madge, where did she go?"

Madge widened her eyes, still continuing the twisting, slippery words of the chant, and gave Murphy a significant look.

Raith turned, back stiffening in apprehension, to face Murphy.

Madge should have warned Raith about me. If he'd blown off old Ebenezar's lethal magic, he had defenses out the wazoo. I didn't even try to blast away at him with power.

Instead I swung the shackles once over my head and brought the flying steel down on Raith's right ear with every ounce of strength in my body. The steel cuffs bit into his flesh with vicious strength and laid him out on the floor. He let out a snarl of shock and surprise. He turned to glare at me, his eyes burning a bright, metallic silver, his torn ear already knitting itself whole again.

I dropped the chains, drew my sword cane, and drove the blade straight at Raith's left eye. The White lord moved his hand in a blur of motion, batting the scalpel-slender blade aside. I drew a sharp cut across his hand, but it didn't keep him from kicking my ankles out from underneath me with a sweep of his leg. He rose almost before I was through falling, and picked up the bloodied shackles, his features set in wrath. I went flat and covered my neck with my hands.

Murphy shot Raith in the back. The first bullet came out the left side of his chest, and must have left a hole in his lung. The second exploded out from between two ribs on the other side of his body.

It had taken less than a second for the two shots to hit, but Raith reversed direction, flashing to one side like a darting bat, and two more shots seemed to miss him. The motion was odd to watch, and vaguely disturbing. Raith almost flowed across the room, looking as if he were being lazy, but moving with unnerving speed. He vanished behind an elaborate Oriental-style screen.

And the cave's lights went out.

The only source of light left in the cavern came from the three black candles at the points of the ritual's triangle, way the hell at the back of the chamber. Madge's voice continued its rippling, liquid chant, an edge of smug contempt somehow conveyed in it, her attention focused on the ritual. Thomas's bruised body twitched as he looked around, eyes wide behind the gag in his mouth. I saw his shoulders tighten as he tested the chains. They didn't seem to give way for him any more than mine had for me.

Murphy's voice slid through the darkness a moment later, sounding sharp against the steady, liquid chant of the entropy curse. "Harry? Where is he?"

"I have no idea," I said, keeping the point of the sword low.

"Can he see in the dark?"

"Um. Tell you in a minute."

"Oh," she said. "Crap."

Chapter Forty-one

Raith's voice drifted out of the darkness. "I can indeed see you, wizard," he said. "I must admit, a brute attack was not what I expected of you."

I tried to orient to the sound of Raith's voice, but the Deeps had the acoustics of, well, a cave. "You really don't have a very good idea about what kind of man I am, do you?"

"I had assumed that White Council training would mold you a bit more predictably," he admitted. "I was certain you'd have some kind of complex magical means of dealing with me without bloodshed."

I thought I heard something really close to me and swept my slender sword left and right. It whistled as it cut the air. "Blood washes out with enough soda water," I said. "I've got no trouble with the thought of spilling more of yours. It's sort of pink anyway."

Murphy was not talking, which meant that she was acting. Either she was using the sound of my voice to get close to me so that we could team up or she had gotten a better idea than I of Raith's location, and she was stalking close enough to drill him in the dark. Either way, it was to our advantage for the conversation to continue.

"Maybe we can make a deal, Raith," I said.

He laughed, low and lazy and confident. "Oh?"

"You don't want to push this all the way," I said. "You've already eaten one death curse. There's no reason for you to take another if you don't have to."

He laughed gently. "What do you propose?"

"I want Thomas," I said. "And I want Madge. You stop these attacks and leave Arturo alone."

"Tempting," he said. "You want me to allow one of my most dangerous foes to live, you want me to surrender a competent ally, and then you would like me to permit the erosion of my power base to continue. And in exchange, what do I receive?"

"You get to live," I said.

"My, such a generous offer," Raith said. "I can only assume this is some sort of clumsy ploy, Dresden, unless you are entirely deluded. I'll counter your offer. Run, wizard. Or I won't kill the pretty officer. I'll keep her. After I kill you, of course."

"Heh," I said. "You aren't in good enough shape for that to be so easy," I said. "Or you wouldn't have let me stall you while we batted bullshit back and forth."

In answer, Raith said absolutely nothing.

The bottom dropped out of my stomach.

And, better and better, the chant rolling from Madge's lips rose to a ringing crescendo. A wild, whirling wind rose within the center of the circle, catching her hair and spreading it in a cloud of dark-and-silver strands. As that happened, the tempo of her words shifted, and they shifted from that other tongue into English. "While here we wait, O hunter of the shadows! We who yearn for your shadow to fall upon our enemy! We who cry out in need for thy strength, O Lord of Slowest Terror! May your right arm come to us! Send unto us your captain of destruction! Mastercraftsman of death! Let now our need become the traveler's road, the vessel for He Who Walks Behind!"

The rest of my stomach promptly followed the bottom, and for a second I thought my sense of logic and reason had vanished with them.

He Who Walks Behind.

Hell's holy stars and freaking stones shit bells.

He Who Walks Behind was a demon. Well. Not really a demon. The Walker was to a demon what one of those hockey-masked movie serial killers was to the grade-school bully who had tried to shake me down once for lunch money. Justin DuMorne had sent the Walker after me when we'd had our falling-out, and I'd barely managed to survive the encounter. I'd torn apart He Who

Walks Behind, but even so he'd left me with some unnerving scars.

And the ritual Madge was using was calling that
thing back.

Madge picked up the sacrificial knife and the silver
bowl. The whirling wind gathered into a miniature thun-
derstorm hovering slowly over the triangle where
Thomas was bound. "See here our offering to flow into
your strength! Flesh and blood, taken unwilling from
one who yearns to live! Bless this plea for help! Accept
this offering of power! Make known to us your hand
that we might dispatch him against our mutual foe—
Harry Dresden!"

"Murphy!" I screamed. "Get out of here! Right
now! Run!"

But Murphy didn't run. As Madge raised the knife,
Murphy appeared in the light of the black candles, darting into the circle, the knife in her teeth, the gun in one
hand—and in her other, the keys she'd taken from the
last bodyguard. She knelt down as Madge screamed out
the last of the ritual in an ecstasy of power. Murphy had
crossed the circle around the ritual, breaking it. That
meant that whatever magic Madge was calling up would
be able to zip right out of it without delay, the second
Madge fed a life to the gathering presence of He Who
Walks Behind. Murphy set the gun down and tried one
key on Thomas's chains. Then another.

"Madge!" Raith's voice snapped in warning. I heard
a flutter of movement that began five feet to my right
and vanished toward the circle.

Madge opened her eyes and looked down.

Murphy found the key, and the steel bracelet on
Thomas's right arm sprang open.

Madge kept screaming, reversed the knife, and drove
it down at Thomas's chest.

Thomas caught Madge's knife hand by the wrist, and
his skin suddenly shone pale and bright. She leaned on
the knife, screaming, but Thomas held her there with
one arm.

Murphy picked up the gun, but before she could aim it at Madge, there was a blur, her head snapped to one side, and she dropped to the ground in abrupt stillness. Raith stood over her unmoving form, and bent with businesslike haste to recover her knife, his eyes moving to Thomas.

Fumbling in haste, I seized the sheath of my cane-sword from my belt, grabbing hard at my will, struggling to pull together power through the cloud of raw terror that had descended over my thoughts. I managed it, and normally invisible runes along the length of the cane burst into blue and silver light. There was a deep hum, so low that it could be felt more than heard, as I reached into the power the cane was meant to focus—the enormous and dangerous forces of earth magic.

I reached out through the cane for Lord Raith—

And felt nothing. Not just empty air and drifting dust, but *nothing*. A cold and somehow hungry emptiness that filled the space where he should have been. I'd felt something like it before, when I'd been near a mote of one of the deadliest substances that any world of flesh or spirit had ever known. My power, my magic, the flowing spirit of life, just vanished into it without getting near Raith.

I couldn't touch him. The void around him was so absolute, I knew without needing to doubt that there was nothing in my arsenal of arcane skills that could affect him.

But Madge didn't have any such protection.

I redirected my power, easily found the knife in Madge's hand, and without the circle to protect her, there was nothing she could do to keep me from seizing the knife in invisible bands of earth force, magnetism, and sending it tumbling out of her grip and into the abyss of the chasm near them.

"No!" Madge screamed, staring up at the whirling cloud of dark energy in horror.

"Hold him!" Raith snarled.

Madge threw herself down on Thomas's arm, and as strong as he was, he had three limbs chained down, and not even supernatural strength is a substitute for proper leverage. Not only that, but Madge was desperate. She managed to force Thomas's arm down, and while she obviously couldn't have held him for long, it was long enough. Lord Raith drove his knife down at Thomas's chest.

Thomas howled in frustration and sudden pain.

I rammed more power through the cane and stopped the knife a bare instant after the tip hit Thomas, and pinkish blood welled up from the shallow stab wound. Raith cast a snarl at me and shoved down on the knife, his own skin luminous, and he had the power of a pile driver behind his arms. I didn't have a prayer of stopping him, even if that void around him hadn't been sapping my power into nothingness—so I redirected my own push instead, switching to a right-angle force instead of going directly against Raith, and the knife swept hard to one side as Raith pushed down. It dug a furrow through Thomas's flesh on the way, wetting a good three inches of the blade in his blood, but then Raith's own power drove it down into the stone of the cavern floor, and the steel shattered.

Thomas got his hand free and hit Madge, a back-handed blow that knocked her out of the light of the black candles.

"Harry!" he yelled. "Break the chains!"

Which I couldn't do. My little displays of earth magic were a long way from being of chain-shattering quality. But I did the next best thing.

Raith had to step back for a second, because a shard from the shattering knife had gone through his hand. He ripped it out of his flesh with a snarl, then turned back to Thomas, and as he did I got the bodyguard's keys in a magnetic grip and threw them hard at Lord Raith's face.

Keys are a nasty missile weapon, and any street fighter will tell you so. For fun, get yourself a milk carton and throw a ring of keys at it. You don't even have to throw it very hard. Odds are better than merely good that the milk carton is going to have holes in it and that milk is going to be dribbling out everywhere.

And eyelids are way thinner than milk cartons.

Raith got a bunch of keys in the face and they hit him hard enough to make him scream. I caught them again on the rebound and sent them zipping back at him, as if they'd been fastened to rubber bands tied to his nose. I don't care how superhumanly sexy you are, if you're a vertically symmetrical biped, you don't have much choice but to react when something tries to put out your eyes.

I pummeled Raith with the keys until he ducked out of the light of the black candles, and then I sent them darting over to Thomas. I shouted his name as I did, and he reached up and caught them with his free hand. He shook one out without delay, and started freeing himself of his chains.

It was just then that the swirling clouds over the empty triangle coalesced into the vague outline of an inhuman face—one that I recognized from the darkest hour of my past and the nightmares it had inhabited since. That demonic mouth split into an eerily soundless scream, as if it had created a sudden void of sound rather than the opposite. That hideous face oriented on the very edge of the remaining candlelight—upon Madge. The cloud surged forward and down, sprouting sudden rows of almost toothlike spines as it did. Madge sat up, raising her hands in a useless gesture of defense. The demonic cloud shot itself forward and into her mouth. The spines tore at her, and Madge struggled to keep it out of her, but it was all useless, and not particularly speedy. She had plenty of time to feel it as the demonic killer, the guiding mind who had been behind the entropy curse, flowed in its semigaseous form into her mouth and throat and lungs, then extruded savage spines and tore her apart from within.

Madge didn't manage to get out a scream as she died.

But it wasn't for lack of trying.

Thomas got his arms and legs free and got up, staring in horror at Madge—or more accurately, at the spined cloud still mangling Madge's corpse from within.

Raith hit Thomas from behind, a blur of motion.

There was only a second to see what was happening, but I saw it clearly when Raith seized Thomas by the shoulder and chin, and with a single savage twist, broke his neck.

Thomas fell without so much as a twitch.

"No!" I screamed.

Raith turned toward me.

I dropped my sword, slashed at the air with the cane and my will, and the gun Murphy had taken from the bodyguard flew to my hand.

Raith's face was bruised and torn. Thick globules of pink blood had splattered over his battered features and his dark shirt. He smiled as he started toward me, and the shadows between the candles and my cane covered him.

I aimed more or less at Raith and shot. The flash showed him to me for an instant. I used that single image to redirect my fire and shot again. And again. And again. The last shot showed me Raith, only eight or ten feet away, a look of shock upon his face. The next shot showed him on his knees, clutching at his stomach, where a welter of pink fluid had soaked him.

Then the gun locked open, and empty.

For a minute it was all dark.

Then Raith's flesh began to glow. His shirt was in shreds, and he tore it from him with a negligent gesture. His skin became suffused with a pale light once more, and I saw his body rippling weirdly around an ungainly hole left of his navel. He was healing.

I stared at him tiredly for a minute, then bent over and picked up my sword.

He laughed at me. "Dresden. Wait there for a moment. I'll deal with you as I did Thomas."

"He was my blood," I said quietly. "He was my only family."

"Family," Raith spat. "Nothing but an accident of birth. Random consequence of desire and response. Family is meaningless. It is nothing but the drive of blood to further its own. Random combination of genes. It is utterly insignificant."

"Your children don't think that," I said. "They think family is important."

He laughed. "Of course they think that. I have trained them to do so. It is a simple and convenient way to control them."

"And nothing more?"

Raith rose, regarding me with casual confidence. "Nothing more. Put the sword down, Dresden. There's no reason this has to hurt you."

"I'll pass. You can't have much left in you," I said. "I've given you enough of a beating to kill three or four people. You'll stay down sooner or later."

"I have enough left in me to deal with you," he said, smiling. "And after that, things will change."

"Must have been hard," I said. "All those years. Playing it careful. Never pushing yourself or using your reserves. Not able to risk getting your hands dirty, for fear everyone would see that you couldn't do what your kind do. Couldn't feed."

"It was an annoyance," Raith said after a wary pause. He took a step toward me, testing my response. "And perhaps taught me a measure of humility, and of patience. But I never told anyone what Margaret's curse did to me, Dresden. How did you know?"

I kept the point of the sword pointed at his chest and said, "My mother told me about it."

"Your mother is dead, boy."

"You're immune to magic, too. Guess she just doesn't have a lot of respect for the rules."

His face darkened into an ugly, murderous mask. "She's dead."

I smirked at him, waving the tip of my sword in little circles.

The glow on his skin began to fade, and the darkness closed in with deadly deliberation. "It has been a pleasure speaking with you, but I am healed, wizard," Raith snarled. "I'm going to make you beg me for death. And my first meal in decades is going to be the little police girl."

At which point all the lights in the cavern came up at

the same time, restoring the place to its slightly melodramatic but perfectly adequate lighting.

Lara stepped from behind the screen, her scarlet skirt swaying, sword on her hip, and murmured, "I think I'd like to see that, Father."

He stopped, staring at her, his face hardening. "Lara. What do you think you're doing?"

"Writhing in disillusionment," she said. "You don't love me, dearest Papa. Me, your little Lara, most dutiful daughter."

He let out a harsh laugh. "You know better. And have for a century."

Her beautiful face became remote. Then she said, "My head knew, Father. But my heart had hoped otherwise."

"Your heart," he said, scorn in his voice. "What is that? Take the wizard at once. Kill him."

"Yes, Papa," she said. "In a moment. What happened to Thomas?"

"The spell," he said. "Madge lost control of it when she unleashed it at Dresden. Your brother died trying to protect him. Subdue him, dearest. And kill him."

Lara smiled, and it was the coldest, most wintry expression I had ever seen. And I had seen some of the champs. She let out a mocking, scornful little laugh. "Did you stage that for my benefit, wizard?"

"It was a little rough," I said. "But I think I got my point across."

"How did you know I was watching?" she asked.

I shrugged. "Someone had to have told Raith that bullshit about the accident with the gun," I said. "You were the only one who could have done that. And since this confrontation was going to be pivotal to your future, regardless of how it turned out, you'd be an idiot not to watch."

"Clever," she said again. "Not only is my father drained of his reserves, he is unable to recover more." She lowered her eyelids, her eyes glittering like silver ice as she did. "Quite helpless, really."

"And now you know it," I said.

I gave Raith a very small smile.

Raith's expression twisted into something somewhere between rage and horror. He took a step back from Lara, looking from her to me and back.

Lara traced her fingers in light caresses over the sword at her hip. "You've made me the cat's-paw for you, Dresden. While making me think I had the advantage of you. You've played me at my own game, and ably. I thought you capable of nothing but overt action. Clearly I underestimated you."

"Don't feel bad," I said. "I mean, I look so stupid."

Lara smiled. "I have one question more," she said. "How did you know the curse left him unable to feed?"

"I didn't," I said. "Not for certain. I just thought of the worst thing I could possibly do to him. And it wasn't killing. It was stealing. It was taking all of his power away. Leaving him to face all the enemies he'd made—with nothing. And I figured my mother might have had similar thoughts."

Raith sneered at Lara. "You can't kill me," he said. "You know that the other Lords would never permit you to lead the Court. They follow *me,* little Lara. Not the office of the Lord of House Raith."

"That's true, Father," Lara said. "But they don't know that you have been weakened, do they? That you have been made impotent. Nor will they know, when you continue to lead them as if nothing had changed."

He lifted his chin in an arrogant sneer. "And why should I do that?"

Silver light from Lara's eyes spread over her. It flowed down the length of her hair. It poured over her skin, flickered over her clothing, and dazzled the very air around her. She let her sword belt fall to the ground, and silver, hungry eyes fell upon Lord Raith.

What she was doing was directed solely at him, but I was on the fringes of it. And I suddenly had pants five sizes too small. I felt the sudden, simple, delicious urge to go to her. Possibly on my knees. Possibly to stay that way.

I panicked and took a step back, making an effort to

shield my thoughts from Lara's seductive power, and it let me think almost clearly again.

"Wizard," she said, "I suggest you take your friend from this place. And my brother, if he managed to survive the injury." Her skirt joined the belt, and I made damned sure I wasn't looking. "Father and I," Lara purred, "are going to renegotiate the terms of our relationship. It promises to be interesting. And you might not be able to tear yourselves away, once I begin."

Raith took a step back from Lara, his eyes racked with fear. And with need. He'd totally forgotten me.

I moved, and quickly. I was going to pick Murphy up, but I managed to get her moving again on her own, though she was still only half-conscious. The right side of her face was already purple with bruising. That gave me the chance to pick Thomas up. He wasn't as tall as me, but he had more muscle and was no featherweight. I huffed and puffed and got him into a fireman's carry, and heard him take a grating, rattling breath as I did.

My brother wasn't dead.

At least, not yet.

I remember three more things from that night in the Deeps.

First was Madge's body. As I turned to leave, it suddenly sat up. Spines protruded from its skin, along with rivulets of slow, dead blood. Its face was ravaged shapeless, but it formed up into the features of the demon called He Who Walks Behind, and its mouth spoke in a honey-smooth, honey-sweet, inhuman voice. "I am returned, mortal man," the demon said through Madge's dead lips. "And I remember thee. Thou and I, we have unfinished business between us."

Then there was a bubbling hiss, and the corpse deflated like an empty balloon.

The second thing I remember happened as I staggered toward the exit with Thomas and Murphy. Lara slid the white shirt from her shoulders to the floor and faced Raith, lovely as the daughter of Death himself, a literal irresistible force. Timeless. Pale. Implacable. I caught the faintest scent of her hair, the smell of wild jasmine, and nearly fell to my knees on the spot. I had to force myself to keep moving, to get Thomas and Murph out of the cave. I don't think any of us would have come out of it with our own minds if I hadn't.

The last thing I remember was dropping to the ground on the grass outside the cave, holding Thomas. I could see his face in the starlight. There were tears in his eyes. He took a breath, but it was a broken one. His head and his neck hung at an impossible angle to his shoulders.

"God," I whispered. "He should be dead already."

His mouth moved in a little fluttering quiver. I don't know how I did it, but I understood that he'd tried to say, "Better this way."

"Like hell it is," I said back. I felt incredibly tired.

"Hurt you," he almost-whispered. "Maybe kill you. Like Justine. Brother. Don't want that."

I blinked down at him.

He didn't know.

"Thomas," I said. "Justine is alive. She told us where you were tonight. She's still alive, you suicidal dolt."

His eyes widened, and the pale radiance flooded through his skin in a startled wave. A moment later he drew in a ragged breath and coughed, thrashing weakly. He looked sunken-eyed and terrible. "Wh-what? She's what?"

"Easy, easy, you're going to throw up or something," I said, holding him steady. "She's alive. Not . . . not good, really, but she's not dead. Not gone. You didn't kill her."

Thomas blinked several times, and then seemed to lose consciousness. He lay there, breathing quietly, and his cheeks were tracked with the trails of luminous silver tears.

My brother would be okay.

But then a thought occurred to me, and I said, "Well, crap."

"What?" asked Murphy, blearily. She blinked her eyes at me.

I peered owlishly up at the night sky and wondered, "When is it going to be Tuesday in Switzerland?"

Chapter Forty-two

I woke up the next morning. More specifically, I woke up the next morning when the last stone on Ebenezar's painkilling bracelet crumbled into black dust, and my hand began reporting that it was currently dipped in molten lead.

Which, as days go, was not one of my better starts. Then again, it wasn't the worst one, either.

Normally I'd give you some story about how manly I was to immediately attain a state of wizardly detachment and ignore the pain. But the truth was that the only reason I didn't wake up screaming was that I was too out of breath to do it. I clenched my hand, still in dirty wrappings, to my chest and tried to remember how to walk to the freezer. Or to the nearest chopping block, one of the two.

"Whoa, whoa," said a voice, and Thomas appeared, leaning over me. He looked rumpled and stylish, the bastard. "Sorry, Harry," he said. "It took me a while to get something for the pain. Thought I'd have gotten back hours ago." He pressed my shoulders to the bed and said, "Stay there. Think of . . . uh, pentangles or something, right? I'll get some water."

He reappeared a minute later with a glass of water and a couple of blue pills. "Here, take them and give them about ten minutes. You won't feel a thing."

He had to help me, but he was right. Ten minutes later I lay on my bed thinking that I should texture my ceiling with something. Something fuzzy and soft.

I got up, dressed in my dark fatigue pants, and shambled out into my living room, slash kitchen, slash study, slash den. Thomas was in the kitchen, humming something to himself. He hummed on-key. I guess we hadn't gotten the same genes for music.

I sat down on my couch and watched him bustle around—as much as you can bustle when you need to take only two steps to get clear from one side of the kitchen to the other. He was cooking eggs and bacon on my wood-burning stove. He knew jack about cooking over an actual fire, so the bacon was scorched and the eggs were runny, but it looked like he was amusing himself doing it, and he dumped burned bits, underdone bits, or bits he simply elected to discard on the floor at the foot of the stove. The puppy and the cat were both there, with Mister eating anything he chose to and the puppy dutifully cleaning up whatever Mister judged unworthy of his advanced palate.

"Heya, man," he said. "You aren't gonna feel hungry, but you should try to eat something, okay? Good for you and all that."

"Okay," I said agreeably.

He slapped the eggs and bacon more or less randomly onto a couple of plates, brought me one, and kept one for himself. We ate. It was awful, but my hand didn't hurt. You take what you can get in this life.

"Harry," Thomas said after a moment.

I looked up at him.

He said, "You came to get me."

"Yeah," I said.

"You saved my life."

I mused on it. "Yeah," I agreed a moment later. I kept eating.

"Thank you."

I shook my head. "Nothing."

"No, it isn't," he said. "You risked yourself. You risked your friend Murphy, too."

"Yeah," I said again. "Well. We're family, right?"

"Too right we are," he said, a lopsided smile on his mouth. "Which is why I want to ask you a favor."

"You want me to go back with you," I said. "Feel things out with Lara. Visit Justine. See which way the future lies."

He blinked at me. "How did you know?"

"I'd do it too."

He nodded quietly. Then said, "You'll go?"

"As long as we do it before Tuesday."

Murphy came by on Monday, to report that the investigation had determined that Emma's shooting was a tragic accident. Since no prints had been found, and the eyewitness (and owner of the weapon) had vanished, I wasn't in any danger of catching a murder rap. It still looked as fishy as a tuna boat, and it wouldn't win me any new friends among the authorities, but at least I wouldn't be going to the pokey this time around.

It was hard for me to concentrate on Murphy's words. Raith had partially dislocated her lower jaw, and the bruises looked like hell. Despite the happy blue pain pills, when I saw Murphy I actually heard myself growling in rage at her injury. Murphy didn't talk much more than business, but her look dared me to make some kind of chivalrous commentary. I didn't, and she didn't break my nose, by way of fair exchange.

She took me to an expensive specialist her family doctor referred her to, who examined my hand, took a bunch of pictures, and wound up shaking his head. "I can't believe it hasn't started to mortify," he said. "Mister Dresden, it looks like you may get to keep your hand. There's even a small portion on your palm that didn't burn at all, which I have no explanation for whatsoever. Do you mind if I ask you a personal question?"

"That's working just fine, Doc," I mumbled. "Not that it's had much use lately."

He gave me a brief smile. "More personal, I'm afraid. How good is your insurance?"

"Um," I said. "Not so hot."

"Then I'd like to give you a bit of advice, off the record. Your injury is almost miraculously fortunate, in terms of how unlikely it was that the limb would survive. But given the extent of the burns and the nerve damage, you might seriously consider amputation and the use of a prosthesis."

"What?" I said. "Why?"

The doctor shook his head. "We can prevent an infection from taking root and spreading until we can get you a graft to regenerate the epidermis—that's the main possible complication at this point. But in my professional judgment, you'll get more functionality out of an artificial hand than you ever again will from your own. Even with surgery and extensive therapy, which will cost you more than a pretty penny, and even if you continue to recover at the high end of the bell curve, it could be decades before you recover any use of the hand. In all probability, you will never recover any use of it at all."

I stared at him for a long minute.

"Mister Dresden?" he asked.

"*My* hand," I responded, with all the composure of a three-year-old. I tried to smile at the doctor. "Look. Maybe my hand is all screwed up. But it's *mine*. So no bone saws."

The doctor shook his head, but said, "I understand, son. Good luck to you." He gave me a prescription for an antibiotic ointment, a reference to a yet more expensive specialist just in case, and some pain medication. On the way back to my house, I asked Murphy to stop by the drugstore, where I got my prescriptions filled, and bought a bunch of clean bandages and a pair of leather gloves.

"Well?" Murphy said. "Are you going to tell me what the doctor said?"

I threw the right glove out the window, and Murphy arched an eyebrow at me.

"When I get done with my mummy impersonation," I said, waving my freshly bandaged hand, "I want to have a choice between looks. Michael Jackson or Johnny Tremaine."

She tried not to show it, but I saw her wince. I empathized. If I hadn't been on Thomas's groovy pain drugs, I may have started feeling bitter about the whole thing with my hand.

Monday afternoon I got the Blue Beetle back from my mechanic, Mike, who is the automotive repair equivalent of Jesus Christ himself. Either that or Dr. Frankenstein. I drove the Beetle out to a hotel near the airport to meet with Arturo Genosa and the new Mrs. Genosa.

"How's the married life, Joan?" I asked.

Joan, dumpy and plain and glowing with happiness, leaned against Arturo with a small smile.

Arturo grinned as well and confided, "I have never been married to a woman with such . . . creativity."

Joan blushed scarlet.

We had a nice breakfast, and Arturo presented me with my fee, in cash. "I hope that isn't inconvenient, Mr. Dresden," he said. "We didn't finish the film and the money is gone when I am forced to declare bankruptcy, but I wanted to be sure you received your pay."

I shook my head and pushed the envelope back to him. "I didn't save your film. I didn't save Emma."

"The film, bah. You risked your life to save Giselle's. And Jake as well. Emma . . ." His voice trailed off. He almost seemed to visibly age. "I understand that you may not be entirely free to speak, but I must know what happened to her."

Joan's expression froze, and she gave me a pleading look.

She didn't have to explain it to me. She knew or suspected the truth—that Tricia Scrump had been behind the killing. It would break Arturo's heart to hear it about a woman he had once, however ill-advisedly, loved.

"I'm not sure," I lied. "I found Emma and Trixie like that. I thought I saw someone and ran off trying to catch the guy. But either he was faster than me or I'd been seeing things. We might never know."

Arturo nodded at me. "You mustn't blame yourself. Nor must you refuse what you rightfully earned, Mister Dresden. I'm in your debt."

I wanted to turn the money down, but damn, it was Monday. And Kincaid was Tuesday. I took the envelope.

Jake Guffie appeared a moment later, dressed in a casual suit of pale cotton. He hadn't shaved, and there was a lot of grey in the scruff of his beard. He looked like he hadn't slept much, either, but he was trying to smile. "Arturo. Joan. Congratulations."

"Thank you," Joan said.

Jake joined us, and we had a nice breakfast. Then we walked with Joan and Arturo to their airport shuttle. Jake and I watched them go. He stared after them for a moment. He looked weary, but if it had bothered him to deceive Arturo about Trixie Vixen, he hadn't let it show.

Jake turned to me and said, "I guess you weren't the killer. The police said the shooting was accidental. They pulled up Trixie's record and saw all her trips to rehab. Said that she had probably done something stupid while she was stoned."

"Do you think that?" I asked.

"No way, man. She did *everything* stupid. Stoned was just a coincidence."

I shook my head. "I'm sorry I wasn't able to protect Emma."

He nodded. "So am I, man. She was going to take her medication. Allergy medication. She didn't want to take it with tap water so she was going to the greenroom for a bottle of Evian. She was just standing in the wrong place. Hell of a thing."

"I feel for her kids," I said. "I've done the orphan thing. It sucks."

Jake nodded. "I don't know how they'll get on without their mom," he said. "Not like I have much experience, either. But I can't be such a lousy father that they qualify as orphans."

I blinked for a second and then said, "You wanted to settle down once, you said."

"Yeah. But Emma decided she wouldn't have me."

I nodded. "You going to keep acting?"

"Oh, hell, no," he said. "Silverlight is gonna blacklist me like everyone else. And I can't do that and go to PTA and stuff. I got another job lined up."

"Yeah?" I asked. "What?"

"Dude, me and Bobby are gonna to start up a consulting business. Feng shui."

I had no problem with that.

Next I went with Thomas up to the Raith family homestead north of town. This time we went in the front doors. There were a new pair of bodyguards at the door. They weren't twins, and they didn't have that numb, mindlessly obedient glaze in their eyes. They had evidently been chosen for skill and experience. I was betting on former marines.

"Welcome, Mister Raith," one of the guards said. "Your sister requests that you join her for breakfast in the east garden."

They both stood there waiting to fall in around us, so it didn't exactly come off like an invitation, but from the attention, they might have been as concerned with protecting us as watching us. Thomas took the lead by half a step, and I fell in on his right. I was quite a bit taller than him, but his expression had taken on a confidence and sense of purpose I hadn't seen in him before, and our feet hit the floor in time with one another.

The guards accompanied us out into a truly gorgeous terraced garden, a number drawn straight from the Italian Renaissance, with faux ruins, ancient statues of the gods, and a design overgrown enough to prevent seeing much at a time, the better to spend more time exploring. At the top of the highest terrace was a table made of fine metal wire twisted into looping designs, with matching chairs spread around it. A light breakfast was laid out on the table, heavier on the fruits and juices than was my habit. But then, my habit was usually to eat any leftovers from dinner for breakfast first.

Lara sat at the table, wearing white clothing accented with embroidered red roses. Her hair was drawn back into a loose tail, and she rose to greet us both with outstretched hands.

"Thomas," she said. "And Harry."

"Sis," Thomas replied. "Should I assume from our greeting that there's been a change of management?"

She took her seat again, and Thomas joined her. I took a seat opposite him, so that I could watch his back, and I didn't spare any energy for false smiles. I didn't want Lara to think that we were going to be buddies now, and I suck at faking them anyway.

Lara took in my gaze, her own eyes calculating behind

the smile. "Oh, it's just the usual little family spat," she said. "I'm sure Father is going to be angry with me for a while and will forget all about it."

"And if he doesn't?" Thomas asked.

Lara's smile grew a little sharper. "I'm sure he will." She took a sip of orange juice. "Unfortunately, Thomas, I don't know if he's going to be as forgiving to you."

Thomas inhaled sharply.

"I'm sorry," Lara said. She looked like she meant it.

"You're turning your back on him?" I asked. "On your brother."

Lara lifted a hand. "I do not want to, but my father's antagonism with Thomas is well known. If I am to maintain the fiction that my father is in control of his House, Thomas cannot remain. I'm not going to have you removed, of course, Thomas. But I do have to cut you off. You no longer enjoy the protection of House Raith—in any overt sense, in any case. And I am truly sorry for it."

"The twins," he said. "They put you up to this. They wanted me gone."

"Madrigal did," Lara confirmed. "Madeline didn't particularly care, but she has always indulged his tantrums. And simply put, I needed their support more than I did yours."

Thomas took another deep breath and nodded. "Things might change later."

"I hope so," Lara said. "But for now, there is nothing else I can do. Don't approach me openly again, Thomas. Don't visit. Don't claim Raith as your home. Lose the credit cards, and don't try to touch your accounts. You've got something tucked away?"

"A little," he said. "The money doesn't matter."

Lara set her orange juice down and leaned back in her seat. "But Justine does," she said.

"Yes. Madrigal would love to get his hands on her."

"He won't," she responded. "I swear it to you, Thomas, that I will keep her safe with me. I can do that much for you, at least."

Something eased out of Thomas's shoulders. "How is she?"

"Distant," Lara said. "Very vague and distracted. But happy, I think. She speaks of you at times."

"You'll . . ." His face twisted in distaste.

"Actually, no," Lara said.

Thomas frowned at her.

"Why don't you go see her," Lara suggested, and nodded toward a lower portion of the garden, where I could see Justine, in her wheelchair, sketching something on a pad across her lap.

Thomas rose like a shot, then visibly forced himself to slow down, and went down the winding path to the girl, leaving me alone with Lara.

"He really doesn't belong here, you know," she said. "Like Inari."

"How is she?"

"In traction," Lara said. "In a room with her boyfriend at the hospital. He isn't in much better shape. They're always talking, laughing." She sighed. "It's got all the signs of love. I spoke to her, as we agreed I would do. I don't think Inari will be one of us after all. She said something about doing feng shui in California."

"I didn't know she knew martial arts," I said.

Lara smiled a little, watching Thomas. He was kneeling beside Justine, looking at her sketches and talking. She looked weak but delighted, like when they take terminal kids to Disneyland on those talk shows. It warmed the heart at the same time it wrenched it. I didn't like the way it made me feel.

"Just to be up-front with you, Lara," I said, "I don't trust you."

She nodded. "Good."

"But we've got a hostage crisis on our hands."

"Of what sort?"

"Family secrets. You know mine about Thomas."

Her eyes were unreadable. "Yes. And you know about my father."

"If you spout off about Thomas, I spout off about your dad. We both lose. So I think it would be best if we agreed to truce of mutual honesty. You don't have to like me. Or agree with me. Or help me. But be honest and you'll get the same from me. If I'm about to go hostile, I'll tell you that our truce is over. You do the same. It's good for both of us."

She nodded slowly and then said, "Your word on it then?"

"My word. Yours?"

"Yes. You have my word."

We both tucked into breakfast then, in silence.

Half an hour later Thomas rose, leaned down, and brushed his lips against Justine's cheek. He stood up rather abruptly, then turned and hurried away with tense, pained motions. He didn't look back. As he approached, I got a good look at his face.

His lips were burned and blistered. He walked past us as if we weren't there, his eyes distant.

"He was always a romantic." Lara sighed. "She's protected. The little idiot should never have let himself feel so much for prey. It was that last time together that did it, I imagine."

"Had to go both ways."

"Greater love hath no man," Lara agreed.

We left. Thomas and I got into the Beetle and I asked him, "You okay?"

His head was bowed. He didn't say anything.

"I asked after Inari," I said.

His eyes moved toward me, though he didn't lift his head.

"She's in traction. And she's in love. Gonna be weeks before she and Bobby are going to get to do anything. No crimes of passion."

"She's free," Thomas said.

"Yeah."

"Good." After a minute he added, "No one should have to be like the Raiths. Destroying the people you care about the most."

"You didn't destroy her. And I think Lara really will protect her."

He shrugged, his expression dark.

"You slept much since Saturday?"

"No."

"You need to rest and I need a dog-sitter. I'll drop you at my place. I'll run errands. You drink Mac's beer until you crash on my couch. We'll figure out what you do next when you're rested. Okay?"

"Okay," he said. "Thank you."

I took him back to my apartment and spent the rest of the morning trying to collect on bills a few people still owed me. I didn't have much luck. I spent the rest of the day applying for loans, and had even less luck. Bank guys get so hung up about things like bad credit histories and people who fill in the "occupation" blank of the application with *wizard*. I guess it could have been worse. I could have been filling out the reason the loan was needed with *pay off mercenary for services rendered*.

By the end of the day, my hand hurt so badly that it had begun to cut through the painkillers, and I was exhausted. On the way out of the last bank, I forgot what my car looked like for a minute. I missed my street and had to drive around the block, but I missed it the second time, too. I managed to get home before I completely lost sentience, staggered past Thomas and Mister and the puppy asleep on the couch, and collapsed onto my bed.

When I woke up, it was Tuesday morning.

I found myself nervously looking around for the bright red dot of a laser sight to appear on my nose while I was in the shower with a plastic trash bag over my bandaged hand. I got dressed, got on the phone, and called Kincaid's number, then waited for him to return the call.

It took less than three minutes. "It's Dresden," I told the phone.

"I know. How's the hand?"

"I saw this great Swiss Army prosthesis with all these different attachments, but my hopes got crushed. I'm keeping the original."

"Damn shame," Kincaid said. "You need another contract?"

"Wanted to talk about the last one," I said. "Uh, I mean, I know you said Tuesday, but I'm still getting some assets turned into cash." I wasn't lying to him. I hadn't sold all my used paperbacks yet, or dipped into my comic collection. "I need a little more time.

"What are you talking about?"

"Time. I need more time."

"For what?"

"To get your money," I said, leaving out the word *dolt*. See? I can be diplomatic.

"The money got here hours ago."

I blinked.

"You can pay me twice if you like," Kincaid said. "I won't stop you. Anything else?"

"Uh. No. I don't think so."

"Don't call me again if it isn't business." He paused. "Though I want to give you a piece of advice."

"What's that?" I asked, cleverly hiding my confusion.

"She went down pretty easy," Kincaid said. "Mavra, I mean."

"Yeah. 'Cause of your groovy cutting-edge vampire-hunting weapon, I guess. Thanks."

"It's paid for," he said. "But I mostly gave it to you to make you feel better. And to make sure you didn't shoot me by accident."

"What about what you said about how cool a weapon it was?"

"Dresden. Come on. It's a paintball gun. Mavra's world-class bad news. I expected it to chew apart newbie vamps, sure. You think Mavra would have tottered on out of the smoke to let you kill her? Nice and dramatic like that? If you buy that one, I got a bridge to sell you."

I got a sick, sinking little feeling in my stomach. "It was her," I said.

"How do you know?" he asked.

"Well. Because . . . she was wearing the same outfit," I said. "Son of a bitch. That sounds really lame, even to me. One corpse looks a lot like another. It could have been a decoy."

"Could," he said. "So my advice to you, Dresden. Watch your back."

"Gee. Thanks."

"No charge." He paused for a second as someone

spoke in the background, then said, "Ivy says to tell your kitty hello for her." He hung up.

I put the phone down, thoughtful. When I turned around Thomas was sitting up on the couch. Silently he offered me the business card with Kincaid's account number and the amount of the bill on it.

"Found it in the laundry," he said.

"You didn't have to do that," I said.

"I know," he replied.

"You really have that much money?"

He shook his head. "Not anymore. That was pretty much everything I'd set aside. I hadn't made a lot of plans for independence. I figured I'd either be dead or running things. I've got about fifty bucks to my name now."

I sat down on the couch. The puppy snuffled me with his nose and wagged his tail in greeting.

"Where are you going to go?" I asked.

"I don't know," he said. "Guess I can do what my cousin Madrigal does: find some rich girl." He grimaced. "I don't know what to do."

"Look," I said. "You really saved my ass. Crash here for a while."

"I don't want charity."

"It isn't," I said. "Think of that money transfer as a rent payment. You can have the couch until you get your feet under you again. It'll be crowded, maybe, but it isn't forever."

He nodded. "You sure?"

"Sure."

Later Thomas went to the grocery store and I went down to the lab to talk to Bob. I filled him in on events.

"You're sure?" Bob asked. "It was He Who Walks Behind?"

I shivered. "Yeah. Thought I'd killed him."

"Walkers aren't killable, Harry," Bob said. "When you tore him up before, it banished him from the mortal realm. Might have hurt him, made him take time to heal up. But he's still out there."

"That's comforting," I said. I unwrapped my burned hand.

"Yuck," said Bob.

"Can you see anything about the injury?" I asked.

"Burned meat and nerve damage, looks like," Bob said. "Hmm, I think it still has reflexes, though. I bet you could use it a little if you did it without thinking about it."

I frowned. "You're right. I think I did during the fight with Raith. But look at this." I opened my stiff fingers with my right hand.

There was unburned flesh there, just as the doctor had observed. What he didn't know was that the unharmed flesh was in the shape of a sigil in angelic script—the name of one of the Fallen angels. Specifically, the same entity imprisoned in an ancient silver coin, at that very moment trapped under two feet of concrete and half a dozen warding spells on the far side of the lab.

"Lasciel," Bob said. His voice was worried.

"I thought she was locked up. I thought she couldn't touch me from there, Bob."

"She can't," Bob said, bewildered. "I mean, that's *impossible*. There's no way she should be able to reach out from there."

"Sounds kind of familiar," I muttered. I wrapped up my hand again. "But that's what I thought too. And my staff is acting weird. When I start to run power through it, I'm getting excess heat. The runes start glowing like embers and there smoke curling up out of them. Seemed like my workings with the staff were coming out a lot bigger than I wanted, too. Did I blow something on the preparation?"

"Maybe," Bob said. "But, uh. Well, it sounds a lot like Hellfire. I hear that some of the Fallen really love it."

"What?"

"Hellfire," Bob said. "Uh, it's sort of an alternate power source. Not a pleasant one, but man, you could really turbocharge violent spells with it."

"I know what Hellfire is, Bob."

"Oh. Right. Why are you using it then, Harry?"

I said through clenched teeth, "I don't know. I didn't mean to. I don't know what the hell is going on."

"Hell," Bob said. "Heh. You made with the funny, boss."

I had involuntary access to Hellfire. How had *that* happened?

Lasciel's sigil on my left palm was the only cool spot on my burning hand.

Hell's bells. I shook my head and headed for the ladder back up.

As I left Bob said, "Hey, Harry?"

"Yeah?"

The orange lights in the skull glowed eagerly. "Tell me again about Murphy's ass."

Thomas came back from the store later that day. "Got the puppy a bowl and a collar and food and so on. Nice little guy. Real quiet. Don't think I've heard him whine at all." He tousled the puppy's ears. "You decide on a name?"

The puppy cocked his head to one side, ears tilted up with interest, dark little eyes on my face.

"I never said I was keeping him," I said.

Thomas snorted. "Yeah. Right."

I frowned down at the puppy. "He's tiny. He's grey. He doesn't make much noise," I said after a minute. I dropped to a knee and held my hand out to the little dog. "How about Mouse?"

Mouse bounced straight up in a fit of eager puppy joy and romped over to lick my hand and chew gently on one of my fingers.

Thomas smiled, though it was a little sad. "I like it," he said.

We started putting groceries away, and it was the strangest feeling. I was used to being alone. Now there was someone else in my personal space. Someone I didn't mind being there. Thomas was all but a stranger, but at the same time he wasn't. The bond I sensed between us was not made weaker by being inexplicable, no less absolute for being illogical.

I had a family. Hell, I had a dog.

This was a huge change. I was happy about it, but at the same time I realized that it was going to be a big adjustment. My place was going to be pretty crowded, pretty fast, but once Thomas got into his own apartment, it would be more normal. I don't think either one of us wanted to be tripping all over each other every time we turned around.

I felt myself smiling. It looked like life was looking up.

I had started feeling a little crowded already, sure. But I took a deep breath and brushed it back. Thomas wouldn't be here too long, and the dog was certainly a lot smaller than Mister. I could handle a little claustrophobia.

I frowned at a giant green bag and asked Thomas, "Hey. Why did you get large breed Puppy Chow?"